THE ACCURSED KING

Book Four of
The Plantagenet Legacy

by Mercedes Rochelle

*Thou schalt be cursid goynge in, and
`thou schalt be cursid goynge out.*

*Deuteronomy 28:19
Wycliffe's Translation of the Bible*

BOOKS BY MERCEDES ROCHELLE

Heir to a Prophecy

The Last Great Saxon Earls Series
Godwine Kingmaker
The Sons of Godwine
Fatal Rivalry

The Plantagenet Legacy Series
A King Under Siege
The King's Retribution
The Usurper King
The Accursed King

THE ACCURSED KING

Book Four of
The Plantagenet Legacy

by Mercedes Rochelle

Cover art: from Chroniques de France ou de St Denis, Royal 20 C VII f. 134v. Reproduced by courtesy of © The British Library Board

Contents

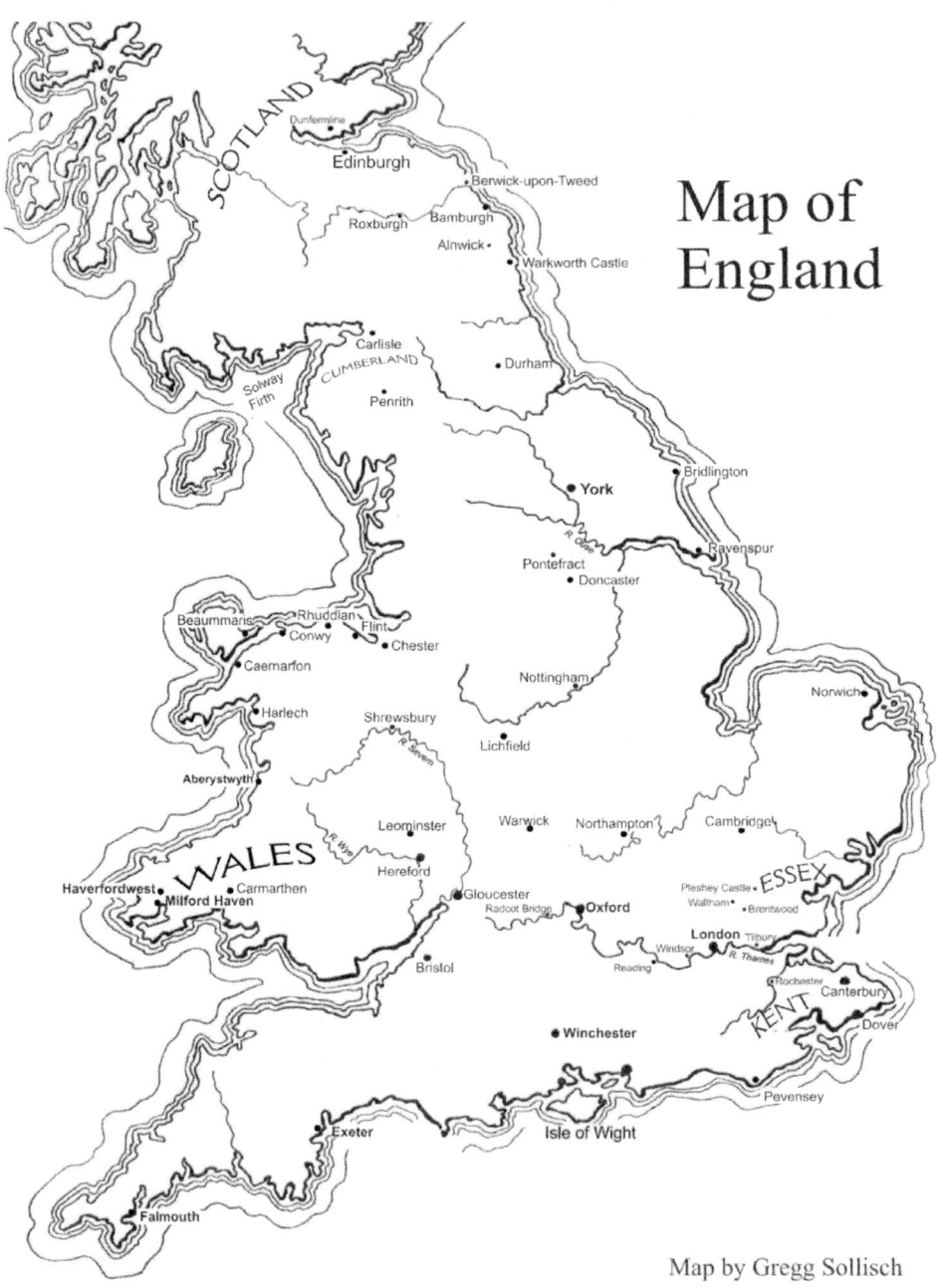

Map of
England

Map by Gregg Sollisch

CAST OF CHARACTERS

ALBANY, ROBERT STEWART, DUKE OF: Younger brother of King Robert III, Regent of Scotland

ARUNDEL, THOMAS FITZALAN, 5th EARL OF, 10th Earl of Surrey, son of Earl Richard Arundel

ARUNDEL, THOMAS, Archbishop of Canterbury and Lord Chancellor of England, Uncle of Thomas Arundel 5th Earl

AUMALE, EDWARD DUKE OF: See York

BARDOLF, LORD THOMAS, 5th Baron Bardolf, supporter of Henry Percy

BEAUFORT, HENRY, second son of John of Gaunt and Katherine Swynford, Bishop of Lincoln, Bishop of Winchester, later Cardinal

BEAUFORT, JOHN, EARL OF SOMERSET (in 1397), Eldest son of John of Gaunt and Katherine Swynford, one of the Counter-Appellants of 1397, created Marquis of Dorset in 1397* (reverts to earl 1399)

BEAUFORT, THOMAS, Earl of Dorset (in 1412), DUKE OF EXETER (in 1416), Youngest son of John of Gaunt and Katherine Swynford

BURGUNDY, JOHN THE FEARLESS, DUKE OF: Son of Philip the Bold, made Duke in 1404. Cousin of King Charles VI

CHARLES, DUKE OF ORLÉANS, Nephew of King Charles VI, son of Louis Duke of Orléans

CHARLES VI KING OF FRANCE, Valois king, (reign 1380-1422), nicknamed "the Beloved" and later "the Mad"

CONSTANCE, LADY DESPENSER, Widow of Thomas Despenser who was killed by the mob during the Epiphany Revolt. Sister to Edward, Duke of York.

CLIFFORD, SIR WILLIAM, Percy retainer, commander of Alnwick, Warkworth and Berwick, son in-law to Lord Thomas Bardolf

EDWARD DUKE OF YORK: See York

ERPINGHAM, SIR THOMAS, Served John of Gaunt then Henry IV; accompanied Henry into exile and back. Also served Henry V and fought at Agincourt.

FITZALAN: See Arundel, Thomas

HARRY PERCY, aka HOTSPUR, son of Earl Henry Percy, Earl of Northumberland

HENRY IV, KING OF ENGLAND: Son of John of Gaunt, Duke of Lancaster

HENRY OF MONMOUTH (Hal), PRINCE OF WALES, Oldest son of Henry IV, Duke of Cornwall and Earl of Chester, later King Henry V

HUMPHREY OF LANCASTER, later Duke of Gloucester (in 1414), 4th son of Henry Bolingbroke, b.1390

ISABELLA OF VALOIS, Queen of England (married 1396 aged 7), daughter of Charles VI of France

JOANNA OF NAVARRE, QUEEN OF ENGLAND, 2nd wife of Henry IV, originally Duchess of Brittany

JOHN OF LANCASTER, later Duke of Bedford (in 1414), 3rd son of Henry Bolingbroke, b.1389

LOUIS, DUKE OF ORLÉANS, brother of King Charles VI, murdered on order of the Duke of Burgundy

MARCH, EARL OF, see Mortimer, Edmund

MORTIMER, EDMUND IV, second son of Edmund Mortimer, 3rd Earl of March. He was uncle to the 5th Earl of March and defected to the Welsh Rebels

MORTIMER, EDMUND, 5th Earl of March and 7th Earl of Ulster, (born 1391) thought by many to be the heir presumptive to the throne after Richard II. He was son of Roger Mortimer, 4th Earl of March (d. 1398). Mortimers were descended from Lionel, second son of Edward III, through his daughter Philippa (the female line)

MOWBRAY, THOMAS DE, 4th EARL OF NORFOLK, son of Thomas Mowbray 1st Duke of Norfolk

OLDCASTLE, JOHN, Knight and friend of Henry V. Lollard leader

ORLÉANS, LOUIS I Duke of: younger brother of King Charles VI of France, nephew of the Duke of Burgundy

PERCY, HENRY, 1st EARL OF NORTHUMBERLAND: 4th Baron Percy, father of Hotspur

PERCY, SIR HARRY a.k.a. HOTSPUR: Son of the Earl of Northumberland

PERCY, THOMAS, 1st EARL OF WORCESTER, younger brother of the Earl of Northumberland. Uncle to Hotspur.

RICHARD II, KING OF ENGLAND, son of Edward Plantagenet the Black Prince and Joan of Kent, living in exile in Scotland

ROBERT III, KING OF SCOTLAND, born John Stewart, also Earl of Carrick before ascending the throne

ROBERT STEWART, DUKE OF ALBANY: See Albany

RUTLAND, see York

SCROPE, RICHARD, Archbishop of York

SERLE, WILLIAM, Esquire of Richard II's chamber, killed the Duke of Gloucester under Richard's orders. Sent letters from Scotland after Richard's usurpation, claiming the king was returning with an army

SOMERSET: see Beaufort, John

THOMAS OF LANCASTER, later 1st Duke of Clarence (in 1412), second son of Henry IV, b.1387

WESTMORLAND, RALPH NEVILLE, 1st EARL OF, created earl in 1397, rival northern magnate to the Percys, brother in-law to Henry IV

YORK, EDWARD, 2nd DUKE OF, eldest son of Edmund Langley, 1st Duke of York. One of the Counter-Appellants of 1397, Duke of Aumale (or Aumerle or Albemarle) in 1397* (reverts to Earl of Rutland, 1399), Duke of York in 1402

CHAPTER 1

23 July, 1403

The axe fell with a solid thud, cleanly severing the head of Sir Thomas Percy. King Henry IV watched the execution from the castle ramparts with tears in his eyes. It was just two days since the Battle of Shrewsbury where another Percy, the famous Harry Hotspur, went down under a flurry of blades. His naked body was now propped up between two millstones near the city gate—having been unceremoniously torn from his temporary grave to thwart rumours of his survival. Henry had refused to look at him, certain that Harry's staring eyes would condemn him, even in death. They had been friends once, a circumstance that made this whole situation more tragic than he wanted to admit. And Thomas, whose deportment had been flawless up until a week ago, disturbed him even more. Henry had done his best to save his life, but his closest advisors flew into a fury, calling the man traitor, and worse. The best he could do was commute the execution to mere decapitation rather than the full penalty, hanging, drawing and quartering.

This whole bloody rebellion caught the king totally by surprise and he mourned the loss of his valiant enemies more than they deserved. What had he done to merit their rancour? Surely they had their disagreements, but nothing so venomous as to warrant an attack on his throne.

And what about Hotspur's father, the Earl of Northumberland? If he had been present the outcome of the battle would have been much less certain. It was a terribly close call; only Hotspur's death determined who had won the day. Where was the earl and why hadn't he shown up?

Henry shook his head. He would think about that later; for now, he had more important things to worry about. His son and heir had been struck in the face by an arrow and had continued fighting until the end of the battle. Only then had he collapsed into the arms of his friends. The royal surgeons, confounded by the injury, professed themselves incapable of extracting the arrowhead from the base of Hal's skull, behind his cheek. In desperation, Henry had sent a messenger to London, ordering the famous surgeon and metalworker John Bradmore to be released from prison; the man had been caught counterfeiting, of all things. Then Bradmore would be brought to Kenilworth, where Hal would be waiting for him—if he survived the trip.

Unfortunately, Henry didn't have the leisure to sit by his son's side and wait for him to live or die. With Henry Percy on the loose, the rebellion still had a chance to succeed. He had to deal with the recalcitrant earl without losing another minute. He had already sent a messenger to the Earl of Westmorland, telling him to block Northumberland's progress, wherever he might be. But some tasks required the presence of the king and besides, Percy could be anywhere. Presumably he was coming south from Northumberland, but Henry could leave nothing to chance.

The king was right about one thing: Henry Percy was on his way south, though that wasn't his original plan.

Two months before, he and his son had their eyes on lands given to them by King Henry—Douglas lands, all in Scotland. Both Percys knew the king's offer was a hollow gesture to keep them quiet; they had to conquer the region themselves before they could claim it. It didn't help that they were owed a huge amount of money from their previous two years as wardens. Their resources were not infinite! Repeated requests for payment fell on deaf ears; the exchequer was hampered by the urgency of the Welsh rebellion, they were told. As far as King Henry was concerned, they were on their own; he had even sent a letter telling Percy he wasn't going to come north—he had business in

London. That was just fine; as far as Percy was concerned, he needed money, not the king's dubious help.

Nonetheless, they couldn't resist the opportunity. Hotspur had laid siege to the Tower of Cocklaw in Teviotdale, deep into Douglas territory. Unfortunately, things hadn't gone well and the garrison put up a strong resistance. Frustrated, Hotspur negotiated with the tower's captain and they agreed upon a six-week truce. If Scotland's governor, the Duke of Albany didn't relieve the castle, they would surrender to the English. Meanwhile, Percy's army withdrew to England's side of the border.

It was Hotspur's idea to use the six weeks to organize a rebellion against King Henry. Rebellion! Even now, Percy was mystified about the abrupt change of plans. However, he knew his son still harboured deep resentment about the way the king had treated him the year before—demanding that he turn over Douglas and other hostages taken at Homildon Hill. It wasn't a pretty scene and Harry had stormed out, threatening to see the king next on the battlefield. Percy hadn't taken this tantrum seriously when he heard about it later, but perhaps he should have.

Harry gave another argument that never failed to provoke his temper. He rightly pointed out that the Earl of Westmorland was showered with favours—and money—while the Percys were constantly shuffled aside. It didn't take a huge leap of understanding to see where *that* was going. Westmorland, after all, had married the king's half-sister, Joan Beaufort, which brought him into the royal family.

Up until recently, Ralph Neville was a minor nobleman compared to the Percys. He had only been made Earl of Westmorland six years before. The Percy family had always held the clear advantage in the North—that is, until Henry's coronation. And only just recently, the king took the captaincy of Roxburgh away from Hotspur—which had been granted for ten years—and gave it to Westmorland. This was the most insulting affront, but not the only one.

As usual, Harry's fervour carried the day. Before he knew it, Percy had been talked into rebellion and his son was off to

3

Chester to raise an army, leaving his father to guard the border in case the Scots launched a counter-offensive. They knew from Percy's brother Thomas that the Prince of Wales resided in Shrewsbury with only a token garrison; Harry should be able to capture him easily. It would take a few days for the news to reach the king in London, then at least another week to gather his forces, ride out and try to rescue his son. Once Percy learned Harry was on his way from Chester, he would bring down his army from the north so they'd trap the king in a pincer movement.

But something went wrong. Only a couple of weeks after Hotspur left, one of Percy's retainers rode into camp—all in a lather. Concerned, the earl moved up to take the reins of his horse.

"What ho, Alan? I thought you were in Nottingham?"

The rider dismounted, turning his horse over to a squire. "I was. So was the king."

"What? He's supposed to be in London. Come. Into my tent. I have some ale." Gesturing for him to follow, Percy led Alan to his pavilion, pulling aside the flap. "What was Henry doing in Nottingham?"

The other accepted a full mug. "They tell me at the last minute he changed his mind and decided to leave for Scotland. To help you." He took a long draught.

"By the blood of Christ, this changes everything. We had it all planned out." Crossing his arms, Percy started pacing. "He's much closer to Shrewsbury now. Our timing is all wrong." He stopped, rubbing his temples. "I've got to think."

"That's not the worst of it," Alan said.

"There's more?"

"Someone told the king that Hotspur was raising an army. He abandoned his plans for Scotland and immediately turned west to rescue Prince Hal."

"West? Oh, no." Percy collapsed onto a bench. "I won't be able to get there in time." He covered his face with his hands and Alan watched him worriedly, saying nothing. Finally, Percy glanced up. "I'm getting too old for this." And suddenly he looked every one of his sixty-two years. His thick, close-cropped

4

hair and beard were entirely white, and the wrinkles cut deep into his weathered face. His blue eyes were rheumy. "My Harry," he said. "He may have over-reached himself this time." He stood. "No matter. We have to go now. Maybe there's a chance I can help him."

Without another word, Percy left the tent, shouting orders. "We're breaking camp. There's no time to waste." His captains were used to obeying him and soon everyone was in motion, taking down tents and packing their bags.

Sir Thomas Bardolf, Percy's friend and ally, came running up. "What has happened?"

"The king is on the move and he's headed to Shrewsbury," Percy said, mopping his head. "He was supposed to be in London. You know how fast he travels."

"Hotspur is at risk," Bardolf said, turning to others who approached. "We need to get on our way as quickly as we can." The baron was always there when Percy needed him, and once again the earl felt a surge of gratitude for his friendship. He always knew what to do. Bardolf was a big man, blond and brawny like a Norseman, and his intelligence was matched by his courage.

"We will not wait for reinforcements," Percy declared, putting a hand on Bardolf's arm. "We'll gather troops as we move south." He was like a man possessed, running back and forth, pointing and scolding. Before long, Percy's small force was moving. It was over sixty miles to the southern border of Northumberland and they would pass through many Percy estates which would swell their numbers as they picked up supplies.

By the time they entered Yorkshire, the earl's army amounted to several hundred men, all mounted and riding hard. They had just passed through his Cleveland estates, about forty miles below Newcastle, when they spotted a large army in the distance, spread across a long hill. Percy's men came to a halt, trying to maintain some sort of order.

"Westmorland," groaned the earl. "It must be him." He wasn't prepared for this. How dare that upstart block his way! How was he ever going to live with this humiliation?

Bardolf was perceptive enough to see the dilemma. "Let me go speak to him under a flag of truce," he said. "I can manage this."

Percy glanced at him appreciatively. For once, he was willing to step aside. "I think you're right," he said. "There's only one reason he gathered an army. The king must have sent him."

Summoning a handful of followers, Bardolf rode to the waiting army while Percy stayed back, grumbling in frustration. If he had to fight now, who knows what condition he and his army would be in when it came time to extricate his son? Yet it was clear there would be no way around Westmorland.

The two forces were far enough apart that Percy couldn't see very clearly what was happening. After what seemed like hours, Bardolf turned and rode back with his companions while the enemy sat unmoving on the top of the hill. At least they respected the flag of truce.

Finally, Percy couldn't sit still any longer and he kicked his mount forward. As he neared the others, Bardolf gestured for his companions to continue and he pulled his horse to a stop, waiting. The other riders passed Percy, intent on looking the other way. His heart sank.

The earl rode up to Bardolf and stopped next to him, their knees touching.

"They outnumber us," said the baron. A gust of wind blew hair into his face and he ran his hand across his forehead, pulling it aside. He seemed unwilling to go on.

"Did the king send him?"

The other nodded. "The Earl of Westmorland has orders to stop you, to apprehend you if you insist on going any further."

"I've got to get to my son," Percy insisted, "one way or the other."

Bardolf shook his head. "We're too late, Henry. A battle was fought at Shrewsbury. Fought and lost."

Percy sucked in his breath. "Harry?"

"He was killed on the battlefield. They captured your brother Thomas and beheaded him the next day."

Percy swayed in the saddle and Bardolf put out a hand to steady him. "Westmorland gives us one hour to turn around and leave."

"God in heaven. What am I to do?"

Bardolf tightened his grip on Percy's arm. "What else is there but to avenge them? Not today, Henry. Today we must conserve our strength." Another blast of wind threatened to blow the weakened earl from his saddle. "Come, my Lord. We must away."

Barely aware that he was being turned around, Percy allowed his friend to direct him back to his army. "Retreat," Bardolf commanded, and the soldiers, happy to be spared a battle, spread the word down the ranks.

Percy finally summoned the strength to speak. "Go back to your homes," he declared, his voice a mockery of its usual tone. He didn't really care that Bardolf had been the first to order his men to disperse. There was nothing to fight for.

It was the first time in his life Henry Percy experienced despair. He didn't know what to do.

While the Earl of Westmorland was busy securing the North, King Henry made his way to his stronghold at Pontefract, which he reached early in August. This time he brought his third son with him, who had turned fourteen that year. John was a quiet, studious lad—never any trouble—who followed his father's wishes without question. He had bright, intelligent eyes, a quick smile, and knew how to listen. Henry had decided that John's charge would be the North, especially since Henry Percy could no longer be trusted. It was time for his son to be placed under the tutelage of Westmorland.

It was good that his boys earned their spurs at a young age, much as he had done. Whenever Hal recovered from his terrible wound he would continue his duties in Wales. Thomas, next in line, was serving as lieutenant of Ireland. He would make John Warden of the Scottish Marches. There only remained Humphrey, and he was still young, yet.

7

At Pontefract, the king found a packet of missives from the earl, bringing him up to date about Percy's movements. After being turned back, the earl made a desultory stop at Newcastle, then continued on to his stronghold at Warkworth, another thirty-five miles north. Henry decided to send his recalcitrant earl a letter, commanding him to come in person and meet him at York—without any armed followers. He promised Percy he would suffer no harm until he had the opportunity to present his case before parliament. The king then issued orders forbidding his own troops from plundering Percy's tenants in the North—he didn't want the same kind of looting he saw after the Epiphany Rising, three months after his coronation. He sent orders to all the ports telling them not to make any payments to the Percys due from customs. With these preparations satisfactorily brought about, Henry continued with his train to York.

Bardolf found Henry Percy alone in his solar with a cup of wine in his hand, staring at the empty fireplace. He had been like this on and off for days, and the garrison was understandably restless as a result. Percy's men expected guidance from him; this was a side of the earl no one had seen before.

Sitting next to him, Bardolf cleared his throat. "My Lord, I have a message from the king."

Turning his head, the other focused his eyes. "He sent a messenger? Why not an executioner?"

Bardolf sighed. "I would say he values you more alive than dead. Here is his letter."

Listlessly, Percy took the missive and read it before dropping his hand onto his lap. "He wants me to debase myself," he said. "He's already killed my son and my brother. He won't be happy until I crawl to him on my hands and knees."

"Perhaps." Bardolf reached for the pitcher, pouring himself a drink. "I doubt it. Stripping a man of his dignity can cause more grief than satisfaction, in the long run. Besides, he has no proof of your complicity."

"Raising an army is proof enough."

"I would say not. You were in your own lands."

"True enough." Percy straightened in his chair. "You think I should go?"

"I don't see where you have many choices. So far, Henry has kept his word—unlike King Richard. He promised you no harm. You may not find favour right away, but he can't forget how loyal your tenants are to you."

A crooked smile crossed Percy's face. "They are, aren't they?"

"Here is what I propose. If your fortresses hold out for you, they will be your strength. Send all your captains a message. I'll take the letters, myself. Even if they are ordered to surrender to the king, they can refuse. After all, they are entrusted with the keeping of your castles by Letters Patent, which could only be broken by *your* express command. That should give the king's servants something to think about. Henry can't afford to lay siege to your fortresses, especially with the rebellion in Wales occupying the royal attention."

"And if I behave myself, he's bound to acquiesce." Percy nodded. "It's a good plan. I think you should take my grandson, young Henry, to William Clifford in Berwick for safekeeping. The man is a bulldog. He won't let my only heir out of his sight." He let out a heavy sigh. "You're right. I don't have much choice. I'm in no mood to fight with the king or his minions."

He stood, stretching, before turning to his friend. "I am in your debt. Gramercy, Thomas. I am in your debt."

Henry Percy rode to York with a small retinue, more to keep up appearances than provide any protection. The king had specified they were to go unarmed, and he knew better than to disobey. The city was surrounded by a stone wall, originally built by the Romans and recently restored by Edward III. The spires of the cathedral rose above the battlements, almost glowing against the emerald blue sky. As they approached Monk Bar, which faced the northeast, Percy held up his hand, causing his men to stop. He was looking at the top of the gatehouse, and the others followed his gaze, gasping in dismay. There, mounted atop a tall pole, the decapitated head of Harry Hotspur gazed over the countryside with glazed eyes. King Henry had made sure that his disgraced earl would get the message.

Percy sat there a long time, swallowing back his tears. If only he had convinced his son to stay home. If only he had gone with him! He couldn't remember their last words before Harry rode off, all puffed up with pride. He did recall shaking his head in exasperation, wondering why he had gone along with this half-baked scheme—not that he could have stopped Harry once he made up his mind. It was a big risk, but they had always been risk-takers. If his son had succeeded, the rewards would have been immense. If King Henry had met his end at Shrewsbury, they would have crowned young Mortimer, the rightful heir to the kingdom. Then the Percys would finally have had a king they could control, rather than the increasingly peevish Henry Bolingbroke. The boy was only twelve years old, after all, and kept in close confinement by the king. He was ripe for the picking.

But now that it had all come crashing down on his head, their aspirations seemed petty—loathsome, even. Poor Harry. What a shameful end to such a promising career. What a terrible vision for a broken-down father.

"How can I go on?" he asked nobody in particular. "This should never have happened."

No one knew how to answer him. They all sat quietly astride their tired horses, wishing themselves anywhere but behind their degraded master.

Finally, he roused himself. "Let's get this over with," he said. "The king awaits."

Percy was met by the steward in the courtyard of the Franciscan Friary, which stood between the King's Landing on the Ouse River and York Castle. This magnificent complex was large enough to house a parliament, and the royal household comfortably filled its chambers. The king sat on a throne in the great hall surrounded by courtiers. Percy's disgrace was to be witnessed by all.

Henry's face was expressionless as the earl approached. Kneeling before the throne, Percy bowed his head. "I come in all humility to submit myself to your Majesty's will."

Pursing his lips, the king gazed at the earl's bent head. He was all too cognizant of their respective positions not four years ago when he landed at Ravenspur—an outlaw—with a handful of followers. Then he had been totally at the mercy of this very man, whose duty was to arrest him. That would have marked the end of any glorious return from exile. But instead, father and son welcomed him with open arms. Without Percy and his army of the North, his venture probably would have foundered. Who would have expected things to transpire like they did?

"What drove you to turn against me?" he said to Percy.

Swallowing, the earl looked up at him, tears in his eyes. His mouth worked a moment before he spoke the words that would haunt him the rest of his life. But his son was beyond harm, and he needed to save himself. "Sire, I had naught to do with this uprising. My son Harry acted without my consent."

Henry raised an eyebrow. Of all the things he expected Percy to say, a flat-out denial was not one of them. He didn't believe a word of it. "You had nothing to do with it?" he repeated in a dubious tone.

Percy looked at the floor, shaking his head. "It was his undertaking. He had his reasons."

"I daresay he did." Henry glanced over his shoulder at Sir Thomas Erpingham, his closest adherent. A slight shake of the knight's head confirmed his own disbelief. "Well, Earl Henry, I promised you the opportunity to bring your case before parliament and I will keep that promise. However, in the meantime you shall remain in my custody. Tomorrow we leave for Pontefract."

Percy was not surprised that he was to be Henry's prisoner; in fact, he expected it. He was spared any shackles, though his door was guarded as he slept. The following day, he was closely accompanied by two guards as the royal train moved on to the king's most formidable castle. The earl wondered if he would be lodged in the same cell as the unfortunate King Richard.

But no, this was not Henry's intention. Once settled into Pontefract, Henry formally demanded Percy surrender all his castles to the king's commissioners. He was deprived of his office of Constable, which was conferred on the king's young son John who had already been appointed Warden of the East March—Hotspur's former command.

Confident that Bardolf had matters well in hand, Percy submitted to Henry's demands. It was harder to stomach the distribution of his son's possessions to the king's favourites, as well as his brother's estates. Once all this was done, Percy was sent to Baginton, a small castle in a little town bordering Coventry. There he was to wait until parliament was called for January, five months thence.

CHAPTER 2

Prince Hal sat propped up in bed, admiring the servant girl who was busy rearranging things on his table. He was too weak to get up yet, but he was well enough to have memorized every inch of his confining room. His only amusement was the banter of his favourite retainers, who insisted on staying at Kenilworth castle with him. And of course he welcomed the ministrations of Angela, who brought all his meals, fed him, and helped change his clothing. Her hands were gentle and her smile inviting. He only wished he could do something about it.

Turning, Angela brought over a serving tray and sat on the bed next to him. Hal reached out and touched her sleeve. "You're wearing a new tunic," he said. "It's very pretty."

Blushing, the girl picked up a napkin and laid it across his chest. "I'm happy you noticed. You must be feeling better."

"I am." He opened his mouth, waiting for his first spoonful of porridge. The surgeon who saved his life, Bradmore, had insisted he eat soft foods until his wound healed better. He knew that the hole in his cheek was terrible to look at. Was Angela repelled by it? Or was she just good at hiding her disgust? Of course, he reminded himself, the only thing that mattered was that he was still alive. A mangled face was a small price to pay for the miracle of his survival.

Angela spooned the food into his mouth and wiped a dribble from his chin. "Do you remember anything that happened?" she asked.

"The operation? Bradmore gave me a soporific that worked very well. I'm sure he didn't want me to move. I can't imagine how any man could have such a steady hand."

"Are you in constant pain?"

He opened his mouth for the next spoonful. "Mostly. But let's not talk about me. How old are you, Angela?"

13

"Seventeen, my Lord."

"Call me Hal. Remember?"

"Oh, I'm sorry. I'm the oldest girl in my family. I have three sisters younger than me."

"Have your parents found a husband for you yet?"

She blushed again, "I'm not in a hurry to marry."

Moving his hand, he placed it on her leg. "You're very pretty, you know." Blond-haired and blue-eyed, she had just the kind of look that pleased him. "I like having you take care of me."

Glancing at his hand, she filled another spoonful. "Maybe you don't need me to feed you anymore."

"Of course I do. Otherwise, I'd spill porridge all over myself."

"Well, as long as the doctor orders it…"

They heard a commotion outside the window and Angela got up to check. She turned to Hal with a look of confusion. "There's a richly dressed lady stepping out of a litter," she said. "She has a whole party of retainers with her."

At that moment Sir John Oldcastle, one of Hal's loyal soldiers, came into the room. "My Lord, the queen has come to visit you."

"The queen?" Hal coughed. He barely knew the lady; she had only been in the country about seven months. She had married his father by proxy ten months before that but needed to stay in Brittany until the regency was settled in favour of her son. Hal had been fighting in Wales all that time; he didn't even attend their wedding. "What could she possibly be doing here?"

John turned at the sound of footsteps. "We're about to find out. Angela, take the food away."

The girl was already in motion and Hal barely noticed as she removed the tray. Queen Joanna came into the room, nodding briefly and looking around; two maids followed her in, while Oldcastle brought over a chair.

"You are very kind," Joanna said graciously, pulling the seat closer to the bed. She spoke in French and Hal wondered if she knew any English yet. "Your father is stopping here on his way to Wales. I came to join him. Kenilworth is a beautiful castle, isn't it?"

"It is, my Lady. I'm sorry I'm in no condition to entertain you."

"Nonsense. I'm glad to see you sitting up. Your colour is good."

She cocked her head and studied him while he tried not to squirm under her scrutiny. Stuck in bed, he hadn't had a decent bath and he felt dirty and unkempt. How he must smell to her! Joanna, on the other hand, looked fresh and sprightly, even though she had just been traveling. She pulled off her outer veil and handed it to a maid, adjusting her circlet. The queen was not beautiful, but pleasant enough to look at. She exuded tranquillity, which put him at ease despite himself, and her eyes were an amazing shade of violet. "That's better. It is warm today."

Hal had nothing to say and his hand unconsciously went to his cheek, almost as if he wanted to hide the injury.

"I understand we almost lost you," the queen said. "That would have been a great tragedy. Your father loves you so."

Blinking, the prince wondered if that was true.

"How is the wound healing?"

"Slowly," he sighed. "They kept placing probes soaked in honey into the hole to make sure it healed from the bottom up. It took three weeks before the puncture completely closed, and I could barely move for fear of disturbing it. I'm just now able to sit up in bed."

"Ah. I came at the right time. You will need someone to keep you company, and we can finally get to know each other."

Hal wasn't sure he agreed with her, but he didn't have much choice. He wasn't even sure how he felt about having a stepmother.

Hearing a disturbance at the door, she turned. "Oh look, here is Humphrey," Joanna said, holding out an arm. Shyly, the youth moved up to her and put a hand on her shoulder.

"Little brother," Hal said, happy to see him. "You've grown." At thirteen, Humphrey was the youngest and smallest of his siblings. He seemed to be at ease with the queen.

An uncomfortable silence wrapped around them until Hal patted the edge of his bed. "Sit, Humphrey. What have you been doing, now that John is off to Northumberland?"

Plopping down beside the invalid, Humphrey gestured to the queen. "I have been accompanying my Lady to her new estates so she can administer them better."

Joanna nodded. "You are very good with numbers," she said. "It always helps to know what one's officers are doing."

"And Thomas Erpingham has been teaching me military skills," Humphrey continued, warming up, "so when father gives me a command I will be ready." He looked uncertainly at Hal. "What exactly happened to you?"

"Well," Hal sighed, "I was on the left wing at Shrewsbury. Once the battle was underway, we charged up and attacked the rear of the enemy's force, throwing them into confusion. Unfortunately, as I was giving orders an arrow must have glanced off someone's helm. I had my visor raised and it struck me in the face." He shuddered at the memory. "One of my knights pulled the arrow out, but the point was stuck in the bone of my skull. I fought on because my men needed a leader. It was all I could do not to pass out. Afterwards, I don't remember."

Humphrey studied his wound. "I see war is not always glorious."

Hal's smile was crooked. "It rarely is. We do our duty."

Pulling back, Humphrey nodded. "Undoubtedly, I have much to learn. Father is taking me to Wales after he comes here."

"Wales," said the Prince. "It'll be a while before I get back there."

Not sure what else to say, Humphrey wandered away, but Joanna seemed content to linger. Resigned, Hal decided to make the best of it. After all, she was here to stay, so to speak. In England, that is. He knew very little about her.

"Just how did you meet my father," he asked, mildly curious.

A sad smile crossed her face. "He stayed with us in Brittany before he returned to England after his exile. We got to know each other while the ships were prepared. My husband,

Duke John, provided the means for Henry's return. Poor man died a few months later."

"And your son? How old is he?"

"He's thirteen now. They made him Duke of Brittany when his father died."

"Weren't you regent?"

"Yes, you are right." Joanna rearranged her skirt, hiding her discomfiture. She wasn't proud of leaving her sons behind. "The Duke of Burgundy took over his tutelage, freeing me up to marry your father."

"You left everything behind to come here. That was quite a sacrifice."

She nodded. "It wasn't an easy decision. But I fell in love with your father the day I met him, despite the fact I was married to another. John was a good husband, but he was more than twice my age and ours was a political marriage. Your father offered me a chance for real happiness."

"I see," said Hal, still dubious. He hadn't seen that side of the king. Was his father the kind of man who inspired such devotion? He just couldn't imagine.

For the next couple of days, Joanna spent much time in Hal's chamber. She brought along her sewing and made herself comfortable, sharing stories and asking questions. Bradmore checked on his patient several times a day, answering the queen's questions about his operation. Hal listened too, since he had no knowledge of that day. Joanna's observations were concise and insightful. He discovered he liked this clever, practical lady. He couldn't help but notice she also treated his little brother like she really cared for him. Hal was too old to need a mother. Still, he appreciated that she could be a means to unite him with his father, who had been too much of a stranger all his life. Perhaps he should give her a chance.

On the third day King Henry showed up, riding ahead of a small army he had gathered as he moved south. Hal could hear the commotion from his bed, and Joanna got up and looked out the window. "There he is," she said happily, "in the courtyard. Of course, he can't take two steps without someone accosting him."

She adjusted her veil and smoothed her skirt. "How do I look?"

Hal grinned. She was like a young girl. "Beautiful."

They could hear laughing and shouting in the great hall below, then footfalls coming up the steps. Henry stopped in the doorway, beaming with happiness at the sight of his wife. Catching himself, he turned to Hal.

"Oh, my son." He strode to the bed and dropped to one knee.

Looking at his concerned face, Hal felt a jog in his memory. He reached out a hand. "Did you watch over me after the battle?" he asked.

Henry nodded with tears in his eyes. "I thought I was going to lose you. I slept on a cot next to yours."

"You spoke to me," Hal said, his eyes distant. "I'm not sure what you said."

"I told you how much I love you. How proud I was. How much you meant to me."

Joanna knelt beside him with a hand on his shoulder. "He's so much better now, even the few days I've been here."

Henry turned and put an arm around her waist. "I missed you so." He kissed her cheek. "I'm happy you two had the opportunity to be friends." He stood, pulling her up. "My dearest wife."

Hal watched curiously as they kissed deeply. This truly was a side of his father he had never seen. He wasn't sure how he felt about it. All his life he had built up a defensive wall against this man, keeping him at arm's length. First, the neglect. His father was never around—never showed him the attention he needed. When he did give his children some time, his partiality toward Thomas, Hal's younger brother, was painfully obvious. To make matters worse, Hal was deeply resentful about the whole Richard II situation, even though it put him in line to the throne. He had loved the old king, who seemed more like a father than the man in this room. But now, all of a sudden, Henry acted like the parent he always wanted. Was he missing something?

The loving pair turned to him, arm in arm, glowing with happiness. Hal could concede theirs looked like a perfect union; he had rarely seen his father smile after he took the crown. This was a great improvement; Henry was relaxed—handsome even.

"I'll be fine," Hal said. "I know you haven't seen each other since before the battle. You have much to catch up on. I'm tired anyway."

Glancing at each other, the king and queen happily took him up on his offer and left the room without a moment's hesitation. Hal leaned back, bemused. Then he closed his eyes; he really was tired.

Someone cleared their throat. His eyes flew open and he saw John Oldcastle leaning against the door frame. Hal was always glad to see him, and today was no exception. Campaigns had a way of bringing men together, and they had both served in Wales since the beginning of the rebellion. Oldcastle had a jaunty, clever way about himself that always put others at ease, though Hal knew he was a deep thinker behind that carefree grin. The prince was always trying to draw him out, but John was maddeningly guarded, as if he had something to hide.

Hal waved his friend over and Oldcastle pulled up Joanna's chair. "I'm ready to come back into the world," the prince said. "Tell me. What is happening in Wales? Why is my father traveling there?"

Shrugging, John leaned over to straighten Hal's pillow. "He didn't bring a large enough army to suggest a long campaign. My thoughts are that he just wants to reinforce our presence in the south after Glyndwr's strong showing just before Shrewsbury. We have to maintain our hold on Carmarthen or we'll lose it all." He got up to pour himself some wine. "What's more worrying to me right now is the activity in the north. They've been burning English towns in Flintshire and Shropshire. I just heard yesterday they have laid siege to Rhuddlan and Flint castles."

"Where King Richard was held," muttered Hal.

"What's that?"

"Nothing. So they might extend their raids into Cheshire and Herefordshire."

"God forbid. I hope not. But it's a real possibility. It seems, at the moment, the whole country is in rebellion. Glyndwr may be only the figurehead, but he has a lot of support."

"This is going to require more attention than we've given it so far."

"And a lot more money."

"That's what I'm worried about. My principality," Hal muttered. "Supposed to sustain my rank. Drivel. In King Richard's time, Wales contributed a great deal toward the exchequer. Now, it is nothing but a constant drain on our resources." He squirmed, trying to make himself more comfortable. "I wish I were there, John. This inaction is driving me mad."

Oldcastle smiled at him sadly. "I'm afraid you have a long wait, my friend."

Henry and Joanna locked the door behind them and threw their arms around each other, kissing deeply just like young lovers. Pausing to look at her, Henry pulled off the veil and touched her hair gingerly.

"You're really here," he said softly. Then he swept her up and strode over to the bed. In a moment they were entangled in the covers. "I would have come to you right away, but I had to finish with that damned Percy."

"I know," she said, touching his face. "Just hearing that you were alive and well was enough. So many days of uncertainty! I must have worn a rut in the floor, pacing back and forth."

"Poor dear. We were so far from London."

"And I heard about Thomas Percy. That was such a shock."

"More than the others." Henry leaned back, taking her hand. "He was solid as a rock. Never complained. I never knew he was unhappy." He turned his head toward her. "Or maybe he was torn between me and his family. I just don't know. I didn't want to execute him. My supporters clamoured for his death."

"Tell me what happened."

Henry sighed. "To think I was on my way north to help Percy with the Scots. I had absolutely no idea what was brewing. It was just good fortune my course took me closer to Shrewsbury—closer than London, that is. And that a scout caught up with me at Nottingham. One day's difference and I would have travelled in the opposite direction. I never would have gotten there in time."

"So you collected troops on your way west?"

"Yes. As it was, Hotspur was already besieging Shrewsbury when I showed up. He pulled back and prepared for battle. I spent the whole next day negotiating with them, to no avail. We didn't engage until evening."

"And by night it was over."

"Yes, though even then I didn't know who won the field. Not until we found Hotspur's body."

Joanna nestled her head against his neck. "It's just not right. You did everything you could for them."

For a moment his lips trembled. "I was very fond of Harry. You couldn't help but love him. But he never forgave me for that altercation we had over his hostages. It was my fault and I deeply regret it."

"And what about his father?"

"My Mattathias?" He grunted. "He may slip from my grasp yet. I cannot prove he was part of the conspiracy. He denies everything, even though Westmorland caught him and his army on his way south. I'll let him stew in prison until parliament meets, though I doubt he will change his story. That friendship, too, is broken forever." Rolling over on his side, Henry gathered her to him. "One by one my magnates have fallen by the wayside. Who can I depend on? Northumberland and York are as slippery as eels. Arundel, Norfolk, and Warwick are just boys. The Hollands are gone, as are the Earls of Gloucester, Stafford, and Oxford."

"Thank God for the Beauforts," Joanna murmured.

"Yes. And Archbishop Arundel. And Westmorland."

"See, you aren't completely alone."

"And, most importantly, I have you," Henry said, placing his chin on top of her head. "Why are we wasting time? Roll over and I'll unlace you myself."

John Oldcastle was mostly right. King Henry was expecting more trouble from Wales—especially since the French were sending reinforcements due to some treaty they had cooked up between them. Recently the Count de St. Pol—married to Richard II's half-sister—had landed a French force on the Isle of Wight. Fortunately, the locals drove them off with heavy losses. St. Pol was allied with Louis of Orléans who had declared himself Henry's eternal enemy. Whether here or in Guyenne, it seemed every French offensive had Orléans behind it.

That wasn't the only thing on the king's mind. Unfortunately, rumours of Richard II's return had not been extinguished after the battle of Shrewsbury. He was coming back, people swore, to claim his throne at the head of an army. It obviously didn't happen, though Hotspur did his damnedest to convince his recruits the time had come.

Henry had done everything in his power to convince nay-sayers that the puppet-king in Scotland was an imposter. A pseudo-Richard, as he liked to call him. One would think Richard's elaborate funeral would have convinced people he was truly dead. But no, if anything, the speculation had redoubled in intensity. Annoyingly, letters kept coming from Scotland bearing King Richard's seal. It seemed like everyone who was anyone received a message proclaiming his triumphant return. Where were they coming from? And why?

Maud de Vere, Countess of Oxford took Richard's letter seriously. No surprise there; hadn't her only son Robert shown himself the king's most loyal friend? He had suffered exile and death in Richard's cause. In the late summer after Shrewsbury, she brought her letter to Colchester, showing it to Geoffrey Storey, the abbot of St. John's. "See? I would know this seal anywhere. It is truly his."

Storey held his wooden spectacles before his eyes. Then he looked at her, unable to hide his excitement. "This is truly encouraging. Let me send a man to Scotland to verify whether King Richard still lives." His eyes widened. "Of course! I can send the very man who claims to have freed the king from Pontefract and brought him to Scotland. William Blythe! I know where to find him."

The countess rubbed her hands together. "Send for him at once, Father. Let us be the ones who reinstate the king."

Blythe showed himself more than willing to take the trip, and Maud gave him a ring, so Richard would know it was her who sent the messenger. Meanwhile, she authorized hundreds of white hart badges to be fashioned so she could distribute them to her followers.

By November, Blythe was back. He assured Countess Maud that Richard was alive and well.

"Does he support our movement to bring him back?"

William took a deep breath. "Well, he didn't object. I believe he wanted to wait and see. He would be in great danger if things went awry."

Nodding wisely, Maud accepted this answer. "One cannot blame him. Once we prepare the way, he can safely return."

Blythe's report removed the last hesitation from many irresolute supporters. The Abbot of St. John sent a message to the Duke of Orléans, inviting him to bring an army and land on the coast of Essex. Local insurgents would be ready to lead him to victory. The duke's response was favourable and more letters crossed the Channel, firming up their plans.

A meeting was called at Colchester, and it was attended by a large number of partisans. Disgruntled monks and abbots, local gentry from miles around crowded into St. John's, ready to throw money and men into the cause.

The countess stood beside Abbot Storey, who took control of the meeting. She was known far and wide as a tenacious woman with strong opinions, and she rarely hesitated to throw her weight behind a cause she believed in. Her mere presence was enough to energize the crowd.

"We have been communicating with the Duke of Orléans," Storey said proudly, and waited while everyone applauded. "We have a date! He and St. Pol will land an army at the Port of

Ipswich in the River Orwell on 28 December. The duke will be bringing Queen Isabella with him to be reunited with King Richard!" More applause. "The usurper is watching the southern coast and will not expect any activity from this direction."

The attendees need not know that their leaders spoke from their hearts rather than any specific instructions from King Richard. Surely once he saw the movement in his favour—and the presence of his wife—he would keep the promise he made in his letters.

"In preparation for the French," the abbot went on, "the week before Christmas William Blythe and the countess's servant John Stanton will destroy the beacons along the shoreline to prevent any alarm being given at the critical moment."

The plans were welcomed with enthusiasm, and everyone set off to raise as much support as they could muster. The French may be their traditional enemy, but they remembered the truce Richard had signed when he married Isabella. With the old king back on the throne, the truce would be stronger than ever. Peace would reign once again.

What the conspirators didn't know was that a discouraged St. Pol had already reneged on his promise and was on his way to Paris. Already their plans threatened to come unravelled.

Nonetheless, Louis of Orléans wasn't necessarily discouraged. As usual, he was operating on many levels. Without the help of St. Pol he was less sure of success. On the other hand, he cherished any opportunity to make life difficult for King Henry—even though the possibility of overthrowing him was remote. He regretted the day he signed a treaty of alliance with Bolingbroke, way back when the duke was in exile. How was he to know that Henry was going to murder his liege lord? He had suffered universal censure ever since, and couldn't shake the indignity of his misplaced friendship. He swore Henry would pay.

And then there was the stubbornness of Isabella. After Jean Creton came back from Scotland with the disappointing news that the man thought to be Richard was an imposter, Isabella still would not be moved. She clung to her hopes that her precious husband was alive. Now she had reached childbearing years, the princess of France was a valuable commodity and Orléans wanted her to marry his son Charles. It didn't matter that they were first cousins; it was easy to get a dispensation from the Pope. There must be a way to convince her.

So when the enterprise of England was suggested by the Countess of Oxford, Louis of Orléans had an idea. Travel across the Channel was capricious this time of year, but Isabella hopefully wouldn't know that. Perhaps he could convince her of his good intentions and still sway her to his side, once the adverse weather forced them to stay in port. It was a gamble but worth it. He travelled to Paris and visited with his niece in the royal palace at L'Hôtel de Saint-Pol. Curious, Isabella sat quietly while he laid out his plans.

"Of course, my dear, it is in all of our interests to be certain whether King Richard is truly with us or not. But it's been almost four years now. You can't wait forever."

Isabella wasn't so sure she agreed with him, but she inclined her head.

Encouraged, Louis picked up her hand. "We have been approached by certain, um, opponents of Lancaster with an invitation to invade England. These allies of King Richard are claiming he intends to return from Scotland at the head of an army."

Her eyes went wide and her mouth turned into a little "O". *Such an innocent girl*, Louis thought, *even after all her trials*. Sent away to a strange country at age seven, married to a king old enough to be her father, forced to watch him lose his throne, then his life. He couldn't help but feel sorry for her, despite his ulterior motives. "For you, I'll agree to do this," he went on. "Let us go to England, you and I. You will head this campaign. If what they are saying is true and King Richard comes back to claim his crown, you will be reunited." *Against all odds*. "But if it is not true and King Richard doesn't come, I hope you will agree to marry my son."

Isabella knew he was making a bargain with her. This could truly be her last chance. Wiping a tear, she nodded her acquiescence.

So everything was in place to invade England on 28 December. Isabella thought that the number of ships waiting at the port in Antwerp was disappointingly few, but she had faith that Duke Louis knew what he was doing. She stood at the forecastle of the duke's ship, clutching her cloak and trying to ignore the wind beating about her head. Even in the harbour the water was choppy. Ships rocked, threatening to bang into each other. Her teeth chattered and her feet were cold but she wouldn't budge, hoping that by sheer will she could move the fleet across the Channel. Finally, her uncle came up beside her. "Come, child. We will go nowhere tonight." He took her by the shoulders and led her into the captain's quarters. By then, she was too miserable to argue.

The next day was the same, as was the day after. 28 December came and went and still the weather was against them. Isabella began to despair, but she refused to let her uncle know. Finally a messenger came from England, for the wind was behind him and his ship crossed quickly.

Duke Louis brought the messenger into the cabin where Isabella sat, sipping on a hot bowl of broth. "I thought you should hear this," he said gently.

Looking up, the princess was afraid to ask. She saw from his face the messenger did not have good news.

The man bowed quickly. "I come from Ipswich, my Lady," he said. "There is no sign of King Richard. The Duchess of Oxford is in despair that you have not landed."

Glancing at her uncle, Isabella frowned. "Is King Richard waiting for us before he comes down from Scotland?"

"I know not, my Lady. He has sent no word."

"No word. We can't give up yet, uncle!"

Opening the door for the messenger to leave, Louis sat across the captain's table from her. "I can't afford to pay my soldiers much longer to remain idle. We can give it another week, but if the weather doesn't improve, we must accept that God is not in favour of our venture. It's the best I can do, my dear." She started to cry and he stood, anxious to get away. Let the girl have her moment of grief.

By now Isabella concluded that, as far as her uncle was concerned, this half-hearted effort to accommodate her turned out for the best. He could say that he had tried. If it was meant to be, the weather would have cooperated. She hated to admit it, but her resolve was crumbling. Perhaps it really was time to reconcile herself to a new life. Charles was only a boy, but she could do worse.

On the other side of the Channel, the conspirators held onto their forlorn hope and continued to plot and plan for another three months. Inevitably, this secret couldn't stay under wraps forever, and some unknown person told the authorities. The main collaborators were arrested and the countess found herself in disfavour. Luckily for her, the king was busy with the Welsh rebellion and the government didn't take the conspiracy seriously enough to give it much attention. Under the auspices of Queen Joanna, Countess Maud and the abbots were pardoned, and the four men tried for treason were found not guilty. All had learned their lessons.

As for Isabella, she was unaware that the Duke of Orléans had already sent his petition to the Pope—even before they set out. It took another six months, and on 5 June she married Charles, Count d'Angoulême. She wept bitterly the day her hand was given to her new husband. Sympathetic courtiers assumed she cried to lose the title of queen of England in order to become a mere countess. But those closest to the princess suspected that her heart still belonged to King Richard and always would.

CHAPTER 3

In January of 1404, the fifth Parliament of Henry IV's reign was called at Westminster. Henry Beaufort, Bishop of Winchester—and the king's half-brother—opened the session as chancellor. He presented a long list of woes.

"I give you the reasons why you have been summoned," Henry Beaufort said, standing in front of the king. Dressed in his ecclesiastic garments, he filled out his robe quite nicely, having succumbed to a rich diet of beef and thick sauces. Nonetheless, he had a big frame and could carry the extra weight. "Immense expenses have been incurred in many parts of the kingdom. The exchequer is desperately short of funds. The rebel Owen Glyndwr has extended his activities in both the north and south of Wales, endangering many royal castles. France continues to threaten our coasts. Only last month, we uncovered a plot where the Duke of Orléans was planning to land in Essex. The French were blown back by bad weather, thank God." He blessed himself.

"That is not all. Payments to the garrison at Calais are seriously in arrears. Income from overseas trade is drying up. Thomas of Lancaster, the king's son, requires funding in Ireland. The northern castles continue to resist the king's authority." He took a deep breath. "With the combined wisdom of the Lords and Commons, the king trusts that the best means might be taken to raise taxes for the country's defences."

Sitting in his high-backed chair, Henry watched the faces of the Commons. None of these complaints were unusual, though the king knew he was increasingly held responsible for the lack of prosperity. Promises made at his coronation in good faith could not be kept—all for a shortage of funds. Not counting minor disturbances, he had had to deal with three major crises in the first three years of his reign: the Epiphany Revolt, the Welsh Rebellion, and most recently, the Percy revolt which ended at the Battle of Shrewsbury. Every one of these was an unforeseen drain on his resources. Last years' taxes were barely enough to cover the costs of the royal household, notwithstanding all these extra burdens. Add to this he had arranged the marriage of his daughter Blanche to Louis, son of the new Holy Roman Emperor. It was a critical recognition of his kingship; too bad he was forced to demand feudal aid so he could meet the dowry's first instalment.

The good news was that most of the members of parliament were retainers or dependents of Lancaster. They were not his enemies. He had been very careful to appoint sheriffs and judges who owed him loyalty. Admittedly many lacked training and were less than successful in their positions. Tax collection had suffered as a result. However, this would improve as time went on and their fidelity was more important than experience.

After the preliminaries were dealt with, it was time to address the Percy situation. The earl had been brought to Westminster from his prison at Baginton and was introduced into the hall, while men strained their necks to get a good look at him. Brought up to the bar in front of the Commons, Percy stood straight and tall, belying his age and rumoured mortification.

Arnold Savage, speaker of the house, cleared his throat. "You are brought here, Earl Percy, to answer for your part in the recent rebellion led by your son, Sir Harry Percy. How do you answer?"

Percy momentarily turned his squint on the speaker before looking at the faces in the crowd. "My lords," he practically bellowed, "you see before you a humble man, bereft of his son and brother who led a rebellion without my knowledge. When I was made aware of the situation, I began raising troops to come south and attempt to make peace between my son and the king. In that, I was too late."

He stopped, listening. The members talked amongst themselves, and the voices were not hostile. He took heart. "The Earl of Westmorland intercepted me and informed me about the Battle of Shrewsbury. This was the first I knew of it. I turned back to my home. After I arrived, the king sent for me and promised I would suffer no harm if I surrendered and agreed to present myself before parliament. King Henry is a man of his word, although I was detained these many months."

The murmuring increased. Sitting on his throne, Henry frowned at the favour the earl found with both the Lords and the Commons. He didn't particularly believe Percy's story, but he had no proof to the contrary. Although he had sent officers to take possession of Percy's castles, almost all the captains continued to defy royal orders. Unrest was everywhere, especially after the rebels returned home from Shrewsbury. He had neither the men nor the funds to pursue any kind of campaign in the North.

Witnesses were brought forward and made statements concerning the rebellion and its aftermath. There was much confusion and little consensus as to who was where and when. Finally, at Savage's request, Henry agreed to stop for the day so the Commons could confer.

The next morning, the king was presented with a petition.

"Your Majesty," the speaker said after Percy had been brought forward. "The Commons feel that the Earl of Northumberland has shown commendable behaviour in presenting himself for your judgment. We feel there is not enough evidence to accuse him of treason. We petition you to grant Earl Henry Percy a charter of pardon and restore all his lands. However, we do feel that the earl has trespassed concerning the Statute of Liveries. He illegally distributed his crescent badge to a large number of men who had gathered to accompany him as an army. We therefore suggest you impose a fine at your discretion."

It was up to Henry, now. He took his time coming to a decision while the attendees squirmed with impatience. He couldn't suppress his disgust that Percy was going to get away with his aborted aid to Hotspur. The earl's popularity with the members of parliament was puzzling. Was this some kind of statement against his own rule? Did they approve of his actions? The king glanced over at Percy, who stood looking at the floor with his hands clasped—the picture of humility. He had lost a son and a brother; had the man suffered enough?

For a moment, Henry allowed himself to remember all that he owed to Northumberland. Without Percy there would have been no crown to protect. Perhaps he should give him one more chance. This would be the best opportunity to show mercy, a quality Henry most wanted to be associated with.

The king stood. "Earl Percy, I shall pardon you the charge of trespass and remit the fine. In accordance with the suggestion of my faithful Commons, I restore all the lands you possessed before my coronation. Any domains granted to you after 1399 shall remain with the crown. The estates of your son Harry Percy and your brother Thomas Percy remain forfeited on account of their open treason. I will not restore to you the constableship, nor the wardenship of either of the Marches." He held out his hand so the earl could kiss his ring. "Now I am prepared to accept your oath of allegiance."

Swallowing his mortification, Henry Percy knelt before the king and gave his oath. He knew things could have been much worse. He also knew that he would probably never recover the power and authority he had possessed before the rebellion. The future looked uncertain, but at least he had survived. The Percys were not finished, yet.

William Serle stood before King Richard, fists on hips, grimacing at the man who barely deigned to notice him. It didn't matter to his former master that he had crossed Scotland to see him, lumbering through snow and sleet to reach this God-awful Dundonald Castle, home to sheep and goats and surly cottars. "Even now, after I sent dozens of letters with your seal," he spat, "even after the Countess of Oxford sent a messenger to confer with you..." No reaction. "Even now," he insisted, "that they are distributing your badges in expectation of your arrival... even now, that the French are gathering to invade England—" His voice was getting louder and louder. "And you tell me you are not going? You lost your chance at the Battle of Shrewsbury. This is your moment! Rouse yourself!"

Stroking the black cat in his lap, Richard turned a weary eye on his visitor. "I never promised to put my neck into that noose," he said. "I see no purpose in it. I told Harry Hotspur I was not coming and he went on to fight that terrible battle anyway." He shuddered. "How many people are going to die in rebellion against Bolingbroke? I don't want to be any part of it."

In face of Richard's recalcitrance, Serle's anger ebbed away. "I sacrificed everything for you," he said sadly. "I have nothing."

For a moment Richard looked at him curiously. "Why did you do that?"

The other blinked. "I believed in you."

"Why? I don't believe in myself."

Serle shook his head. Of course, the real reason he went to so much effort was the reward he envisioned at the end. Why else would he have accepted the unsavoury task of killing the Duke of Gloucester, back in 1397? And when he discovered Richard's whereabouts after the escape from Pontefract, he had offered to send letters under Richard's name in an attempt to raise support. He never really considered that Richard would resist, once it was demonstrated the people wanted him back. "I warn you, this is the last time I will ever aid your cause."

"That is good. I don't want your aid. I am better left alone." He bent over and picked up a letter, holding it out to Serle.

"Here. Take this back. I don't want it. Go to France. We have allies there. Maybe they will help you."

Letting out his breath in disgust, Serle turned his back on Richard and left the room. He meant what he said. It was time to fend for himself. He had no allies in Scotland, nor did he want to stay a minute longer in this barren country.

He'd been thinking about this for a long time. He would pay a visit to Sir William Clifford, lieutenant of Berwick, just over the border. For six years Clifford had served alongside Serle in Richard's household, and his current opposition to King Henry was well-known. There was no way Clifford would surrender Berwick, just because the Earl of Northumberland stood in royal disfavour. Perhaps he could be persuaded to countenance a more serious defiance against the usurper. Or, failing that, Serle would beg the man to help him escape to France.

Serle practiced his argument all the way to Berwick. Clifford was a rogue, just like himself. Surely his old friend would welcome him, just to spite Henry Bolingbroke. After all, the whole Richard debacle—with the king's sealed letters sent to every possible ally—was not the only offense held against him. It was public knowledge that Serle had been involved with the Duke of Gloucester's murder. This made him the most wanted man in England.

Berwick had the dubious honour of changing hands between Scotland and England for hundreds of years. The town was in terrible shape; it had been besieged and blockaded and even sacked on occasion. Stone walls were crumbling in many places and the port needed repairs. Even so, Berwick was considered important and its castle, with royal apartments and great hall, was refortified within its own circuit of walls.

Serle had been here before, and he knew his way around. The place was well guarded, but he gained an introduction with a minimum of aggravation. However, when he was led into the captain's chamber, he was immediately overcome with uneasiness. Clifford was seated across from the door with a half-eaten meal in front of him. His greeting was more of a snarl, and there was no mistaking the unsympathetic look in his host's eye.

Although Clifford offered a chair to his guest, the old camaraderie was gone. Serle sat gingerly. He had already noticed the two guards flanking the door, holding halberds. The room was oppressively hot from the fireplace. No one offered him any refreshments. The scent of chicken made his stomach growl; he wished he could lean over and snatch a few unwanted pieces.

Clearing his throat, Serle got right to the point. "I've come from Scotland."

"Oh? What have you been doing there?"

Frowning, Serle cleared his throat a second time. Since Clifford was one of the recipients of his letters, he was pretty certain the man knew what he was up to. Serle realized with a start that he had forgotten to consider Clifford's opportunism. "I was helping, um, King Richard."

"The pseudo-Richard? What a waste of your talents."

Serle didn't know whether Clifford was being complimentary or sarcastic. "It was for the cause," he said, lamely. "Well, a lost cause, as you can see. I need your assistance, Sir William."

"Really? What is it you want?"

"I need help getting to France."

"Hmm." Clifford scratched his chin. "I think not." He nodded to one of his guards.

"What?" Serle sat up, looking around. The guard grabbed his arm.

"Before I start abetting a criminal, I need to do some investigating."

"I'm no criminal!"

"Of course not. If you were a criminal, I would put you in the dungeon. Instead, you will be my guest." He gestured for the guard to take him away. "Don't worry. I won't harm you."

Serle was locked into one of the tower chambers overlooking the Tweed. It was a long way down, and he knew there would be no escape.

Serle couldn't have known that Clifford was waiting for the Earl of Northumberland to show up. Both of them had received a summons to the king at Pontefract; Percy was still under suspicion despite parliament's acquittal, and Clifford needed to answer for his refusal to surrender Berwick. Because Clifford held the castle for Percy, it stood to reason that they should go together. And now he had a bargaining chip: Serle's treason would make Clifford's resistance almost innocuous by comparison.

Clifford had been taking care of Percy's grandson and heir Henry, ever since Bardolf brought him there after the earl surrendered to the king—along with the message to hold out against any royal interference. The boy was well-behaved and provided good company to his own son. He provided another reason for Percy to detour via Berwick; the earl wanted to see the lad.

Two days after Serle was escorted to his temporary lodging, the Earl of Northumberland arrived with a handful of knights and a blast of trumpets. The earl dismounted, throwing his reins to a page. He had to stretch for a moment, trying to shake off the stiffness in his back. Clifford greeted him in the castle entranceway, calling for young Henry. The lad was waiting for his summons and ran into the hall, letting out a yell of excitement. Percy dropped to one knee and Henry threw himself into the old man's arms. The earl buried his face in Henry's hair to hide his tears.

"Look who's here," Percy said, turning around.

"John! Ralph!" Young Henry could barely hide his excitement. These were his cousins, sons of Hotspur's younger brother Thomas who had died in Spain. They were all orphans now.

"Go, Henry," said Clifford. "Show them your new horse while we talk."

Percy looked longingly at the boys as they ran out of the room. "I brought those two because the king demanded hostages," he said. "I won't let him have Henry. I don't care what he says."

Clifford nodded. "He stays here, then."

"For now." The earl sat heavily on a bench. "The king doesn't trust me any more than I trust him." He sighed. "He means to have his way this time. He means to take Berwick."

"I won't make it easy on him, though I daresay you're right. But I have something he wants very badly, and he will have to pay dearly for it."

"Oh?" Percy raised an eyebrow. "What's that?"

"William Serle."

"Serle? You can't be serious."

"He showed up on my doorstep, out of money and looking for help. The fool. He's under lock and key now."

"Well, that's a stroke of good fortune. Poor bastard. I wouldn't want to be in his shoes."

Clifford shrugged. "He should have thought about that before he came begging for favours."

The next day the party was on its way to Pontefract. Percy and Clifford led a score of horsemen, pennons flying overhead, with a small train of packhorses to make the 160 mile trip to Lancaster's stronghold. Unhappy to be left behind, young Henry waved goodbye from the castle battlements. The other two boys rode their own horses, and the unfortunate Serle was tied to his mount, flanked by guards. No amount of pleading had softened the resolve of his gaoler, and he had fallen into a deep depression, which at least made him easier to manage.

King Henry had been at Pontefract for a couple of weeks already. Percy's party clattered into the castle bailey, chased by barking dogs and grooms who made haste to secure the horses. Dismounting, the earl lifted the boys from their palfreys and turned them over to the castellan, who shouted orders and directed servants to care for them. Taking one last glance, Percy strode to the keep, followed by Clifford, who instructed his guards to stay behind with Serle.

King Henry sat enthroned in the great hall as the newcomers were introduced. He nodded formally as they bowed before them, as though they were strangers.

The earl expected nothing less. He wasn't entirely sure he would escape unscathed, even at this late date.

"Well, you finally came." Nobody was sure which of them he was talking to. "There is the matter of Berwick, which must be delivered to the new warden, Sir Robert Umfraville."

Percy straightened. "Sire, I am prepared to do so provided the parliament grants me and my heirs—forever—property of equal value elsewhere."

"Hmm. We can consult parliament when they next meet. Now, my Lord Clifford," Henry added, his eyes narrowing, "I understand you have held back 4000 marks of Hotspur's goods that have been forfeited to the crown."

"Your Majesty, the sum is not nearly so large!"

"And you have taken custody of Hotspur's son."

"Yes, at the earl's request."

Henry frowned again. Although parliament had forced his hand, he was not ready to trust Percy any farther than he had to. Exhibiting that distrust, however, invited more trouble.

"Sire," Clifford ventured, interrupting Henry's thoughts, "as I am aware of your exasperation concerning...the mammet in Scotland, I have arrested William Serle and am prepared to offer him as a token of reconciliation."

"Serle?" Despite himself, Henry forgot all his complaints. This man had been a thorn in his side for years. There was no one on earth he'd rather have in his power. "You have Serle?"

"I do, your Majesty. And I hope we can work out a compromise concerning your trifling objections."

"Surely, surely. Where is he?"

"He is held prisoner in town."

"Bring him in. Bring him in."

Clifford gestured to one of his men who immediately left the room. "Now, Sire, in face of your objections..."

"You may keep wardenship of young Percy for now," Henry said, "and Hotspur's goods will help defray the costs. Come November I will send Umfraville to take possession of the town of Berwick."

"But I shall continue to maintain the castle."

Henry glanced at Percy who was doing his best to keep his face neutral. "For now."

In due time, William Serle was brought into the hall. The man looked worse for wear; they had not treated him gently. The guard shoved him to his knees.

Leaning forward in his throne, Henry studied the prisoner. "You have caused no end of trouble to me and the country. What say you, William Serle?"

Still on his knees, Serle glanced at Percy who ignored him. No help there. He cleared his throat. "Sire, when King Richard was captured at Flint Castle, I appropriated his seal and kept it on my person when I fled to France." He hesitated.

"Yes? Then what?"

"I had heard that Richard escaped his prison and so I went to find him in Scotland."

"And did you find him?"

Once again Serle looked at Percy, then Clifford. He wasn't sure how much he dared admit. What could he say that would save his life?

"I repeat my question," Henry said impatiently. "Did you find him?"

"No, Sire." Serle lowered his head. "I found an imposter."

"Ah." Henry leaned back. "And you chose to send letters to Richard's possible supporters, stamped with his seal. For what reason?"

There was no way out. Serle paled, though Henry could detect a look of hatred in his eyes. "My fortunes lay with the late king. I had hoped to re-establish myself."

"By fomenting rebellion?" Henry's voice went up an octave.

"I saw no other way. There are many in the country who still support Richard."

"I think you deceive yourself. And now that your wretched letters have ceased, they will have nothing to rally to. Do you not agree, Sir Henry Percy?"

Surprised, Percy nodded, looking at Henry as if for the first time. Did the king still suspect him of treason? Had he used up all of Henry's good graces?

The king wasn't finished. "There's still the question of the Duke of Gloucester's death." His voice took on a threatening tone. "Are you aware that John Hall related the circumstances of his murder in my first parliament?"

"Who?"

"Hall. The Duke of Norfolk's servant."

Serle shook his head. "I don't know who you are talking about."

"He guarded the door while you strangled the duke with his own neck scarf. To death."

His eyes widening, Serle rocked back, still on his knees.

"Your guilt has been affirmed. John Hall paid the price for his part in the murder."

"My guilt." Serle's throat was suddenly dry. "I was following King Richard's orders."

"Then you admit you were his instrument."

"Sire, I had no choice."

"We always have a choice. William Serle, I accuse you of treason. You shall suffer the extreme penalty of the law." He hesitated. "No, that won't be sufficient. Listen to me."

Two guards flanked the prisoner, waiting for the king's pleasure.

"We need to make an example of William Serle, and convince the people, once and for all, that King Richard is dead. Take him to London along the same route we brought Richard's funeral hearse. Drag him on a hurdle through the streets of Pontefract, Lincoln, and Norwich, then through the towns in Suffolk, Essex, and Hertford. In each of these towns, hang him by the neck and cut him down while still alive. Not until he reaches London will we subject him to the full traitor's punishment: he shall be hanged, disembowelled, beheaded, and quartered.

Stunned, Serle didn't react as the two guards dragged him to his feet. Then he panicked. "No! Sire, have pity on me! I have done wrong but I repent! I am your faithful servant!" With superhuman strength he broke free and threw himself at the king's feet. Henry gestured for the guards to take him away.

Percy and Clifford were appalled. Never had anyone been subjected to such an onerous punishment. They knew the king was making an example of Serle for their benefit. Too many rebellions had embittered the king—and the Percys bore as much guilt as anyone. But more than that; this terrible punishment was pure revenge, though the earl could see that the king still wasn't appeased. It would take more than the execution of one man to conciliate him. Henry Percy was walking on a knife's edge and he knew it.

Clifford, on the other hand, congratulated himself for a timely intercession.

CHAPTER 4

Apparently the king's ferocious order for Serle's execution was enough to satisfy him for the moment. Percy and Clifford were abruptly dismissed with a warning, and they rode away from Pontefract as quickly as they could, glad to be alive and free. As expected, the king retained the earl's two grandsons as hostages for his good behaviour. Percy relinquished them with great regret; Henry was no longer the man he had once known. There was a streak of cruelty to the king he had never seen before. How could he ever have thought he could control John of Gaunt's son? But even Gaunt had his limitations; King Henry apparently had none. Unlike his father, the king would not back down if hard pressed.

They decided to ride to York with their retinues while Percy contemplated his next move. At the moment, he felt rudderless. On the one hand, at least he hadn't lost his earldom. If he behaved himself, he could still worm his way back into the king's council. That is, if he wanted to. He had income from his remaining estates. His earldom was vast. Couldn't he be satisfied with that?

Percy frowned, looking up at a flock of geese squawking over his head. Who was he fooling? Prestige was everything. Without the power that came with the wardenship, his life had little meaning. For generations his family ruled the North like kings. He made the laws in the Scottish Marches; his word was unquestioned. How could he now accept less?

It galled him that the king had appointed Prince John as Warden of the East March. Worse than that, the boy had been given many of Hotspur's forfeited lands. Harry's death would have no meaning if he took this humiliation like a beaten dog.

The boy was unknown to him, but he obviously had no experience. How old was he? All of fifteen? Did he have the force of his older brother Hal? Or was he to be just one of Westmorland's creatures?

This would not do. The earl was more than ever convinced that his only hope was to finish what Hotspur had started. There would no middle ground here.

It was only twenty-four miles north to York, through some of the most beautiful landscapes in England. Taking their time, they camped overnight under a midsummer full moon, enjoying the sweet smell of honeysuckle permeating the air. Percy pulled off his boots and leaned back against his saddle. "To think it's already been a year since Shrewsbury," he mused. "I haven't accomplished a thing."

"Something tells me that's about to change," said Clifford. "I can see that look in your eye."

The other sighed. "I think I'm coming back to life. I had the heart torn out of me."

"Things will never be the same without Harry. But you have his son to live for."

"Poor boy." Percy smiled briefly. "He shows promise, doesn't he?"

"He won't let you down. You'll see."

Strange thought. They both wondered whether Percy would live to *see* him grown, after all.

By the next afternoon, they arrived at York. "I hope Archbishop Scrope is in residence," Percy said, as they entered through the towering Micklegate Bar, followed by their retainers. The narrow street was crowded, made worse by the merchant stalls lining both sides in front of the houses. People yelled at the shopkeepers, dogs barked, geese honked along the side of the road. A goat ran in front of Percy's horse, followed by a lad with a stick. Their pace slowed as people tried to get out of their way.

Percy raised his voice. "In the last parliament, the king suggested the government take possession of some church lands to fund the exchequer. As you can imagine, that created quite a controversy, led by our dear archbishop."

"Glad to have missed it," Clifford said, swinging his whip to ward off an annoying peddler.

"I believe we will find a sympathetic ear. Let us try the archbishop's palace." They headed toward the minster; the palace was just on the other side.

Percy had sent ahead to notify Scrope of his approach. Luckily, his timing was perfect. They were welcomed by the archbishop himself, who seemed genuinely happy to see the earl. He was dressed in a simple black cassock trimmed with red buttons and a red sash belt. Past the age of fifty, he was naturally balding and didn't need a tonsure. Scrope held out both hands as Percy dismounted.

"It is good to see you, my Lord. I feared the king would have your head."

Percy gave him a wry smile. The archbishop was famous for speaking his mind. "He very nearly did, your Grace. As it is, I had to leave two of my grandsons as hostages."

"That is a shame. Come, come inside. I have made provisions for all your men. Welcome, Sir William." He put a hand on Clifford's shoulder and led them up the stone stairs. "We have much to talk about." He gestured for his servants to take care of the horses.

Scrope hadn't seen the Earl of Northumberland since before Shrewsbury. Although Percy wouldn't be happy to be reminded of his loss, he was prepared to talk about it. In fact, he knew the subject couldn't be avoided. Besides, he needed to see if the archbishop was sympathetic to his cause. As he and his men settled down to a welcome repast, he pulled out a satin-wrapped parcel from his pouch.

"I brought this for you," he said, handing it to the prelate. "A gift from the good brothers at Alnwick Abbey."

"Ah, this is most beautiful." Scrope held up a pearl-studded crucifix. "Precious. I must write a letter of thanks."

"They are most grateful for your grace's undaunted stance against King Henry's policies. His attempt to appropriate the church's properties would set a terrible precedent."

"Indeed." Scrope wrapped the gift back in its satin. "Although I can't take too much credit. Archbishop Arundel is our most powerful ally. Without his help our cause would be lost."

The conversation was going in the right direction. Percy stole a glance at Clifford. "Nor do I think parliament will make any progress if they think they can fill the exchequer by taxing our poor merchants in the North."

As Percy suspected, this was a subject close to Scrope's heart. "It's outrageous," the archbishop declared. "My people can barely scrape enough together to meet normal taxes. These new demands will plunge us into penury. I understand that all pensions and annuities from the exchequer have been suspended for lack of funds." He lowered his voice. "King Henry has much to answer for."

"And we were both instrumental in putting him on the throne," Percy added, his voice even lower. "To my lasting regret."

Scrope looked hard at him. "Your son," he said, crossing himself, "tried to put things to right. We have candles burning at his grave day and night."

Percy lowered his head, closing his eyes. "He never could accept the usurpation. And now it's up to me to carry on his struggle."

Shocked, the archbishop put a hand on his arm. "You cannot be in earnest."

"I am in deadly earnest. This country is going in the wrong direction. The court is shamefully extravagant, wasting great sums of money when the taxes ought to be dedicated to paying our garrisons and protecting our borders."

Shaking his head, Scrope was obviously divided. "Your chances of success are slim."

"I'm not so sure I agree with you." Percy sipped his wine. "Owain Glyndwr is having more success than ever before. Our cause joined to his could prove Henry's undoing."

"I'm not sure his undoing should be our goal. A popular uprising could force the king to take notice and change his policy. Without civil war."

"Of course, of course." Percy knew better than push things too far at this early stage. It was enough that Scrope could be persuaded to support him. Of that, he was sure.

Leaving York, Percy and Clifford rode into Northumberland. The earl stopped at Warkworth Castle, his favourite residence, while Clifford continued on another thirty-eight miles to Berwick. Almost immediately after he settled in, Percy sent messengers to local magnates, arranging meetings to determine a level of support. He was still deep in his preparations when he received a summons to the January 1405 Great council. He read it with mixed feelings. It was encouraging to be back in the king's good graces—for what it was worth. On the other hand, his feelings toward Henry were unchanged. If anything, he felt more hostile than ever. Percy was under no delusions about getting his old authority back. King Henry had made it clear that Prince John was in the ascendant now.

Striding across the room, he handed the summons to Bardolf, who was watching him curiously. "I can't do it," he said, mostly to himself. "I no longer want to play Henry's game. He'll throw me a bone now and then while giving my assets to that... boy. I've already lost Berwick and Jedburgh. I'll never see the equivalent in exchange like he promised. There *is* no equivalent."

Bardolf looked over the parchment with a frown. "What will you do?"

"I've been in communication with Owain Glyndwr. He's in a strong position to threaten the king. If I throw in my lot with him..." He looked hard at Bardolf who retained an ambivalent expression. "I want you to go in my place," he said decidedly. "I will write a letter to Henry complaining about my health and the difficulty of traveling so far south in the depths of winter." He gave Bardolf a wry smile. "You are a much younger and heartier man, and better able to withstand the rigors of such a journey."

The other grunted. "While you take the easy route to Wales?"

Letting out a guffaw, Percy had the good graces to look abashed. "Well, Henry doesn't need to know about that part. I can't see why he would object to the substitution. You've been on his councils before."

"Perhaps. He will take note of your absence."

"Ah, my friend. You'll know how to appease him. Meanwhile, I have a rebellion to plan."

Henry Percy rode south as a common traveller on a palfrey bred for long distances; his small escort was similarly dressed. No livery was in evidence. He had high hopes that after speaking in person with Glyndwr they would come to some sort of understanding. After all, during the early stages of the Welsh revolt he and his son had communicated with Owain many times. They were always in favour of a negotiated peace, and on more than one occasion they cobbled together a reasonable treaty to present to the council. It could have worked and saved a lot of killing. But again and again, the king would have none of it. The government's short-sightedness was the reason Hotspur resigned his post as Constable in North Wales.

Well, now Percy would negotiate for his own interests. Last he had heard, the Welsh leader was at Harlech, on the west coast of Wales, which the insurgents had recently captured. He hoped this was still the case, for it worked in well with his objective to stop by Carmarthen on the way. There was another person he had to speak with first: Edward, Duke of York, who had recently been made Lieutenant of South Wales. Even though Edward was King Henry's first cousin, he was still under suspicion for his part in the almost-fatal Epiphany Rising, just three months after Henry took the crown. Yes, he exposed the rebellion—belatedly. But why was he involved in the first place?

Henry couldn't manage without York; he had a shortage of peers as it was. By placing him in Wales, he gave the duke a position of responsibility. Edward would also be on the fringes, where he would not have much opportunity to cause trouble. Nonetheless, York's talents were wasted there, and Percy suspected he was none too happy with this assignment. The only commission worse than Wales would have been Ireland. The earl was willing to gamble that Edward might be brought over to the rebel point of view, for his prospects could use a little boost.

The Duke of York welcomed Percy like a long-lost brother. He had reportedly been short of funds, but it was evident he hadn't let penury impact on his lifestyle. He had put on a considerable amount of weight, much of which had gone to his face. Forget about his chiselled profile; York now sported a double chin which he unsuccessfully tried to hide under a beard. However, his beady eyes were as alert as ever. He put an arm around Percy's shoulders and led him into his solar, warmed by a welcome fire that kept the winter chill at bay. Like most castles, Carmarthen was built for defence, not comfort.

"I am so sorry about Harry," York said, pouring wine into Percy's chalice. "He was a lion of a man. There will never be another like him."

Percy relaxed, encouraged by his host's respect for the king's enemy. He took a sip, enjoying the rare vintage. "My son will never be forgotten. He had his own way of doing things and I had to respect his wishes, even unto death."

"So I hear you weren't there?"

"At Shrewsbury?" Percy shook his head. "No, I fear Harry was precipitous this time. He started without me. As usual, luck was with the king."

"Hmm." York took a sip of wine. "I understand it was very close."

"It was." The earl stole a sideways look at him. "If my son had had his way, young Edmund Mortimer would be on the throne. He is the rightful heir, after all."

"Instead of a prisoner."

"Ah, yes. Safely out of sight. That's three rebellions against King Henry in so many years. Not an auspicious beginning, is it?" Percy watched York squirm, cognizant of the man's participation in the Epiphany Revolt. And his betrayal of it. *Did the duke have any regrets? How far could we push him?* "If Mortimer was king," Percy said slowly, spinning his cup, "I wonder how different things would be?"

For a minute the other didn't respond; he stared off with unfocussed eyes, as though weighing his options. Finally he sighed, putting down his wine. "They couldn't be much worse— at least for me. I'm owed thousands of pounds for my service in Guyenne. And the situation here is even more deplorable! I've already sold all my plate to pay for maintenance of my troops. And it's still not enough. Now I have to mortgage my lands to make up the difference."

Percy was astonished. "And the king your cousin! I thought I was in bad straits!"

"Oh, Henry will take care of his sons first, you can be sure of that. The rest of us can fend for ourselves." He hesitated. "Well, Prince Hal is not much better off than I am, admittedly. But the king won't let him founder."

"Is he back?"

"Yes. He's at Hereford now, fully recovered though he wears a fearsome scar on his face. He's the overall leader here."

"I see." Percy shifted in his chair. "Where does that leave you?"

"Good question. His second in command, I reckon. I dare say there's enough fighting for everyone. Still..." Cocking his head, York studied his guest. "It wouldn't be too much to say I'm feeling a little under-appreciated."

"That wouldn't be the case with Mortimer."

There. It was said. Percy had just committed himself. He held his breath.

"Yeesss." That came out slowly. "With Glyndwr's help—"

"We would be unstoppable. I'm on my way to see him. He's at Harlech, I believe."

"No. Aberystwyth. He just captured it on 12 January."

"Well! Much closer for me."

"Yes. Shameful affair. I understand the poor constable only had twelve men-at-arms and forty-five archers to defend both Harlech and Aberystwyth. How he was supposed to sustain these vital strongholds with such pitiful garrisons is beyond me." York took a deep draught of his wine. "So, what did you have in mind?"

Not sure how much he should share with this slippery duke, Percy took another tack. "Without the boys..."

"The Mortimers." York nodded. "Henry is keeping them close, at Windsor."

"Without them, our plans would come to nothing. Do you have access to the boys?"

York picked up his wine again. "My sister does. She too resides at Windsor under the queen's eye."

"Constance?"

"Oh, yes. Since her husband was killed by the mob at Bristol, she hasn't felt too kindly toward the king."

"Ah." Percy leaned forward. Constance's husband, Thomas Despenser, had been one of King Richard's closest confidants. His participation in the aborted Epiphany Revolt must have been undertaken with his wife's blessing. Constance was a very determined woman; he wouldn't have made such a move otherwise. "Do you think she would help us?"

"I know she would." York spoke with more conviction than he felt, but he was warming to the scheme. "She has always had a good relationship with the Mortimers."

"These are the best tidings yet," acclaimed Percy, his face breaking into a smile. "With Constance's aid, we can free the boys and put them under Owain's protection."

"Meanwhile, we can plan the next steps."

"Exactly. Let me sound out Glyndwr and see what he says. Perhaps my son did not die in vain."

Content that the first part of his plan was in place, Percy travelled the fifty miles north to Aberystwyth. With its diamond shape and its wall-within-a-wall design, Aberystwyth was one of Edward I's most successful fortifications. Unfortunately, built only a few yards away from the pounding surf, the castle was already starting to erode, which might help account for the Welsh's successful capture.

Approaching the castle, Percy drew rein and sat on his horse atop the hill, looking at the sea. The wind blasted across his face, causing him to squint. "This is more blustery than Northumberland," he shouted, barely able to hear himself. "Let's get to shelter!"

The earl and his following were welcomed in the style they were accustomed to, and brought to the great hall. The prince entered soon afterward, preceded by four men-at-arms. Owain Glyndwr was a handsome man, tall and elegant. Descended from two princely dynasties, he carried himself like a natural successor. Even Percy was in awe of him. Unmindful of his own regal bearing, Glyndwr held out his arms in welcome. "A sight for sore eyes," he cried, taking Percy by the shoulders. "Edmund and I were just talking about you."

Owain turned as Edmund Mortimer joined them, clapping the earl on the back. Uncle of the child heir, Edmund was the acting head of the Mortimer family and had recently joined forces with the Welsh, marrying the daughter of Glyndwr—notwithstanding the fact that he was originally taken prisoner. Or maybe because of it. King Henry had sworn he would never ransom Mortimer, declaring him a traitor after England's most shameful loss at the Battle of Pilleth in 1402. That didn't give Edmund many options. Hotspur, at least, had championed his cause, which was another reason Percy's son turned rebel.

"How fares my sister?" Edmund asked. He hadn't seen her for many years, since she married Hotspur.

"She took Harry's death very hard," Percy said as they led him up the steps to the dais, set with chairs under a blazing heraldic banner quartered with four lions rampant. Next to this hung the Red Dragon of Cadwaladr, associated with King Arthur. Percy glanced at the flags and took a seat, glad to finally rest. "The king has suggested a few potential spouses for your sister, to keep her out of trouble. So far she is resisting." He shook his head. "Alas, since all Harry's lands were forfeited to the Crown, she is practically destitute. I do what I can for her, but I'm not in a good position, either, after Shrewsbury." He glanced at Glyndwr. "Which is why I'm here, of course."

"Of course," nodded Owain. "I'm hoping you seek an alliance." He paused, waiting for Percy's nod. "You know, we recently signed a confederation with France. They have sent us some troops and promise to follow with an army this summer to help our cause."

Percy was hard put to restrain his enthusiasm. "We'll be unstoppable."

Glyndwr did not miss his excitement. He leaned toward Percy. "Between you in the North, me in the West, the French lending their strength, and Mortimer laying claim to the crown, poor Henry Bolingbroke could easily be caught in the middle. He is none too stable on his throne."

"I have a plan that will make this even more formidable. I have spoken to the Duke of York."

Glyndwr sat back again, surprised. "He is our enemy. How can that man be of assistance?"

"He's not as much an enemy as you think. He is disgruntled with things as they are."

"When is he not?" the other muttered.

"He feels he can fare better under Mortimer's administration."

"Does he now? More opportunity for advancement?" Glyndwr put a hand to his chin, stroking his beard.

"Look at what he faces: four royal sons and a crowd of Beauforts to compete with. There's not much left over for a mere duke."

"And what can he do for us?"

"His sister resides at Windsor."

"Where my nephews are kept prisoner," Mortimer said in wonder. "Now, that is intriguing."

Percy smiled smugly. "And York says he can persuade her to help them escape."

"We'll see," said Glyndwr. "I don't hold much faith in his constancy, but it's certainly worth a try."

"The sooner those boys are in our hands, the better," urged Mortimer.

"We can move forward either way." Glyndwr turned to one of his retainers. "Send for Gruffudd Yonge," he said, then came back to Percy. "He's my chancellor and ambassador to France. He's the one who composed the *Confederation Between Wales and France*. Here's what I propose. Let us form a confederation of our own. The three of us. Let us propose to support each other in making war upon Henry IV. We will be bound together in friendship and shall pursue the honour and advantage of each other. Once we have removed Henry from the throne, I propose that we agree to divide the rule of England into three parts: I and my heirs shall rule the whole of Wales. Percy shall rule the North, and Mortimer shall have the remainder of England. Edmund, you shall be regent until your nephew reaches his majority." He held up his chalice and the others tapped theirs against it.

"And France?" asked Percy. "How do you think they will they feel about our confederation?"

"With Mortimer on the throne, England no longer has a claim to the French crown. They can only benefit from the end of hostilities." Glyndwr smiled knowingly. "They will be our silent partner. I predict our... what shall we call it? Our *Tripartite Indenture* will encourage them to help make it happen." He turned as the door opened. "Ah, here is my chancellor. Gruffydd, we need your acumen. We require another confederation, and you have already drafted the important passages."

Percy was more than pleased. So far, everything was proceeding admirably.

A few letters back and forth between Aberystwyth and Carmarthen and all was arranged. Percy didn't care how York did it; all he knew was that the duke had persuaded his sister to go along with their plan. They had merely to wait for the fugitive princes to show up and their campaign could prosper with the most convincing of figureheads: the future king of England.

CHAPTER 5

Lady Constance Despenser was an unhappy woman. Growing up, she felt unloved by her father the Duke of York. She wasn't particularly close to her brother, the second Duke of York, and her marriage to Thomas Despenser always took second place to his relationship with King Richard. After the usurpation, they might have had a chance together except that he had to get himself involved in that cursed Epiphany Rising which led to his untimely death—again, no thanks to her treacherous brother. Her subsequent entanglement with the handsome but young Earl of Kent only left her pregnant and abandoned. And now she was living a life of relative obscurity at Windsor Castle, neither prisoner nor free, ignored by one and all. Nearing thirty years old, she was still handsome, with high cheekbones and an oval face. Her eyes, however, gave away a haughty disposition, her only defence.

Boredom was her most tenacious enemy. So when a letter came from her brother she was intrigued, despite herself. The courier also had a verbal message for her that couldn't be trusted to paper. Since the king and his household had gone to Eltham for the holiday celebrations, security was at a minimum. It was simple for Constance to find a private room for them to talk. After sitting the courier down with food and drink, she read the letter, which was very brief. *So typical,* she thought. *My brother is such a schemer.*

"So what does he want?" she asked. No need to be polite.

"My Lady." He swallowed a bite. "My lord the duke has a request to make of you. He knows you are unhappy here."

Constance grimaced; it was true, but how would her brother know?

The courier ignored the look on her face. "The duke wonders if you would find life in Wales more suitable to your needs," the man went on. "He has been approached..."

She didn't realize that she had crumpled the paper. "By whom?"

"Suffice it to say that the Prince of Wales would be more than interested to put the Mortimer heirs under his protection. And their uncle Edmund has been most anxious for their welfare."

She wasn't interested in making this easy on anyone. "The Prince of Wales? Which one?"

"Owain Glyndwr, my lady."

"And how does this benefit my brother?"

The courier took another bite of his dinner. "Your brother languishes as lieutenant of South Wales. In fact, he is nearly ruined in the king's service. The Prince of Wales offers substantial benefits for both the Duke of York and yourself once the true heirs to the throne are removed from their illegal imprisonment. And brought to Wales, of course. To safety."

"Hmm." Constance was surprised at how her stomach jumped at the thought. She knew she shouldn't trust her brother. But here was an unexpected chance to start a new life. She hated Windsor Castle. She knew King Henry was suspicious of her, which made for an uncomfortable existence. On the other hand, she and Edmund Mortimer had been friends from before her marriage. What was there to stop her?

Eyeing her carefully, the courier put down his spoon. "Well?"

"Let me think. Those boys are locked in at night."

"It shouldn't be too hard to hire a locksmith—especially now, during the holiday festivities."

He was right. Security was slack. Constance allowed herself a slight smile. "What is your name?"

"Milton."

"All right, Milton. I'll do it. Come back tomorrow night with four horses; I'll have to bring my son Richard, too. At midnight. Do you know the postern gate by the curfew tower?" The man nodded. "Meet us there. We'll be ready."

Once she made up her mind, Constance was very efficient. She had a sum of money set aside, and a locksmith was found in town willing to help for a hefty fee. Waiting until after dark, she met him at the postern gate which only opened from the inside. Together they went to the wing of the castle where the boys were held. The lock on their door was a simple mechanism and he quickly had it open; taking his fee, he turned and disappeared without a word.

Constance slipped into the room and the two Mortimer boys glanced up from their board game, lit by the fire. Looking at their innocent faces Constance felt a surge of pity. Edmund, the older, was thirteen and Roger was eleven—too young to be hostages. They really didn't deserve this life; she was glad to help them escape.

"I'm here to take you away. To your uncle in Wales."

Edmund stood. "In secret?"

"Yes. My brother's servant is bringing horses. They are to meet us at midnight."

"Is Richard coming?"

"Of course. You can ride, can't you?"

The boys looked at each other. "Not very well."

"All right. My son will help you. Pack your things in a bag and bring an extra cloak. We'll be traveling through the forest."

Roger let out a little whine but his brother shushed him. "It'll be an adventure. You'll see."

"I'll wait. Let's stuff something under the covers so it looks like you are sleeping."

Encouraged, the boys followed her direction and the three of them made their way to Constance's chambers, where Richard was waiting. She packed her jewels, money, and warm clothes and, taking one last look around, opened the door. No one was in the hallway.

"Come on. Stay near the wall."

Quietly, the four of them made their way down the stairs and along a covered colonnade until they reached the end. Fortunately, there was no moon and the sky was cloudy, so Constance felt relatively well-hidden. But she couldn't stop her teeth from chattering, though whether it was from cold or fear she didn't know. She paused at the hooting of an owl, then chided herself. There was no point in being jumpy. "This way," she said, trying to sound confident. Crossing the bailey, they found the postern gate. Milton was waiting outside, as promised. He had brought an escort of six men.

Letting out a sigh of relief, Constance shuffled the boys through the door and with a little boost, the Mortimers were settled into their saddles. Then they were off.

Milton was familiar with the area—a great reassurance, because Constance had no idea where they were headed. They stuck to less-travelled paths and rode through the night, which was hard on the Mortimer boys because they could barely stay awake, much less stay in the saddle. Two of their escorts put the children in front of them on their own mounts. Just before dawn the party was forced to stop because the boys could go no farther. They found an abandoned farmhouse and made improvised beds with straw under their cloaks. Milton had brought enough food for three days and after a few hours' sleep, they broke their fast and then mounted again. The lads knew how serious this was and continued without complaining.

They rode the whole next day, though a fresh batch of snow slowed them down. Constance was in despair that their tracks were obvious to anyone following. But what could they do? Face west and keep going. And trust to their luck.

Unfortunately, their luck ran out. Toward nightfall, they could hear the pounding of hooves behind them, and the party spurred their horses to dash forward. All of them knew they were doomed. Two of the escort kept going, preferring to save their own necks. The rest turned and faced the new threat; Milton and the others drew their swords and bolted forward, hoping to overawe their pursuers.

Constance took advantage of the situation to encourage the boys to follow the fleeing men. Shouting for them to hurry, she started off with a jump, but a thump behind her betrayed that one of her charges had fallen from his horse. Cursing, she turned around and saw Roger lying on his side in the snow. That was the end of their escape, and she went back, dismounting and pulling the boy to his feet. She wiped the tears from his face as the other two gathered around.

"I'm so sorry," Roger gasped.

"It's all right, child. No one is going to hurt you." She wasn't so sure about herself.

They could hear the fighting still, though it was hard to determine what was happening among the trees. Their allies were outnumbered and as Constance watched in despair, two men fell to the ground. A few more sword strokes and two others threw up their arms in surrender, leaving their last companion fighting until he fell to his knees.

It was over. Everything had been for naught. Both the Mortimers were crying as the king's men lifted them back onto their horses. Constance shook off any help and mounted her own by herself.

"Where are you taking us?" she asked.

"Back to Windsor. The king will decide what to do with you."

It was one of those rare days that King Henry allowed himself to relax. Their Christmas celebrations at Eltham had been extended another month to allow for the wedding ceremony of one of Queen Joanna's lady-maids. They had since moved on to

Kennington, just south of London. Unable to sit still for too long, Henry was poring over the accounts relating to the queen's dower. When they had married, two years before, Henry had granted her an annuity of 10,000 marks, or £6666—easily a quarter of the royal household's expenses. Although it was the largest dowry ever given to a queen of England, he was so thrilled to have her by his side he didn't care what it cost. Unfortunately, this unpopular gesture was impossible to fund, and after one year it was already £3000 in arrears. The only way to make up the difference was to bestow estates and land forfeited by traitors or acquired in other ways.

Queen Joanna sat by the fire, playing on her lute which always comforted her husband. He looked up at her and smiled, when the door opened behind him. Turning, his smile fell to a frown. It was Erpingham and the man's expression meant no good.

"What is it this time?"

"A message from Windsor." The knight came forward and held out the paper.

Henry took it and squinted, holding it close to his face. "God's blood," he exclaimed. "When will this ever end?"

"What happened?" Joanna put her lute aside and stood up.

"The Mortimer boys. That cursed Constance has carried them off. I should have known she couldn't be trusted."

"When?" Joanna put a hand on Henry's shoulder.

"During the night. Constable Waterton discovered their empty room this morning. They are several hours ahead of us." He looked at Erpingham. "Where would they have gone, do you think?"

"To Wales, most likely. Their uncle might have had a hand in this."

"We must go. I can't sit here and wait."

Erpingham smiled grimly. "I've already ordered the horses to be saddled."

Henry picked up Joanna's hand and kissed it. "So much for my day of rest. Meet me at Westminster, my dear. I'll be there in a few days."

Wasting no time, Henry muttered at the inconvenience and mounted his waiting steed. Erpingham was with them as well as John Beaufort, the Earl of Somerset. It was a snowy night and very cold, but there was no helping it so the king and his six followers bent their heads into the wind and kicked their horses into a canter. It was twenty-eight miles to Windsor; they stopped at Brentford and changed mounts then continued for the rest of the night. All knew that Henry wouldn't slow down; he had enough energy for ten men.

Sir Hugh Waterton was waiting for them and called the grooms forward. A crowd of young men ran up and took the weary horses as the riders dismounted. They followed the constable into the great hall. Henry allowed a servant to remove his cloak as Hugh handed him a mug of mulled wine.

"What have you learned so far?" the king asked, fighting his weariness.

"As soon as I discovered the boys were missing I sent my men after them. Because of the snow, their tracks were easy to follow. They were headed toward Wales. Then I sent my message to you."

"You haven't heard back yet?"

"No, Sire. I suggest you get some rest. I will notify you as soon as they return."

Henry nodded. "We can't take any chances. Issue an order for the arrest of Lady Constance Despenser and her accomplices. Wake me in four hours."

Once he was alone in his bed with the curtains drawn, Henry discovered he couldn't sleep. This was the first time he allowed himself to think about what had happened. At first he felt a frisson of anger, but it soon turned into sadness. What had he done to deserve yet another slap in the face from his own family? Constance was his first cousin, for God's sake. Hadn't he shown her enough forgiveness after the Epiphany Rising? He could have deprived her of all the Despenser estates after her husband was killed by the mob. But he didn't. He even allowed her custody of her son. They were never particularly close, but he expected a shred of gratitude from her.

He rolled over, pulling the covers tighter. And what about her brother? Surely Edward of York had a hand in this disaster. Of that, he had no doubt. Who else could persuade Constance to attempt such a dangerous enterprise? With that tongue of his, the man was the devil incarnate. Too bad he was so useful! And Henry had few enough titled nobles to rely on without losing the Duke of York for yet another unprincipled scheme.

But why? What did they have to gain? What more did they expect from him?

It took a day and a half before a bedraggled party showed up at Windsor. Tired but triumphant, Waterton's scout led the two Mortimer boys on one horse, followed by Constance and her son. The lady refused to look at the king.

Pulling the exhausted boys from their mount, Waterton fussed over them like a mother hen. "You're shivering," he chided. "We'll get you out of those wet clothes and into a bath." He turned the lads over to a servant while a groom helped Constance from her horse. She straightened before the king, trying to retain her dignity. It wasn't easy; her cloak was soaked through and dirty around the hem and her hair spilled out from under a crooked hood.

Henry took one look at her then turned away. He gestured to the scout. "Tell me what happened."

"We caught up with them in the woods near Cheltenham, Sire. They were riding hard and we had to attack them. We killed two of her servants but two got away. The rest surrendered."

"You have done well, my man. Hugh, reward him for his good service." He gave another sidelong glance at Constance. "Make sure they are all ready to travel to London on the morrow," he said. "Have John Beaufort take them to Westminster for trial."

Constance shuddered. She may have been temporarily spared a dressing-down by the king, but her punishment was only delayed. She saw Henry's look of disdain.

Four days later, Constance was brought before the king's council at Westminster. She had had time to regain her dignity and swept into the room, chin held high, though no one looked favourably upon her. Henry sat at the head of a long table flanked by his great officers as well as the Archbishop of Canterbury, John Beaufort, and Edward of York. She quickly squelched a look of surprise when she saw her brother.

Chancellor Langley stood. "Lady Constance Despenser, you are brought here to answer for the treason of abducting the young Earl of March and his brother and plotting against the king. How do you answer these charges?"

Glancing at York, Constance took a deep breath. "My lords, I cannot deny that I attempted to free the Mortimer boys from their imprisonment. They have done nothing to justify incarceration and deserved to be united with their uncle."

"You were taking them into rebel territory."

"I was taking them to my estates in South Wales."

"Which had risen in rebellion!" Langley's voice went up in volume. "How did you arrange their escape?"

Unwilling to compromise her brother, Constance held her tongue.

"You must answer or face serious consequences. I repeat: how did you arrange their escape?"

Frowning, Constance lowered her head a moment. "I hired a locksmith."

"A locksmith?"

She nodded.

"And you spirited the boys away in the middle of the night. Two men have been killed because of your foolish plot. And the locksmith will lose a hand. By law." Langley paused as the clerk recorded his words. "Who is behind this plot?"

Again, Constance pursed her lips.

"The king does not believe you planned this alone. Who else is involved in this abduction?"

"No one," she said.

"Do you really expect us to accept this? Who persuaded you to attempt this treason?"

"I did it on my own." She looked over at her brother who was busy inspecting his nails.

King Henry caught that glance. He shifted in his chair. "My lord of York, what are your thoughts on this matter?"

Thus singled out, York glanced up uncomfortably. He stood. "I do not know, Sire. The Lady Despenser had her reasons."

"You knew nothing about this venture?"

"Sire, you have my loyalty."

"And your loyalty to your sister?"

"My sister speaks for herself."

In the midst of this exchange, Henry noticed that Constance was getting more and more agitated. This talking in circles was doing York no good at all. "I repeat," the king said. "Do you assert that you knew nothing about this conspiracy?"

"This is the first I learned about it."

"Stop!" Unable to stomach her brother's faithlessness a minute longer, Constance dropped her sullen behaviour. She pointed at Edward. "My brother, the Duke of York, has instigated this plan. It was he who brought the suggestion to me."

"That is a lie!"

"It was you who arranged everything. I was just your instrument."

"You foolish girl. I did nothing of the sort." York looked around, appalled at the expressions he saw. No one believed him.

Henry was unsurprised. "You deny all knowledge of her actions, yet Lady Despenser accuses you of initiating this plot. You can't have it both ways, cousin. What was your involvement?"

Starting to sweat, York wiped his forehead. "I admit I had heard rumours but regrettably did not act upon them."

"He persuaded me to abduct the boys to further his aims." Constance stamped her foot.

"You lie," Edward retorted, his voice rising.

"I would have done nothing without your guidance."

York threw out his arms, turning to the others. "You can see my sister is trying to deflect the blame onto myself. What possible motive could I have had?"

"What motive could *I* have had?" she retorted, pointing at Edward. "You are the one who is lying. I challenge you, Duke Edward, to trial by combat. I call for a champion to step forward and do battle for me. My cause is just! If my champion is worsted in the lists on my behalf, I give myself up to be burnt alive. Will anyone in this room take up the cause of a wronged woman?"

Lady Despenser's voice rang clear and sharp, but she was not a popular figure in the court and had not bothered to make many friends. Men looked down at their hands, at the door, the king—anywhere else but her. Edward's gloating smile increased her humiliation.

She looked around in consternation. "Will no one stand as my champion?"

The hush in the room stretched interminably. Finally, a voice she did not immediately recognize broke the silence. "I will defend the Lady Despenser." Constance turned around, grateful but puzzled. The young man strode forward and threw down his gage before the duke. "The Lady is innocent and I challenge you to take up arms against me."

Edward's smile widened. "Gladly, Squire William Maidstone. Though I warn you, your cause is desperate."

"No more desperate than you are," William snarled. "How dare you discredit this woman? Where is your sense of honour?"

"We are not speaking of honour here. We are speaking of treason."

"The treason you share with me, if any is spoken of," interjected Constance. "You are as guilty as I am!"

"I will prove your lie against this poor man," York shouted, pointing at her.

"Enough!" King Henry jumped to his feet. "I forbid this travesty. Squire William," he said more gently, "you have done this lady a great service but I will not permit this to go on. I acknowledge and thank you for your gallantry."

William bowed first to the king, then to Constance before backing from the room. Henry faced the Duke of York. "There is more to this situation than I originally suspected. Thomas of Lancaster," he called to his son, gesturing him forward, "take the Duke of York to the Tower until the circumstances can be more thoroughly investigated. Guards, escort the Lady Despenser back to her quarters."

Both Edward and Constance stared at the king in consternation before they were hauled away. Henry refused to look at either one of them. "We have wasted enough of our time," he said to the council. "Let us move on to our next order of business."

Later that evening, Henry sat alone before the fire in his private solar, wishing he was back at Eltham. Westminster Palace was not his favourite residence. Originally built on Thorney Island in the middle of a swamp, it was infested with vermin and in constant danger of flooding. The stuffy odour of mould permeated the older rooms. The roof leaked and the windows were drafty. But since most of the government's offices were permanently seated here, he had to make the best of it. He poured himself some wine while he waited for his prisoner. A knock was followed by Constance Despenser, who attempted to sustain her usual haughtiness. The guard closed the door behind her and she stood still, looking at the far wall.

He sighed. "Please, cousin. This is difficult enough without your ridiculous behaviour. Sit down."

Letting out her breath, Constance obliged, finding an uncomfortable chair that forced her to maintain her stiff posture.

Henry frowned, annoyed by her conceit. "I don't understand all this. I've given you back your estates, maintained your annuity, allowed you to keep your son. Why would you repay me with such an offense? Do you hate me so much?" He chided himself for the slight complaint in his voice. But he couldn't help it.

"Sire, as I said, my brother instigated this." Her voice was dull, unemotional.

"Why did you agree?" snapped Henry, losing his patience.

She hesitated. "They didn't deserve to be locked up," she said finally.

The king refused to believe her. "There's more to this story."

For once, she looked directly at him. "Yes and no. My Lord. In your rush to take the throne, you trounced on everyone who stood in your way. Those unfortunate boys. My father. My brother. King Richard who should never have died. What is my poor indiscretion compared to the sins on your soul?"

Henry compressed his lips, taken aback. "That is quite enough, Lady Despenser. By your own admission, you have committed treason. I'll spare your wretched life because of the love I bore your father, who deserved more charity than you ever showed him. As for the Mortimer boys, you did them no favour. Now that I see how vulnerable they are, I shall send them to Pevensey Castle where I can surround them with better security."

She gasped, shaken by the repercussions of her escapade. She started to speak and was forced to clear her throat. "What shall happen to me?"

"Don't worry. I am not a monster. I'm sending you to Kenilworth Castle. If you show good behaviour, I may be prevailed upon to forgive you someday." He turned around in his chair. "Guards!"

The door opened immediately. "Take Lady Despenser back to her quarters. In the morning, she is to be sent to Kenilworth. Watch her closely."

Daunted, Constance went quietly. She was exhausted and defeated but managed to summon up a look of bitterness as she left the room. Henry didn't care. He had had enough of his ungrateful cousins. Too bad he still had to deal with Edward. This was one man he needed in his government. Now he, too, had to be taught a lesson. Again.

After giving it much thought, he sent for Erpingham. The old knight could be relied upon to use his discretion. He alone, aside from the archbishop, knew the true story of King Richard's escape. Loyal from the beginning, Erpingham had served John of Gaunt in Spain and Scotland and stayed with Henry in France during his exile.

Always near at hand, Erpingham stepped into the room with a slight bow. His jet black hair was greying now around the temples and his weathered face bore more wrinkles than Henry wanted to acknowledge. But he was as robust as ever and showed no signs of slowing down.

"Join me, Thomas," said Henry, waving at a chair. "It has been a long day."

Nodding, Erpingham helped himself to a cup of wine as he sat with a grunt.

"I suppose you know why I asked for you."

"Edward of York?"

Henry puffed out a breath. "That's it. Confound him, he would sell his own mother if it proved to his benefit. We already saw how far his loyalty stretched to his sister."

"Too bad he's so useful to you."

"Exactly my problem. Not to mention that I don't exactly have a surfeit of dukes running around." Henry poured himself more wine, making a face at the nearly empty pitcher. "Thomas, I don't have the patience to deal with him again."

"He's at the Tower?"

"On his way, at least. I would have you go and see him. Find out his story. I know he's hiding something. I'm inclined to send him to join the Mortimer boys at Pevensey. Let's give him some time to think it over."

Edward, Duke of York admitted he knew about the conspiracy to abduct the boys, but he never let the name of Percy cross his lips. Careful as ever, he wanted to make sure he ended up on the winning side of this conspiracy, whatever happened. If he refrained from compromising his collaborators, they would recognize his loyalty—if they prevailed. If they met with disaster, no one would know any better and Henry would eventually pardon him. He need only be patient.

Erpingham questioned him at length, then finally gave up. He was transferred from the Tower to Pevensey Castle—a cold and unforgiving fortress. The king allowed him some books and writing utensils and he settled down to work on his beloved project: translating Gaston Phoebus's *Livre de Chasse* into English. That would keep him busy.

It didn't take long for word of the failed rescue to reach Glyndwr. Percy had tarried at Aberystwyth, waiting for developments. This first blow to his ambitions hit him hard, but they had gone too far to abandon their plans. Dining in a private chamber with Owain and Edmund Mortimer, Percy was encouraged by the Welshman's confidence.

"Unfortunate though this is," said Owain, "the absence of Edmund's nephew need not change our intentions. Once Henry is out of the way, we'll have the lad in our possession, regardless. In any case, Edmund would rule in his nephew's interest until the boy reaches his majority. Let us continue to perfect our *Tripartite Indenture*. It is almost complete."

And so they progressed. By the end of February 1405, the three leaders of the proposed ruling council over England and Wales convened a ceremony, dressed in their finest. They presided over a small gathering of mostly Welsh gentry who had come to witness this important event. Glyndwr's chancellor read out the text of his document:

"The lords Owain Glyndwr, Earl Henry Percy, and Sir Edmund Mortimer shall henceforth be joined to one another by the bond of a true federation and true friendship. Each of these lords shall procure the honour and advantage of one another and in good faith prevent any losses and distresses that shall come to the knowledge of any of them." He went on for a while in this vein until he came to the division of the kingdom. "It is unanimously agreed that Owain and his heirs shall have the whole of Wales from the Severn coast where the River Severn leads from the sea, north directly by the high road to the source of the River Trent, thence to the river commonly called the Mersey, thus encompassing the Marcher territories. The Earl of Northumberland shall have to himself and his heirs the counties of Northumberland, Westmorland, Lancashire, Yorkshire, Lincolnshire, Nottinghamshire, Derbyshire, Staffordshire, Leicestershire, Northamptonshire, Warwickshire, and Norfolk. And Lord Edmund shall have the whole of the remainder of England entirely to himself and his successors."

Thus, the whole country was divided up between these three lords, who swore to defend the kingdom against all men, except the most illustrious prince, Charles of France. They duly swore an oath to observe the conditions of the indenture and affixed their seals to the document. The conspiracy against King Henry was entering a new phase.

CHAPTER 6

Fortified by his compact with the Welsh, Henry Percy returned to the North to raise support from his loyal retainers and disgruntled vassals. His captains had already demonstrated their commitment to him when the king tried to take over Northumberland's castles. King Henry would never win the hearts of his fellow countrymen; Lancaster had little understanding of the Northern Marches. John of Gaunt had tried and failed to govern this territory and his son would have no better luck.

On the other hand, Percy reasoned to himself, the Earl of Westmorland was encroaching on his domains. His family had been prominent office-holders in the region since the reign of Henry III, though none had risen as high as Ralph Neville. *He* was the man most to be reckoned with, and now that he was Prince John's advisor his position was more entrenched than ever.

On the way home, Percy needed to stop over at York. He had resolved to pay another visit to the archbishop. If Scrope could be persuaded to add his voice to the northern rebellion, he would confer a mantle of respectability otherwise lacking. Percy knew the man was relatively non-political. But recent clashes between the king and clergy over taxation were still unresolved, as well as unrest among the merchants for the same reason. This would be a good time to bring their grievances out into the open.

Archbishop Scrope welcomed the earl guardedly. Percy inwardly winced at his restraint, so different from the last time they had met. But he had no choice; he must stay his course. The archbishop kept the conversation neutral while they sat down to dinner and helped themselves to a platter of roasted squabs. There was another guest at Scrope's table, and at first Percy was annoyed at the intrusion. But once introductions were made, he immediately saw a new opportunity.

"This is Thomas Mowbray, son of the old Duke of Norfolk," said Scrope, gesturing to a lad of around twenty years of age. He had his father's craggy nose which made him easily recognizable. "Thomas," said the archbishop, "meet Henry Percy, Earl of Northumberland."

Thomas's mouth moved into something resembling a quick smile before he resumed a sullen demeanour. Percy observed him curiously. It was unknown whether King Henry would have recalled Mowbray from exile; the duke died in Venice just before Henry's coronation. It appeared his son had already developed a bad attitude, if this behaviour was any indication.

Why not put him to the test? "I understand the king made Westmorland Earl Marshal," Percy said, trying to appear sympathetic.

Thomas grimaced. "For life! He's serving in that military capacity," he said bitterly. "King Henry allowed me to retain my hereditary title but not the rank, claiming I was too young." He took a sip of wine. "I think we know the real reason."

Nodding, Percy took a bite of his bird, savouring the taste. "You have a valid complaint," he agreed in his most conciliatory tone. "Many of us would like to bring our grievances to the king's attention. Especially here in the North." He gestured to the archbishop.

"Oh?" Mowbray glanced first at Percy and then at Scrope. "Do you include yourself in that number, your Grace?"

After a moment the archbishop nodded. His eyes darted from Percy to the door, as though he wished his guest gone.

"If you were to join forces with York," Percy said, leaning forward and pointing his knife, "that would give added impetus to the movement."

"Me?" Thomas put his wine down, flattered.

"Of course. Henry can't ignore his nobles. You'll reach your majority very soon, won't you?"

"Well, yes."

"And you'll take your seat in Parliament as 4th Earl of Norfolk. This would be your first opportunity to be heard."

Scrope cleared his throat. "What are your plans, Earl Henry?"

Percy turned his attention to the archbishop. "I'm just coming back from Wales," he said.

"Oh?" Scrope wondered where the earl had gone after their last meeting but had refrained from asking.

"Owain Glyndwr was a most gracious host. We have much in common."

"Indeed." The archbishop sighed, resigning himself to the conversation. "And what might that be?"

"Let us be honest with each other." Percy took a sip of his wine, glancing at Scrope over the edge of his cup. "The Welsh, the Northerners, even your York merchants…as you say, all of us suffer hardship under Lancaster's administration. The government is insolvent, and rather than give us any consideration, they squeeze us relentlessly for our hard-earned money. If King Henry had negotiated with Glyndwr instead of imposing even more hardships on the Welsh, he wouldn't be spending all his resources fighting a rebellion."

Scrope contemplated his clasped hands. "There is much in what you say."

"There is much you can do," Percy urged. "You are the voice of the downtrodden. If you rouse the merchants of York— if you take up arms to redress these wrongs—your standing will give credibility to their protests. When Earl Thomas Mowbray and the Welsh add their voices to our alliance, we will become too forceful to ignore." He set his mouth, conjuring up another argument. "After speaking with Owain Glyndwr, I am certain that if England is returned to good rule, the Welsh will also make peace."

Scrope rested his chin in his hand. "What you say bears consideration. It is true the king beggars the merchants with excessive customs duties and forced loans." He moved his hand to his cheek, looking aside at Percy. "It's true. His exactions are crippling every class of citizenry in York."

Percy nodded. "You can post a manifesto that the heirs of nobles should be restored to their rightful inheritance and honours." He glanced meaningfully at Mowbray. "And insist that King Henry's avaricious and greedy counsellors should be removed. You will demand that knights and burgesses should be properly elected to parliament, instead of the king's personal nominees."

"You're right," said the archbishop, gaining enthusiasm despite himself. "I can inspire the men of York to support our cause. But wait," he muttered, slumping in his chair. "I'm not a military man. Nor are our citizens."

"That is no matter." Percy pushed his plate away. "I will furnish the main fighting force and bring them down from the North. We will set a date to join our armies together here, say at Shipton Moor just west of York. This puts you in easy reach of my Tadcaster estates. My levies will join your supporters at the end of our march and you will fill out their ranks, making us numerically formidable. Meanwhile, Glyndwr will keep Prince Hal tied up in Wales so he cannot join forces with his father."

"I see," said Scrope, not really comprehending all of it. But Percy was an old hand and obviously knew what he was doing. "I will consult with local leaders and determine their level of support."

"I know you can inspire them," Percy assured him. He knew when to stop. Let matters take their own course, for now.

By morning, the earl departed; he was satisfied that he had accomplished his mission. He suspected Scrope had spent much of the night at prayer, for as the archbishop bade him farewell, a look of determination on the prelate's face indicated a new resolve.

It was just as well; Percy was already planning the next step. He hadn't bothered to confide his deepest concerns to his new allies; they needed encouragement, not uneasiness. But there was still the Earl of Westmorland to be dealt with. If Percy's enterprise was to have any hope of success, Westmorland would have to be taken out of action.

Time was of the essence. As soon as Percy returned to Warkworth he summoned his retainers and local lords to a war council. He sent letters to the far edges of Northumberland, calling in old favours and promising redress of King Henry's misrule. He welcomed Lord Bardolf—who had quietly slipped away from Westminster—and four of his most trustworthy North Yorkshire knights, Ralph Hastings, John Fauconberg, John Fitzrandolph and John Colville. Clifford came south from Berwick, along with Robert Umfraville.

Umfraville was the new Warden of Berwick town and had been one of Percy's retainers for years; unfortunately, Percy was unaware that he had also been retained for life by the king. These days, it was not at all unusual for a man to serve more than one master; it was like an attorney having more than one client. As warden of the town he had been working closely with Clifford who was captain of the castle. There was no problem between them, since so far his instructions from King Henry had not interfered with the day-to-day routines.

During the meeting, Umfraville sat quietly and listened while the earl outlined his plans; he wasn't about to call attention to himself.

"I need four hundred men to capture the Earl of Westmorland and render him powerless," Percy was saying. "He stands in the way of our objectives. I know many of you have lost lands and influence to that upstart."

He wasn't exactly an upstart, thought Umfraville.

"Once we capture Westmorland," Percy went on, "my good Yorkshire knights"—he nodded at the four men who had come with Bardolf—"have agreed to gather their forces near Tadcaster. Archbishop Scrope will be waiting for them at Shipton Moor, near York. Our combined forces will thenceforth march south, and our numbers will be swelled as we pass through Thomas Mowbray's lands." Barely able to contain his enthusiasm, Percy rubbed his hands together. "We shall finish what my son started. My scouts tell me that King Henry is in Hereford arranging his next Welsh campaign. If the king chooses to turn around and march to confront us—which I expect—Owain Glyndwr will keep Prince Hal occupied so he cannot join his father. We shall outnumber the royal forces and take them down. Then we shall raise up the Mortimers, the true heirs to the crown."

Watching the general hubbub, Umfraville did not join in. The plan was a bit sketchy. Did Northumberland really think removing Westmorland would make the difference between success and failure? A lot could happen between now and then. But no matter what Percy was planning, it sounded too much like treason. Most of the men present were antagonistic to the Neville clan, so they found Percy's objectives perfectly acceptable.

Umfraville, on the other hand, felt no such animosity toward Westmorland. Over the years he had seen the growing rivalry between these two powerful families. Up until now, it didn't affect him. But all of a sudden, he found himself in the opposing camp and he didn't like it. If it was a matter of siding with either Percy or the king, there really wasn't any choice. Why should he stick his neck out to satisfy Northumberland's ambitions? On the other hand, if he were to step in and thwart Percy's insurrection, the king would be eternally grateful.

Not wanting to give himself away, Sir Robert stayed through the feast, making sure to water his wine. No need to dull his senses. Fortunately, he had taken lodgings in town, so when he and his retinue retired for the night, no one thought twice about it.

Once they arrived at the inn, he pulled one of his squires aside. "Hardyng," he said to the man. "I want you to ride hard for Sir Hrolf Eure's castle at Witton le Wear and give this message to the Earl of Westmorland." He handed the man a letter with his seal. "I know he is staying there. It's vital he learns that Henry Percy plans to march on Witton with four hundred men and capture him unawares. I will stay here so as not to raise the alarm and join him when it's safe to do so."

Knowing the importance of his mission, John Hardyng bowed and went to saddle a fresh horse, leaving Umfraville to plan his next move. He was an ambitious man—always ready to volunteer so he could be an eye-witness to major events. He served Hotspur until his death, and now Umfraville, keeping a chronicle that glorified and pleased his patrons. Someday, he'd be finished with his annals and he hoped they would gain approval from a future master—maybe even the king.

Ralph Neville, the Earl of Westmorland was a practical man. He had served King Richard II faithfully and received his earldom in 1397 as a result. But when Henry Bolingbroke landed at Ravenspur, he supported the usurpation. He had to; there was no other way to ensure his rival, Henry Percy, would not triumph at his expense. At the time, it was important for Neville and Percy to keep an eye on each other. As expected, their uncomfortable alliance didn't last long.

On the very day of Henry's coronation he was made Marshal of England for life. Of course, his marriage to Bolingbroke's half-sister Joan had a lot to do with his success—and continued loyalty. And now, he was given charge of the king's son John—a reliable way to stay attached to the royal affinity.

He looked over at the fifteen-year-old lad who was helping himself to a second serving of stew. John was the third son of King Henry, a likable boy who knew how to listen and showed good potential as a fighter. John had already been given the title of Warden of the East Marches alongside Westmorland's posting as Warden of the West Marches toward Scotland. Together they would impose law and order on the borders. And, following in his brother's footsteps, John would soon be ruling in his own right.

The prince looked up at him with a smile when the knock of a servant brought their heads around. A messenger was announced from Sir Robert Umfraville. Sir Hrolf, Westmorland's host, beckoned the newcomer forward. The man bowed but extended the missive toward Westmorland.

"What's this?" asked the earl. "Oh, Hardyng. This letter must be important for your lord to part with you." He noted the seal before opening the missive. A look of concern turned to a frown, bringing John to his feet.

"I knew this was going to happen." Westmorland handed the note to his nephew. "That damned Percy. He's stirring up another rebellion and seeks to get me out of the way. Or worse." He stood, adjusting his belt. "I appreciate your hospitality, Sir Hrolf. Alas, Percy will be marching here with a small army just to capture me. I must be on my way tonight. He's up to no good."

Putting an arm around John's shoulders, Westmorland gave a squeeze. "Thanks to Umfraville, we'll have a head start. We'll ride to Durham; it's only fifteen miles."

Calmed by his uncle's cool demeanour, John thanked their host in his turn and hurried to alert his men. Westmorland watched him leave the room and picked up his cup, gesturing toward Sir Hrolf. "I'll know soon enough what we're up against. I may need your assistance," he said. "This is one rebellion too many. Percy can't be allowed to get away with it this time."

"You can count on me," said Hrolf. "Northumberland won't get any satisfaction here. He can break his head against my castle walls as much as he wants."

Nodding his thanks, Westmorland quickly assembled his men and they were soon on their way, disappearing into the night.

The day after making his plans, Henry Percy led four hundred men south the sixty miles to Witton le Wear. He was accompanied by Umfraville, Bardolf, and many of his high-ranking retainers. All were mounted and lightly armed; after all, they only had one man to capture. Well, two, counting Prince John. He wasn't sure what he was planning to do with the lad; maybe he wouldn't even be there. They stopped for the night at Newcastle, where Hardyng quietly joined them on his way back from Witton; he gave Umfraville his report and promptly fell asleep for a couple of hours before joining the army. He hadn't been missed.

The next morning they continued on their way, riding hard over well-travelled roads for the most part; speed was more important than stealth.

Or was it? Percy was so confident he would take Westmorland unawares that he underestimated his victim. He was a little surprised that the gates of the castle were closed, but wasted no time in announcing himself.

"Sir Hrolf Eure," he bellowed, facing the twin towers. "I have come to relieve you of your guest." It was a small fortification and the earl was certain they could hear him. "Open the gates. I demand entrance."

After a short wait, the knight himself appeared at the battlements. "Earl Percy," he shouted back. "Move on. There is nothing for you here."

"I beg to differ. I have come for the Earl of Westmorland."

"He departed last night."

79

"What?" Percy whirled around, frowning at Bardolf. "You told me he was here," he said in a low voice.

"He was." The other stepped forward. "Do you expect us to believe you?" he shouted up.

"Why not? If he was here, he would confront you."

Facing away, Percy felt his first pang of anxiety. "He would," he said to his companions. "But I need to be sure."

Umfraville put a hand on his arm. "Let me enter the castle and search for him. I'll see if there is any sign of his men."

Squinting his eye, Percy nodded upwards. "He might detain you," he said uncertainly.

The knight waved a dismissal. "If he has nothing to hide, why would he?"

After a moment, Percy turned back to Eure. "Will you give permission for Sir Robert Umfraville to enter?"

"I know Sir Robert. He may enter alone. Step back, the rest of you."

They cooperated and Hrolf gestured to one of his men. "Open the gate for Sir Robert."

Surrendering his sword, Umfraville glanced up at the portcullis as he entered through the battlements. Sir Hrolf came down the stairs to meet him.

Robert nodded his greetings. "Westmorland couldn't have had a more gracious host," he said. "I know he received my message. My man returned this morning."

Hrolf had trouble hiding his confusion. "So why do you ride with Percy?"

"I serve King Henry first. Percy is so confident he can't see past his self-conceit. I want no part of this rebellion, and I thought I could be more useful going along with his plans. With Westmorland free, Percy has much to worry about."

"And you have come inside—"

"To convince Percy that his bird has flown."

"Then you are welcome, Sir Robert. Do you have time for a cup of wine?"

"Gladly."

Umfraville permitted himself a few minutes rest, then took his leave of Sir Hrolf, who was only too glad to see him off. He rejoined Percy who had been pacing before his men.

"Well?"

"Westmorland is gone, and so are his men." He pulled Northumberland aside. "The earl intends to raise a force against you."

"God's death!" Percy whirled away from him then came back. "How did he find out?"

Umfraville shrugged. "It could have been anyone."

"I know, I know." The earl looked at Bardolf. "This changes everything." The men surrounding him started all speaking at once, and Percy put his hands over his ears, grumbling to himself and walking away. They all followed him. Still within sight of the castle walls, the earl straightened and pointed back the way they had come. "There's nothing we can do now except reorganize ourselves. Let my Yorkshire knights continue to gather their forces. For the moment we'll go back to the safety of Warkworth."

Unwilling to brook any argument, Percy remounted, gesturing for his soldiers to follow. The other leaders looked at each other, knowing when it was useless to object. This was such a major setback, there was no knowing what he would do.

Sir Hrolf Eure watched them disperse, shaking his head. Ever since Shrewsbury, Northumberland had shown more indecision than ever in his life. It was fortunate for Hrolf that the earl wasn't a vindictive man. He wasn't prepared for a siege.

Although Westmorland rode to Durham for safety, he wasted no time forwarding a dispatch to King Henry, in Hereford. The king received the message just as he was composing a letter to Hal about his troop dispositions in the upcoming campaign.

Passing the messenger, Queen Joanna came into the room and stopped at the door. As usual, Henry sat at his desk, but this time he was leaning forward, forehead in his hand, shoulders hunched. She approached quietly and started rubbing his neck.

"Bad news?"

He let out a sigh, leaning back and resting his head against her stomach. "The worst. I knew this was going to happen."

"Don't tell me it's another uprising."

He moved his head to one side as she concentrated on a stiff muscle. "The North this time. Percy waited just long enough for me to announce this campaign against the Welsh. He knew I'd be hard-pressed. Ouch!"

"Sorry." She shifted her grip.

"He tried to attack Westmorland with four hundred men, but Ralph was warned in time and got away. Damn that man! Can't he just once put England before his own selfish ambitions?"

"Will you go on to Wales?"

Henry shook his head, grabbing her hand and kissing it. "Thank you, my dear. No. There's something very wrong and I can't take a chance. I'm going to have to abandon this campaign and ride for Pontefract." He sighed. "I've invested so much here. For every pence we lose in revenue we spend twice as much trying to contain the Welsh. I can't afford to do it again. Such a terrible waste."

"Can Hal manage on his own?"

"Of that, I have no doubt. This is his patrimony now; he'll earn his spurs with me or without me. For now it will have to be without me."

The king immediately dispatched a messenger to Pontefract, ordering its castellan, the loyal Robert Waterton, to find Henry Percy and discover what was going on. Anxious to prove himself after the fiasco of Richard II's escape, Waterton personally set out for Warkworth.

Even though he would have liked to have disappeared, Umfraville knew that would have been a mistake. Until Percy made a decision one way or the other, Westmorland would be like a blind man. So he travelled back to Warkworth with the rest of the little army, suspecting that a resolution wouldn't be long in coming. And indeed it wasn't.

When Robert Waterton arrived at Warkworth Castle, he sat on his horse in thought for a moment; his escort waited behind him. Percy's banners fluttered atop the keep, announcing that he was in residence. That was good; at least they didn't have to ride all over Yorkshire looking for him. Turning, Waterton gestured to his next in command. "Stay out of sight," he ordered. "If I fail to return by midnight, don't wait for me. I want you to immediately report back to Pontefract. The king is expected there."

"But, my Lord—"

"No, if all is well I will come for you myself. If Percy is guilty of wrongdoing, he will take me prisoner. I would, if I were in his place."

The other started to object again, but to no avail. His captain was already on his way.

Henry Percy was none too pleased when Waterton was announced. He knew the decisive moment had come. Although in the interim he had put out great effort to gather support from Northumberland, not as many magnates came forward as he had hoped. He was seated on the dais in his great hall when Waterton strode forward. No welcome was extended to the constable.

"King Henry sent me," the newcomer announced, neglecting to bow. "He seeks to understand the meaning of reports he keeps hearing about your activities."

"Activities?" Percy looked down at his interrogator. "What activities are you referring to?"

"I shall speak bluntly, Earl Percy. Your attempt to capture the Earl of Westmorland smacks of rebellion."

Percy pointed to a man-at-arms next to him who bent down to hear a whispered order. Waterton watched the man descend the steps and exit the hall.

"I shall speak bluntly as well, Lord Robert. Your appearance is quite inconvenient and I must retain you." Waterton turned as four soldiers approached, halberds in hand.

"Don't worry, your stay will be comfortable." Percy nodded at the guards and Waterton glowered at him before following his warders.

After watching the men leave the hall, Percy stood. "Come, my lords," he said. "This can wait no longer. Let us meet in the council room."

Robert Umfraville was among the twenty or so men who assembled to hear the earl's decision. Percy looked at each of them in turn.

"Robert Waterton's presence has forced my hand. It is unfortunate that we were unable to remove Westmorland; he will wreak havoc on our enterprise. There's only one option at this point: I must go north to Scotland and enlist their aid."

The room was silent. Percy didn't know whether it was from shock or relief.

"This does not need to be the end," he said with less conviction. "But we must be certain of success."

Bardolf was the first to speak. "What about the others?"

"In Yorkshire? They are gathering men from Cleveland and Topcliffe. They can carry on without me until I bring help from Scotland. In fact, it might be better for everyone if our names weren't associated together—until after we triumph."

Grimacing, Bardolf narrowed his eyes. "And Scrope?"

"He'll be all right. York's purpose is to swell the ranks of our Cleveland rebels. He won't make any moves until the rest of the army is in the field."

Bardolf shrugged. "We'll have to leave at once."

"I intend to. We'll take a small force so we can travel faster. We'll take Waterton along with us; once we lodge him at Berwick, he'll be no threat."

This was the moment Umfraville was waiting for. Assuring Percy he had to collect his own resources, he made his excuses and left for his estates. Once safely away, he and his men rode hard for Durham.

CHAPTER 7

Durham Castle was well guarded, but Umfraville was known to all and immediately gained access to Westmorland and Prince John. The earl was at a table piled high with instructions to his captains, and his face lit up when the newcomer was admitted.

"Robert!" He exclaimed. "I am so glad to see you! I have been gathering strength for a confrontation with Percy. Lords Fitzhugh and Eure are already here."

The prince turned from the window. "You have good news for us, I trust," he said.

"Most encouraging. You are free to march south and confront the rebels."

Westmorland put down his quill. "What about Percy?"

"You no longer need to worry about him. The way is clear. Percy has decided to go north and beg the Scots for aid."

"Surely not!" exclaimed John. "That would be madness!"

"One would think so," said Umfraville. "To be honest, I think he's going there to save his own skin. He saw that his cause was already lost once Waterton showed up at the king's behest." He removed his gloves, placing them on the table. "Of course, Percy arrested him."

"I thought it was a bad idea to send Waterton," Westmorland mused. "King Henry needed confirmation, as if Percy's attempt to abduct me wasn't enough of a warning. Now Waterton needs rescuing."

"He's beyond help, I'm sorry to say. They are taking him to Berwick. Though I don't think Northumberland means to harm him."

"I hope you're right."

"I don't know what got into Percy's head. The fool couldn't be bothered warning his Yorkshire partners." Umfraville barely restrained a look of contempt. "He seems convinced they will carry on without him, until he returns. If he ever does."

"Who are they?"

"Four knights. Hastings, Fauconberg, Fitzrandolph, and Colville. They are gathering strength from his Topcliffe and Cleveland estates. Without Percy in command, I suspect they will be rudderless."

"Good men, but not great leaders. So much the better." Westmorland gestured to John. "Tell our captains to prepare to march south. If we move quickly enough, we'll be able to catch our Yorkshiremen before they even know their leader has fled."

"There's more. Archbishop Scrope is rousing support from York. I believe he will wait for them at Shipton Moor."

"I know where that is. It's about six miles northwest of the city. If fortune favours us, we can stop the Topcliffe rebels then continue on to York."

"Yes, deal with them separately. Their numbers promise to be quite substantial."

Once Archbishop Scrope came to terms with Percy's rebellion, he embraced it wholeheartedly and made it his own. Hadn't he been resisting the king's burdensome taxes for quite some time? He preached about the evils afflicting the kingdom, starting in his own cathedral; then he took the word to smaller churches. The more he sermonized, the more ardent his convictions grew. Then he issued a manifesto and had many copies made so he could nail them to the gates of the city, church doors, and even alleyways and street corners. He sent copies to curates of surrounding villages so they could preach to their congregations.

His manifesto was respectful and reasonable; he had refrained from direct accusations. Rather, he stated simply and effectively all the ways the government should improve the hardships of the people. The document was only a beginning; he was confident that, with the might of his followers, he would achieve the attention they most obviously deserved.

Mounting the steps before Saint Mary's Abbey in York, Scrope gave his most pointed speech yet. Finding a voice he didn't even realize he possessed, he raised both arms to encompass the notables and churchmen surrounding him.

"I am not rebelling against the king," he insisted as the citizens gathered before him. "No, I am complaining about King Henry's avaricious and greedy counsellors, gorging themselves on the wealth ordained for the common good. We shall demand that the king remove the intolerable burdens imposed on the clergy. But that's not all. I protest against the king's unbearable taxes and forced loans!" He was pleased at their reaction. "I denounce the excessive customs duties and oppressions that are crippling the people of York."

The citizens shouted encouragement. They needed this opportunity to express their grievances. Up until now, they felt they had no outlet for their resentment. And here was their most respected prelate, taking their side. "I protest against the crown's abuse of purveyance," Scrope shouted. "Suppliers are forced to hand over their goods to the king's representatives who fail to pay them. This should never be permitted!" His words were received with applause, for many of the offended merchants were in his audience.

Raising his chin, Scrope responded fervently. "We shall insist that proper knights and burgesses should be elected to parliament instead of royal favourites. Our needs must be addressed! The sons of nobles should be restored to their rightful inheritances and honours," he added, pointing to Thomas Mowbray who stood uncomfortably next to him. "It is time we overturned the evils threatening this kingdom!" He waited until the cheering died down. "If our demands are put into practice, England will be better able to resist foreign enemies and protect our trade. Even the Welsh promised to make peace if our country returns to good rule."

The archbishop knew what was important to his flock. "Any who might fall defending this sacred cause will be guaranteed full remission for their sins."

That was it. Almost every man in York capable of bearing arms swore they would join his movement. He knew this was not an effective fighting force. On the other hand, their numbers and enthusiasm must count for something once the Topcliffe rebels joined them. According to schedule, they were to gather at Shipton Moor and await the others who should appear by 28 May.

On the agreed-upon date, the archbishop donned a borrowed breastplate and went out into the streets, crosier in hand, exhorting the people to follow him. He was surrounded by members of his household including the archdeacon of York, his vicar-general, and several clerics. Singing old crusader songs, Scrope led a growing multitude of priests, monks, and townsmen through the city gates. They armed themselves as best as they could with spears and old swords, shovels and axes. At the front of the army rode Earl Thomas Mowbray and two of Percy's prominent knights. Sir William Plumpton and Sir Nicholas Hall came fully armed, mounted on stallions draped in flowing caparisons. A third Percy knight, Sir Thomas Cattall, flaunted a banner with the five sacred wounds on a silver background. The presence of Northumberland's vassals gave the archbishop more comfort than he was willing to admit.

Chanting psalms and blessings to his growing band of followers, Scrope felt his heart swell with pride. At his word alone, these trusting folk came by the thousands to support his cause—and theirs as well. Accompanied by minstrels and trumpeters, the citizens of York progressed to Shipton Moor. Wagons full of supplies followed them, carted by local merchants amply paid by the archbishop. The line of marchers stretched for miles along the narrow road, and they gathered what firewood they could as they passed through the forest. Once they reached the moor they spread out; some erected tents, while others slept under the stars. Scrope glanced up at the clear sky, grateful that the good Lord granted them fine weather.

The next day dawned just as beautiful as the morning before, and Archbishop Scrope put on his regalia, wandering through the multitude who seemed happy enough. As they munched on their breads and fruits, he blessed them and offered words of encouragement.

"I am expecting Sir Ralph Hastings and John Fauconberg today with their levies from Topcliffe and Cleveland. King Henry will not be able to ignore our demands!" Cheers went up as the archbishop spoke in his most reassuring voice, all the while trying to pretend he wasn't the least bit concerned about the lack of communication from the Percy leaders.

But he was concerned. Already he sent out scouts along the main roads, looking for any sign of the expected army. He wasn't prepared to face the king alone; he certainly wasn't prepared to do battle without experienced leaders. This had never been the plan.

As the afternoon drew on, he decided to hold mass, and to that end sent out heralds who gathered as many townsfolk as were willing to attend his service. Standing on the only small hill on the moor, Scrope led the singing of psalms and ostentatiously blessed the multitude who patiently listened to his prayers. Evening drew on and the atmosphere of merriment continued to pervade the gathering, enhanced by wine that was distributed through the archbishop's generosity.

Already feeling the strain, Scrope shared a supper of cold meats with young Mowbray. Pouring more wine into the earl's cup, he looked around to make sure no one was within earshot.

"They should have come by now," he said into Mowbray's ear. "I can't help but be concerned."

The other turned in alarm. "They were supposed to be here first?"

"Oh yes. They should have been here yesterday, or today at the latest. It was all arranged ahead of time."

"They must have been held up."

"I hope it's no more than that. What am I going to do to keep these men occupied?"

"My God, I don't know. Wine and food and more musicians would help. And prayers."

Scrope made a face. "I didn't expect to feed everyone for more than two days."

"We're running out of food?" Mowbray looked toward the wagons.

"Not yet. But soon."

"You had better send for more!"

Letting out a heavy sigh, the archbishop gestured to a pair of priests who got up heavily from their blanket. This was not the kind of life they were used to.

"How are our foodstuffs holding out?"

The older of the two shook his head. "You told us to be generous. By tomorrow it will be gone."

"This won't do." Scrope fought down his panic. "Theo, arrange for these wagons to be taken back to York and refilled. I'll see it gets reimbursed from the cathedral funds."

"Are you certain, your Grace?"

"We have no choice," Mowbray broke in. "Otherwise they may start deserting."

Muttering, the priests withdrew. Scrope stood wearily. "I had better make the rounds. Will you join me?"

Doing his best to reassure his people and remind them of why they were there, Scrope spent hours on his feet—cajoling, sharing stories, listening to complaints—before falling, exhausted, into his bedroll. Mowbray had given out long before, and once again the archbishop had to remind himself that the legitimacy conferred by an earl was worth more than the man himself. Mowbray wasn't much help, but he was only a lad.

Day two was no better than day one. Scrope preached the sermon of his life to great applause. He held two masses and encouraged others to stand forth and berate the king, extoll the virtues of Henry Percy, and sing to keep their spirits up. He walked through the crowd, trying to ignore the smell of excrement pervading the air—especially when he neared the edges of the assemblage. No one had prepared for any kind of sanitation. People were dirty and unhappy, but at least they perked up when he bent over to talk with them; he even greeted many by name. Come nightfall, the archbishop was so hoarse he could barely talk, and he fell asleep without his accustomed wine. He didn't know how much longer he could hold out.

The next morning dawned cloudy and chill. There was no wood for fires on the moor and people were complaining. The wagons had come back half full, they had run out of ale, and Scrope could see a lot of men wandering around, bored and restless. His eyes lighted up when he saw Sir William Plumpton spurring his horse forward. The three Percy knights had gone to see if the main army was anywhere in sight.

Plumpton pulled rein and reached down for a wineskin. Scrope waited impatiently while he took a deep draught and wiped his mouth.

"Well? Did you see anyone?"

The knight nodded. "It was too far away to distinguish any coat of arms, but a large force is coming from the north."

"Finally!" Scrope raised his arms. "Announce it to our assembly. The wait is over!"

Word travelled fast from one end of the moor to the other. Scrope's company had grown to over seven thousand and they covered the ground in a dense, colourful mass. The archbishop could be proud that he had delivered what he promised, and more. His exhaustion was forgotten.

Men had risen to their feet and gazed anxiously to the north. In time, an army came into view and Scrope strode back and forth in front of his gathering, praising God and offering blessings. He waved at the other Percy knights who approached at a gallop, but their evident haste had a sobering effect. Something was not quite right.

When Sir Nicholas Hall was within earshot, he pointed at the approaching army. "It's not ours!" he shouted. "The Earl of Westmorland approaches!"

Sir Ralph Neville and Prince John did not dawdle after learning about Percy's movements. Gathering local levies to augment the prince's troops, they made their way to York. Topcliffe, a small village on the River Swale, was directly on their route, and Westmorland hoped to catch the gathering army unprepared. As they came within sight of the river, the earl was satisfied to see that the recruits were spread out haphazardly across the fields, without even posting guards. No leadership! Percy would have made short work of this bunch.

Once Westmorland appeared with his troops, the rebels blew their horns and dashed about, lining up surprisingly fast with their backs to the river. There were several thousands of them—about the same size as the advancing force. Percy's knights, recognizable in their heraldic surcoats, rode back and forth calling encouragement. But these troops weren't ready for a battle; they had little heart for Northumberland's cause without his presence. Already, men on the edges of the lines began to slip away. The dribble became a flood of anxious men, and before long the rest of the rebels threw their weapons to the ground and held up their arms in surrender. Not a blow was struck. Aside from the four Yorkshire knights, Westmorland didn't even bother to take prisoners; he had more important things to do and didn't need to be hampered. Warning the chastened Yorkshiremen not to break the peace again, he allowed them to disperse and continued on his way to Shipton Moor. It was only twenty miles further.

The moor sat across from a boggy plain sloping down from the edges of the Royal Forest of Galtres. It was from that height the Earl of Westmorland paused and looked down at the large gathering. At first he was quite taken aback by the size of Scrope's force, but it looked more like a mob than an army. He ordered his troops to settle down for the night.

Prince John came up to him while he stood observing the rebels.

"Their army is larger than ours!" he said.

Westmorland stroked his chin. "I don't see any escutcheons, knight's banners, or even pennons," he mused. "No cavalry that I can see. I believe this is an army of peasants and townspeople. They could do us some harm, but they are no match for our fighters." He put a hand on John's shoulder. "I suspect the good archbishop might be willing to negotiate. We'll try in the morning."

Westmorland wasn't the only one observing the enemy anxiously. Archbishop Scrope had to fight hard to keep his panic from interfering with his train of thought. This wasn't what he signed on for! Where was Henry Percy? Where was the Yorkshire army? What was he doing all alone, facing the might of the Earl of Westmorland?

For once, Mowbray had nothing to say and the archbishop felt pity for his companion, though there was nothing he could do to reassure him. Westmorland was Mowbray's sworn enemy. The young earl had never intended to confront him from a position of weakness. Ralph Neville would like nothing better than to squash him underfoot like a bug, and they both knew it.

Percy's few knights gathered around them as well, totally disheartened. Much as he would have liked to, Scrope couldn't hold them responsible. They, too, were let down by Northumberland.

"What are our options now?" said Scrope to no one in particular. "They are fighting men. We are not equipped to take on an army all by ourselves."

"All we wanted—" Mowbray cleared his throat. "All we wanted was to be heard. We needed a show of strength to make the king recognize our grievances."

"It's true," said Scrope, taking heart. "We have done no wrong. We have been peaceful in our deportment." He almost believed his own words. "We're not rebels...we are merely making formal protests."

That night, the mood of his army was far from encouraging. Men crouched around their little fires, barely acknowledging the archbishop as he passed through. They didn't have enough food to last much longer, and it didn't take a leap of understanding to recognize they were in trouble. Scrope walked as quickly as possible, trying not to answer any direct questions. He found that he couldn't lie to the men, nor could he hide his worry. He was glad the darkness shrouded his face.

So the next morning, as Scrope and his clerics were finishing breakfast, they were relieved to see a small group of envoys approaching under a flag of truce. The rebels quietly parted their ranks and let the newcomers ride up to the archbishop, who threw back his shoulders and tried to assume a dignity he no longer felt. For a moment the spokesman sat on his horse and studied the archbishop appraisingly. Scrope refused to lower his gaze.

"My lord the Earl of Westmorland sends me to ask why you have chosen to gather in warlike array?" asked the envoy.

Scrope pursed his lips. He was defeated already and he knew it. "I would rather have peace than war," he started, dismayed that his voice came out at a higher pitch than he intended. "But I dare not approach the king without the support of my followers. We have a manifesto of our grievances against the king's government. Here, I have a copy for you." Scrope turned and impatiently gestured for someone to bring him the document. After a little fumbling around, a cleric brought the manifesto from the tent. He handed it to the archbishop who in turn gave it to the man on the horse. "Here. Take this to the earl and tell him to read it."

The envoy accepted the document and jerked his head at his companions, who all turned and rode silently away. The rebels watched them uneasily.

Taking a deep breath, Scrope faced his companions. Some looked at him with disappointment, others with relief. Few wanted to fight. Mowbray was most obviously upset.

"What else could we do, my son? We have been let down. If I commanded this gathering of ill-prepared Yorkshiremen to attack, I would be condemning many to a senseless death. We are no match for Westmorland's soldiers."

Mowbray nodded, looking at the ground. "I fear this will not end well."

"Take heart," said the archbishop, though he might as well have been reassuring himself. "Our cause is just and our arguments are reasonable. Besides, my spiritual office will be our shield."

"And who will protect me?" Mowbray mumbled.

Scrope shot him a worried glance. "We all fight for the same cause. We shall stand together."

The wait was interminable. They ate a dismal lunch and once again Scrope started his pacing when someone announced the return of Westmorland's envoy.

"Quick, my breastplate." The archbishop gestured to his cleric without even turning around. As two men buckled the armour on, Scrope squirmed uncomfortably. He wasn't used to the weight, but at least he would look the part of a commander.

The messenger bowed from astride his horse. "The Earl of Westmorland has been very impressed by your manifesto. He requests a personal conference in full sight of both armies so he can learn more about your suggested reforms."

Scrope gave Mowbray a look of triumph. "There. I knew the great earl was a reasonable man."

Mowbray leaned over to whisper in his ear. "It could be a trick."

The other shook his head. "He is a worthy knight," he whispered back. "I would not deign to mistrust my old friend and neighbour."

Shrugging, Mowbray stepped back, lowering his head in acquiescence. Scrope held out a hand for his crosier. "I will come accompanied by ten attendants, as long as the Earl of Westmorland agrees to the same."

"He has assured me he will agree to your terms. He hopes to meet you directly." And at that, the envoy turned his horse and rode back to the waiting army.

Percy's knight, Sir William Plumpton, volunteered to accompany the archbishop, as well as eight others and a reluctant Mowbray. Flying the banner of York, the little group set out on foot, for the distance was not great. As agreed, Westmorland met them in the open ground accompanied by Prince John and his own retinue.

The two leaders observed each other impassively. Westmorland had the impression that Scrope was at the end of his resources and anxious to find a way out of his predicament. The man's lack of pretension was almost pitiful. At the same time, Mowbray's sour expression convinced the earl he had already won the day, though he made it a point to ignore the lad.

"Archbishop Scrope," said the earl in his most forbearing voice. "I read your manifesto and find it to be justly framed. No sane man could help but support your assertions. Don't you agree, John?" he added, turning to the Prince. Totally under Westmorland's influence, John nodded.

The archbishop's grateful smile spread to his eyes. "I am comforted to hear that, my Lord. I believe the king will understand we only seek to make the people's voices heard."

"Of course, of course. For myself, I intend to do my utmost to induce the king to implement your proposed reforms. Now tell me; I could use some further clarification on this item here..." and he pointed to the manuscript. Scrope enthusiastically gave an explanation while the earl waited for him to finish, confident that the tension was beginning to ease.

"Thank you for that, your Grace." He held out his hand and Scrope shook it with both of his own. The earl patted him on the back and looked over at John; he jerked his head toward Mowbray. The prince got the idea and approached the nervous young man.

"We finally get to meet," he said. "Your father and mine went back a long way."

Mowbray caught himself frowning and bit his lip. "That's true." He was trying to think of something else to say when Westmorland saved him the effort.

"Well now," the earl said, clapping his hands together. "Now that our task is done and we are in agreement, let us drink together in the open so all may see we are friends." At that, his servants brought up tables and benches and started pouring wine into cups. Sitting comfortably at the table, Scrope gestured to his side for Mowbray to join him.

The small talk went on for a while, and then Westmorland leaned forward. "Now that everything is settled between us, why not announce to your army they can return home?" Without waiting for an answer, he beckoned to Sir Henry Fitzhugh. "Sir Henry, tell the former rebels they need not wait for the archbishop's return; he will sup with me this night. There is no more necessity for their services; they are free to go."

Mowbray stiffened and put a hand on Scrope's arm. The archbishop was just as uncomfortable, but he knew he didn't have much choice. He had to trust Westmorland's integrity. His heart sank as Fitzhugh mounted his horse; this was a disgraceful end to a glorious crusade. Scrope turned and watched helplessly as the knight crossed the short distance to the waiting army.

Fitzhugh rode back and forth before the archbishop's faithful followers, gesturing toward the city. After only a brief hesitation, they started slipping away from the field—first in ones and twos, then in groups, and finally all together in a mad dash for freedom. Scrope tried to stand but someone pushed him back onto the bench.

"My dear archbishop," Westmorland said mildly, "it's over. You may not know this, but I already have the Yorkshire knights, Ralph Hastings, John Fauconberg, John Fitzrandolph and John Colville in my custody. They were never going to meet up with you. Your cause was lost before I even reached Shipton Moor."

Stricken, Scrope lowered his head, at a loss for words. They had all been betrayed—first by Percy, and now by Westmorland.

"King Henry is on his way and you may make your case to him. I will do my best to speak on your behest. It must tell in your favour that you spared so much bloodshed at the last."

Raising his eyes, the archbishop looked hard at Westmorland. The earl could not hold his gaze. He turned to his guards. "Take Archbishop Scrope, Earl Thomas Mowbray, and Sir William Plumpton to Pontefract Castle," he said. "Prince John and I must return to Durham in readiness for Northumberland's attack."

Little did Westmorland know that Northumberland had other ideas. Taking his grandson and heir, Henry Percy was heading north to the Scottish border and safety.

CHAPTER 8

King Henry wasted no time in riding north with a small retinue. By forced marches he made it to Worcester the next day, then Hatfield, and finally Derby, where he learned about the rising at Shipton Moor. He wrote to his council in London telling them to meet him at Pontefract, including Chief Justice Gascoigne, who would be needed to hold a trial for the traitors.

It wasn't until later that Thomas Arundel, Archbishop of Canterbury heard the news. He listened with horror as the messenger described what he knew of the Scrope rebellion and the arrest of the archbishop. Stepping forward, Arundel fixed the man with a hard gaze. "What happened to the prisoners?"

"Your Grace, I believe they are on their way to Pontefract to meet the king."

"Pontefract." Arundel turned away. "I must go before something terrible happens."

Before the day had ended, Arundel was on his way north in the company of his most reliable servant. Prepared to ride day and night, the archbishop donned his everyday clothes and bid his companion to bring extra food. They had 185 miles ahead of them. And what would he encounter at the end?

When Henry arrived at Pontefract, he learned that Scrope and Mowbray had already been imprisoned there. By then, the king had amassed a small army along the way and was accompanied by Earl Arundel—who had grown into his father's shoes since the usurpation—and Sir John Stanley, steward of the royal household. Thomas Beaufort, the youngest of Henry's half-brothers, was already waiting for him. Taking his fellow nobles into his private chambers, Henry paced the room while waiting for a quick supper to be laid. Then he dismissed the servants and turned to his brother, hands on his hips.

"Well?" He didn't even try to hide his annoyance.

Beaufort was just lowering himself to his chair and paused halfway. "The prisoners arrived yesterday. Westmorland and Prince John have gone back north to clean up any remaining rebellious activity."

"All right. What about York?"

"The city has been quiet." He sat the rest of the way.

"I intend to keep it that way. Stanley, I want you to take half our forces and march to York. Put the city under martial law until I get there. I have to finish this business first. You may go, Sir John."

Taking a reluctant look at the food, the steward left the room. Beaufort cleared his throat. "Sire, Archbishop Scrope begs an interview with you."

Henry raised his eyebrows. "What can he possibly say that will mitigate his actions?"

"As far as I am concerned, nothing. He is a traitor."

Turning to Arundel, Henry shifted his weight to his other foot. "And what do you think?"

"He deserves no mercy."

"I agree with both of you. No. I will not see him."

"He still hides behind his spiritual office," Beaufort prodded. "Shall I take away his crosier?"

Henry's eyes flashed. "Yes. He no longer deserves it."

Needing no other encouragement, Beaufort took a quick bite of food then left the room. Henry had been very good to him, and he took any rebellion personally.

The archbishop and Thomas Mowbray were being held in a receiving chamber, surrounded by surly guards. Beaufort thought they were being treated too well, but he knew they wouldn't be staying here long. When he burst into the room,

Archbishop Scrope stood, drawing himself up to his full height. He was wearing his everyday ecclesiastic garments and leaned on his crosier. Events of the last week had totally worn him out.

"Will King Henry see me?" he asked.

Beaufort's lip curled. "The king has nothing to say to traitors. You will be tried and condemned as you deserve."

"That is not for you to decide. I insist you take me to see the king."

"Didn't you hear me? He will not see you." He strode forward and put a hand on the staff. "He has instructed me to take this and give it to a more worthy priest." He tugged on the crosier but Scrope wouldn't let go.

"This is my staff of office and I won't relinquish it!"

"And I say you will!" Beaufort pulled it out of Scrope's hand but the archbishop seized it back, tugging hard.

"Take your hand off my crosier! You have no right to it!"

"Mind your manners, priest! Give me your staff." And he twisted it, trying to pry it loose. Scrope would not let go and his antagonist tipped the crosier forward, striking him on the head. The archbishop dropped to the floor and Mowbray dashed up to him. He bent over the old man, grasping him by the shoulders and helping him sit. Both of them looked up at Beaufort who jerked his head in disgust before turning away, prize in hand. None of the soldiers dared stop him.

"Are you all right?" Mowbray slipped his arm around Scrope's shoulder.

Nodding, the archbishop clambered to his knees. "I'll have a headache for a while. My pride is damaged more than my pate. What an awful scuffle."

"It truly was. Shameful." Mowbray rose, pulling the other with him. "Sit, please. He gave you a good blow."

Scrope didn't argue. He let the other support him as they moved to a bench and sat heavily.

"I'm sorry, my son. I didn't expect us to be treated so badly." The archbishop shook his head. "I feel so responsible."

Mowbray agreed but remained silent.

"I don't know what is going to happen," Scrope continued. "Our demands were not unreasonable. Anyone could see that. We must rely on the good sense of King Henry."

"Perhaps he is only trying to scare us."

Scrope let out a grunt. "It's working."

It's possible that many would have wondered what happened to King Henry's good sense. There was a look in his eye that defied argument. He was short-tempered with all his servants, and anyone who delivered fresh tidings was dismissed without a second word. He drank heavily that night without eating more than a morsel. In the morning he insisted they take their prisoners and all his forces and move forward another thirty miles to Bishopthorpe, the archbishop's own manor. As this was only three miles from York, no one could misunderstand Henry's intentions.

The citizens of York, already dismayed by Stanley's arrival with a small army, panicked to hear of the king's approach. They gathered around city hall, looking for leadership. Men who had, just a few days before, mustered proudly with their brothers for the archbishop's cause, now grumbled about his betrayal. Their wives carried squalling babies in their arms as toddlers clung to their skirts. As the mayor stepped onto the portico, their grumbling turned into a sort of wail that swept back and forth like the surging sea.

He held up his arms. "Please, please, my good folk. Do not panic."

Somewhat reassured, they quieted down.

"Let us go to the king ourselves. We will demonstrate our humility and beg his forgiveness. King Henry is a reasonable man!"

"What if he has us arrested?" someone shouted.

"All of us? If we stand together, he must listen to our pleas. Stay in your filthy rags. Go as you are. Follow me, citizens of York!"

Gesturing to his secretaries, the mayor marched down the steps and along the main street. For lack of any better idea, the others followed him, men, women, children and all. There was no cohesion to their cries but an eerie, continuous lamentation. They streamed out of the city gate, barefoot and bareheaded. Some pointed their swords down in a position of submission; others held up their hands in surrender and still others tied a rope around their necks.

When Henry learned that the citizenry was approaching, he directed his horse toward York and stopped when in view of this ridiculous spectacle. His officers lined up behind him.

Men and women cried and sobbed, and as they came within earshot they flung themselves to their knees and crawled forward, begging the King's pardon. It was pathetic—and elicited the opposite effect than they desired. Sitting on his stallion, Henry had to fight the urge to trample them underfoot.

"Wretches!" he cried. "Fools and miscreants! You dare to rebel against my majesty then expect me to forgive you because you grovel like the curs you are!"

The king's unkind words only served to make them yowl more. He sat his horse for a few minutes then pointed toward York. "Get ye gone! Go back to your miserable city and await my pleasure."

Terrified at the king's anger but relieved they were spared for the moment, the chastened citizens rose to their feet and backed up, crowding into each other in their desperation to get away. Not bothering to watch, Henry turned his horse around and rode through his own retinue, who moved aside to give him space.

The king's party continued on to Bishopthorpe, dragging along their prisoners who were tied to their mounts. Scrope was thrown into a prison cell beneath his own residence, with a tiny window barely letting light reach the floor. Mowbray was confined in the next room.

The archbishop fell to his knees in prayer, but he could barely concentrate on the words. He was ashamed he had never once considered prisoners who had been detained here, bereft of light or heat in the winter. The cell was filthy, with mouldy hay in the corner and a wooden bucket for night soil. It stank of excrement and vomit. In his arrogance he had thought himself above such mortification; was God punishing him? As he watched the evening light fade in the little window, the seriousness of King Henry's wrath bore down on him like a shroud. This was the side of the king he had never known— never suspected. Then he remembered the fate of Richard II, and he despaired.

The next day was filled with putting together a commission to pass judgment on the rebels. Because Westmorland and Prince John were still in the North, Henry appointed Thomas Arundel and Thomas Beaufort as deputies. They would be in charge of the tribunal. There was much uneasiness in the room, although most of the council were ready to give Henry the answers he was looking for. Then there were the others; among the king's closest advisors sat a handful of bishops, who hovered together for support.

The king sat at the head of a long table, dressed in his formal robes of office. This was not to be a casual session. "We are here to determine the guilt of the foul traitors Archbishop Scrope and Sir Thomas Mowbray, who led the citizens of York in rebellion." He looked hard at the men closest to him and was surprised when Justice Gasciogne stood. The Chief Justice had been summoned specifically to officiate at the trial.

Aware that everyone was staring at him, Gasciogne picked up a book and held it to his chest. "I cannot in good conscience participate in these irregular proceedings," he stated flatly. "Neither the king nor any of his subjects can legally pass sentence upon a bishop of the Church. This matter should be under the authority of the Pope."

Henry was speechless. Already he met with resistance, and the hearing hadn't even begun. Gasciogne bowed and left the table, walking out of the room amid total silence. Henry leaned toward Thomas Beaufort. "We can't let this stop us. Who can take his place?"

Turning to his other side, Beaufort's eyes rested on Sir William Fulthorpe, an up-and-coming lawyer whose father had been a judge. He had adequate knowledge of the law. Fulthorpe nodded briefly.

"Sir William will take the Chief Justice's place," Beaufort assured the king. "We may proceed."

"That is good," Henry said, relieved. "Earl Arundel, would you please give this commission the details of Scrope's rebellion." He leaned back in his chair, watching the faces of his council. Arundel's report was brief, since he was reading from a letter written by Westmorland. That was the extent of his knowledge. The men listened intently, staring at Arundel; no one wanted to look at the king. When the earl finished, the Bishop of Carlisle raised a hand.

"Yes, your Grace," Henry said. "What do you have to say?"

"Sire." The bishop glanced at his fellows. "Before the, um, Yorkist gathering, I received a letter from Archbishop Scrope. His message was only one of reform, not revolt. He complained of the government's insolvency, its excessive levies against the church to make up the difference—"

"What do you think causes my insolvency?" Henry burst out, his face red. "At the moment I learned about this revolt, I had been about to lead a double attack against the Welsh insurgents! Do you have any idea how much that campaign cost the exchequer? And I had to call it off to deal with *his* rebellion! Do you realize how much money is squandered on uprisings like this? Badly needed money!" He threw up his hands. "We're wasting our time. Get on with it!"

Totally cowed, the bishop sat down. The tone had been set and the council proceeded to listen to additional witnesses brought forward, condemning Scrope's behaviour. The archbishop's manifesto was read aloud, though no one dared comment on its contents. As the sun was setting and the commissioners grew restless, Earl Arundel stood.

"My Lords, the king thanks you for your attention in this matter. Now that all the evidence has been presented, it is time to take a vote," he declared.

The men around the table squirmed uncomfortably. This was all happening too fast.

Arundel started with Thomas Beaufort, seated next to him. "Do you declare the prisoners guilty or not guilty?"

Beaufort stood. "Guilty," he stated categorically.

Nodding confidently, Arundel pointed to the next man. He was Lord Grey of Ruthin, not happy to be drafted into this commission. "Guilty or not guilty?"

The knight stood slowly, looking at the others for support. No one returned his gaze. Then he regarded the king who was glaring at him. He swallowed. "Guilty."

"Good," said Arundel, then moved on to the man next to him. "Guilty or not guilty?"

The third man, Lord Willoughby, could feel the heat in the room rising. By the same measure, his courage was fading. Everyone knew Scrope was doomed. Why risk one's neck for a lost cause? "Guilty," he rasped.

The precedent had been set. One by one, each commissioner found it easier to pronounce judgment on Scrope and his accomplices. By the time the voting worked its way over to the bishops, they stood as a group. The Bishop of Carlisle spoke up. "Sire, this court is outside of our jurisdiction. We are not in a position to pass judgment upon our spiritual superior."

For a moment King Henry was tempted to arrest the bunch of them. He grasped his sceptre and his mouth moved, though he succeeded in clenching his teeth instead of breaking into an oath. Beaufort moved behind him and whispered into his ear. "We don't need their vote."

Closing his eyes, Henry let out a deep breath. What was one more irregularity in this irregular trial? "My Lord Bishop," he said finally, "out of respect for your holy office, you are all excused."

The bishops practically fell into their chairs. Henry ignored them. "Go on, my Lord Arundel."

The earl nodded to the king. "This court finds Archbishop Scrope, Earl Thomas Mowbray, and Sir William Plumpton guilty of treason. We will resume in the morning to determine sentencing."

It was over. The commissioners filed out to partake of supper, which was laid for them across the hall. Few had an appetite, but there was an inordinate amount of wine consumed that evening.

Henry did not join them, He went back to his chamber and dismissed all his servants—even William. Filling a mug with undiluted wine, he hoped to drown his anger. This was just too much. Percy, he could understand. The man was a lost cause and should never have been pardoned by parliament. But Scrope? If the archbishop felt confident enough to lead a rebellion, where would it end? He assisted in Richard's resignation, for God's sake. He should have been one of Henry's most reliable supporters. How could such an adherent turn against him?

The wine didn't help, although he initially dozed in his chair. Henry kept waking up and lumbering to the chamber pot to empty his bladder, until finally a restless sleep overcame him. Sometime during the night his squire came back and lay down on his usual pallet at the end of the bed.

His uneasy slumber was broken by a persistent banging on his door. He was jolted awake, though his eyes didn't want to open. The sun was just beginning to rise. Groaning, Henry propped himself up against his pillows and drew the covers around him. "Find out who it is," he muttered to his squire who was climbing to his feet. "It must be important."

Still half-asleep, William opened the door. He stumbled aside when a dishevelled and dirty Archbishop Arundel pushed his way in. The archbishop's cloak was stained from the road and he even had bits of straw tangled in his hair. Henry stared at him, his mouth open.

"What happened to you, man?"

"Sire." Arundel strode to the bed and threw himself to his knees. He was still gasping for breath. "I've ridden day and night to reach you before something terrible happened. Excuse my appearance; I slept a few hours in a stable before I rode the last stretch."

"Get up, get up." Henry reached over and plucked a piece of straw from the archbishop's head. But Arundel refused to move.

"I've come to warn you—no, to plead with you. I know Archbishop Scrope has greatly offended. But please, Sire, do not be the cause of his death. The punishment you would incur in the afterlife... do not risk your immortal soul for such an unworthy deed."

Taking his hand away, Henry shook his head. "You don't understand. This has to stop."

"But my Lord, think of what people will say! Look at Henry II after Becket was killed! Do you want to bring this disaster upon yourself? Do you want to be known as the man who killed both an anointed king and an archbishop? Surely not!"

"Calm yourself, Thomas. You are overwrought."

"As your spiritual father, I claim the right to be consulted. Yes, Archbishop Scrope has erred. But leave his judgment to the Pope, or at least to parliament! At your peril, do not foul your hands with his blood!"

Coughing, Arundel leaned against the bed. Henry threw back the covers and slid aside, bending over the exhausted archbishop.

"Come, come. You are exhausted. Get up, Thomas. I hear you. Get up." He helped Arundel to his feet. "You must go to bed. You need rest. Get some sleep. Nothing will be done without your advice. Go. Rest."

As is often the case after a great effort has been made, Arundel was ready to collapse. Henry put an arm around his waist and walked him to the door, turning the archbishop over to his servants. "Make sure my dear friend is well taken care of," he said, holding out his hand as they shuffled away.

Once the archbishop was out of hearing, Henry gestured to one of his guards. "I need you to summon Sir Thomas Erpingham at once. Then have the servants lay out breakfast for five. Have the Earl of Arundel, Sir Thomas Beaufort and Sir William Fulthorpe join me when it is ready."

Erpingham slept nearby and appeared almost immediately; it looked like he was already awake. Once again, Henry was grateful for his constancy. "Help me on with this tunic, would you?" He stretched his arms as Erpingham raised the garment over his head. "Did you see him?"

"Archbishop Arundel?" Erpingham nodded, straightening out the back. "My door was open a bit and he slipped past, doing his best to appear invisible. I was expecting your summons."

"You can imagine, then, that he was trying to stop me."

"I would expect nothing else. He would naturally try to protect his fellow archbishop."

Henry reached for his belt and tightened it himself. "I sent him off to bed."

Erpingham nodded, saying nothing.

"Come, sit with me." Henry adjusted a pillow in the window seat and leaned against it. "Scrope certainly has a comfortable bedchamber. Too bad he will no longer be able to enjoy it." He frowned. "Thomas, what he did is indefensible. If I let him get away with it, there will be no end to future rebellions."

110

"That is so. But perhaps a higher authority—"

"The Pope? I've been down that road before. Look at Bishop Merks. He was sentenced to death for his role in the Epiphany Rising, but the Pope reversed his decision. And then there was last year's parliament. They forced me to absolve Percy for Shrewsbury and give him back his castles and lands. Look where that brought us. No, I can no longer afford to let others make my decisions for me."

Erpingham nodded again. "You do realize that if you go through with the execution, it will darken your reputation forever."

"Perhaps. People have a short memory."

"Not always. Not with such an eminent prisoner."

Henry pursed his lips. "He should never have raised his city against me. What was he thinking? Half the demands he made had already been addressed by parliament."

"That is true. To be honest, I think he was part of a larger movement. It can't be by chance that this happened at the same time as—"

"Percy." Henry spat the word. "All the more reason Scrope and Mowbray have to be condemned. Let Percy's man Sir William Plumpton join them on the scaffold, since he was part of this debacle. The guilt shall be on Percy's conscience, not mine."

A knock on the door was followed by a bevy of servants who set bread, cheese, and fruit on the table. Within a few minutes, the others showed up and Henry rose with a sigh. "Thank you, Thomas. I needed to clear my head."

Erpingham joined the others at the table but Henry contented himself with an apple. He took a bite while pacing the room.

"We must get this business over with at once," he said finally. "Today."

Stopping in mid-chew, Beaufort swallowed hard. "Has something happened?"

Henry grimaced. "Archbishop Arundel. He rode all night from London just to stop me. At the moment, he has gone to bed. I want this done before he wakes up."

Everyone stared at him.

"What more is to be said?" the king said defensively. "Sentence the prisoners and we will summon the people of York so there will be no doubt of my anger. Find a field beside the city and execute them." He turned away and walked to the window.

Suddenly Henry's diners lost their appetite. Erpingham stood and gestured for the others to leave. As he paused at the door, he heard Henry call his name.

"Have my horse ready. I must see this through."

There was no mistaking Henry's wishes. The commission and its leaders assembled and the three prisoners were brought before them—not to give their side of the story, but to listen to their sentences. All three men stood bareheaded, ragged, and malodorous. Still, they did their best to appear undaunted. Scrope held his head up, observing his opponents.

Fulthorpe stood, pointing at the prisoners. "Archbishop Scrope, Earl Thomas Mowbray and Sir William Plumpton, you have been taken openly in the process of raising an army of rebellion against King Henry of England. You have been branded traitors and are to be executed at once. The king has graciously sentenced you to the block rather than impose the maximum penalty."

"Sir William," interposed Scrope, "I must state to this honourable assembly that I meant no harm against the realm nor the person of the king."

"Take them away," insisted Fulthorpe, gesturing toward the condemned men.

But Scrope hadn't finished, "I pray that God will not take vengeance on the king or his house for my death!" he shouted as a soldier took him by the arm. Many were later to remember his words. Did he mean the opposite of what he said? It sounded more like a curse than an intercession.

Scrope asked to have his crosier and was quickly refused. Three sorry-looking nags were brought out for them, and one of Henry's knights hoisted the archbishop up to ride bareback. A halter with a rope served as a bridle. The other two were similarly served, and they rode straight-backed out the gate of the archbishop's own residence, stopping momentarily to see the huge throng waiting for them. The crowd was eerily silent.

Nudging the mounts forward, sixteen guards flanked their three prisoners while the onlookers parted to let them through. Riding beside the archbishop, Thomas Mowbray let out a groan. "How wretched we are," he muttered. "How could things have come to this pass? Dear God, I wish I were dead already."

Scrope looked at him with composure. "My son, the death-pain will last but a moment. Be comforted that you will die in the cause of justice. A higher judge awaits and you will be found worthy." He ventured to glance over the crowd who blessed themselves as they passed. Already he felt like a martyr.

At the southwest corner of York where the high road entered the city, the prisoners were directed into a field belonging to the nuns of Clementhorpe. Archbishop Scrope took in a deep breath as a slight breeze made waves across a field of barley. The sweet smell of grass reminded him that this was to be his last comforting sensation before leaving this world. The good sisters' crop was soon destined to be trampled underfoot, just like his mortality. Scrope saw a man placing a block on the ground in front of the nuns' windmill, which sliced through the air with a deep whoosh.

The prisoners dismounted and were prodded toward the executioner. Whoosh, the mill affirmed, almost speaking with the voice of God. The headsman knelt before the archbishop, holding the long handle of his axe. "Forgive me, your Grace," he said. "I have been imprisoned fifteen years in York and they agreed to release me if I perform this deed. I would not have chosen this task but I dared not refuse." Whoosh was the only sound he heard in response.

Scrope was about to answer when he glanced over the man's head. King Henry sat on his horse a short distance away, watching intently. His face told Scrope everything he needed to know. There would be no reprieve. This was truly the end. Tearing his eyes away from the king, the archbishop put his hand on the executioner's head. "I forgive you, my son. You are only the instrument of the king's will. I ask you only one thing: give me five blows at the neck in memory of Christ's five sacred wounds."

"The Earl Marshal is to be executed first," spoke one of the guards who pushed Mowbray forward. Trembling, the earl bowed his head for a blessing.

"I will see you in paradise," said Scrope, making the sign of the cross. He pursed his lips while Mowbray lay his head on the block, stretching out his arms. The execution was quick and they pulled the body away, still pumping red. The metallic smell of blood permeated the air. They retrieved the head so it could be placed high on Bootham Bar. Plumpton soon followed; his head was destined for Micklegate. Then it was the archbishop's turn.

Refusing to look at the king, Scrope put his hands on the executioner's shoulders and kissed him three times. "Remember what I said," he whispered, then knelt before the block and made a prayer.

"It is for the laws and good government of England that I die," he called out to the crowd with a slight smile on his lips, taking pleasure in having the last word. Then he stretched out his arms and placed his neck on the block.

The executioner gave him four taps, barely breaking the skin on his neck, then struck him hard and true the fifth time. Scrope's head fell, holding that faint smile, while his body rolled over on its right side. The windmill swept over his remains. The crowd groaned.

Henry leaned over to Erpingham. "Archbishop Scrope has paid for his treason with his life. I do not need to abuse his corpse as well. Make sure these people disperse, then I will permit his vicars to bury his body in the Minster." The knight nodded and the king laid a hand on his arm, almost absently. "I am going into York. There is much to do before we leave tonight."

"Tonight?"

"There is no time to lose. I must catch up with Percy. Have the army ready to follow tomorrow. Also, send a messenger to Pontefract. I want to bring the big cannons with me. This time we lay siege to Percy's castles. They will surrender if I have to blast a hole in their walls." Nodding, Erpingham started to turn his horse when Henry's grip tightened. "Send Beaufort over to me."

Thomas Beaufort was overseeing the removal of the bodies when Erpingham caught up with him, pointing to Henry. Nodding, he hastened over to the king.

"Is there anything you need?"

"Yes. There's no time for me to return to Bishopthorpe. I am going to finish my business in York and continue on tonight toward Ripon. Have my things brought."

Beaufort looked at the sky. "It threatens rain."

"All the more reason for me to move quickly." He hesitated. Both of them knew there was more. Henry gave his brother an eloquent look.

"You want me to talk to Archbishop Arundel," Beaufort said quietly.

"If I spoke to him now, it would only get ugly. He needs time to…consider."

The other shrugged. "I'll do what I can to soften the blow."

"It would be better coming from you," Henry said, not entirely convincingly.

Nodding, Beaufort turned to leave.

"I thank you, brother," Henry said. That much, at least, was sincere.

Beaufort rode slowly through the silent townspeople who trudged away from the execution site. They didn't look angry— just stunned. And fearful. Henry wasn't finished with them and they knew it. He wondered what business the king had in York; it probably had something to do with reprisals.

His was going to be a thankless job and Beaufort didn't look forward to dealing with an angry archbishop. Arundel was an intimidating man. Why would Henry make him do this? For the first time Beaufort doubted the king's courage. But no, he told himself, shaking his head. Perhaps Henry was just being wise. Nobody wanted to face recriminations. However, there was something more to this situation. It was quite possible that Arundel's unwelcome visit had propelled Henry to act precipitously. If it were to come to accusations, both of them might say something they would regret later.

Taking his time when he reached Bishopthorpe, Beaufort gave orders to prepare for the campaign to the North. The king's bed and other furniture had to be packed up. Purveyors would need to get a head start so the royal household would be properly fed and housed. Horses needed to be groomed, and their equipment readied. Once this was done, a reluctant Beaufort found his way to the archbishop's chambers. The exhausted man was lingering over dinner. Arundel had bags under his eyes, he hadn't brushed his hair, and he was positively drooping. Beaufort had never seen him like this. He sat quietly across the table, pouring himself a drink.

Arundel looked up with bloodshot eyes. "I see the king has gone."

The other nodded, pretending to enjoy the wine. "He intends to go after Henry Percy this very evening."

There was a long pause. "Tell me, Thomas." The archbishop tried to keep the accusation from his voice.

Beaufort put down the cup. "It's over, your Grace. The prisoners have been put to death."

For a moment Arundel stared at him. Then he put a hand over his chest. "No. He couldn't. He promised me."

At a loss, Beaufort cleared his throat. "They were declared traitors. At least they didn't suffer the full penalty."

The archbishop took a ragged breath. "Tell me everything." He spoke with authority, his voice belying his appearance.

Beaufort hesitated. "They sentenced them this morning. Scrope, Mowbray, and Plumpton. The prisoners were placed on horses and rode out to a field next to the city walls. They were decapitated, the archbishop last. The citizens of York were ordered to attend."

"Did he suffer?"

The other shook his head. "It was over quickly. There was no pain."

Putting his knife on the table, the archbishop lowered his head. "He was my friend. More than that, Thomas. I gave him his first ecclesiastic appointment thirty years ago. Scrope was no traitor."

Fighting back tears, Beaufort wanted to defend the king but could find no words.

"It wasn't right," Arundel muttered. "The king has made a terrible mistake. He had no authority to put the archbishop to death. God will punish him."

Despite himself, Beaufort made the sign of the cross. "He had his reasons…" He paused. Something was not quite right. Arundel wasn't listening.

Still clutching the garment over his heart, the archbishop leaned dangerously to the side. Beaufort jumped up and caught the man before he fell out of his chair.

"Help me!" he shouted. "I need help!"

The door slammed open and two servants ran in. They supported the archbishop as best as they could and together the three men jostled him into bed.

"Call a doctor," Beaufort gasped. Arundel was breathing irregularly.

After what seemed an interminable time, a physician came in and put a hand on Arundel's forehead. He felt the man's neck, lifted his eyelids, and listened to his heart. Then he checked the forehead again. "He's feverish."

Heaving a sigh, Beaufort drew himself up. "I must go. Do what you can. In the king's name, summon whatever assistance you need."

Shaking his head, the doctor called for a cloth and a bowl of water. He could tell this wasn't going to be easy.

CHAPTER 9

There was no satisfaction to be had in the aftermath of Scrope's execution. King Henry frowned at the Mayor of York who did his best to appear submissive rather than terrified. After signing pardons for five of the archbishop's clerks, he gave the mayor his full attention.

"At first, I was angry enough to raze this city to the ground," he said, keeping his voice threatening. "But I think you have learned your lesson. Nonetheless, I am suspending your liberties, and expect this city to pay a fine of 500 marks to obtain my pardon."

The mayor let out a breath. This was truly a king's ransom, but it certainly could have been much worse. Given time they could manage it. He bowed, trying to hide his relief.

"I need 200 marks at once to cover my household's expenses for the upcoming campaign," Henry added. "You may start by collecting jewels and money from the archbishop's personal treasury."

Still bowing, the mayor gulped down his objection. "Yes, Sire," he gasped.

"While you are collecting the funds, I shall speak to your keeper of spirituals. He shall exercise supervision over the diocese of York until we appoint a new archbishop."

A few more pieces of business were tended to before the mayor returned with 100 marks. "This is all we can collect at the moment," he apologized.

Standing, Henry accepted the funds. "I shall send Chief Justice Gasciogne and Sir Thomas Rempston after this is all over to make arrangements for collecting the arrears," he said simply. Then he was gone, along with all his councillors.

Riding out through Micklegate bar, King Henry and his retinue took the road to Boroughbridge. They had only gone a couple of miles when the clouds turned black. Lightning struck close by and the blast of thunder was deafening. Stinging rain smote them in the face. The wind quickly grew punishing and both riders and horses slogged forward, their heads lowered. One of Henry's knights rode up beside him.

"Shall we turn back, Sire?"

"No." The king clutched his reins. "We'll lose too much time."

No one dared argue with him and they resigned themselves to a miserable ride. The road led them over Hessay Moor and the storm hit them with its full fury. There was nothing to stop the wind but they could see a strand of trees in the distance. Suddenly a particularly violent gust knocked Henry back in his saddle and he almost lost his seat. The knight was beside him again.

"We'll never make it to Ripon at this rate." Henry shouted to be heard. "Let us halt at the nearest manor for the night."

Relieved, the men picked up their speed as best as they could but they didn't get far. The River Nidd crossed the road in front of them; already it had risen beyond its banks and flowed through the woods, making it hard to distinguish where the channel was. This was normally a shallow current and easily fordable, but today was not a normal day. This little river was torrential, dragging branches downstream along with the occasional tumbling log. The king's party huddled under trees, pulling their cloaks higher. The horses stood with their heads down; no one dared move forward.

"This can't last long," Henry shouted again. Rain ran in rivulets down his hood in front of his face. The others agreed dubiously. As if to argue with him, lightning flashed with another explosion of thunder; the horses jumped and skittered to the side. As their riders wrestled with the reins they heard the crash of a heavy tree and the air was filled with a smoky, burnt smell.

"It can't happen twice," someone yelled.

"We'll be all right," the king tried to reassure them. "Look, it's passing already."

They craned their necks, looking around, and it seemed that this time, Henry was correct. With one last blow, the rain suddenly diminished—at least to the point they didn't feel threatened. After a few more minutes, even the river receded a bit.

"We can't stay here all night," Henry said. "Let us try it." The men looked at each other, afraid to argue. Henry knew his companions were annoyed at his insistence, but he needed to put as much distance between himself and that terrible execution as possible. There was no going back.

They waited a bit longer until the intimidating debris had passed and the water visibly subsided. The king was the first to urge his mount forward, and the others followed. After a hesitation, Henry's horse waded into the current. The water buffeted them for a moment, and as they moved forward the animal was forced to swim a short distance, but he soon got his footing and gained the other side. Water poured from the saddle. Seeing his progress, the other horses followed. All were soon across and immediately started forward at a trot. They were anxious to get under a roof. Fortunately, they caught sight of a twinkling light in the distance.

"Does anyone know what this is?" Henry called.

Someone behind him spoke up. "Yes. That is Green Hammerton. It's an old village with a small manor house."

"That will have to do. I don't think our horses can take much more."

A stone farmhouse offered a welcome shelter, and Henry's party crowded into the parlour while the servants brought the horses to the barn. The king's hosts were quite overwhelmed by the honour, and after a modest supper they offered up their own sleeping quarters, which Henry gratefully accepted. This had been a long day and everyone was exhausted. The servants threw their damp cloaks on the rushes and were soon asleep, but the king tossed and turned for over an hour before falling into a fitful doze.

The storm continued on and off, rattling the shutters, and Henry grew restless again, when suddenly he let out a yowl. "Traitors! Traitors! You have thrown fire over me!" He wasn't entirely awake but he was flailing his arms and screaming in pain. "My skin! My skin is burning! Traitors!"

Leaping to their feet, the servants converged around his bed. Henry's squire, William Phillips, struck a flint and lit a candle, and when he brought it closer to Henry's face the others gasped. Big red blotches spread across his cheeks and forehead, even extending to his neck. The flickering light made it difficult to see in detail. "It's burning," Henry cried. "Someone is trying to kill me!"

The servants looked at each other, sharing a silent conviction. This was not an assassin. It was God's retribution for the killing of Archbishop Scrope.

"Get some wine," called William, coming to his senses. Another squire ran to soak a cloth in water. They tried to catch Henry's arms and force him to relax.

"Sire, no one is trying to kill you," said William in a soothing voice. "I was here all the time." Someone poured wine into a cup with a shaking hand. "Here. Drink this." He helped Henry sit and took the cup, holding it to his mouth. Henry grasped it with both hands.

"My face is burning," the king said after taking a sip. He looked up at their host who stood in the doorway.

Walter turned around. "Do you have a salve?" he asked. The man disappeared into the darkness. Walter placed a wet rag over Henry's forehead and patted his cheeks while waiting; soon their host came back with a little clay pot. Speaking in a soft voice, Walter dipped his fingers into the salve and spread it over the angry patches. Breathing heavily, Henry leaned back with his eyes closed.

"I'll have more wine," he said finally, and everyone breathed a sigh of relief that his voice was normal. "My God it hurts."

William sat on the side of the bed while the king held the wine in his lap. "Did you have a bad dream?" he asked.

Henry shook his head. "I don't remember."

"Maybe it has something to do with the storm. The lightning."

Opening one eye, Henry looked at him for a moment then closed it. "It appears I'm the only one affected." He shook his head slowly. "No, I know what you are thinking. God's judgment upon me. Does it really work that way? I've seen so many wicked men go unpunished." He took a sip of wine. "Or does it take an especially vile sin to catch His attention?"

William sat quietly, not knowing what to say.

Henry reached out and patted his leg. "The salve is working," he said. "Stay with me a while. I don't want to be alone." He handed over the wine.

Eventually Henry drifted off to sleep, and William laid his cloak on the floor next to the bed. When he awoke just after dawn and clambered to his knees, he was surprised to see Henry watching him, still propped up against the wall. It looked like he had been awake for some time. He wasn't any better; in fact, he looked even worse. Although the red blotches had crusted over somewhat, the inflammation had spread even farther, joining all the patches together.

"Are you all right, Sire?"

"All right? I don't think I'll be all right ever again. Even talking hurts. Can you put some more salve on my face?" He grimaced. "We have to get out of here. When we reach Ripon, I'm sure we can find a physician."

Their hosts could only spare a lean breakfast, but Henry did not complain. William gave them a small bag of coins for their trouble and the king's party prepared to leave. Henry wrapped a cloth around his head and pretended he was not in pain. No one dared speak to him and they rode in silence to Ripon, which was only a few miles further on. The trees were still dripping but the rain had blown itself out and the company was forced to move slowly along the muddy path which no longer resembled a road.

Ripon was blessed with a large gothic minster, and Henry directed his followers to the nearby palace. The king was once again in agony and desperately needed a place to rest. The chaplain immediately took in the travellers; Henry was put to bed and a physician summoned. By then, the king's illness had become general knowledge, and people were anxious to leave him alone. The word *leprosy* had already spread among Henry's entourage, and only William was brave enough to sit by his bedside.

On the second day, the lesions looked worse; they had even spread to his hands. Henry was despondent and turned away whenever anyone entered the room. At least the fierce pain had subsided somewhat and he was able to sleep. His limbs were heavy and his knees and ankles were swollen. Standing was a struggle—not that he tried very hard. Henry was totally exhausted. By the third day his skin started to heal and he turned his thoughts to business once again. His physicians assured the dubious witnesses that the king did not have leprosy, and men returned to their service, though they were anxious to stand apart from the king's bed.

Henry sent orders to the sheriff of Yorkshire to raise levies on the instant and await the king's arrival at Newcastle; the army that had initially followed him from York was already on its way north. Provisions for the troops were to be forwarded from Norfolk and also by sea. Properties belonging to the Earl of Northumberland and Lord Bardolf were declared confiscated. It was assumed that Percy was headed to Berwick, the northernmost fortified town in England. Henry would get there eventually; but first he must bring Percy's castles to submission.

By the end of a week, Henry was fit to travel again. When he emerged from his sickbed his men were relieved to see that he almost acted like his old self. However, his face was still covered with sores, many of which resembled large pimples. He mounted his horse and spurred forward with his usual energy, and they were hard put to keep up with him. The next day they had reached Durham. In another two days he was in Newcastle.

Up to this point, Percy's exact whereabouts were still unknown, but the king was about to be enlightened from an unlikely source. It was after supper; as usual, the king gave a couple of hours to local petitioners. It didn't matter where he was staying; he considered making himself available to his countrymen an important attribute of his rule. Henry liked to lean on a cushion against a sideboard and speak informally to whoever was admitted.

He was surprised, nonetheless, when the mayor of Berwick was introduced, hat in hand. The man was sixty miles south of where he should have been. The mayor bowed low to the floor, keeping his eyes down. "Sire," he began hesitantly, "I come from Berwick with distressing news. Earl Henry Percy tricked his way into town before I knew he was in rebellion."

Stopping with a cup of wine halfway to his mouth, Henry glanced at Erpingham and Norbury, who were deep in conversation across the room. "Thomas. John. Over here," he said, jerking his head. "Tidings about Percy."

The mayor briefly looked over his shoulder and then back to the king. "When the earl showed up with three hundred men and asked permission to enter, I had the feeling something was amiss."

"Were his men in possession of the castle?" asked the king.

"Yes, and also Percy tower. But our town is loyal to you."

Henry nodded briefly.

"So I told the earl that as long as he was faithful to you, he was welcome into town. He replied that he was perfectly loyal to the king, but was having a disagreement with some of his neighbours. He said it would be better for us if we were to let him in and put ourselves under his protection." The mayor coughed, looking at the wine on the sideboard longingly. Henry gestured for a servant to pour a cup.

"I thank you, Sire. As I was saying, I hesitated to answer him, but he told me I had better let him in or he would force his way, regardless. What could I do? As I said, his men occupied the castle and I feared he would put the town to the torch." He looked worriedly at Erpingham who was approaching with a frown. "It wasn't long before I discovered the true reason for his presence. They forced the keys from my hand and threatened to imprison me. I upbraided the earl for deceiving me and begged him to let me leave."

Straightening, the mayor seemed to gain courage from the wine. "Sire, I told the earl I would not eat or sleep in my bed until I had justified myself before your highness. He let me go and I came here directly."

"Hmm. Sit, my good fellow." Henry pointed at a chair. "I accept your explanation. I suspect he wouldn't have released you unless he wanted me to know he was on his way to Scotland."

Relieved, the mayor sat.

"Do you think he's challenging you?" asked Erpingham, changing his glance from the mayor to the king.

"Percy? I suspect he thinks he still has some kind of hold over me. My Mathathias, indeed." Henry shook his head, a look of regret on his face. "Remember that? He kept signing his letters like an Old Testament demagogue. He wanted to be a father to me. Even then he was misguided. He was using me for his own ends, and I let him. I owed him much, but that's over." He put a hand on the mayor's shoulder. "Percy is a formidable man and we won't underestimate him. He is not finished yet.

However, once we march on Berwick, if he isn't already gone, he won't stay around to defend the town against me. That's one fight he knows he would lose." The king smiled grimly. "I merely have to convince the men in the castle their cause is lost."

The king sent messages to the garrisons at both Alnwick and Warkworth to surrender. Unsurprisingly, they still held out for Percy. Alnwick was commanded by Clifford who told the king to win Berwick first. No matter; their turn could come. While Henry waited for an answer from Warkworth, he made his headquarters at Widrington, just a few miles away.

King Henry had been looking forward to an opportunity to use his artillery. He had seen the big guns at work on the continent when he travelled with the Teutonic Knights in Prussia, back in the 1390s. Over the last couple of years the Privy Wardrobe had been adding guns of different sizes to its collection. Thousands of pounds of charcoal, saltpetre, and sulphur for gunpowder had been carefully stored in dry barrels. Henry was anxious to see these ordinances in use, and he ordered six cannons to be brought from Pontefract.

Young Humphrey had arrived with the artillery, finally deemed old enough to attend his first campaign. As the prince climbed on top of the thousand-pound iron fowler, giving it a thorough inspection, Henry gave him a fond smile. He would have liked to have done the same thing himself.

Hearing a noise behind him, the king turned.

"I have Warkworth's response," Erpingham said, holding out a letter.

Reading it, Henry shrugged. "They have a lot of confidence in that worm-eaten fortress," he said. "When will these people learn? Well, at least we'll give these guns a workout." He patted the barrel. "But first, let's bring up the two-ton bombard. I want to see what it's capable of."

"You mean *George*?" Erpingham smiled. "I've been anxious to see that one in action, too. I understand it'll throw a stone weighing one hundred and twenty pounds."

"It will take two men just to load that stone." He rolled up the letter. "Well, we shall see how many shots from our cannons it will take for them to surrender. What do you think?"

Erpingham scratched his chin. "I would say six or more."

"And I say five or less. What do you think, Humphrey?"

Jumping down, the prince pretended to concentrate. "Three!"

"All right. Thomas, would you like to wager?"

"A gold noble says six or more."

"Done!" Henry shook his hand. "Let's get moving."

Warkworth Castle stood at the top of a sloping hill, surrounded on three sides by the Coquet River, with a deep moat protecting its front. It was a large fortification, and well-defended. But this was not to be a siege; Henry wasn't prepared for that. He was determined to prove the might of his firepower. Archers on the castle wall presented an ever-present problem, and the gunners needed protection as they set up. They staked wattle hurdles to the ground with a hinged wooden shield in the middle, the size of a door—to be set in front of the cannon and opened when the gun fired. The crew set up a tall timber A-frame to hang pulleys from. They strung ropes between the pulleys and a nearby capstan winch.

Twenty horses strained to pull a wagon carrying the impressive bombard. This was a monster of a bronze cannon, its meter-long barrel wrapped with iron rings. It was seated upon a heavy wooden box—more of a cradle—with chains wrapped around the barrel to hold it in place. Men slipped the pulley ropes under the cradle—mounted on thick blocks—and turned the capstan so the whole contraption could be lifted from the wagon. Big wooden wedges were brought up to hammer underneath the box in order to lift it for aiming, and huge timbers weighted with stones were placed behind it to absorb the shock.

Using a long iron bar, they nudged the bombard into place. Meanwhile, soldiers fired *handgonnes* mounted to poles, aimed at the defenders. They didn't do much damage at this distance, but made a very satisfying clamour.

Henry couldn't restrain himself; he tightened his belt and joined in. A soldier filled a bag with gunpowder and used a long rod to shove it into the chamber to the back of the barrel. Then he hammered a sheepskin wad to hold the gunpowder in place. Two gunners loaded a stone onto a rope sling and raised it to the barrel, while the king guided it into the mouth. A pile of huge stone balls was stacked by the side waiting to be used.

"Stand back, Sire, and put your hands over your ears," said the gunner, who did the same. Another came forward, poured a tiny bit of priming powder into the touchhole and stepped back, wielding a long pole. He blew on a slow-burning fuse at the end and lowered it into the hole. After a few seconds, a flame of fire shot straight up from the breech, and another flare blasted from the barrel along with a huge burst of smoke and a deafening explosion. The cannon, its butt end supported by the timbers, jumped up and settled at a slight angle.

Henry held his breath until the stone ball slammed against the castle wall, shattering into a thousand fragments. With a resounding boom, a number of stones broke away but the wall stood firm. He turned to Erpingham.

"One," said the knight. "I'm sure it gave them a good scare."

Because it took so much preparation to fire the bombard again, they had no choice but to resort to the smaller cannons. Humphrey followed the gunners, asking questions as they prepared each cannon. The smaller guns performed with plenty of noise and smoke, but still the walls held. The fourth cannon cracked an iron ring when it went off.

"That's four," Erpingham said smugly. "This gun is done for the day."

"No worries, Sire," said Henry's artillery master Gerard Sprong. He was one of four specialists brought over from Germany. "We will have it fixed up for the next time."

Henry gave Erpingham a sour smile. "I may have been a bit overconfident."

"Nonetheless, if they surrender without a fight, it will save lives."

In the end, Henry lost the wager but won the day. *George* performed perfectly well, and after its second shot, even though more fragments flew from the wall, the damage was minimal. After seven shots had been discharged from the cannons, the ramparts were still intact but the defenders raised a white flag. They sent out a herald who bent his knee to the king.

"Sire, we performed our duty to our master the Earl of Northumberland, but we recognize your superior claim. We submit ourselves to your royal grace."

Much though Henry would have liked to hang a few rebels, he saw the value in offering mercy. Word would travel to the other castles about his clemency if the defenders surrendered without a fight—and were spared.

"Very well. I will permit the garrison to pass out with horse and harness, but all weapons are to be left behind."

Leaving Sir Robert Umfraville in charge of Warkworth, Henry's army proceeded north and arrived at Berwick in five days. He was to discover that much had happened since the mayor reported Percy's unwelcome appearance.

Filled with anxiety, the Earl of Northumberland watched Bardolf ride off to Scotland with young Henry in tow. His grandson was the last link he had to his precious, long-lost Harry, but Berwick was no longer safe for the boy. "Work out the best deal you can with Albany," he had said to Bardolf. "See how many troops they can send down on short notice; King Henry won't be long in coming. I trust they will give safe refuge for my grandson; make sure you arrange the same in Scotland for both you and me, just in case." He had given the boy a long hug and a kiss on the cheek, and told him he would follow in due time, after his business was finished here.

"Use Berwick as a bargaining chip, if you must," he had said as a final instruction, slapping the horse on its rump. There was no more to be done, and he allowed himself a last pang of sadness as his grandson turned around with a wave. Look what he'd been reduced to! His loss of influence was devastating. Things couldn't have gone more wrong. That damned Westmorland! If it weren't for him…

Percy grimaced. No point in fretting over something he couldn't help. What was important now was salvaging what he could of his declining fortunes. He sent scouts south to discover the whereabouts of King Henry and to gauge the commitment of his remaining allies.

Berwick was an occupied town now, but business proceeded much as usual. Percy passed the ensuing week inspecting the fortifications which were in poor shape, having withstood many sieges from both Scotland and England. Berwick was surrounded by two miles' worth of wall—mostly made of earth, stone, and lime. It was a pitiful defence at best. Several small towers looked out from its circumference, the largest being the Percy Tower. This was connected to the castle and was approached through town and over a drawbridge; the little enclave was surrounded by its own wall. This was the only part of the town permanently occupied by Northumberland's troops, and the earl spent most of his time shoring up its defences.

After ten days, Bardolf was back, accompanied by the Earl of Orkney and three hundred Scots. All were mounted. Percy and his captains met them at the main gates, armoured and riding horses decked out in their full heraldic blazonry, mostly for show. Although the Scots entered the town without resistance, tension was high. The leaders followed Percy to the castle while the soldiers rode behind them, not in any particular order but fairly restrained.

Leaning over to Bardolf, Percy said, "You have done remarkably well. You got here sooner than I expected."

"They were anxious to take advantage of your invitation. I have secured safe-conducts for us. I sent young Henry to St. Andrews, where he was put under the tutelage of the Bishop. He will have good company; the king's son James is there too."

"We may end up there as well," said Percy, turning as Orkney approached. "We shall see."

The soldiers were billeted with the unwilling populace. Inns soon filled up with rowdy interlopers, demanding service and offering no payment. The local officials had their hands full stopping fights, which more often than not escalated into full-scale brawls. This was all to be expected; Percy wasn't concerned. After all, part of the deal Bardolf made with Albany would entail giving free rein to the Scots. They would get their plunder one way or the other.

The next day, Percy received word about Archbishop Scrope. There was no keeping it a secret; bad news travelled fast. He looked up from the message, his face pale.

"Westmorland. He scattered all my forces. Christ in heaven, the king executed the archbishop." He stared at Bardolf. "I can't believe it. What was he thinking?" He spoke in a hushed voice. "Scrope, Mowbray, and Plumpton. He decapitated them in a field outside of York. I never expected that to happen."

The Earl of Orkney cocked his head. "Your king shows no mercy," he said. "Is this the end of your rebellion?"

"I…yes. No doubt Henry is on his way. He knows I am here."

"Then we must finish our business and return to Scotland. You will come with us, I presume?"

"Yes." Percy handed the letter to Bardolf. "There's no future for me here."

As expected, the Scots commenced their pillaging. The residents of Berwick were quick to react, having been through this many times before. Some of them escaped across the bridge to Tweedmouth, a fishing village on the south bank of the river. Many locked themselves inside their homes. The hardier citizens threatened Scots with swords and axes, though organized resistance was impossible. The fighting went from street to street, house to house. The Scots were thorough, taking their loot and setting fire to the buildings—all except churches and religious houses. Percy's garrison barricaded themselves in the castle.

However, the pillaging was abruptly cut short when trumpets blared, announcing the approach of King Henry's army. As they had many times before, the raiders withdrew just as quickly as they came, leaving the exhausted townspeople to pick up the pieces as best as they could. The Scots were soon on the road, taking Percy and Bardolf with them.

When King Henry appeared he found the lower town a smoking ruin. Survivors had formed a bucket brigade from the river, trying to douse the fires. Some shovelled dirt onto the flames and others dejectedly picked through the rubble. The king put his men to work helping the unfortunate citizens. It was clear many had lost their homes. Meanwhile, he sent a herald up to the castle and demanded its surrender. Stubbornly, the garrison refused and the king moved his cannons down the main street, past the sweating workers who barely noted his progress.

Despite himself, Henry was glad he brought the artillery, even though it was a lot of trouble. The big guns fought them every inch of the way. They required a large number of horses and oxen to pull them and were constantly getting stuck in the mud. Still, the novelty hadn't worn off, and he was invigorated by their power. There was nothing like it. A few well-placed shots from the smaller cannons blew a hole in the wall surrounding Berwick castle, and as his men were preparing to infiltrate the enclave, Henry ordered them to wait until *George* had its say.

The bombard was brought up and carefully prepared as the defenders watched apprehensively from the battlements. They had never seen a cannon this size before and didn't know what to expect. Too soon, they found out. With a gigantic blast, a huge stone ball crashed against Percy tower, shaking it to its foundation. As the men watched in horror, the stones shook and slowly crumbled, then the whole side collapsed into itself. Henry later learned that a man climbing the stairs was crushed to death.

As the dust settled, the garrison raised a flag of surrender and opened the gates for the king. After interrogating the captain, who was brought to him in chains, Henry discovered that Percy had disappeared—no one knew where. His resolution hardened along with his bitterness. Although he permitted the garrison to evacuate, the king hung the leaders and sent their heads to Newcastle, York, and other towns to be mounted over their gates as a warning.

It was all done in two days, then Henry retraced his steps to Alnwick, the last major Percy holdout. Hearing of Berwick's fall, Clifford surrendered the stronghold without dissension. Content with his successes, Henry was ready to return to Newcastle.

In the far reaches of Scotland, news travelled slowly and Richard of Bordeaux felt removed from the troubles of his former kingdom. Dundonald Castle, on the western coast, was exposed to the worst of the gale winds, but tight shutters and a roaring fire kept the chill at bay and gave him a sense of security. This evening Richard looked sympathetically at King Robert, who sat down with an obvious effort. No one understood the Scottish monarch better than he. They were both failed kings, living out their sad existence in comfortable exile—one, a virtual ghost, neither dead nor alive, the other a weak-willed shell, resigned to have left the rule of Scotland to his imposing younger brother.

Robert sighed, putting his feet up. "I did it. I sent off my only surviving son to safety."

"To St. Andrews?" Richard asked.

"Yes. The good bishop is a man of honour and integrity. He won't let my brother Albany get his hands on the boy."

Richard crossed himself. "You really think Albany was responsible for the death of David?"

"My beloved firstborn?" Robert wiped a tear from his cheek. "If I hadn't been so foolish as to permit my brother to imprison him in the first place—to teach him a lesson, he said. Bah! I should have known. How he hated my son." He sighed again. "But not again. He won't have a second chance."

Richard leaned forward and put a hand on Robert's arm. It was terrible; rumours had it that David was starved to death in a prison cell. "I know it was difficult for you. James is a sweet boy."

"I can't protect him here." He patted Richard's hand. "I appreciate your sympathy. There's so much strife between my nobles, I'm not even sure he'll be safe at St. Andrews. Perhaps I should send him over to France."

"That's a big risk."

"I know. Pirates. So many things can go wrong. I just don't know what to do. Or who I can trust."

The king was interrupted by a knock at the door. His steward peeked into the room. "Sire, you have some visitors. I believe it would behoove you to speak with them."

"Oh, just as I was getting comfortable." Robert groaned as he pushed himself up. "I'll be back. Save some wine for me," he added with a slight grin.

Closing the door behind him, Robert recognized his visitors with a start—or at least one of them. Henry Percy and a tall, burly Norwegian-looking fellow stood before him, dressed in traveling clothes. Percy looked more like a commoner than a nobleman, his face brown from the sun and much more weathered than the last time he saw him. His grizzled hair was pure white now. But his eyes still shot fire.

"This is my friend, Lord Bardolf," Percy said, gesturing to his companion. "We come from the Duke of Albany in Stirling and are passing through on the way to Wales."

"Oh?" King Robert was always on his guard at the mention of his brother. "Is he well?"

"Very well. He gave us a safe-conduct and agreed to protect my grandson. Henry's in St. Andrews with your son James."

"You saw James?" The king wiped his eye again.

"Yes, we spent some time there. The boys are getting along just fine."

Robert sighed. "I am happy to hear that. Sit, my Lords, and tell me why you are here."

Percy sat on the edge of a chair. "As I said, we are on the way to Wales. Our intent is to renew the struggle against King Henry, both in Wales and on the continent. I wanted to pay my respects to King Richard and tell him we are working in his interests." He exchanged glances with Bardolf. "King Richard knows Owain Glyndwr. I would tell him that the Welsh prince continues his fight against King Henry. He has not been forgotten."

Robert wasn't so sure Richard would consider this good news—or even that he cared. But an earl was certainly of higher stature than Richard's previous supporters. He stood, putting a finger to his lips. "Let me speak with him."

He slipped through the door again, closing it quickly. Richard hadn't moved and he looked up, somewhat interested.

Glancing at the door, Robert cleared his throat. "There's someone here to see you."

"Oh?" Richard's voice took on a note of suspicion.

"Yes. The Earl of Northumberland."

"What?" Richard leapt to his feet. "Percy?"

136

Surprised at his reaction, Robert took a step back. "What's the matter?"

"Send him away!"

"What? Why?"

Increasingly agitated, Richard started pacing. "I never want to see him again. Never! That traitor!"

"Surely you don't mean it. He's come a long way."

"How dare he expect me to welcome him? After what he did to me? Don't you see? He betrayed me! I won't see him. Send him away, I say!" His voice was so shrill that Robert winced.

"He's in the next room."

"I don't care! He can go to hell!"

Daunted, King Robert put a hand on the latch. "Are you sure?"

"Make him go away!" Richard picked up a candlestick and threw it. It slammed against the wall.

Taking that for an answer, Robert got out as quickly as possible. Percy and Bardolf stood staring at him. They couldn't help but hear.

"I'm sorry," the king said. "He's never acted this way before."

Henry Percy picked up his walking stick which had been leaning against the wall. "I had hoped to make amends by espousing his cause. I should have expected this. Do you think he'll change his mind later on?"

Something else crashed against the door. Robert shrugged. "I don't think he'll relent."

Percy didn't think so either. "Sire, when he has calmed down, let him know I'm on my way to Wales. I will continue to work for his restoration in the hope that someday, he will forgive me."

Clearly he didn't want to linger and King Robert was relieved. Too bad he couldn't help the man. On the other hand, no need to involve himself in someone else's business. He had enough worries of his own.

If he only knew! David Fleming—one of Robert's last remaining supporters—showed up a few weeks after Percy passed through. His tidings were not good. The Douglas clan was rearming, having gained a promise from Albany that he would not interfere if they were to break the truce with England. This caused their enemies near the border to put themselves into a state of preparation for any kind of warfare. Perhaps it was time to send young James out of the country for safekeeping, as they originally planned if matters grew unsettled.

King Robert agreed. He resolved to send the eleven-year-old prince to France, which was the best place to educate a noble of his rank. "Take care of my boy," he said with tears in his eyes. "I fear I may never see him again."

Fleming knelt before the king and pledged he would do his utmost to see James to safety. Under his guardianship, as well as the Earl of Orkney and a strong party of barons, the prince was secretly removed from St. Andrews. The party travelled through Lothian to North Berwick, a seaside town on the Firth of Forth. From there they boarded a little rowboat and crossed one mile of choppy water to the island of Bass Rock, which stood in the middle of the Firth within view of Douglas's castle of Tantallon. This isolated island looked like a giant lump in the sea, over a hundred meters tall. Its craggy sides were almost vertical, offering only the tiniest of landing places for the prince's boat. But it held a proud fortification of stone that had been in the Lauder family for centuries, and offered shelter to the fugitive James. It took a month until a merchant ship could be found to pick up the young prince—a month during which the grateful but uncomfortable party were crammed into accommodations designed for many fewer residents. Fortunately, James had no trouble diverting himself with rock climbing and observing the gigantic colony of gannets that covered the stones with droppings.

The little party embarked in the middle of the night, and David Fleming bade farewell to his charge, trusting the truce between England and France that had not yet expired. They should be able to cross the Channel in safety.

Unfortunately, it was not meant to be. After two days at sea their ship was seized by English privateers and Prince James was easily identified and taken prisoner. As they were later to learn, the pirates were instructed to be on the lookout for him; the Duke of Albany had a long arm. The unfortunate captives were brought to London, where they were imprisoned in the Tower. Now King Henry had two prizes: Albany's son Murdoch and Prince James. With these hostages, his problems with Scotland had just been resolved.

Unfortunately for David Fleming, on his way back from North Berwick his party was ambushed and he was killed. His long-term feud with the Douglas clan provided timely revenge for Albany.

It took a week for the news of the prince's misfortune to reach the King of Scotland. At that moment, Robert had been dining with Richard. A messenger came into the room and the king turned to him, chalice in hand.

"Who has sent you?" he asked uneasily.

"I come from the Duke of Albany," the messenger said, bowing.

Robert looked at Richard. Somehow, he knew. Something had gone wrong.

"Is it about Prince James?"

The messenger bowed again. "Sire, the duke has sent me to tell you that a ship carrying Prince James has been captured by the English. Why the prince was on the ship in the first place, the duke does not know."

Robert stared at him for a moment then dropped the chalice; it splashed wine all over the table, but nobody noticed. Groaning, Robert leaned forward, grasping his chest. Richard jumped up and put his hands on the king's shoulders.

"What happened to my son?" Robert gasped, his voice a croak.

"Sire, our informant tells us that he has been taken under the protection of the King of England."

"Protection. Richard, did you hear that?" Gasping for breath, Robert started coughing.

"Get help!" Richard cried. "Can't you see? The king needs help!"

Hearing his voice, two chamber grooms dashed into the room and shouted for more aid. Another three followed and together they picked up the king and carried him from the room. Richard went with them.

"Take heart," Richard said softly as they lay Robert in his bed. The king stared back at him, his eyes like two saucers. "No one will hurt your child."

"He trusted me." Robert tried to sit up but Richard pushed him back against the pillows.

"Shh. You did the best you could. At least he is out of Albany's influence." Richard knew that was not much help, but he couldn't think of any better reassurance. "Together we'll write a letter to King Henry tomorrow. Perhaps he will let you ransom your son. We know he's in bad need of funds."

"Perhaps. Dear Lord, what have I done?" He closed his eyes. "What have I done to deserve this?"

For five days the king lay in his bed, praying, refusing food, and bemoaning the fate of his child. Richard sat at his side and tried to comfort his old friend, but he could see Robert was failing. Finally, the king beckoned him closer, for his voice was almost gone.

"I'm sorry I can no longer shelter you, my friend," he murmured. "We've had some good talks together and you are the only one who understands me." He coughed and reached for a glass of water. After taking a few deep breaths he went on. "My brother will most assuredly bring you back with him after I am gone. He'll take good care of you, never fear. You are a useful pawn." He almost laughed. "Though you may find yourself very much alone."

"It matters not," Richard said, taking the glass. "What matters is that you get better."

"No, that's not possible. The world has no use for me. I've already requested they bury me in a midden and write, 'Here lies the worst of kings and the most wretched of men' on my grave. I don't deserve to be buried with my betters." He reached for Richard's hand and squeezed it. "Now I will sleep and if God wills it, I won't wake up."

Reluctantly, the bygone King of England bent over and kissed the dying man on the brow before leaving the room. Robert had been kind to him, and Richard owed him his very life, for what it was worth. No one else would have taken him in and indulged him these last five years.

Robert got what he wished for; he never woke up. The Duke of Albany duly came to Rothesay Castle, collected the body, gave him a quiet funeral and buried the king in Paisley Abbey, which had been founded by the Stewarts.

Then he summoned Richard, who had attended the funeral. Shorn of all vainglory, Richard quietly presented himself. Albany looked him up and down. "Of course you can't stay here anymore."

Richard looked back appraisingly. Just a few years younger than Robert, the duke's short hair was mostly grey, his nose was a little flattened and his skin pockmarked. Not an ugly man, exactly, but certainly not pleasing to the eye. He had a habit of not looking at a person directly, which gave the impression of untrustworthiness—amply justified by his behaviour. He may have been competent—even a good governor, many said—but Richard suspected his words could be read on many levels.

"I am at your mercy," Richard said carefully. "King Robert told me you'd take good care of me."

Albany laughed briefly. "He knew me very well. And he was very fond of you. Yes, Sir Richard. I have already prepared your chambers at Stirling Castle. You'll have a good view of the courtyard."

"I would bring the king's dog with me. And his cat."

"Of course. Bring anything you need."

Richard shrugged. Hopefully his chambers would be more accommodating than at Pontefract. Not that he had much choice. He truly was at Albany's mercy.

Fortunately, the governor did not have any nefarious plans. Richard was comfortably housed in the castle and pretty much allowed to go where he wanted, as long as he stayed on the castle grounds. That was all right with him. His needs were few and he didn't want to talk to anyone. This was also a good thing, because he was destined to live there in relative obscurity for the next thirteen years.

CHAPTER 10

After having dealt with the northern rebellion, King Henry retraced his steps until finally he returned to Kenilworth, where Joanna was waiting for him. Of all the challenges he dealt with this year, facing his wife an altered man was the moment he dreaded the most. By then his flesh had mostly healed, but he was so afraid she would find him repulsive he nearly changed his plans. But no, that wouldn't be fair. They had married for better or worse.

He and his retainers clattered into the courtyard amidst the barking of dogs and honking of geese. Throwing himself from the saddle, he turned over the reins to a groom and practically ran up the stairs, for he had truly missed his queen. Best to pretend nothing was wrong and get it over with.

As the king entered the great hall, flanked by Thomas Erpingham and John Norbury, he was gratified by the cheer that greeted them. Looking around, he spotted Joanna at the far door with her ladies. She had dressed up for him, wearing her most becoming dark green velvet gown with matching silk veil trimmed in gold, her hair wrapped in braided cylinders nestled against her ears. Long sleeves trailed on the floor.

Henry held his breath as she approached and curtseyed before him. Then she looked up, eyes glowing. He took her hands and raised her, searching for signs of shock. Was it there behind that smile or was she just good at hiding it?

"Welcome back, my lord. I have missed you." Joanna leaned forward, presenting her cheek for a kiss.

Henry smiled in turn, feeling a little crack in his chapped lip. He hoped she didn't notice. The routine was all very normal, stepping through the crowd, exchanging pleasantries, then moving into the feast hall for dinner. Henry didn't know how he managed it all, pretending that no one was scrutinizing his face or talking about him behind his back. When they finally sat at the head table, he took Joanna's hand and kissed it while a servant poured the wine.

"You haven't asked me about my illness."

She nonchalantly took a sip. "I trust you'll tell me all about it."

"What have you heard?"

She shrugged. "All sorts of things which I chose to ignore. The timing was unfortunate."

He grimaced. "You heard that much, then."

"Oh, yes. The bishops were most bothersome."

"What did they say?"

She hesitated. "They feared for the Church after the execution."

He grunted. "The church isn't in danger. They fear for their skins."

"No doubt. I understand many supported Scrope's cause." She stroked the back of Henry's hand. "They say you are suffering from God's punishment."

Sighing, Henry nodded. "I fear the same thing, myself. How could I not?" Then he shook his head in denial. "He should never have led a rebellion against me. I had to make an example of him."

"Hmm." Releasing his hand, Joanna took a bite of her roasted swan. "Was he really such a threat to your crown?"

He grimaced. As usual, his wife went right to the heart of things. "It was one rebellion too many. He raised the whole city of York against me!"

"But were they prepared to fight a battle?"

"They were going to join Percy. They were all going to march south and..." He hesitated.

"And what?"

"I'm not entirely certain. It never got that far. I'm sure it didn't bode well for me. But enough was enough. This constant defiance had to end. By the time Archbishop Arundel reproached me, I was so furious I couldn't think straight. It was as though I had to go through with the execution just to prove myself."

"That's not like you. You must have been under a great strain. Could this be the cause of your attack?"

He nodded imperceptibly, considering.

"Here." She took a piece of swan and brought it to his lips. "You've lost weight."

Later that evening, in the privacy of their bedchamber, Henry leaned back against his pillows. Joanna had taken the brush from her lady's maid and dismissed all her servants. She sat on the edge of the bed and continued her brushing.

"You're so beautiful," Henry said.

She twisted around and studied him. "Tell me about it, dear. How bad was it?"

"It felt like someone poured fire on my skin." He shuddered. "Then my joints swelled up and I couldn't walk. I don't know which was worse."

Shaking her head, Joanna put the brush down and leaned against him. "I wish I was there."

"Oh no, no. I must have been terrible to look at. Even now, when I'm mostly healed, I'm afraid you find me fearsome."

"Not at all." She rolled over. "Never. I love all of you, not just what's on the surface."

She reached for him but he stopped her hand. "Oh, no, my dear. This might be infectious."

"I'll take my chances."

"But I won't. Wait until I'm completely healed. How can I embrace you if I'm worried about spreading this terrible disease?"

"Well…" Disappointed, Joanna sat back up and reached for her brush again. "If you insist…"

"Your health is more important than mine. I need you to be well. What if I have l-l-leprosy." He could barely get the word out.

Shocked, she stopped and stared at him. "Is that what your physician said?"

"He didn't know. He didn't dare say."

"But you got better."

"I did. It must be something else." He didn't sound convinced. "But if God is truly punishing me…"

This time Joanna didn't argue. "I heard that miracles have been reported at Archbishop Scrope's grave," she whispered.

"I don't believe it." Again, he couldn't hide his lack of conviction. "People will do anything for attention."

"I'm sure you're right," she said with certainty. Her faith in Henry was absolute. But what about his faith in himself?

Henry spent a month at Kenilworth, and just before he was ready to leave for London Archbishop Arundel made an appearance. When he was announced, the king looked out the window, cursing his bad luck that he wasn't already gone. He knew he would have to face Arundel sooner or later, but it was easier to put off this unwelcome meeting. Leaving York without taking leave of the archbishop was not the least of his guilty blunders.

Joanna came up behind him and put a hand on Henry's shoulder. "You must see him, you know."

"I know, I know."

"Maybe it won't be so bad. Enough time has passed."

Looking up with a lopsided smile, he closed his book. "Enough time for him to come up with some real scathing remarks. I'm no match for his eloquence."

"He's more sensible than that. You'll see."

Sighing, Henry straightened his surcoat, adjusted his belt, and ran a hand over his hair. Giving Joanna one last look, he went into the outer chamber where the archbishop was waiting.

His first glance made him stop short; Arundel was gaunt, pale, and a little bent over. Henry wondered if he looked just as bad.

"Thomas," he said, holding out a hand. Arundel got out of his chair and prepared to kneel but Henry stopped him. "Sit, my friend. I understand you have been very ill."

With a look of relief, the archbishop sat back down. "I've never been sicker in my life," he said.

Henry didn't know where to start. "Have you…have you completely recovered?"

"I've been very careful not to do too much."

"That's good. That's good." Unable and unwilling to apologize, Henry decided not to say anything at all. It was up to Arundel to direct the conversation.

Equally ill at ease, the archbishop cleared his throat. "The cathedral chapter at York elected Chancellor Langley as the next archbishop."

"Yes, I approved that."

"Um, yes. Well, Sire, the pope disapproved. That's why I am here. He published a bull of excommunication against yourself, Chancellor Langley, and all those who counselled or agreed to Archbishop Scrope's death." Arundel held it up; the pope's seal swung back and forth from a red cord.

Though he was expecting as much, Henry was still struck dumb by the news. No matter what happened, he considered himself a good man of the church. Sitting down across from Arundel, he reached for the document.

"No," the archbishop said, rolling it up. "I have decided not to publish this, in the interests of public order. It would unsettle the whole country and we need time to come to terms with the aftermath of this rebellion."

Henry couldn't hide his relief. But it was time to make amends. "Thomas," he started, but the other held up a hand.

"It was a grievous situation. But I leave it to God to pass judgment, whose will is inscrutable." The look in his eye betrayed these words, but Henry was grateful, nonetheless.

Sometimes it was better not to delve too deep. "Unfortunately," Arundel went on, "the people have already come to their own conclusions, based on your..." he made a gesture at his own face." The best I can do is mitigate the situation. My first responsibility is to the Church."

Henry held his breath. Arundel was coming to the crux of the matter. He knew that without the archbishop's active support he might not survive, politically. He was expecting some sort of demand.

"We must reverse all the recent attacks on the liberties and property of the Church," Arundel went on. "No more assessing extra tax liens against the clergy. No more threats to take away our lands." He paused, stroking the crucifix hanging from his neck. "Most importantly, I need your backing in the church's crusade against Lollards."

Ah. Henry sat back. He could work with this.

"And in return," the archbishop went on, "I will do my best to discourage all this attention around Scrope's tomb. I will attempt to bring you back into the Church's good graces." He looked appraisingly at Henry. "I am prepared to take a more active part in the government, in the face of your...troubled health."

Despite himself, Henry blushed. During the last few years, the archbishop had concentrated on his ecclesiastic concerns and left the governing to others. But things were different now. God willing, this illness would subside. Too bad he couldn't count on it. No one wanted an incapacitated king. He might need someone to carry on if he had another attack; there was no one better for the job and they both knew it.

"I am glad to have you back," Henry said. "Your terms are more than acceptable."

After four years of fighting, Prince Hal could congratulate himself for having turned the tide of the Welsh rebellion—

almost. Although during the previous season the Welsh seemed invincible with the help of a small French army that had overrun South Wales, their allies had grown disenchanted with the poor plunder, bad food, and terrible weather. Already they were streaming back to France. Hal was given a fresh commission as lieutenant in Wales along with a welcome influx of badly-needed cash, as well as more than three thousand new soldiers.

Swollen with arrogance, the Welsh experienced their first major setback near Usk on 23 April, St. George's Day. A thousand men were killed including one of Glyndwr's sons. It was rare that the English could engage the Welsh in a pitched battle, and they were surprisingly able to follow this up with a second win. This ill-fated Welsh debacle was led by the Earl of Northumberland and Lord Bardolf, who tried and failed to make a good impression on their new host. But pitched battles did not ensure success. The English had to regain control over major strongholds, especially Aberystwyth and Harlech. Meanwhile, guerrilla warfare continued, and Hal couldn't be everywhere at once.

Parliament had been scheduled for spring, and Hal was expected to attend. As his most crucial responsibilities for the Welsh war eased up, he became more and more interested in the working of government. He needed to be ready when his time came. So in the 1406 Parliament, he watched with interest mixed with indignation as the Commons went on the offensive against his father.

King Henry was expecting trouble but he got much more than he anticipated. How could he be held responsible for three years of bad harvests? The rains were worse than anyone ever saw in their lives. Along the Thames, dykes and causeways were broken between London and Greenwich. The Severn had flooded and 800 acres of grain crops were destroyed. At York, the Fossbridge had been destroyed. Roads and bridges were washed away in the Fen country. All of England was in terrible condition. Revenue from the wool trade had collapsed.

Large sums of money had been spent this last year, but nothing had been done to secure peace for trade; the seas were awash with French pirates. From Guyenne to Wales to Scotland to Ireland, they experienced nothing but ceaseless war. And now the king wants more taxes? Where was the accountability? And that wasn't all. Members of parliament harangued him about the costs of the royal household. They insisted he expel all foreigners from France and Brittany, including most of the queen's servants and courtiers.

Henry's temper had reached the breaking point, and the Commons realized they had gone too far. The speaker, Sir John Tiptoft, stood up and gestured to his fellow members. "Sire," he said, "we ask to be forgiven if we have given you offense." He lowered his head in supplication.

For a moment it looked like their contrition might not be enough. Grinding his teeth in frustration, Henry turned aside, picked up a cup of water and took his time drinking it. Then he handed the cup to Archbishop Arundel. "All right. I accept your apology. This session is adjourned until after Easter. We will reconvene in three weeks' time."

Heaving a collective sigh of relief, the members dispersed to their homes. Many would reunite anyway on Sunday, 25 April at Windsor Castle— just before the next session began. It was the annual feast for the Order of the Garter, and all the companions were expected to be there. No new members were made this year, though that didn't detract from the colourful pageantry embellishing this event. All twenty-six knights wore a full-length dark purple cloak, or mantle, with an ermine collar. A badge of St. George's cross on a shield, encircled by a garter, was sewn onto the left shoulder. A wide gold collar made of heraldic knots and roses encircled their shoulders, hung with a pendant of St. George slaying the dragon, known as the *Greater George*. Beneath their mantle, all wore a long red tunic; black velvet hats completed the ensemble.

First, a grand feast was held, then afterwards the members processed through Windsor castle, from St. George's Hall to the chapel. There they attended a service of thanksgiving.

Henry's sons had all been made Knights of the Garter at his first parliament, and they hadn't seen each other since the previous year. After the Garter ceremony, Henry moved on to his hunting lodge at Windsor Park. He invited his sons for dinner, just the four of them and himself.

Hal planned to join the king ahead of time before the others showed up; he had much to discuss and many questions. Opening the door, he was disappointed to see that his brother Thomas was already there, deep in conversation with Henry at the table. Their father had his hand on Thomas's arm and as Hal entered the room, the smile on Henry's face disappeared.

"Come and sit down, son," Henry said. "We were just talking about the fleet. I have heard good reports about Thomas's first commission as admiral." He was smiling again.

Sitting across the table from them, Hal reached for the wine. "Was there any action?"

Thomas gave him a sour look, detecting veiled criticism. "French pirates were threatening Dover. We gave them a merry chase back to the continent."

"I see." Taking a sip, Hal stretched his legs. "I wonder if those were the same Frenchmen that departed from Wales. They could well have been looking for more plunder."

"I wouldn't be surprised." Thomas was turning back to his father when John and Humphrey came into the room.

Henry stood, holding out his arms. "Ah, now we are all together. I swear, both of you have grown a foot!"

Grinning, John nudged his brother. "He's growing faster than I am. But I am better looking!"

Henry hugged both of his boys, then held them at arm's length. John was always the prettiest of his children, with his blond curls and blue eyes like his mother. He was seventeen years old now, and his brother was sixteen. Humphrey took after his father, a little stouter than John and darker of complexion. His brown eyes were piercing and his eyebrows on the heavy side. He had yet to be given a position of responsibility, and Henry knew he was anxious to prove himself.

Thomas, on the other hand, was more inclined to take life easy. So far, his performance in Ireland had been lacklustre; perhaps he just hadn't been given the right opportunity to prove himself. Regardless, thought Henry, he looked every bit the prince—with that handsome face, compelling smile, dimpled chin, and deep-set eyes that took in everything around him. Not like Hal, small and wiry with a pointed nose and that unfortunate scar. Dear God he was hard to look at. Even so, Henry had to admit that Hal was thoroughly efficient and promised to be a great soldier.

"Sit, everyone. We have so much to talk about."

As the servants came in with their first course, Henry held up his cup. "You have all made me proud. My sons." He drank quickly, trying not to notice the way they scrutinized him. He knew they were searching for signs of his recent illness, but hoped to avoid the subject. Oh, what was the point? He took a big sigh; might as well get it over with. "I am doing well. You can see." He cocked his head at Thomas who nodded.

"You look hale," the other lied, shooting a warning glance at Hal.

"The doctors have bled me when I needed it," Henry assured them, "and check my urine regularly. They watch me like a hawk." He chuckled. "I dare say they watch each other just as closely. Nothing gets past them."

"You're better then?" asked Hal.

"God willing." Henry blessed himself. They all followed. For a moment silence settled on the room.

"All is quiet in the north," John said lightly, changing the subject. "Since you retook Northumberland's castles, my job has been much easier."

"Percy has moved on again," Hal added. "After he got trounced in Wales, he slipped across the Channel to France. I doubt he'll find much support there."

"I think his power is broken," Henry nodded. "John, I intend to award you some of his estates."

"That will help." John laughed briefly, "My coffers are empty."

"As are mine," Thomas said.

"Yours?" Hal couldn't restrain himself. "You haven't been in Ireland in over two years."

"I've been covering for the Earl of Somerset while he's been ill," Thomas answered defensively.

"That's only been for four months. What about the rest of the time? Why should you get paid when John and I have been exposing ourselves to all sorts of hardships?"

"I sold all my plate to pay my soldiers in Ireland!"

"I did the same! So did John! You came home and left the governing to a deputy!"

"Father had other tasks for me." Thomas turned to Henry who nodded uncomfortably.

"Then you should be paid for those tasks, not as lieutenant of Ireland, where you have performed abysmally."

"Sons, sons," interrupted Henry. "This should be a reunion. We don't need to ruin it by bickering."

Grumbling, Hal sat back, taking a drink of wine.

"That's better. Now tell me about Owain Glyndwr. I understand he held his own parliament at Aberystwyth…"

Henry and his sons got through their unhappy reunion and he was preparing to return to the next parliament session at Westminster. He sent a message to his council that he planned to arrive the following day, but as he and Joanna were taking a last stroll around the park, he suddenly felt a twinge in his right leg. He stopped.

Joanna was alarmed by the look on his face. "What is it, my dear?"

"Something's wrong. We need to go back."

Taking their time, they returned to the manor house, but the more he walked, the more Henry needed to lean on the queen's arm for support. She waved to William Philips, who was trailing them with a pack of courtiers.

"William, the king needs help."

Breaking into a run, the squire and another dashed up and put Henry's arms over their shoulders, supporting him the rest of the way to the building. Once inside, he and the queen lowered Henry into a chair.

"Summon the physician," Joanna said, waving the curious onlookers away. She leaned over her husband. "What is it?"

"Both of my legs," he said, trying to sit up straight. "They were tingling at first, and now they are going numb. I'm afraid they are starting to swell."

William knelt. "We'll have to get your hose off. Can you walk?"

"I'll need help."

Turning, the squire gestured to some of the servants who lingered nearby. "We need to carry the king to his bedchamber." Three others stepped forward and they carefully picked Henry up; he wrapped his arms around their necks. He couldn't hide a grimace of pain but kept silent.

Once they settled Henry into bed and the physician arrived, the king gave up his show of bravery. He gasped in pain as they undressed him and his head lolled back. Joanna sat at his bedside and dabbed his forehead with a damp cloth, but he didn't seem to notice.

"Is this the same as before?" she asked William.

The squire looked puzzled. "The skin irritation came first."

"At least he is spared that, for now." She gasped when the physician rolled down his hose. The legs were indeed starting to swell, from his thighs to his ankles. "What could it be?"

The physician touched his knee tenderly. "The joints are inflamed. We need to keep him cool if possible."

Putting damp cloths on his legs, they did the best they could to slow down the swelling.

Henry opened his eyes briefly before telling Joanna how tired he was. "I'm sorry. I don't want you to see me this way."

"Nonsense. You're not the first sick person I tended."

He squeezed her hand then let out a gasp. "Damn legs. Let me sleep. I'll be better in the morning. I have to go to Westminster." His words slurred, but Joanna decided to let it pass. He was clearly exhausted.

But the next morning he was no better. Joanna accompanied the servants into his bedchamber; they carried a little table which they put on his lap so he could eat breakfast while in bed. Henry was already awake and he smiled bravely at her while they busied themselves around him.

Dismissing the servants, she sat on the bed. "Henry? Are you all right?"

His smile gone, he reached for her hand. "It's as bad as the last time," he said slowly. "With all the pain, I can't think straight."

Blinking away tears, she fluffed his pillow. "Can you eat?"

"I don't know." He picked up a piece of bread and looked at it for a moment before putting it in his mouth. Taking a bite, he had trouble swallowing but he finally got it down. "Maybe something softer," he said.

Calling the servants, Joanna told them to bring porridge. And the physicians. Then she took his hand again.

"We'll get through this."

"I need to write to Westminster."

That was a good sign. "Let me help you." She went across to the desk and found a piece of paper. "If it's all right with you, I'll tell them—"

"Tell them I've been struck with a malady in my leg and cannot ride. Tell them there will be a few days' delay before I can attend parliament."

"Very good. That will give you time to recover."

"I think the Duke of York is still at Windsor Castle. See if he will come."

The physicians arrived shortly thereafter and Joanna went off to find the duke. Freed from all pretence, Henry was much more forthcoming. "Something has happened to my head," he admitted. "I am not myself. My mind is confused."

"One grand accesse," said the Italian physician. "His humours are imbalanced."

"Apoplexy," said the other one. "That explains the legs."

Both of them thought *divine punishment* but neither put it into words.

"He needs to be bled at once," concluded the first doctor. "Then we should purge him with an enema."

"Yes," the other nodded, "then I will prepare an herbal oil to apply to his limbs."

As they were discussing this, Joanna returned with the Duke of York. Henry gave her a crooked smile. "I will be well soon. Don't worry."

York looked from one physician to the other. "You're not going." That was a statement, not a question.

Henry shook his head. "You can be my representative. The queen shall send you with a letter to the council. It's nothing serious. I just need some rest. I will follow in a few days."

Bowing, the duke refrained from asking any questions.

"And tell no one," Henry added, wincing as one of the physicians touched his leg.

"Sire, I am at your service."

There was nothing else to be done. York took his letter and went on ahead, though for the first several days no business was conducted at Westminster. Finally, at the end of the week,

Arundel, York, and the Lords opened parliament without the king. The Commons would assemble later.

It took four days for Henry to feel well enough to get out of bed. Thanks to the ministrations of his physicians, his head cleared and the swelling diminished a bit in his legs. He was in great pain and could barely walk, but he needed to be in London. It was too soon to face the recalcitrant Commons; Henry did not have enough energy for that. Nonetheless, he could stay nearby so he could be consulted.

"As long as I am accessible," he said to Joanna, "they can do routine transactions, and I can send my responses under the privy seal. I will make an appearance when absolutely necessary."

Over the objections of his doctors, the king insisted they carry him in a litter the seven miles to the Thames. The royal barge was waiting. He and his household sailed downriver, past Westminster, to the London palace of Chancellor Langley. He was to stay there on-and-off for the next two and a half months.

Three weeks after he settled in London, Henry dragged himself to Westminster. He had decided to announce his decision to transfer most of the daily work of government to a continual council of seventeen. This was meant to be temporary—at least until next parliament. He was bound to be better by then, he assured the members. Archbishop Arundel would take the leading role, supported by the Duke of York, Henry and John Beaufort, the chancellor, treasurer, keeper of the privy seal, chamberlain, and many others trusted by the king. Prince Hal and Prince Thomas would also be present.

Meanwhile, parliament took four months off from June through October, giving Henry the opportunity to go on pilgrimage to local shrines. He received blessings, kissed holy relics, and doused himself with holy water. He could ride for short distances and moved very slowly, praying daily for relief. None came.

Parliament reconvened one last time that year, and it took them until a few days before Christmas before they granted the subsidy Henry needed. But it came at an even bigger cost: this state of uncertainty could not go on. It was apparent to all that King Henry was no longer capable. Word had leaked out concerning his dubious health. Even his mental state was suspect. Something had to be done.

Assuring the king they were working in the best interest of the country, parliament passed a constitutional document called Thirty-One articles. Henry was to give up all control of the government, including his own household. The council would rule in his name until the next parliament. No one would be permitted to come to him with disputes, requests, or appointments—not even his own servants. A certain number of council members would be obliged to stay with him at all times to oversee the chamber expenses. He was not allowed to make gifts to anyone. Because the king was required to be accessible to the public, Wednesdays and Fridays were proclaimed as the days he could transact business, and then only in the presence of council members.

No king had ever been given such restrictions. On the other hand, no king had ever been so ill. Henry was humiliated, but there was nothing he could do. He truly *was* as helpless as a babe. He still couldn't walk without support, and there were times his attention wandered. He needed a great deal of sleep. His doctors kept experimenting with new and promising treatments, and he submitted to every discomfort in the hopes that this would be the one to cure him.

At Christmas, King Henry went to Eltham, his favourite palace. He felt like a failure—a weak and despondent man. The Long Parliament, as it came to be called, had accomplished next to nothing—except to render him useless. Its expenses were almost as much as the pitiful grant of taxation he had sacrificed so much to achieve.

On the other hand, Henry was still king, even if he did not rule. Notwithstanding his mortification, the government had rallied behind him. At the very beginning of his reign, Henry had promised to rule with the advice of his magnates. It was ironic that his ill health forced him to keep that promise, belated though it was. If he lived through this, they would find a way out of this mess. If he died, there was a new act of succession in place declaring Hal as heir to the throne and his children after him.

The Lancastrian dynasty was assured. He had done at least that much.

CHAPTER 11

Aberystwyth Castle was built on a rocky promontory overlooking the sea with an excellent harbour. One of Edward I's Ring of Castles intended to control the rebellious Welsh, Aberystwyth featured two concentric curtain walls with round towers at every point. The inner ward was shaped like a diamond instead of the usual rectangle. The outer wall consisted of a twin D-shaped barbican, mirrored by a second D-shaped gatehouse on the inner wall. In its day, Aberystwyth was a formidable fortress, but exposure to the elements and lack of funding contributed to its disrepair. The main gateway, drawbridges, and outer bailey curtain walls were badly in need of repair, though the Welsh had attempted to patch up its defensive capabilities.

The English had settled in around the castle several weeks ago, but the Welsh were still able to receive occasional aid by sea. This was worrisome; after three years, it remained to be seen whether the English had the means to recover it from the rebels.

Prince Hal believed he would be successful this time, especially as he watched the unloading of the artillery, sent to aid his task. Five guns were on the ship from Bristol; the king's 4½-ton cannon—called *Messenger*—caused the most excitement. They also received 538 pounds of powder, 971 pounds of saltpetre, and 303 pounds of sulphur.

The cannons came with German gunners, dressed in short hauberks and bascinet helms; they were cocksure, strutting fellows who wasted no time ordering other soldiers around. But these big guns were such an innovation that no one seemed to mind too much; they gathered around the ordnances, pointing and speculating and asking a gratifying number of questions.

Putting a hand on *Messenger's* barrel, Hal turned to Sir John Oldcastle who was peering into the muzzle. "Don't let that thing blow your head off," he joked.

John smirked, throwing his head back to fling the hair from his eyes. "Never fear. When this thing fires, I'll be far away."

"So will I. My father loves these big guns but I'm not sure I trust them. Come. I'm hungry." Hal headed toward his pavilion. Then he paused, gesturing at the cannon. "We'll put these to use tomorrow morning," he said to the gunner. "Let's hope this scares the Welsh into submission. I don't look forward to a long siege."

If the artillery failed to dislodge them, the next step would be to requisition more ships and fully blockade the castle—an expensive proposition, especially considering money was practically non-existent. Hal and John worked their way over to the prince's tent; they were happy to see the squires putting together a meal for them.

"The fighting in South Wales goes on apace," John said, sitting before a cooking fire. "To tell you true, I don't think these big guns are going to make a difference in the face of all this skirmishing." He held out a mug for a servant to pour ale. "You chase down one pack of knaves and they disappear, only to crop up on the other side of a mountain, burning and pillaging. Towns that would remain loyal do so at their own risk and pay the consequences sooner or later."

"You of all people know only too well," Hal agreed. He pulled off a boot and rubbed his foot. "But it seems to me you have come out ahead of late. While I've been wasting my time in Hereford writing incessant letters to my father's council, you're out there in the field doing the important work. I don't know what I'd do without you."

"I thank you for that. I get enough practice."

"Ha! But you also know that once we recapture all our fortifications, we'll be able to gain a measure of control. If we only had the money…" Hal's face took on a faraway look. "I'm tired of this conflict, John. Six years is enough. God's blood, the more we fight the more we destroy their capability to sustain a livelihood—and pay their taxes." He threw a piece of wood on the fire. "If I'm tired, they must be exhausted. How much longer can they hold out?"

"I wish I knew."

The next morning, the bombardment started with the sun. The smaller guns went first, peppering the fortress with round balls six inches in diameter. Aside from making a lot of noise, they didn't do much damage against the stone walls. Hal stood behind *Messenger*, arms crossed, watching as the gunners loaded a stone ball into the cannon barrel.

"You had better step back," the captain said, waving to the prince. "Hold your hands over your ears and keep your mouth open. Takes the pressure off." He made a joke to his mate that Hal couldn't quite hear. No matter. Grabbing Oldcastle by the elbow, Hal moved to a safer place.

Soon they were ready to fire the gun. The soldiers took a step away and one of them extended a long pole with a lighted piece of hemp on the end. He lowered it to the touchhole. A couple of seconds later the ball was expelled from the muzzle with a huge discharge of smoke and flame. The blast was tremendous, and Hal was glad he listened to the gunner's advice. They watched the projectile fly through the air and slam into the stone wall, throwing shards of rock in every direction. The men cheered and Hal looked at his friend, impressed.

The captain strutted up, clearly enjoying the effect his artillery made on the English. "Now we have to wait for it to cool off," he said, "before sponging out the inside so we can make sure it's clean. Come back in two hours and we'll do it again."

Hal returned as directed, with somewhat more enthusiasm and much more caution. Intent on their job, the cannoneers efficiently loaded another stone into the chamber and announced they were ready. Stepping to the rear, Hal put his hands over his ears and waited expectantly while the soldier put the fuse into the touchhole.

Suddenly, a blast blew him back onto his rump. With a huge ball of fire, the cannon exploded into what looked like a thousand pieces, throwing up a black cloud of smoke shrouding everything in view. Men flew through the air—some with shards of iron driven into their flesh, others on fire, screaming.

Oldcastle scrambled to Hal on his knees. "Are you all right?"

Shaking his head clear, the prince let John help him up. "Yes, yes. Oh, dear Lord. Look at them."

As the smoke cleared, the bloody scene drove even hardened soldiers to turn away and vomit. The centre of the cannon barrel was bent and mangled from the force of the explosion. The air was filled with the stench of sulphur. The ground beneath the gun was scarred and black. Those closest to the blast were dismembered, while others writhed in agony, their clothes on fire while men tried to extinguish the flames. The captain, so proud and cocky just a minute before, sprawled on the ground, his eyes open and his head caved in.

For a moment Hal bent over, hands on his knees. Then he straightened. "John, help me carry this man to the surgeon."

He knew the others didn't need direction from him as soldiers ran forward, aiding those who were wounded and picking up the bloody pieces of those who were beyond care. From a distance they could hear the Welsh cheering behind the castle walls.

"They won't be celebrating for long, I promise you," Hal muttered. "The cannons won't finish this; tomorrow we'll send for the rest of the ships and blockade those bastards."

The men who survived were patched up and placed inside a tent, reserved just for them. The victims were given a mass burial with proper services read by the resident priest. The king's cannon was dragged out of the way and replaced with one of the smaller guns. The effect was not as exhilarating, but at least none of the cannons exploded again.

A total blockade was soon in place. Within three weeks, the rebels inside Aberystwyth were nearing the end of their resources. Finally, on 12 September, the commander Rhys Ddu—The Black—sent an envoy to Prince Hal offering to negotiate terms.

"This time it's for real," Hal told Oldcastle. "We need witnesses. Send a letter to my cousin, the Duke of York, at Carmarthen." York had recently been recommissioned as sub-Lieutenant for south Wales. "Also, I would have the Earl of Warwick here, and we need to notify my father who is in York. Notify the leading Marcher Lords in Wales. The timing is such that we can all travel from here to the upcoming parliament at Gloucester."

Eager to see the end of the conflict, the great lords gathered at the camp—all except the king who was too far away. The gates to Aberystwyth opened and the distinguished party met the proud but tattered Welsh commanders led by the swarthy Rhys Ddu. Master Courtenay held mass, then the council gathered around a large table inside the castle.

Rhys stood, a parchment in hand. "My gracious lords, here is our proposal. If our Lord Owain Glyndwr does not relieve us by 1 November, we will deliver up the fortress with its guns and artillery and perform homage to King Henry. In return, we ask that you refrain from assaulting the castle in the meantime." This was no more than Prince Hal expected. As far as he knew, Glyndwr was too far away to relieve the garrison. Agreeing to the terms, the English and Welsh signed the document.

Within days, Hal and his large company were off to Hereford, then to Gloucester. Honouring their agreement, he left

120 men-at-arms and 360 archers to guard Aberystwyth with orders to refrain from making any attacks. Many of the ships had tasks elsewhere and couldn't be tied up in a profitless blockade, so they were released. Security was relaxed.

Alas, this was to have unfortunate consequences. Once again, the Prince of Wales was able to hide his movements. Immediately after Hal and his army had safely gone, an outraged Glyndwr returned unexpectedly. Owain slipped into the castle and declared that he had nothing to do with the proposed surrender, then declared Rhys Ddu and his supporters to be traitors. A few hangings proceeded to re-establish his authority.

Blissfully ignorant, Hal planned to plead his case at the 1407 parliament and secure enough resources to put an end to the Welsh rebellion once and for all. His father's health was not improving, and he felt the need to involve himself more in the workings of government. What if the inevitable happened before he was prepared to take over the rule of England?

Parliament started with the usual bickering and criticizing—in the king's absence. As expected, Henry moved at his usual torturous pace. One of the reasons he was late was the difficulty in traveling; he went by boat whenever possible, which made his itinerary more circuitous. And he required more resting time between stretches. Happily, he was expected any day.

But there was one big difference in the complaining this year. The Commons had reluctantly begun to recognize that they could no longer blame their grievances on the king. He had been inactive for a year. None of the decisions had been made by him. It was the council's performance they began to scrutinize.

The speaker had his points all written down. "The exchequer has recorded that the Easter term this year has provided the lowest level of revenue for the last seven years. We would like to know how the taxes collected last year have been spent. They were supposed to last until Michaelmas of next year, and yet here we are already, in need of another subsidy."

Archbishop Arundel would have none of it. As head of the council, he drew himself up in a righteous rage.

"How dare you find fault with our work!" he bellowed. "We have selflessly volunteered our services in the most thankless job ever imagined. You are singularly lacking in gratitude and do not deserve our consideration. We shall demand to be released from this burden!"

This was a setback no one counted on. Fortunately, news of the king's arrival precipitated a recess, and the following day all reassembled, with tempers under control. The king entered the hall at Gloucester on his own two feet, but he needed a staff to lean on and his steps were shuffling and uncertain. It was a sobering sight, for he could no longer even pretend that he was hale. Henry took his place and listened carefully, although actually he had been well prepared by Arundel the night before.

"I have made a decision," the king said once everyone was ready for his response. "I shall release the council from their oaths. With their permission, I will ask them to continue as a favour to myself until I am prepared to take up the reins of government." This was a technicality but an important one: if the council no longer operated under oath, no legal action could be taken against them. The level of mistrust was undiminished, but no one could see a good alternative.

In the end, King Henry received the subsidy he was looking for, though he was forced to make a major concession that perhaps was inevitable. For the first time in the history of parliament, the Commons were awarded the ability to conduct business on their own—without the presence of the king, or even the Lords. This right would be guaranteed for the present and all future parliaments.

Parliament had been scheduled at Gloucester so that Hal could go back and forth to Wales, and the prince proceeded to do so. However, the first time he returned to Aberystwyth, he learned that the November surrender was off the table. Some of the prince's soldiers had deserted by then, and Hal was hard put

166

to re-establish the blockade as before. But with the help of the Duke of York, the siege went on and Hal would be able to mind his duties at Gloucester. Aberystwyth would hold out for almost another year, and by the time it really surrendered, Glyndwr was long gone.

CHAPTER 12

Across the Channel, Louis of Orléans was too busy with the affairs of France to give much thought to his ongoing feud with Henry. He brushed aside his disappointment that French support of Glyndwr had proved expensive and largely unproductive; providing a constant annoyance to the English king was satisfying enough. He returned to Paris for the winter, leaving his wife and children safely ensconced at Château-Thierry in the country.

It was St. Clement's day, 23 November. Isabeau of Bavaria, the Queen of France was ill and in mourning for her twelfth child, who died at birth ten days before. Louis hoped to cheer her up by arranging a supper at her Hôtel Barbette in the Rue du Temple. A merry party gathered, with all the most fashionable cavaliers and dames, who diverted the queen with pleasantries and songs of love. Despite herself, Isabeau smiled and engaged in a little wordplay, trying to forget her unhappiness for a few hours.

Around nine o'clock, a messenger was admitted. Louis recognized him; his name was Courteheuse, one of the king's valets. He bowed to the queen and then turned to the duke who was sitting beside her.

"Monsieur le Duc d'Orléans, I come from his Majesty. He requests your presence at once at St. Pol to discuss most urgent business."

"Ah, Madame la Reine, I must go." Kissing the queen's hand, Louis rose immediately.

Outside the room, two of his squires waited for him. "The king commands," the duke said, reaching for his black furred cloak. "We must go quickly." Not pausing for an answer, Louis made his way outside and waited while his squires brought up one horse for the both of them and his own palfrey. He looked up, noticing the sky was overcast. It was very dark and the streets were already deserted.

"There you are. Good. Let us go." He mounted and started off at a fast walk, his squires behind him. Three valets carrying torches followed, but they were on foot and had trouble keeping up. The buildings were shuttered for the night and only an occasional sliver of light from barred windows lit the street. Louis didn't mind. As they rode down the Rue Vielle du Temple, he was fiddling with his gloves and humming to himself.

They came to a place where the road widened around a well in the centre. Without warning eight muffled men sprung out from the shadows and ran at him. Thinking they were thieves, Louis shouted, "I am the Duke of Orléans!"

"That's who we are looking for," yelled one of them, and struck with an axe, severing Louis's bridle hand. The duke shrieked, and another man slammed an axe into the back of his head. They pulled Louis from his horse and a third axe cleft his skull to the teeth, spilling his brains over the frozen paving stones.

The squires' horse sidestepped, shied and bolted. The valets carrying the torches stopped when they reached the opening and two of them turned away and ran. The third dashed forward, pushing aside one of the attackers and threw himself onto the duke, not realizing he was too late. He vainly tried to protect his master but found himself in dire trouble, for by now the murderers were stabbing again and again with their daggers.

"Murder! Murder!" shrieked a witness from a window overhead.

"Shut up, you damned woman!" yelled one of the murderers. "Shut up!"

Frightened for a moment, the woman withdrew. The attackers heaved the valet aside and dragged the mangled duke over to the well, propping him up against the stones. His head lolled to one side. They picked up the still-burning torch and brought it closer to make sure he was truly dead.

At that moment, a burly man in a red hood came out of the house across the street, known as the Hôtel de l'Image de Notre Dame. He raised an axe one more time and brought it down on the duke's head. "Give me that torch," he growled. "Let's go! He's dead."

The murderers were interrupted by a clatter at the end of the street; the squires, having gained control of their horse returned with the duke's palfrey. They assumed he had fallen off.

The man in the red hood stepped forward. "Be gone! Or you shall share his fate." He pointed to the dead man.

Terrified, they turned and fled, crying out, "Murder! Murder!"

Their task finished, the red-hooded man threw his torch into the Hôtel, setting it on fire. They all fled down the Rue des Blancs Manteaux, scattering caltrops on the ground to deter anyone from giving chase. At the same time, the woman started screaming "Murder" again, and the poor valet lay on the ground, crying, "My master! My Lord!" Soon his voice failed and he, too, was gone.

One of the squires ran to the queen with the terrible news. Thrown into a panic, Isabeau begged her brother Louis of Bavaria to carry her to a litter and convey her immediately to the Hôtel de St. Pol. There she was lodged in a chamber next to the king for safety.

Awakened by the noise, he came out himself to see what the matter was. The queen threw herself into his arms, crying hysterically.

"They have murdered your brother," she sobbed. "Poor Louis, he was just having dinner with me and your valet bid him to come see you at once on urgent business. They must have ambushed him on the way."

"See me? Who said that?"

"Courteheuse. I saw him myself."

"The rogue! Find him," Charles ordered, speaking over his shoulder. "Dear God, how can this have happened?" He gently handed the queen over to her lady maids.

Turning, he saw that Count de St. Pol and his chamberlain were watching. "Where is my poor brother?"

They shook their heads, as confounded as he was.

A large crowd had gathered outside the queen's room. Word had already spread about the terrible murder, and most of them were afraid the king would relapse into his mysterious affliction. For the last fifteen years he had slipped in and out of sanity—a condition inherited from his mother. There were times he didn't recognize his wife or children. During one episode he thought he was made of glass. Two years ago, he refused to change his clothes or bathe for five months.

But this night, fortunately, Charles was in his right mind. Seeing everyone's faces, he drew himself up. Tall and slightly overweight with the typical Valois hooked nose, Charles still carried himself with dignity.

"I'm all right," he said. The others sighed with relief. Ignoring their response, he pointed to the chamberlain. "Have the Provost Marshal close the city gates," he said. "Send out patrols. We must find the murderers. We will impose martial law this night." The chamberlain ran to obey and Charles took St. Pol's arm. "We shall walk there. I know it's not far."

"Your Majesty, it's not safe."

"My guards will protect me."

Nodding, St. Pol gestured to the men-at-arms who waited next to the wall, the butts of their halberds on the floor. As the pair passed the guards and exited the hôtel, many other lords and knights hurried up to join them. Another set of guards preceded the king so that by the time they reached the end of the street, their small following had quickly grown into a protective square. Men holding torches lit the way to the Rue Vielle du Temple, throwing a trembling light on the walls of houses. It was not difficult to find the spot where the murder had taken place, for by now the streets were full of people heading in that direction, shouting and exclaiming at the death of a duke. Windows hung open and people leaned out, adding their voices to the cacophony. Men fought the fire at Hôtel de l'Image, slapping it with cloaks and drawing water from the well. Fortunately, the flames did not have the chance to spread, though they cast a lurid light over the street.

As they drew closer, Charles saw that Orléans' household knights and squires were gently picking up the body. One of them had the foresight to bring a white sheet and they placed the duke on it, still dripping blood. His head hung at an impossible angle. Someone finally perceived the king and everybody stopped for a moment. The crowd parted in silence.

The Duke du Barry and the Duke of Anjou shouldered their way forward. "Mon Dieu! It's true," said du Barry, fighting back a sob. Louis was his nephew and he had raised him from a boy. "This is appalling." He bent over the body. "We must get him out of here. Jean," he said to a household knight, "go ahead of us to the Church of the Blanc-Manteaux. It's in the next street. Wake up the monks."

Taking charge, the Duke du Barry put his arm around the king's shoulders. Charles had tears flowing down his face, and he barely reacted. This was a mistake; the king should never have witnessed this terrible scene. Cursing to himself, du Barry turned him over to St. Pol. "Go back, your Majesty," he said soothingly, "I will make sure all the proper rites are observed."

Charles nodded silently and, to the great relief of the duke, allowed himself to be escorted back to his hôtel. Taking one last look, du Barry accompanied the mourners to the church. Orléans' knights carried the body between them. It was a slow procession and the double doors stood open by the time they got there. They passed the lamenting citizens of Paris, who formerly cursed Louis of Orléans for his taxation but now saw him as a tragic hero. Women ran forward to touch the body as they passed, wailing and moaning in grief.

The monks were ready. They placed the body into a coffin lined with lead and set candles all about it, then proceeded to say prayers and sing psalms. The household of Orléans sat vigil with the monks all night.

The following morning, a search of the street uncovered the duke's severed hand. Placing it in a lead box along with scrapings of the poor man's brain, Louis' servants brought it to the church and laid it beside the coffin. By then, all the dukes resident in Paris had shown up at the church—Berry, Burgundy, Anjou, and Bourbon—along with counts and other nobles, as well as the constable of France and several members of the clergy. Officers of the late duke's household covered the coffin with a pall, and the lords carried the casket out of the church; Orléans' squires accompanied them, carrying torches. They proceeded to the church of the Celestins where Louis had already built a chapel for his resting place. A service was held and all the mourners passed by the bier, making room for the king and queen who showed up, all dressed in black silk. As was usual, even the dukes wept for their murdered relative. Burgundy's lamentations were among the loudest. "Never has a more malicious and treacherous murder been committed in this kingdom," he moaned.

Afterwards, the princes of the blood retired to the Duke of Anjou's hotel for a council of state. They summoned the provost of Paris to find out what he had discovered.

"My lords," the man started, overwhelmed by all the great nobles in one room, "I believe I have discovered an important piece of evidence. We interviewed bowl-wives, barbers, tallow-chandlers, and water-carriers. We discovered that one of the water-carriers had supplied the occupants of l'Hôtel de l'Image—the same that was set on fire. He is said to be living at l'Hôtel d'Artois."

Everyone in the room looked at the Duke of Burgundy, for that was his residence.

"As we cannot arrest anyone there without permission from the owner, I have come here to ask for your leave, Monsieur le Duc."

The question was so unexpected that Burgundy couldn't control his face. Normally his eyes were shuttered and his mouth was set in an arrogant scowl, but for a moment his brows rose in consternation. He quickly squelched any surprise, but not quickly enough. The Duke du Berry pulled him aside.

"What do you know about this?"

Looking at the floor, Burgundy was unusually reticent. "I am responsible."

Du Berry couldn't hide his shock. "But why? You just made a pact of friendship with him."

His defences shattered, the duke was at a loss for words. "I was driven by the devil," he muttered finally.

Du Berry broke into tears. "I am losing both my nephews," he exclaimed. This was too much for him to confront.

Overhearing the conversation, Anjou came up behind them. "Could it be true?" he said.

Belatedly summoning his natural swagger, Burgundy drew his cloak around his shoulders. "Orléans had plenty of enemies. Ask Octonville, the treasurer he impeached. He was more than happy to oblige." Glaring at Anjou, he turned toward the door. "Excuse me. I must go to the privy chamber."

He pushed past a puzzled Duke of Bourbon, swept out of the room and down the stairs. Mounting his horse, he summoned his immediate companions—Octonville included, who still wore his red hood. They galloped through the streets of Paris— knocking aside any unwary pedestrians who stood in their way—and out through the northern gates of the city.

The provost was quick to react and soon followed on his heels. His men were nearby and they joined the pursuit, along with the Admiral of Brabant and a growing number of Orléanist knights. But Burgundy had increased his lead and fled at top speed, only stopping long enough to destroy a bridge over the Oise. They crossed the borders of his own lands, arriving safely at his town of Bapaume as the bells chimed one o'clock in the morning.

Three days after the funeral, the heir of Louis of Orléans bravely entered Paris in full mourning, despite the possibility that he could have been the next victim. Young Charles was only thirteen years old but had already taken on the mantle of his father. He rode all by himself, head bowed in grief, atop a black horse. A party of men-at-arms followed at a respectable distance, and an open litter came next, all draped in black. The Duchess Valentina Visconti sat upon it, having eschewed the normal forty days of mourning in isolation. Subjecting herself to censure was as nothing compared to the tragedy of her husband's murder, and she was here to protest to the king. Behind her rode the Princess Isabella, former queen of England and wife of young Charles, also dressed in black. Parisians gathered along the sides of the street and watched them in respectful silence.

The sad procession headed straight to the Hôtel de St. Pol and entered unopposed. They knelt before a chastened King Charles, who had so far done nothing to avenge the murder of his brother.

"Your Majesty, you must give us justice!" Valentina cried, while her son and daughter in-law joined their voices to hers. Although Isabella was the king's daughter, on this day she knelt beside her husband and raised her arms alongside his.

"Father, you must avenge the murder of my uncle," Isabella sobbed.

Charles was at a loss. "Get up, my children," he said. "There will be an investigation."

"He has admitted his guilt!" Valentina was appalled by the king's apathy.

"Duke John will be summoned," Charles tried to assure her. "There will be a trial…"

"He will not come by his own free will! You must take him by force!"

"Rest assured. I will do what I can." The king's face was slack. It was apparent he was in shock over the murder and it looked like he could slide into insensibility at any moment.

Young Charles stood and bent over his mother. "This will do us no good. Maybe he will be in a better state tomorrow."

Sobbing, Valentina nodded her acquiescence. She dragged herself to her feet and allowed her son to lead her from the room. Isabella followed with a last longing look at her father. He was adjusting his sleeve, oblivious to their withdrawal.

After staying a couple of days, Charles and his mother determined that their efforts were futile—at least for the moment. Everyone at court avoided them as much as possible; people preferred to go back to their own business. Judging from hostile looks in the streets, they could see that despite the murder, John the Fearless was still popular in the capital. This was not the time to cry for vengeance. If anything, they felt compelled to leave Paris before their enemies converged upon them.

The unhappy family of a murdered duke made their way to the Duchy of Orléans and settled into Blois Castle on the Loire River. There, young Charles was soon joined by his uncles Berry and Bourbon, the Count d'Alençon, and Bernard VII of Armagnac. They had to plan very carefully how they could best bring down the traitorous duke.

King Henry was going over household expenses with Erpingham when a messenger was announced from France. Both men looked up from the table in curiosity. The man knelt and held out a rolled parchment. "The French ambassador sends his salutations," he said.

Henry glanced at Erpingham before taking the scroll. "Has something happened?" he asked.

"Sire, there has been a murder. The Duke of Burgundy ordered the assassination of Duke Louis of Orléans."

"What?" Henry unrolled the document. He read it for a moment then looked again at Thomas. "Listen to this. 'The duke was set upon by a group of assassins in the street of Paris, just steps from the queen's hotel. They shattered his skull and spread his brains all over the pavement.' Jesus wept." He looked again at the messenger. "And Burgundy?"

"He fled to Flanders. The ambassador promises to keep you informed."

Henry nodded his dismissal and pushed the message over to Erpingham. "What a terrible death. He was my friend once," he said sadly.

"Only as long as it suited him," the other responded.

Henry nodded. "You are right about that. I still remember the letters he sent me." He shook his head as a chill ran down his spine. "He was so self-righteous. Well, at least I no longer have to worry about his endless accusations. No more attacks on English territory driven by personal vendettas." He put a finger on his lips in thought. "Orléans did everything he could to upset the balance of power in Guyenne. Perhaps we should send an embassy to discuss a truce."

"I think that's a wise move."

"How old is his son?"

"Orléans? I believe he is still a boy."

"So much the better. The more they are in turmoil over there, the more they will leave us alone."

"We could use a little peace." Erpingham raised his cup. "Though I suspect it won't last long."

John the Fearless, Duke of Burgundy was known far and wide as a clever man—generous to his friends, ruthless to his enemies, influential, persuasive and unscrupulous. By the time he gathered around himself his brothers, princes of the Low Countries, councillors, knights, and lawyers, he had come up with a much better motive for the murder: the assassination was justified in order to protect the state. He should be rewarded, not persecuted. To help present his Justification to King Charles and the rest of Europe, he enlisted the aid of Jehan Petit, Doctor of Theology at the University of Paris.

After quite a bit of wrangling, Petit was permitted to read his Justification to the royal court in Paris, in the presence of Duke John, the king, and his Orléans enemies. The speech took four long hours to deliver, complete with quotes from the Bible, citations from civil law, and a round of legal arguments torturous enough to turn any brain into mush.

"The Duke of Orléans," declared Petit, "practiced black magic in an effort to kill the king, or at least induce insanity. He made a pact with Henry of Lancaster to help each other usurp their respective thrones. He tried to take over the government of France and imposed heavy taxes on the country, keeping much of the revenue for himself." He pulled out a handkerchief and mopped his forehead.

"To sum up my argument," continued the intrepid Jehan Petit, "my thesis can be presented in the following syllogism: *The major*, that it is permissible and meritorious to kill a tyrant. *The minor*, that the Duke of Orléans was a tyrant. And *The conclusion*, Therefore the Duke of Burgundy did well to kill him."

The widow and children of the victim listened in shock as this glorified sophist smeared their husband and father with malicious accusations. How could anybody take this seriously? The killer was actually defaming his victim! Louis was no tyrant. Burgundy was clearly covering up his guilt with false accusations.

Alas, the king was of a different mind. Was it because of his unsettled wits or did he truly believe his brother was after the crown? Or was he afraid of the Duke of Burgundy? The king didn't know, himself. Befuddled, Charles accepted the Justification at face value and gave the Duke of Burgundy a formal pardon the following day. John the Fearless had literally gotten away with murder. But his enemies were many and they would find a way to come back stronger.

True to her Italian blood, Valentina was not content to accept this injustice. Over the next few months she repeatedly petitioned the king and queen to allow a defence of her husband before the royal court, as well as a list of charges against Duke John for his heinous murder. Finally, her request was granted and the abbot of St. Fiacre read out the challenge which had been carefully prepared by the outraged widow and her noble advisors. The accused was not present; he was far away in Liège with a large army.

Burgundy's absence was not important to Valentina; the purpose of this rebuttal was to influence the king.

"If this crime is not punished," said the abbot, "innumerable evils will ensue. If this unfounded Justification is allowed to stand, in the future everyone will take the law into his own hands and act as judge and executioner." Many in the room voiced their approbation to this statement. Taking heart, the abbot went on, "The king must see the wickedness of our enemy who pleads his case with a drawn sword in his hand. Our opponent had no authority whatsoever to murder so great and noble a person as the late Duke of Orléans. He followed no form of law or justice, and put the duke to death without hearing what he might say in his own defence." He paused while the murmuring in the room increased in volume. "We assert that Burgundy did not murder the late Duke of Orléans for the public welfare, but merely because of his lust for power and from the great hatred he fostered in his heart."

Much more was stated along these lines, ending with the conclusion that "As a matter of course, due to his office, the king must be bound from reason and justice to provide remedy for this abominable deed." The attendees could tell from the king's face that he agreed.

Had Valentina been satisfied with this vindication of her lord, all might have gone well. But her demands for reparation were so outrageous they wouldn't stand on their own. Could she really expect the Duke of Burgundy to allow all of his lands to be confiscated by the crown, as well as permitting his buildings in Paris to be destroyed? And then to be banished overseas for twenty years? All in reparation for a murder he considered justified?

It was only because the duchess had an influential core of supporters that the Great Council agreed to her demands. Once again the Duke of Burgundy was declared guilty. But it wasn't to last long. While all this was going on, his army won a huge battle at Liège, and news of the victory resounded across Europe. Puffed up with his success, Burgundy was informed about Valentina's challenge, and he decided it was time to reassert his authority. His army would support his argument.

Wasting no time, Burgundy directed his troops toward the capital. King Charles and his Council took fright like naughty children and decamped to Tours, where the court could lodge safely. They felt that the Parisians were much too hostile, and the king feared their violence. He had good reason; Duke John had not lost his popularity and returned to Paris to great acclaim. Burgundy was back in the ascendant.

Despondent, the young Duke Charles and his family returned to Blois. Poor Valentina Visconti, overwhelmed with grief, took to her bed and died within a few months. She exhorted her sons never to give up until they avenged the assassination of their father.

The duchess's death made matters much easier for Burgundy. His aim had always been to rule as regent in place of

Louis of Orléans. Finally, the opportunity was within his grasp. It only remained to bring the king under his control—and back to Paris.

However, this took some doing. At first, Charles was reluctant to leave Tours. But Burgundy was persistent. He initiated a series of negotiations that finally ended with a decision for all parties to meet in a neutral location: the town of Chartres. This was to be a hugely public event designed to bring peace to the country.

King Charles agreed, but only on the condition that both John of Burgundy and Charles of Orléans submit to a ceremony of reconciliation and swear to be friends henceforth. Knowing he was the weaker party, the sixteen-year-old Orléans reluctantly agreed and went through the ceremony. However, after it was over he quickly returned to Blois, sullen and resentful. There was nothing he could do for the moment against his triumphant enemy, but he was already planning his next move.

The seeds of civil war had been sown.

CHAPTER 13

The winter of 1408 was the coldest, most miserable in living history. The Danube was ice-bound, as was the Rhine at Cologne. A man could walk over the sea from Flanders to Zeeland. In England, from December to March the country was covered with snow. Birds died off in the thousands, and chroniclers could not write because their ink froze in the pot.

Henry Percy warmed his hands over a brazier, once again cursing their bad luck which had brought them back to Scotland. From Wales they had travelled to France, hoping to raise an army to quash the usurper Henry of Lancaster. At first King Charles and the Duke of Orléans pretended interest, but they soon tired of him. The murder of Orléans threw the royal house into such an uproar that Percy's problems went by the wayside. He fared no better in Flanders and finally decided to cross back over the Channel. He had nowhere else to go. At least in Scotland they had a roof over their head; his most recent ally James Douglas offered one of his peel towers on the border while they planned their next move.

"I've sent letters to the bishops of Bangor and the prior of Hexham," Percy said to Bardolf, who sat gloomily nursing an ale. "They promised to raise support for our cause. But see here." He held up a letter. "This is a response from Thomas Rokeby, Sheriff of York. Remember him?"

His interest piqued, Bardolf raised his eyebrows. "Most certainly. Didn't he serve with you in France?"

"Yes. We've been friends for a long time. Listen to what he says. 'The people of the North are greatly dissatisfied with the usurper. Law and order have completely broken down in the

Midlands. Even King Henry's estates in Stafford and Derby have been attacked. One of the king's tax-gatherers was set upon and stabbed three times in the chest.'" Percy looked up from the letter. "It gets worse and worse. Here, Rokeby says, 'I urge you to gather some Scots and march into Northumberland. Within a few days, Englishmen will flock to your standard.' This could be our moment."

Bardolf shook his head. "You couldn't pick a more miserable time to campaign."

"Ah, but don't you see. It's the last thing King Henry will expect. And with the roads frozen, we'll be able to travel quickly."

"You're right about that. I'm with you. You know that."

Percy smiled gratefully at the big man who had never left his side through all their wanderings. Bardolf's loyalty was one of the only things that bolstered his spirits. But his smile quickly faded. Who was he fooling? His luck had fled long ago, and he had little left to fight for—only that innocent boy he had relinquished at St. Andrews. He couldn't even protect the last living heir to his house. His dreams were haunted by the spectres of those he had discarded and deserted along the way— especially that pathetic Archbishop Scrope, who wouldn't leave him alone. Who would have expected the king to execute the poor man? He had never intended for that to happen.

He folded the letter, putting it under his cup. What else was there to do but move forward? It wasn't in his nature to give up. He'd rather risk all on the throw of the dice. "Let us gather as many local fighters as we can who are looking for action and cross the border. More will swell our ranks, I promise."

As Percy and his faithful retinue crossed the River Tweed into England, their forces were swelled by local monks and chaplains and their congregations who still deplored the death of Archbishop Scrope. Everywhere he stopped, Percy sent out proclamations, claiming he had come to relieve unjust oppression. He called for all those who loved liberty to take up arms and join him. The country folk answered his summons from Northumberland and Durham: knights and labourers, farmers and apprentices. Alas, he waited in vain for members of the baronage to answer his call. Nonetheless, Percy was encouraged by a message from Rokeby promising to join him at Tadcaster on the River Wharfe.

But Percy never made it to Tadcaster. As his army moved south, they found their way blocked at the bridge to Knaresborough, about fifteen miles north. A sizeable well-armed force grimly faced the invaders, and Percy drew rein when he recognized the pennon next to the banner of St. George. Coming up beside him, Bardolf groaned.

"Rokeby," said Percy, hanging his head. "He betrayed us."

"God's wounds. He's in thrall to the king."

"I should have known." Holding up his hand for his troops to stop, Percy took a big sigh. "He seeks to benefit from my downfall. I suspect King Henry has offered him some of my forfeited lands." His face hardened. "But I won't make it easy for him. Come, my friend. I know of a ford downstream."

Percy and his followers spent the night at Wetherby, and his scouts told him that Rokeby had remained in their rear near Knaresborough. But come morning, things had changed; the sheriff was sending out detachments in an effort to contain the rebels. It was time to take a stand.

"Branham Moor," said Percy, looking south, "just west of Tadcaster. There is a long slope and we can position ourselves at the top. My son and I used to hold practice battles there."

They rode the twelve miles to Branham Moor, flanked at a distance by bristling Yorkshiremen. Percy lined up his men along the shallow ridge. The front ranks were mounted and the infantry stood three deep behind them in ordered lines. They were a motley crew, many of them only protected by heavy padded or leather hauberks. At least most held axes and swords and sturdy oaken shields; the cavalry bore spears as well. The earl took his place at the centre under his banner with a rampant blue lion on a gold background. He and Bardolf were fully armoured. As they waited, Rokeby arrived with his army, only slightly larger than the rebels but more heavily armed, though not many were covered with full plate. Neither side had archers.

The sky was mostly cloudy and on the undisturbed moor the snow stood several inches deep. The sun was well past the midway point when Percy decided to move; he knew they wouldn't need much time to finish this battle. Even before Rokeby was entirely prepared, the earl ordered the trumpets to sound and his cavalry lurched forward, lowering their spears. Finding the footing awkward, the horses slid and stumbled but soon caught their stride, throwing great clouds of snow as they dashed down the hill toward the scrambling Yorkshiremen. But it didn't take long for the others to recover and the enemy horse were soon moving forward. Both sides clashed in shrieking chaos. Some of the horsemen kept going and needed to turn around; others were thrown from their saddles. Still others smashed against a rival mount—both horses rearing, some falling to the ground, trapping their riders underneath. Spears shattered, axes bore down onto shields, knights turned their mounts in a tight circle, charging an enemy.

Soon the infantry caught up and joined the fray, some targeting the horses, some trying to pull the knights from their saddles. Many were quickly forced to fight other footmen. Screams rent the air; the snow quickly turned red and the churned up slush caused many to slip.

Still mounted, Henry Percy was in the thick of the fighting, swinging his sword first on one side then the other. He caught one horseman across the neck, pulling his blade away and blocking an axe aimed at his head, while holding up his shield and fending off another. Gasping for breath, he struck at the third fighter when from behind a great blow knocked him forward. Another clout threw him from his saddle. He hit the ground hard on his shoulder and his helmet flew off. For a moment he thought he was finished, when Bardolf appeared beside him and pulled him up by his other arm.

"My thanks," Percy panted, leaning against his friend for a moment. "I'm getting too old for this."

"Stay with me." Bardolf turned around and sank his axe into a mounted man's leg, gashing the leather. At his back, Percy had recovered his strength and fought bravely, but his shoulder was weak and he could barely hold his shield. Bardolf redoubled his efforts to protect the earl.

The ranks were thinning but the focus was on Percy now, and the pair found themselves surrounded by Rokeby's knights. Bardolf was attempting to clear a path through them when suddenly a lance-thrust caught him in the neck and he fell, slashing wildly with his axe. Seeing his friend collapse, Percy hesitated a moment. That pause was his downfall; a war hammer smashed into his temple and he was dead before he hit the ground.

"Percy down! Percy down!" The shouts spread across the battlefield. The rebels fought on for a while but the heart was out of them and on the edge of the fighting they started to turn and run; before long the whole army was in flight, pursued by the vengeful Yorkshiremen. Bardolf tried to stand but went down again under a shower of blows; someone shoved a poniard into his eye slit and he was stilled under a gush of blood. Rokeby let the fleeing rebels go, for there were no hostages worth taking and the threat was clearly gone. Percy was all that mattered.

"Take his head," the sheriff said to one of his knights. "We'll send it to the king. On second thought, send his body, too. I'm sure he'll want to dismember it."

King Henry was in London when he first heard of Percy's rebellion. Immediately summoning his retinue, he left for the North to deal with the new uprising. But Sheriff Rokeby had matters well in hand, and by the time the king reached Stony

Stratford, a few miles south of Northampton, he received word of Percy's defeat—along with the earl's head. The gruesome evidence was delivered in a basket wrapped with a cloth. When Erpingham stepped forward to uncover the face, Henry suppressed a momentary surge of grief. It was just like Shrewsbury all over again. The eyes were closed, at least sparing the king a last look of censure. Henry couldn't exactly call Percy a friend, but their fates were tied together for so long he was almost family.

Things had gone so very wrong. Henry knew he had given too much power to his northern earl and headstrong son. In the beginning, he didn't really have much choice. But as his hold on the crown strengthened, he thought it best to offset their dominance by promoting Westmorland. It was a calculated risk; he was relying on Percy's professed loyalty. Alas, the Percys rejected his efforts just as they had rejected King Richard. He should have known better than to expect anything different.

But he never wanted it to end this way. First Archbishop Scrope and now, an ignominious end to a noble earl. He felt a twinge in his cheek and tried to ignore the discomfort. Every time he let his emotions get the better of him, his flesh broke out in that terrible festering affliction.

"Have it sent to London Bridge with the rest of the criminals," he said, covering up the head again. "He's a traitor and should be treated as such. Cut his body into quarters and send them to Berwick, Lincoln, Newcastle, and York." As Erpingham turned to give the order, he added, "In time, we'll recover the parts and bury him next to Hotspur."

This was the best he could do. He gestured to Norbury, who was about to leave as well. "What about Bardolf?"

"I understand he died in the battle."

"No more than he deserved. Send his head to Lincoln and his quarters should be dispersed also."

Norbury nodded and left to deliver the king's orders, passing Erpingham who was just returning. Henry went to the sideboard and poured himself some wine. "We might as well continue north to mete out justice. I need to be seen."

"Travel will be terrible. The roads are still covered with snow and ice. Are you sure you want to do this?"

"I'm not an invalid," Henry snapped, knowing that he was almost one. "We leave in the morning."

Watching Erpingham bow and turn, Henry immediately regretted his harsh tone. Thomas had been with him all his life; he knew better than anyone what condition the king was in. Lately he had been fortunate; he only needed a walking stick to get around. Even his flesh had calmed down. But he knew it wouldn't last. Over the past four years, on four occasions Henry announced his intention to lead the troops on some expedition or other. And on all four occasions his health forced him to cancel. He knew how this weakness looked to everyone else. How many times he was obliged to travel by barge rather than horse, even he lost track. The king could see people looking askance at him, calculating how long he was going to be able to hold the reins of government.

After working so hard to overcome one rebellion after another, why was God allowing him to falter now? Damn it all...if he had to prove himself by sheer force of will, he was determined to do so.

But he was so tired.

No matter. He went to the North, hanged a few rebels, gave out pardons, and rewarded deserving magnates with Percy lands. Sir Thomas Rokeby was given three of Northumberland's manors for life. Henry also reconfirmed his son John as Warden of the East Marches. There was so much needing to be done.

Henry stopped in Nottingham, where he held an audience with James, the captive king of Scotland. The lad's father Robert III had collapsed on hearing that the prince was captured by the English and died a few days later. Henry felt bad about that, but of course he didn't regret it enough to release James. He couldn't be in a better position to dictate terms. As usual, he would

188

continue to negotiate with the Duke of Albany, much to James's disgust. The lad's uncle may only be regent, but he behaved like a king and was doing his best to make sure young James remained a hostage in England— forever, if possible. Henry was happy for the pseudo-Richard to stay in Scotland forever, as well. So they had an unspoken agreement between them. Because Henry also held Albany's son Murdoch hostage ever since Halidon Hill, he had an extra carrot to dangle before the duke and keep the man honest.

At fourteen years old, James showed amazing pluck for someone in his position. He demonstrated great strength and agility in his martial training, and took no nonsense from anyone careless enough to challenge him. Despite himself, Henry liked the Scottish King though he tried not to show it.

"It's been two years since you captured me," James said, after bowing briefly. "I would like to know what your objectives are."

Henry raised his eyebrows. He certainly had no intention of telling James anything. "Are you comfortable here?"

The Scot made a gesture of dismissal. "I prefer this to the Tower, most certainly."

"How are your tutors?"

"They teach me very well, thank you."

"And your knightly training?"

"It's coming along just fine."

"Well, then. I see no reason for complaint."

James knew his value as a hostage. Could the English king keep him here until he died? "How much is my ransom?"

"That is one thing my ambassadors will be discussing. You may send a letter along with Prince John, if you like. I'm giving him and Westmorland a commission to negotiate a year's truce with your country."

James had trouble hiding his anger. He's the one who should be doing the negotiating, not Albany. But arguing with King Henry would be a humiliating exercise. "I will certainly do so," he said dourly, backing away. At least he had some slight satisfaction knowing that Murdoch's situation was as hopeless as his.

When his business was finished at Nottingham, Henry moved on to Pontefract, then Bishopthorpe and York. By the middle of June, he was back at Windsor. Henry knew he had pushed his body beyond his comfort level, but at least he had sufficiently proven his capabilities to everyone. He had done it. Now he needed a rest. The Archbishop Arundel's manor at Mortlake was one of his favourite stopping places, with its wonderful pastoral view of the Thames. Even better, it was halfway between Windsor and Westminster, so the king could be near his council.

Over the last couple of years, Henry and Arundel had found common ground between them, and old disagreements had faded away. Henry found himself relying on the archbishop more and more—especially since the last two parliaments. Arundel was totally committed to good government, fiercely protective of the king's prerogatives, and endlessly resourceful. Their mutual dependence had deepened into genuine friendship and he had come to prefer staying under Arundel's roof to almost anywhere else.

Most of the household continued to London, while the king disembarked with Joanna, his chamber knights, confessors, grooms, valets, chamberlain, and of course, physicians. It was a small party, comparatively speaking. Of course, Arundel had the resources to host them indefinitely.

The king was almost absurdly happy having nothing special to do. Sitting at a table across from the queen, Henry picked up a deck of cards. "Come, Thomas," he called to Erpingham. "We need you. Who else will join us?"

Joanna rubbed her hands together. "Are you ready to lose more money?" she joked as two more sat down and the king dealt the cards.

"Just wait and see, my love," Henry smiled, picking up his hand. The stakes were usually high at the king's table, and he lost as often as he won.

Before long they were deeply involved in the game as Arundel watched from across the room, seated at his own desk. As usual, he had a stack of papers in front of him demanding attention. But the archbishop didn't mind; he wasn't fond of gambling but never went so far as to try to stop others from enjoying themselves. He was content to listen to the laughter and teasing that accompanied their entertainment.

But the sudden silence brought Arundel's attention to the gambling table. Henry had his back to him, and the others were staring at the king most disconcertingly. Suddenly he started choking and he pitched forward onto the table, scattering cards and coins in every direction.

"Call Recoches!" Erpingham shouted as he jumped up and pulled Henry to a sitting position.

Arundel was already out of his chair, summoning help as the others lowered the king gently to the floor. Henry's breathing started out ragged then quickly became shallower as the physician ran into the room and knelt at his side.

"What happened?"

"He just stopped talking and stared at me," said Joanna, kneeling and brushing his hair from his face. "Then he started choking and fell onto the table, insensible."

"We have to get him into bed. Quickly."

Plenty of hands lifted the king from the floor and he was carried to his bedchamber where the physician carefully removed his outer garments and listened to his heart.

"I don't hear anything," he muttered, then pulled out a feather and put it under Henry's nose. No movement. Recoches looked at Joanna.

She put a hand over her mouth. "Is he…"

He shook his head. "I think the king lives. I've seen this before. We must keep him warm."

This seemed odd considering the season, but a light blanket was brought in and tucked around him. While Recoches busied himself mixing a medication, Joanna sat on the bed and placed a warm damp cloth over Henry's forehead. She spoke quietly to him, looking anxiously for any sign of life. His eyes didn't move and his chest seemed quite still. But his flesh was warm.

"I'm afraid all that traveling did him no good," said Arundel, who had quietly entered the room. "I've been concerned about his health."

Joanna looked at him worriedly. "This is worse than anything we've seen so far."

The archbishop knelt beside the bed. "Pray with me," he said, and the queen lowered herself to her knees. For more than an hour they said their Rosary while the physician sat on the patient's other side, occasionally taking the king's pulse and shaking his head. No one could tell whether he was breathing. The room was terribly still, and the only sound Joanna could hear was the squawking of swans on the river. She put her face into her hands and started to sob.

This was the first time anyone had seen a break in her calm demeanour. It was more unsettling to Arundel than he cared to admit. He put a hand on her shoulder, leaning over concernedly. "Perhaps you would find more comfort in my chapel?" he said.

Trying to blink the tears away, she took Henry's hand. "I can't leave him. You are kind to offer."

"Let me bring you something to sit on." Snapping his fingers, he pointed to his servants who began fussing around the room, lighting candles and carrying chairs. Gently, the archbishop helped the queen to her feet. "Here, let's put your seat next to the bed."

That's as far away as she would go, and Joanna rearranged her skirt, preparing for a long vigil. She turned her head toward the physician, who had bent over his patient yet again. "Anything?"

He shook his head sadly. "He is still warm, at least."

Leaning toward her husband, Joanna spoke softly. "It's not time for you to leave me, my dear. Not yet. We waited so long to be together, you haven't had a chance to get tired of me." She smiled to herself. "There's so much more I need to tell you. But you already know you have made me the happiest woman in the world." She stroked his hand. "I know you can hear me. Come back to me. I need you."

She fancied she saw his eyelids tremble, but in the half-light she couldn't be sure. She sat back in her chair, closing her eyes. After some time had passed, she heard the physician leave the room with the archbishop. They checked in periodically throughout the night, noting that Joanna never left her chair. She had slept many a night like this, sitting with her first husband, though she hadn't expected to do it again so soon.

The sun was starting to rise when suddenly Henry took a big gasp and opened his eyes. He stared in fright at the far wall then moved his head when Joanna softly called his name. Focussing his eyes on her face, his features relaxed.

"Do you know who I am?" she asked.

"Of course. What happened?"

"You collapsed," she said, getting to her feet. "We feared for your life."

"How did I get here?"

"You were carried upstairs." She adjusted his blanket, hoping he didn't see her face. "You were barely breathing."

"Oh, my dear." He held out a hand. "I'm so sorry."

"Sorry?" She laughed through her tears. "That you gave me such a fright? Yes, you should be sorry."

Hearing her voice, the physician burst into the room. "Thank God," he exclaimed, rushing over to the bed. He picked up Henry's wrist, feeling for a pulse.

The king frowned at Recoches. "What happened to me?"

"You're exhausted. Your humours are imbalanced. I must bleed you."

"Of course." Henry held out his hand toward Joanna. "Stay with me, my dear. You give me so much comfort. Though I'm very tired right now."

While the physician prepared to bleed the king, servants came in and did their best to make him comfortable. Joanna sat on the bed, refusing to let go of his hand. Recoches did his ministrations then Henry leaned back into his pillows, exhausted.

"Can you tell me how you feel?" she asked.

"I don't think I can move my legs." He tried to smile. "It'll pass. I'm sure I'll be better by tomorrow."

Alas, everyone knew otherwise. The next day was the same. The ups and downs with the king's condition were becoming all too common. Accustomed to his periods of incapacitation, Henry's servants and clerks carried on with business as usual. As the days passed, they brought messages that required his personal responses and left the rest of the government's business to the archbishop. It was a week before Henry felt well enough to get out of bed, but he was destined to be Arundel's guest for a month.

The king spent the rest of the year traveling around the immediate vicinity, mostly by water, and stayed at the residences of his closest friends. By December he didn't feel much better and decided to recall his two eldest sons, just in case. As usual, Henry spent Christmas at Eltham though celebrations were modest this year. Hal was able to attend, while Prince Thomas was still en route from Ireland.

Henry dearly loved this palace, with its huge great hall hung wall-to-wall with tapestries depicting hunting scenes, ladies in gorgeous gowns and nobles sporting heraldic surcoats. The magnificent carved ceiling was illuminated by tall stained-glass windows gracing both sides of the hall. Mistletoe, holly, and lush garlands hung in every room, and the yule log burned in the hearth. All the guests attended the midnight mass on Christmas Eve, the shepherds' mass at dawn, and again the

Divine Liturgy on Christmas Day. The usual tournament with blunted lances was held on the grounds, and the king was carried to his throne to watch from the special viewing box alongside his queen, Hal, and Humphrey.

Feasting was the highlight of the week, and as usual, the boar's head was carried out on Christmas Day with much acclaim, followed by fish and game hunted on the manor itself. And afterwards, Henry and Joanna entertained their guests by singing together and playing on their lutes, followed by a mixture of minstrels and other musicians. All the way until Twelfth Night the tables were loaded with delicacies, stuffed fowl, oysters, clams, venison, spiced nuts, and washed down with wine and small beer.

But Henry's participation was limited. Most of the time, he sat quietly under his canopy of state at the end of the hall, watching the mummery and dancing. Often and again, the king noticed people pausing in their conversations and studying him thoughtfully, which in itself was debilitating. He was beyond annoyance, though he never got used to the humiliation. The king tired easily every night and waved for his guests to continue without him, but the celebrations were muted.

By mid-January everything was back to normal. Henry chose to stay at Eltham until the council meeting, which was planned for 20 January. Hal spent more time than usual with his father, and they found common ground in their love of music. The prince was a talented lute player, himself, and even wrote a few pieces of music for his father to try out. Joanna and Humphrey often joined them, though the young prince was more content to listen than play. He was a little in awe of Hal and didn't want to draw attention to himself.

All was well until the day before Henry expected to leave for Westminster. When Joanna came into his room that morning, she found the pages standing hesitantly around the king's bed. Henry was propped up, as usual, but his face was expressionless.

"I don't know how long he's been like this," said William. "He seemed to be awake when I came in."

Joanna knelt at the bedside. "Henry, can you hear me?"

No response. The queen looked at her husband's squire. "Not again. Have you called the physician?"

As if in answer, Recoches opened the door. One look at the king and he knew. "Une grande accesse," he muttered to himself. "This one could be fatal."

There was no choice but to repeat all the steps they took in the past. This time, Henry's limbs were heavy and it took many hours for him to recover his senses. He didn't even try to smile at his wife, and the look of fear in his eyes tore at her heart.

"Is he dying?" she asked Recoches, pulling him to one side.

"He may come back," the doctor answered slowly, "but I think we should bring him to Greenwich so he can breathe the fresh air of the Thames."

As soon as the king could be moved, his household carefully brought up a whirlicote and drove the five miles to the river. It was a slow-moving cavalcade, and Joanna worried about the bumpy ride that must have caused him agony with every lurch. She sat beside him, holding his hand. He was conscious and could speak again, though he had little to say. By the time they reached Greenwich he was exhausted.

Carried up to his bed, the king called for Joanna, not realizing she was in the room. He sighed with relief when she threw open the windows and sat beside him on the bed.

"I feel better already," he lied, moving his hand until he reached her own. "But while I am still alert, I think it's time to dictate my will."

There, it was said. This was the signal that even Henry feared his illness was mortal. Wills were only written at the end of one's life, or before a man went to war.

She bowed her head in silent acquiescence.

"Just in case," he added, squeezing her hand. "It would be foolish otherwise. But mark this: I intend to get well."

Smiling through her tears, Joanna took heart. "I'll hold you to that. We'll do this will, for practice sake."

And so it was decided. The king summoned Archbishop Arundel, Prince Henry, Thomas Erpingham, the Duke of York, and his great officers as witnesses. And the queen. As Henry lay back in bed, his scribe dipped the quill in his inkwell and held it, poised.

"In the name of God, Father, and Son," the king started slowly, "I, Henry, sinful wretch, by the grace of God King of England and France, and lord of Ireland, being in my whole mind, bequeath to Almighty God my sinful soul, which has never been worthy to be a man but through his mercy and his grace; which life I have misspent…"

Listening intently to this will which was dictated in English for the first time by a king, Hal was of two minds. Part of him was astonished at the sentiments of unworthiness coming from the mouth of his father. Henry IV was so self-righteous he had no compunction in executing hundreds who objected to his usurpation. Where did this sudden humility come from?

On the other hand, Hal was often impressed by his father's religious zeal and his devotion to the Holy Trinity. Did this contradiction have something to do with kingship? Did a king answer to a different set of divine rules? Was there something he didn't understand? Or was his father a hypocrite?

More to the point, was he? Even now Hal could barely suppress his impatience, though he felt shamed by it. Why didn't his father just face reality? It was obvious to everyone that Henry was getting too feeble to rule. A king needed all of his faculties; how could he control his quarrelsome barons when he could barely control his own body? Couldn't he see his physical deterioration as a sign from God that it was time to relinquish control?

Pursing his lips, Hal chided himself as an ungrateful son. He must learn to show his father more respect. If he survived.

Henry IV did survive, though he would never be the same.

CHAPTER 14

Henry was glad the February days were so cold, as they gave him an excuse not to leave his bed. Not that he needed one, exactly; there was no secret that his legs had pretty much given out—for the time being. His carpenters had built him a chair on four wheels that needed to be pushed around, but he was reluctant to use it. Today, he sat deep in a chair with cushions and a blanket over his lap, listening to Joanna play the lute. His own harp sat unused at his side, though from time to time he put a hand on it. She looked up hopefully, silently willing him to join her, but it just seemed like too much effort.

He looked up with a smile as Hal came into the room, holding up a parchment. It was clear from his face that his son had good news.

"It's from Harlech. The siege is over." Hal handed him the message.

"Ah." Henry held the document close to his face so he could read it better. "Listen to this, Joanna. They captured Owain Glyndwr's wife, his son Lionel, two of his daughters, and three of his granddaughters."

"They are on their way to the Tower," Hal added. "Oh, and Edmund Mortimer died during the siege."

"Mortimer," Henry muttered. "He caused me no end of trouble, may he rest in peace." He crossed himself. "I can't say I regret his passing." He looked at Hal speculatively. "It's time you took young Mortimer in as ward. I shall dictate the order on the morrow."

Bowing, Hal hid his satisfaction. The lad was still years from his majority and would provide a decent income. The younger brother, Roger, had recently died from a fever so the whole estate was conveyed to the elder. Now Hal would have control of his education; he always thought Edmund should be trained as a knight. He wouldn't be a boy forever.

Henry's mind was still on the Welsh problem. "Any word of Glyndwr?"

The other shook his head. "Once again, he has disappeared. It's too soon to relax our vigilance."

"That's for certes. Nonetheless, I think it's just a matter of mopping up, now. I'm glad you're here, Hal. The council needs you. I need you. I think you can leave Wales to your captains."

Hal wasn't sorry to hear that. He was ready to move on to bigger things. No one dared speak of the king's possible demise, but it was on everyone's mind. Hal had noticed the way people consulted *him* now—even deferred to him—since his father's last illness. His recent appointment as constable of Dover Castle, and Warden of the Cinque Ports had served to increase his prestige. And why not? His closeness to the throne dictated that he needed to serve in many capacities before he took on the rule of the whole country. He was determined to be ready.

The rapport between father and son was rare enough that Hal sat down and gestured to the harp. Henry nodded agreeably and Hal repositioned it, raising his eyebrows to Joanna. Gladly, she plucked a familiar tune on her lute and he joined in, nimbly keeping up and improvising a bit. Henry tapped his finger on the edge of his chair and even started singing, pleased that his voice, at least, had not degraded along with his limbs. Servants brought in drinks and cakes for their enjoyment, and the afternoon passed agreeably—that is, until Archbishop Arundel was announced.

Finishing a particularly difficult melody, Hal stopped and leaned the harp against his shoulder, reaching for wine. Suddenly he lost his enthusiasm as the archbishop—pretending not to notice that he was the cause of the interruption—kissed the queen's hand and bowed to the king.

"I heard about Harlech," he said to Hal. "I congratulate you on your successful mission."

The prince nodded his acknowledgement, wishing he was elsewhere. He never could shake his dislike for the man; he was so arrogant—so unlike his nephew Thomas. On the other hand, perhaps Arundel had something important to say and Hal should listen.

The archbishop sat at Henry's desk. "I see you read my report," he said, tapping a small bundle of papers. The king nodded. Satisfied, Arundel went on. "Treasurer Tiptoft agreed that the money has run out from the 1407 parliament and we need to call another."

This was a common complaint; the exchequer was always out of money. But Hal had long ago concluded that some of the funds were not allocated properly. "The Commons will surely object to being called prematurely," he ventured.

Arundel frowned. "It will be preferable to bankruptcy." Dismissing the prince with a lift of his chin, he turned to Henry. "I propose we hold parliament in Bristol this time."

"Bristol!" Hal stood, carefully placing the harp in its previous spot. "What a terrible location."

"Not at all," Arundel said. "Sire, I propose we schedule it for 27 January."

Hal had heard enough. It was obvious to him that the archbishop hoped to keep him in the background. While he was busy managing the rebellion in Wales, that was one thing. But now that he was intent on picking up the reins of government from his ailing father, there could only be one person in charge. And it wasn't going to be that pompous, domineering priest.

As he was leaving, Hal bumped into his brother Thomas who was just coming in. They exchanged hostile looks but neither said anything. Thomas jerked his head toward the door as he sat down in the seat just vacated by Hal.

"What is his problem?"

"Oh, the usual." Henry gestured his dismissal. "He disagrees with the Archbishop."

Frowning, Arundel started writing on a fresh piece of parchment. "He's going to have to learn some self-control," he said. "He's a grown man. He should start acting like one."

It was Henry's turn to frown. Just because the two didn't get along, that didn't mean the archbishop had the freedom to insult his firstborn, friendship or not.

Arundel caught his expression. "My apologies, Sire. That was uncharitable of me." He cleared his throat. "I'm concerned that disagreements might disrupt the council."

The king shrugged. "We shall see. As long as everyone is working toward the same goal, it shouldn't be a problem. Should it?" The last came out as a statement rather than a question. Arundel knew better than argue.

"I'm glad you're back, Thomas," Henry said, changing the subject.

"So am I, father. I've been worried about you."

His heart swelling with tenderness, Henry reached out his hand. He would have to figure out a way to keep his favourite son at home rather than send him back to Ireland, which neither of them wanted.

Arundel kept writing. He'll bring up the topic of parliament at a better time.

As the archbishop suspected, the damage was done. A week later, Prince Hal gathered his closest associates at Coldharbour, an estate just upstream from London Bridge that his father had given over to his use. Formerly belonging to John Holland, half-brother to King Richard, Coldharbour was one of the most desirable mansions in London. With stairs leading directly to the river, it was both grand and convenient. Having spent the last nine years in and around Wales, the prince was beginning to appreciate the benefits of the city.

He had invited his uncle Henry Beaufort earlier than the rest, for they had much to discuss. As Bishop of Winchester, Beaufort had already reached what most churchmen would consider the pinnacle of a career, but he was an ambitious man and intended to go farther. He had already been chancellor once, having given it up to take on his bishopric. Beaufort was also superbly educated, as well as wealthy, urbane, and astute. He and Hal got along famously, and shared an antipathy for Archbishop Arundel.

"He plans to hold parliament at Bristol," Hal said, pouring wine for his uncle. "Bristol!"

"We know what that means. The members will be so uncomfortable they'll agree to anything the king says, just to get out of there." Beaufort took a sip and smiled appreciatively at the taste. His heavy face was just beginning to grow jowls, but he had long ago quit worrying about keeping a trim figure. Since his hair was thinning also, he accepted his rather dowdy appearance.

"We've got to find a way to counteract this," Hal mused. "The upcoming parliament can be crucial to the council."

Beaufort took another sip. "I agree. If Arundel retains control, you'll never have a say."

"It's him or me. Nothing more, nothing less."

"Yes…oh, here's my brother."

Thomas Beaufort came in, shaking rain from his cloak. "It just started coming down," he said, handing his wrap to a servant. "The others are right behind me."

In came Thomas, Earl of Arundel, and Richard Beauchamp, Earl of Warwick, equally wet. Hal stood, striding over to greet the newcomers. The two earls were the up-and-coming next generation, just like he was, and equally desirous to assert themselves. Although Arundel had joined his uncle in their exile, they had come to a parting of the ways over a recent land grant. Richard Beauchamp had served with the prince in

Wales and was proving himself quite the warrior. Hal intended to make both of them leading members in his affinity.

The prince slapped them on the shoulders, bringing them back to the table. Between the two earls and the Beauforts, he felt well supported against the opposite party.

"Now that we're all here," Hal said, "we have three months before parliament. Archbishop Arundel wants to hold it in Bristol so he can force his agenda through. We have to figure out how to get it moved to Westminster."

"His agenda?" asked Warwick.

"Another subsidy. I don't particularly object to that. What bothers me is the way the money is being squandered. I'm certain of it. And he doesn't want to be held accountable."

Henry Beaufort was the first to put forward what everyone else was thinking. "It would help if we had a new chancellor."

The room fell silent; the crackling of the fire emphasized the hush. Even Hal caught his breath. "I doubt whether my father would agree."

"Oh, I don't think we can ever talk him into it. No, we must persuade the archbishop to resign."

"And the treasurer," nodded Thomas Beaufort. "Otherwise, our fiscal policies will fail as ever before."

"I wonder how much persuading my uncle would need," said Earl Thomas. "I don't think he enjoys the position in the first place."

"Agreed. He took the chancellorship to help the king," said Bishop Beaufort. "But if Prince Hal was to step forward…"

"He could go back to his congregation," Hal said with satisfaction. "In fact, if I'm not mistaken, the chancellorship is keeping him from his preferred work, stamping out Lollardy."

"Which he pursues with steadfast devotion," muttered the bishop, who did not share Arundel's piety. He was a worldly man, not a saint.

"I think," added Hal thoughtfully, "I can solicit the aid of Master Courtenay, chancellor of Oxford University. I understand the scholars at Oxford are defying the archbishop's orders against teaching subjects he is trying to suppress. Wycliffe studies, of course." Hal grimaced. He wasn't happy with the Lollards either, but this was more a matter of anti-Arundel policy rather than pro-Wycliffe support. "If I uphold Courtenay's arguments, it will send a message to Arundel that I oppose him."

"Would that be enough to unseat him?" wondered Henry Beaufort.

"Who knows? It's a start, anyway."

Arundel was indeed putting a great deal of effort into his fight against heresy. He had recently unleashed his committee of Twelve whose mission was to ferret out errors contained in Wycliffe's teachings. From way back in John of Gaunt's day, the Oxford scholar Wycliffe had been a thorn in the side of the Church. His followers, called Lollards, believed all sorts of heretical ideas. From denying the Eucharist to teaching his English translation of the Bible, they were a stubborn, irascible group and needed to be put down.

The committee of Twelve censors was a powerful tool. They produced a document condemning 267 of Wycliffe's conclusions, giving the archbishop enough weapons to be used against any level of Lollardy. To emphasize his achievement, Arundel staged a significant book burning at Carfax, in the centre of Oxford.

But this wasn't enough to satisfy him. A group of dissident academics refused to adhere to Arundel's commands and continued to teach what he considered forbidden subjects. As far as they were concerned, they were defending their freedom of intellectual expression. Unfortunately, Arundel only saw them as proof of a heretical sect that needed to be eradicated. Hence, he decided on a visitation.

This was big trouble. An archbishop's right to conduct a visitation was a huge controversy, for it was obvious he meant to impose some sort of discipline. Excommunications had been known to follow on the heels of a visitation—all aimed at teachers of Wycliffe. Oxford jealously guarded its entitlements and was determined to resist any censure. Arundel didn't care about their academic freedom; he was on a mission. Even though Courtenay wrote to the king in protest, the archbishop ignored any opposition and showed up with a large retinue. They headed toward St. Mary's Church, where he intended to make his prominent stand.

With its tall thirteenth-century tower and its cluster of pinnacles, the edifice dominated the surrounding buildings. St. Mary's was the main church of the university, and its parish was composed almost exclusively of colleges. There was no better place to stage his inquisition. Dressed in his full regalia, Arundel marched down Catte Street followed by his minions. But when he reached St. Mary's a large and ugly group of students blocked the door, led by two university Proctors. The archbishop stopped, banging his crosier on the ground.

"I command you to let me pass!" he bellowed, only to be answered by boos and hisses. "How dare you interfere with me!"

Armed with sticks and swords, the students were not in the least cowed. They shouted insults while he stood there, uncertain as to how he should respond but barely able to suppress his fury.

"What do you know about Law and Divinity?" shouted someone. "You never even graduated Master!" That garnered the expected response, and the catcalls echoed against college walls. This was the worst insult of all, for Arundel was sensitive about his lack of education. It was his aristocratic rank that generated his early promotions, not his scholarship.

This last insult pushed him past his tolerance. Raising his crosier again along with his other arm, he seemed to grow in size, resembling an angry prophet of the old religion. "I place this university under the interdict!" he shouted above the clamour. "No one is to enter this church. The clergy is not to perform Divine offices until further notice! I insist you lock the doors and still the bells." His vehemence dampened the enthusiasm somewhat and he was able to turn and make his exit from the situation with dignity.

But if the archbishop thought his demonstration would change the minds of Oxford's recalcitrant students, he was destined to be disappointed. That very night, two Oriel fellows—well-known ringleaders—broke into the Chancellor's office, stole the keys, and opened the church. They held mass anyway and rang the bells, to spite the interdict.

The following day, even more students swarmed the squares and courtyards. When the Dean of Oriel was accosted for the outrage of the previous night, he puffed out his chest and spouted, "Why should we be punished for other people's sins? Devil take the archbishop and break his neck!" Word of his declaration served to antagonize the scholars even further, and their disorder spilled into the streets of the city. Citizens of Oxford gathered in groups and resisted the agitators, for they supported the archbishop and found the students to be troublesome under the best of circumstances. Windows got broken and heads were cracked until finally the local authorities rode horses through town and managed to convince the students that the archbishop had withdrawn and the matter was going to be brought before the king. Their instigator gone, the students stopped their rioting.

A month passed before Courtenay, his Proctors, and the twelve censors met King Henry at Lambeth. Prince Hal attended as well, ready to defend the university's privileges—especially as he saw this as an opportunity to confront Archbishop Arundel. Courtenay was relieved to see him, for Henry was in a righteous wrath.

Sitting under a canopy of state, the king listened to Courtenay with a frown of displeasure while Hal, standing behind his father, debated with himself how to approach the situation.

The chancellor knelt before the king. "I remind you, Sire, that the University of Oxford had obtained a bull from Pope Boniface IX in 1395 granting us an exemption from visitations. We resisted the most recent attempt in defence of our immunity."

Henry was having none of it. "You know that my predecessor refused to verify that bull. And I have not reversed his decision. After your recent abominable behaviour, I see that you don't deserve any special consideration."

Courtenay was taken aback; the king had previously given the university many privileges and gifts including a large gilt cross. He wasn't aware of the extent to which Henry was under Arundel's influence. The king's deference to the archbishop outweighed his usual inclination toward academic freedom— something the chancellor hadn't taken into consideration.

But Hal knew. Looking across the room, he noted the look of satisfaction on the archbishop's face. He leaned over his father's shoulder. "Remember that they say a Mass of the Holy Spirit for you every year in St. Mary's Church attended by all the Doctors and Masters."

Caught short, Henry quickly glanced at his son. This little exchange wasn't lost on Arundel. He stepped forward. "The Oriel students caused especial destruction to the city square," he growled.

"And they have been punished," Courtenay retorted.

"I believe a stint in the Tower might teach your proctors a more valuable lesson," the archbishop answered, pointing to the men in question.

Hal straightened. "Do you really want to send that kind of message?" he said, barely restraining his contempt. "Our universities are supposed to be beacons of light, not thralls to orthodoxy."

"Not at the cost of blasphemy!"

"Your Grace," interrupted Courtenay, trying to mollify the archbishop, "not everyone was behind the recent unrest. Many at the university conform to your directives."

"And Oxford deserves a chancellor who is less combative! Your Majesty, I insist on the resignation of Chancellor Courtenay."

Hal leaned over again. "The man has given you years of good service and I believe he deserves better."

Henry put up his hands. "That is enough. Master Courtenay, I expect a letter of apology. In the meantime, I shall consider the situation and give you my decision. Everyone is dismissed." As was often the case these days, the king was exhausted by controversy and his anger had dissipated.

Hal knew he had done the best he could in the situation, for Arundel was incredibly powerful in his righteous indignation. But at least the crisis had passed without drawing any blood.

In the end, a compromise of sorts was reached, although mostly in the archbishop's favour. Courtenay was permitted to continue as chancellor, but Arundel's visitation rights were confirmed. Unfortunately for the university's freedom of expression, they were obliged to forswear their Wycliffe teachings. At least for the present.

On the other hand, Hal could be satisfied that Arundel knew he was a force to be reckoned with. He wasn't going to go away. There was no doubt that the Prince of Wales was the rising sun, and he had every intention of showing the archbishop there could only be one man in charge of the council.

It was late in the evening and Henry was ready to retire to bed when it was announced that Archbishop Arundel was requesting an interview. Since this was unusual—and even more to the point, since Treasurer Tiptoft had just resigned three days before—Henry reluctantly agreed to see him. He had suspected

Tiptoft's resignation was an ominous sign. Henry waited for his squire to wrap a blanket around his shoulders, then he sat beside the hearth while his other manservants stoked a fire.

"William, you might as well bring us some mulled wine," the king said. "And have the archbishop sent in."

Henry was expecting Arundel to show strain over the events surrounding his visit to Oxford, but he was shocked to see that the archbishop appeared to have aged ten years. He always thought his old friend thrived on conflict.

"Please, sit." The king pointed to another chair.

Arundel was happy to comply. He accepted a cup of wine with a trembling hand.

"Are you ill?" Henry asked, concernedly.

Shaking his head, the archbishop wrapped both hands around his wine. "Not in my body, Sire, but in my mind. I have given this much thought and can't come to any other conclusion."

"Given thought to what? Don't hold back."

That was exactly the conflict. How far could he trust his relationship with the king? Grimacing, Arundel decided it was now or never. "Sire, I don't think I can work with Prince Hal. We just can't agree on issues affecting the welfare of this country."

Henry grasped his blanket tightly. He was afraid of this.

"Thomas—"

"Please, Sire. I hate to interrupt you but I must finish. Hal has many praiseworthy attributes. He's a strong leader, intelligent, decisive…" He hesitated.

"But?"

"He won't listen to me. He has his own ideas and disrespects my experience."

"Ah." Henry wasn't surprised. He knew they didn't get along. And it wasn't just the two of them; Hal had surrounded himself with loyal followers who were also antagonistic to Arundel and possibly even himself. He needed to look no further than his half-brother Henry Beaufort. "But you know I support you in every way."

Arundel nodded, closing his eyes momentarily. "I do know that. Your support means more to me than anything. But from day to day, I just don't have the will to fight him anymore. I want to go back to my spiritual work. I have been neglecting my congregation."

"Take some time away, Thomas. You need a rest."

"No, Sire. It's more than that. I never wanted this job in the first place. You know that. Hal is more than competent to take charge of the council. I have other work to do. God's work." He opened a pouch he was carrying and placed the great seal on a low table between them. "Please accept my resignation."

There, it was said. The words hung like an icicle between them. It wasn't just the council at issue; it was the leadership of the whole country.

"I need you," Henry said softly.

"I'm not going anywhere. I welcome you to stay at my estates any time for as long as you want. I will always be at your beck and call."

"Of course." Henry saw from Arundel's face that it would be useless arguing with him. For the moment. "I shall hold the great seal for a while until you are certain."

"There's no need. I will not change my mind."

"We shall see."

It would be difficult to say whether Henry's stubbornness or Arundel's will was stronger. Several times they exchanged letters as the king tried to get him to change his mind. Several times the archbishop politely but firmly refused. A month passed while the king held onto the great seal, though the need for a new treasurer was even more urgent. On 6 January Henry conceded to Hal's judgment and appointed his son's chosen candidate, Henry Lord Scrope of Masham to the post. The prince knew better than to gloat.

Parliament opened as scheduled on 27 January, and the venue had been transferred back to London, much to Hal's satisfaction. Bishop Beaufort made the opening speech, a job usually undertaken by the chancellor. Henry knew that the time for procrastination had come to an end. If he didn't do something soon, the bishop would be perceived as Arundel's replacement. After all, he had the necessary qualifications. But that would be such an insult to Arundel! He just couldn't do that to his friend.

Summoning Prince Hal, the king forced himself to accept the new situation. His health had not recovered enough to resume his duties, especially in this atmosphere of discord. He knew he should be encouraged that the prince was impatient to take over his royal duties. It was his son's birthright, after all. But what if they disagreed on a fundamental issue? Would Hal listen to him? Was he strong enough to stop him from going too far?

The prince's entrance interrupted Henry's troubled thoughts. He came in carrying a book which he placed onto his father's lap with a flourish. It had a leather cover beautifully embossed, and Henry ran his fingers across the fine grain. He opened to the first page, entranced.

"The Master of Game," he said, looking up. "Is this the book the Duke of York has been working on?"

"Yes, I commissioned a copy for you. It's mostly a translation of Gaston Phoebus's *Livre de Chasse* with additional chapters about English hunting. The illustrations are splendid."

Paging through, Henry wiped a tear from his eye. "It's beautiful. What a lovely gift."

"You need it in your library." Hal smiled, happy to cheer up his father.

Going back to the prologue, Henry read out loud, "To the honour and reverence of you my right worshipful and dread Lord Henry by the grace of God eldest son and heir unto the high excellent and Christian Prince Henry IV." He looked up, trying to hide his envy. Another noble brought into Hal's inner circle. "He dedicated it to you."

Hal didn't notice his father's reticence. "York was a Godsend in Wales. He's a good man."

Henry didn't necessarily agree, having imprisoned the duke for ten months concerning that fiasco with Constance and the Mortimer boys. But he was reminded about why Hal was here. Treasuring the book, he held it in his lap.

"Hal, I've come to a decision. Now that you will be head of my council, you need a chancellor you can work with. I've decided to give the great seal to Thomas Beaufort." He watched his son closely, trying to gauge his reaction. Thomas was the younger brother of Bishop Henry and one of the king's most ardent supporters.

Hal turned away and took a couple of steps toward the window then came back. "I think I understand your reasoning. Yes, uncle Thomas is a fine choice."

Henry had to struggle to contain his surprise. He was expecting an argument. "I will announce it in parliament tomorrow."

Bowing, Hal made to leave but Henry stopped him with a hand on his arm. "I'm sure you will do a fine job with the council. I have faith in your good judgment."

It was Hal's turn to cover his astonishment. He knew his father bitterly resented Arundel's forced retirement. At least Thomas Beaufort was acceptable to the both of them; this was one compromise they could each be thankful for. He only wished that they could come to a deeper understanding despite the change of administration. Perhaps, in time, the king would agree to new measures in order to ease the country's financial difficulties. Measures that Hal wasn't ready to vocalize. "Thank you, father. I will do my best."

CHAPTER 15

Prince Hal had an enormous task ahead of him. He was determined to get the country's finances under control. The problem was not new; there had been a huge deficit since the first year of his father's reign, due mostly to the glut of grants and annuities. When Henry took the throne, he was generous in his efforts to secure support for his fledgling dynasty—overgenerous, in truth, though he acted out of necessity. Many of those annuities were left over from King Richard's reign. They couldn't be cut off; that would be disastrous.

And that wasn't all; the royal household's expenses were totally out of control—especially after his marriage. The queen's promised dowry of 10,000 marks per year was a huge liability. At the same time, purveyors were constantly accused of issuing bad tallies for supplies to the household; the exchequer had to pick and choose who to pay.

That was only half of the problem. Overseas garrisons in Calais and Guyenne were terribly in arrears, as were the soldiers in Ireland, Wales, and the Northern Marches. As usual, the government was run on borrowed money; parliament's collection of taxes was used to pay off loans. Usually the subsidy awarded by parliament didn't stretch far enough. Nothing was left over for current expenses, so more loans had to be taken out.

With Prince Hal's new ministry, the Commons were ready to move forward with some unorthodox methods to tap new resources. What about the clerical wealth, which had been the subject of so much controversy in the Wycliffe years? Talk about an embarrassment of riches! And they were only referring to the landed wealth of the Church, not the money earned for tithes, which should be enough for the clergy to live on.

These discussions had been floating around for some time, but Arundel's rigid policies in defence of the Church had clamped down on that approach. But now that his heavy hand had been lifted, the Commons put together a proposal for ecclesiastic disendowment that was breathtaking. The redistribution of the Church's wealth would benefit everybody, and the crown would be totally self-sufficient. Getting back to the basics would enhance the spirituality of the clergy who had become much too worldly while they enjoyed lives of pleasure and idleness.

Prince Hal wisely stayed mute regarding this controversial proposal. The king, on the other hand, shut it down immediately. He absolutely forbade any discussion on the matter. Many of the higher ecclesiastics in the House of Lords were understandably outraged. The Commons retreated from their experimental position in a sulk. They had lost the first battle.

Archbishop Arundel was uncommonly silent. He knew the king had a dilemma. Henry was dependent on the Commons for granting new taxation; if he pushed them too hard, he would have another fight on his hands. Although Arundel no longer led the council, he was still active in the House of Lords. How could he best support the king? There was a good chance Hal would be looking for any opportunity to cause him embarrassment, so he had to be careful.

Nonetheless, something needed to be done. Arundel would have to make a statement so definitive that nobody would bring up this despicable proposition ever again. Disendow the Church? It smacked of Lollardy and needed to be nipped in the bud. This was the best time to make a gesture in the cause of orthodoxy, and secure the king's position while he was at it. The more he thought about it, the more the perfect solution came to mind.

Determined to make his point, Arundel called a Convocation attended by the most important ecclesiastics and nobles in the land. It just so happened that he had an obdurate heretic at hand, snugly detained inside an episcopal prison and awaiting his trial. John Badby may have been an unlettered layman—in fact, he was a tailor—but he had already demonstrated a defiance that promised a good showing.

In the house of the Friars Preachers of London, Badby was brought in, filthy from his imprisonment. He stood before both archbishops and most of England's bishops, as well as notable lords including the Duke of York, Thomas and Henry Beaufort, and Henry Chichele of St. Davids. It was no accident that many of these witnesses were partisans of the prince, though Hal was not present.

The accused stood unperturbed with his hands tied behind his back, looking around, not terribly impressed by the august spectators. Arundel stood on a platform and ostentatiously held out a scroll, waiting for the murmuring to die down.

"John Badby, you have been accused of the crime of heresy, openly maintaining your erroneous opinions and refusing correction. It is in the interests of this court to instruct you in the true teachings of the Church. We seek to persuade you to accept the doctrine of Christ." He paused, waiting for his words to sink in. "You are accused of maintaining that the sacred host, consecrated by the priest at the altar, does not become the true body of Christ. You believe that the material bread remains unchanged after the sanctification. Do you still affirm this heresy?"

Having heard this a thousand times, Badby was undisturbed. "Your Grace, it is my belief that it is impossible for any priest to make the body of Christ."

Arundel wanted to make sure the accused understood the charges brought against him, and had them read out another time. "Do you still affirm this heresy?"

"Your Grace, these words surely cannot be taken literally. I believe in the omnipotent God in Trinity. If every host consecrated at the altar be the Lord's body, then there would be twenty thousand Gods in England. But there is only one God omnipotent."

This familiar Lollard rhetoric antagonized Arundel, though Badby only spoke as his logic instructed him. Ignoring the signs that he was going too far, the prisoner continued, "With Christ sitting before his disciples at supper, I would greatly marvel that if any man had a loaf of bread, broke it into little pieces and gave each man a mouthful, that the same loaf should afterwards be whole."

Rearing back as if to strike, Arundel pointed a finger at him. "You take the name of the Lord in vain! I ask you again, John Badby, whether you will renounce and forsake your opinions and adhere to the Christian faith? Consider it well, for your soul is at risk."

Unmoved, Badby shook his head. "I stand by my beliefs."

"Very well." The archbishop turned aside and consulted with the Bishop of London. The witnesses waited expectantly. Coming back, Arundel had composed himself once more. "It is our decision to adjourn this case for one week, in which time we shall keep the prisoner in safe custody so that he can carefully reconsider his heretical opinions. We shall reconvene at St. Paul's Cathedral on 5 March."

This decision was a surprise to some, but in truth Arundel needed the time to acquire a royal warrant for Badby's arrest and execution, since he showed no signs of recanting. The Church had the power to declare him a heretic, but it did not possess the legal ability to condemn a man to death. That was up to the state, and Arundel knew the king was behind him.

He also wanted more time to garner as much public attention as possible. St. Paul's was certainly a larger and better-known venue. It was also within walking distance to Smithfield, a site reserved for public executions.

On 5 March, the attendance was the same, at least as far as bishops and prominent laymen were concerned. Overall, there were many more onlookers, and the archbishop had worked himself into a righteous frenzy. He would prove that Badby was deserving of death. Luckily for him, the prisoner, by all indications, aspired to martyrdom.

The demonstration began with the usual pronouncements and the usual denials. But Badby went one step further. "I maintain that the Eucharist is of less value than a toad or spider. At least these last are living things. Anything created by God is more worthy than a man-made image."

The grumbling amongst the spectators was gratifying to Arundel's ears. "Do you understand the enormity of your pride?" he roared. "You presume to pit your own limited intellect against those who are infinitely better qualified to comprehend the mystery of Christian doctrine! Who are you to re-interpret the sacred mysteries of the faith?"

Badby shrugged. "Your doctrine is also man-made and hence open to interpretation." The crowd noted that he was irritated by something on his face, and although his hands were still tied he tried to rub his cheek against his shoulder.

"Look," said someone nearby. "It's a spider."

Others gasped in surprise. A fairly large black spider ran across his lips and back again.

"The devil," people whispered, pointing. Everyone knew that spiders were familiars of those in league with Satan. Try how he would, Badby couldn't shake the annoying critter.

Arundel nearly burst from excitement. "Look there," he exclaimed, "now we will see who is teaching this man to speak."

There was no denying it. Badby had proven his guilt.

"I declare this Convocation at an end," Arundel declared. "The Holy Spirit is totally absent from this man, and he has proven himself beyond redemption. I declare John Badby a heretic and turn him over to the authorities." In a lower voice, he said, "I beg you, my lords, that he does not suffer the death penalty."

This last statement was a matter of form, and everyone knew he would be very disappointed if the laymen obliged. It was time for the government to do its duty.

As the attendees dispersed for their mid-day meal, Bishop Beaufort borrowed a horse and rode across town to Coldharbour, where he knew Prince Hal was in residence. There was little time to spare, because the crowd would soon be moving to Smithfield to witness the notorious burning of an accursed heretic. This was to be the climax of Arundel's show trial, and Prince Hal would be conspicuous by his absence.

Hal was eating a private meal with his friend John Oldcastle at the moment. He gestured to the table, obviously unsurprised by Beaufort's entrance. He knew what was happening at the moment.

Shaking his head, the bishop sat, leaning forward. "The inevitable has come to pass. They are going to burn John Badby. At once."

Frowning, the prince put down his knife. "At Smithfield?"

The other nodded. "It's to be a very public execution. They are setting up a stage for the leaders to watch from."

Hal quickly glanced at Oldcastle. "You think I should be there."

"I'm afraid so," Beaufort said. "People would wonder why you were absent. Arundel's triumph will be complete."

"Hmm." Hal tore off a piece of bread. Beaufort was significantly more experienced than he was and Hal had already embraced him as a mentor. He rarely rejected his uncle's advice. "The whole point of this demonstration is to chasten the Commons after their attempt to disendow the clergy. I realize that."

Beaufort shifted his shoulders uncomfortably. "I know you had no part in that, but your, um, ambivalence confused people. They don't know where you stand."

"On the side of orthodoxy!" This came out a little too quickly and Hal took a deep breath. "I just don't want to be associated with Arundel."

The bishop let out a snort. "That's not likely."

Hal smiled, embarrassed. "All right. I didn't take sides with or against the Commons because I wanted to see which way the wind was blowing. Or rather, to see how malleable they were. You and I both know their suggestions were preposterous."

Raising his eyebrows, Beaufort reached for a piece of cheese. "Maybe Arundel is doing you a favour. They are bound to be more compliant after this."

"Maybe he is. Perhaps I can turn this disaster to my advantage." He glanced sideways at the bishop. "Do you think Badby is totally irredeemable?"

"Who knows? People can change once they look death in the face."

After a moment's further consideration, Hal pushed his plate aside. "All right. I'm coming." He turned to Oldcastle. "Are you ready?"

John shook his head. "No, Hal. Go without me."

The prince couldn't suppress a look of annoyance. "What?"

"I cannot witness such a scene."

"Of course it's not pleasant. For anyone."

Oldcastle sighed. He had done his best to keep his religious feelings to himself, but he knew Hal suspected his leanings toward Wycliffe's teachings. "The burning of heretics is unconscionable. It's barbaric. It's not something we should practice in this country."

"I believe that is a discussion for more learned minds than ourselves," Beaufort broke in. "As long as the Pope does not discount it—"

"That does not make it moral," Oldcastle retorted. He put a hand on Hal's arm. "Please, my Lord, don't ask this of me."

For a moment Hal was tempted to insist, but the look in his friend's eyes deterred him. "All right. Watch yourself, John. There may come a time I cannot protect you."

A shiver shot down Oldcastle's spine. "I'm not the stuff of martyrs," he said. "I'm a soldier." He poured himself another drink while Hal took a last sip of his own and followed Beaufort from the room. Once they were safely gone, John pulled a small book from his pocket and opened it to a well-thumbed passage. It was a book of psalms, translated into English, and he read it silently, his lips moving with the words. Unfortunately, this time it gave him little comfort.

Just north of the city walls, Smithfield was an open space so large it would take about ten days for a yoke of oxen to plow it. Every August since the time of Henry I, the famous Bartholomew Fair brought people from all over the country. Otherwise, Smithfield was most often used as a horse market, and sometimes it hosted sporting games and tournaments. This was the site where King Richard II met the infamous Wat Tyler and disarmed the great revolt. The Scottish rebel, William Wallace, was hanged, drawn, and quartered under the elms in the far northwest corner. And now it was to witness the only other burning of a heretic in Henry IV's reign. William Sawtrey, a relapsed priest, was burned nine years before, but that episode was carried out with very little ceremony.

Hal took his place on the stage along with the others, most of whom walked over from St. Pauls. Although not acting in any official capacity, the prince's attendance was unquestionably accepted due to his rank. Arundel looked askance at Hal but proceeded to ignore him, and Beaufort as well. As they watched, Badby was brought forward and forced to step onto a gridiron, underneath which was piled a heap of faggots. They chained him to a stake and lowered a large barrel open at both ends—its purpose to concentrate the heat and smoke and accelerate the victim's death more humanely. The barrel reached to his waist.

A dirge was heard rising above the muted muttering of the crowd, and the doors of St. Bartholomew's church—located on the western edge of Smithfield—flew open. The prior, bearing the Host, was followed by twelve priests, each holding aloft a lighted torch. They made their way to the heretic, hoping to transform him with the Sacrament.

As the priests gathered before the stake, Hal felt a sudden urge to join them. He whispered in Beaufort's ear, "If I can persuade Badby to recant, no one can find fault with me, could they?" The bishop shook his head, wondering what Hal was up to. That was good enough. The prince jumped down from the stage and made his way forward.

The prior continued in his mission, unaware of Hal's presence. "We call upon you, John Badby, to renounce your heresy and take the Lord into your heart. God shall forgive you if you recant your erroneous proclamations! Save your soul! There is still time to accept the Church's teachings." Even though the prior made his most eloquent pleas, Badby shook his head, unyielding.

Hal couldn't restrain himself any longer. He stepped forward as the prior was moving aside. The prince was a tall man, and had an aura about him that couldn't be denied. It was partly because of his rank, but there was something else which drew all eyes. His bearing was that of a soldier and a nobleman, his reputation that of a paladin—the scar on his face a silent testimony to his bravery. Even Badby, covered in chains, stared at him.

"Listen to me," Hal said to the heretic. "I urge you to uphold the beliefs of the Holy Church. Doing so will ensure your release!"

"I cannot, and save my soul," said Badby sadly.

"Your words are offensive to pious ears and seductive to simple minds. Because you have confounded the truth of God, today the Lord confounds you. Admit your errors before you are thrown into the fire!" Hal's conviction was poignant. Even the recusant shook his head in distress.

"To my last breath I stand behind my beliefs," exhorted Badby.

Defeated, Hal stepped back and gestured to the executioners. Two men came forward with their torches and set fire to the faggots. They caught quickly and the flames licked up the outside of the barrel, though more made their way inside. Black smoke rose and encompassed his body. Trying to withstand the pain, Badby leaned his head back against the stake and gritted his teeth, but the heat was too much for him and he shrieked.

Hal was horrified. "Stop!" he cried. "Stop the fire! Remove the wood!"

There wasn't much time to spare. The executioners rushed forward with their iron bars and raked the wood out from under the gridiron. Still smouldering, the faggots were pushed aside.

"Raise the barrel," gasped the prince as he paced back in forth before the prisoner. Badby was already half-unconscious and barely noticed as the executioners grunted in their efforts to pull the ropes attached to pulleys. Fortunately, they hadn't burned away as yet.

Disregarding the heat, Hal leaned toward Badby, grabbing him by the chin. The heretic opened his eyes halfway.

"John Badby, you have suffered the agony of the fire," the prince said. "Here is your last chance. Save yourself! If you conform to the Church's teachings, you will receive spiritual salvation. And I offer you more: your life and a pardon. Renounce your heresy and I will give you an annual pension of three pence a day for the rest of your life. Do it now!"

Badby's eyes had closed again and Hal gave him another shake. "This is your last chance at redemption. Take it!"

The prisoner was conscious enough to respond. Once again, he shook his head. "I stand by my beliefs," he croaked. "I will not recant."

Taking his hand away, the prince took a step back. He was glad no one could see his bitter disappointment; he had willed the man to renounce his heresy and been firmly rejected. He was forced to face his own humiliation. He had failed. And now he had two choices: stop the burning altogether, or go ahead with it. There was no time to think about repercussions. Both choices were terrible. But the man *was* a heretic.

Placing a hand over his eyes, he gestured with the other to the executioners. "Go ahead. Finish the job."

They were ready. Without hesitation, they lowered the barrel onto the gridiron and pushed the wood back into place, refreshing it with new faggots. The priests began their dirge again and Hal stepped amongst them, reassured by their presence. He refused to leave and watched in dismay as Badby started wailing again. The flames worked their way up his clothes and his hair caught fire, causing his screams to increase in pitch until they gave out altogether. His body pitched forward, held up the chains. There only remained the crackling of the fire and the stench of charred flesh. John Badby was dead. The heat was so fierce the witnesses stepped back, watching in nauseated fascination as the corpse was consumed.

When Hal finally turned away, he saw that Arundel was nowhere to be seen. The archbishop had achieved his goal, and Hal wondered how much satisfaction he gained from this terrible spectacle.

Bishop Beaufort waited for him and together they made their way through the crowd; the witnesses parted before the prince, somewhat in awe. Hal barely noticed. "I need to walk back," he said. "That was terrible."

The bishop was equally revolted, for he was against the whole practice of burning heretics. "That was an admirable gesture," he said, dropping a coin into a beggar's hand as they passed.

Hal looked over at him, his face pale. "Was it? I don't know. Did I do the right thing?"

"By trying to stop it or insisting that it go on?"

"Both. I couldn't help myself."

Beaufort took his question seriously. "You did the Christian thing," he said, not very convincingly. "I'll tell you this: you took the archbishop's thunder away."

"Ah!" A glimmer of satisfaction broke through. "If only I had succeeded."

"That was outside of your control. But your demonstration made a stronger impression than all of his bombast."

"Well…" they walked a bit before Hal took a deep breath. "I wish I could have seen his face." He put an arm through Beaufort's. "I couldn't have done otherwise, you know. I mean, to let them burn the poor bastard. I would have brought the bishops and archbishops down upon my head. And my father. Oh, I cringe at the thought."

The other smiled grimly. "You are so right."

"And truly, my orthodoxy may be firmer than I thought. I felt no satisfaction from his burning. Though I'm not sure how I would have felt if I had released him to continue his heretical ways. Perhaps it's for the best."

The bishop wisely made no response. What kind of king was his nephew going to make?

CHAPTER 16

On Palm Sunday, 16 March 1410, John Beaufort, Earl of Somerset died quietly at the Hospital of St. Katharine's by the Tower, having made his will only a few hours before. His widow Margaret Holland kept a third of his lands for her dowry, which was a good thing as she had six children to raise—one of whom was to be the father of Margaret Beaufort, future mother of Henry VII. John Beaufort was the eldest of Gaunt's illegitimate children—which made him Henry's half-brother. They grew up in the same household. John had travelled with Bolingbroke when they traipsed across Europe in the '90s. He was the one who arranged for ships to be ready when Henry touched down near Dover on his return from exile. Of all the Beauforts, King Henry loved him the most and was devastated at his death, which only made his own health problems worse.

The king retired to Archbishop Arundel's palace at Lambeth to mourn his brother's passing. However, many of Somerset's vacant offices needed to be filled at once—most importantly, the Captain of Calais town. Two days after Beaufort's death, the Prince of Wales was appointed to this important post, and Sir Thomas Beaufort continued in command of the Castle of Calais. Hal's appointment was a great benefit for the garrison, for he finally had direct control of financial resources and made sure that a new subsidy was voted for repairing and strengthening the castles and catching up on their wages.

While all these preparations were going on, civil war was brewing again in France. The ghost of the murdered Louis of Orléans had not been appeased. His son, Duke Charles had tired of demands for justice that went nowhere. John the Fearless had shouldered his way into the French government, trumping up charges of treason against the king's grand master, Jehan de Montagu—one of Charles's staunchest supporters. Jehan was arrested and beheaded in front of a huge crowd, then his body was hung up on a gallows by an iron chain. The people saw Jehan as another corrupt official, so they cheered for their saviour the Duke of Burgundy. After that, it had been easy for the duke to purge the rest of the royal officials and replace them with men of his own choosing. The king was helpless to resist. Once Burgundy took control of the dauphin as well, his triumph was complete.

But this only made his enemies more determined to get rid of him.

Unfortunately, the young Duke of Orléans experienced yet another tragedy in his personal life. His beloved wife, Isabella of Valois, died in childbirth in September of 1409. She was only twenty years old and had experienced more travail in her life than most people twice her age. Charles consoled himself that he made her happy at the end. She rarely spoke of King Richard, and they had tacitly agreed to look forward rather than backward. Who would have known that she had so little life left to enjoy? Their daughter lived, though she gave Charles scant comfort. The bereaved duke wrote his most eloquent poetry to his beautiful duchess, and it was many months before he roused himself to confront his perpetual enemy. The Duke of Burgundy had only gathered more power in the interim.

It was time for Charles of Orléans to take a stand. Much to many peoples' surprise and Burgundy's consternation, he decided to marry the eleven-year-old daughter of Bernard VII, Count of Armagnac. The count was one of the most brutal protagonists of a blood-thirsty age. Little Bonne was also the granddaughter of the Duke du Barry, which bonded Charles even closer to his great-uncle and natural ally. Seven months after the death of Isabella, Charles's engagement was solemnly ratified at Gien, on the Loire, in the company of his new father-in-law, du Barry, Brittany, Anjou, Alençon, and the other members of their alliance. From then on, they were officially known as the Armagnacs.

Not only did the new league vow to raise five thousand men-at-arms and four thousand archers to be used for the good of the kingdom, they also published a manifesto. They pledged to rescue the King of France and the dauphin from the Duke of Burgundy and restore them to power. Both sides of the conflict housed their soldiers in and around Paris, and although they didn't come to blows, they inflicted great damage to the towns and villages they took possession of. Ultimately, the Duke of Burgundy was obliged to withdraw his forces, resolving to ask the English for help against his enemies.

Actually, *both* parties decided it would be a good idea to solicit aid from England, unwittingly starting a pattern of negotiation that would continue for years. King Henry entertained first one then another set of ambassadors, promising nothing to either one. There was much more he needed to learn. Obviously something had happened to upset the delicate balance of power in France. Had King Charles slipped into madness again? Which faction had control of the government?

For the last several months, Henry's primary concern had been the threat both sides posed to Calais. In fact, he had recently gone to great expense organizing an expedition to stop a looming French invasion. He intended to lead it himself, this time. An order had been issued for all vessels of thirty tuns portage to be brought to London, ready to sail. The barons of Cinque Ports were to provide their required fifty-seven ships outfitted with twenty men each, fully equipped.

And now he was suddenly approached by these very enemies? How sincere were they? Which of them would offer a better settlement?

Undeterred, Armagnac's ambassadors returned to France to prepare for the next round of diplomacy. Burgundy's envoys, on the other hand, had different instructions. Finding Henry's responses too lukewarm, they turned to Prince Hal. The king was not consulted.

Hal welcomed Burgundy's embassy at Coldharbour. "My Lord the Duke of Burgundy sends his greetings," the lead ambassador Guillaume Auclair said smoothly, "along with this gift." He handed the prince a carved box. Opening it, Hal beheld a beautiful dagger nestled in a black velvet cushion. The carved handle was wrapped in gold wire and embedded with a huge ruby.

Admiring its jewel-encrusted sheaf, Hal's eyes glittered when he drew the blade. "This is truly a magnificent present. Please tell your master I am very grateful for his thoughtfulness."

"He will be quite pleased," the other said, taking a seat with his associates. Hal gestured to his servants who brought in wine and comfits. "Do try the ginger," he said, leaning over and picking up one of the sugar-coated titbits.

As his guests relaxed, Hal studied them carefully. "I understand there is a bit of uneasiness in Paris."

Guillaume shrugged. "There is always uneasiness in Paris. But you are correct, my Lord; our capital is under siege at the moment and the enemy threatens to take over."

Hal nodded. "And what does your master request from us?"

"My Lord's antagonists, led by the Duke of Orléans, seek to gain control of the king. Naturally, this would cause great harm to our country. With your help, the duke can repel the insurrection and free our capital of this threat."

"You wish for us to send a force of arms?"

"That and much more. The Duke of Burgundy seeks an alliance. He is prepared to offer you the hand of his daughter Anne in marriage."

Hal sat up in his chair. It wasn't a royal marriage, but the next best thing. Burgundy was a very wealthy man. "That is generous. What does he propose as a dowry?"

"At this stage we are not authorized to make any firm proposals. However, we trust you will send your own envoys with us when we return to Burgundy."

"We shall do so. Will the duke assist us with full recovery of Guyenne?"

"That is certainly within the realm of possibility. And of course my master is prepared to pay the expenses of your expedition for our aid."

"That is commendable. I shall have the Earl of Arundel call on you tomorrow to arrange a return embassy."

This was a good first audience. Within a few days, all had been agreed upon and Arundel gathered a sizeable entourage. He departed for Burgundy to confer with the duke. Hal waited until they were safely gone before consulting with his father.

The prince knew he had been a little precipitate. But surely the king would understand! Hal was at the head of the council and was expected to act with dispatch. He prepared his words carefully so as not to offend. Fortunately, he caught Henry alone.

"Father," he said, pulling up a chair, "I have been approached by Burgundian ambassadors who have presented me with a fair proposal."

"Oh? I wonder what they said to you that they neglected to tell me?"

"The Duke of Burgundy has offered me the hand of his daughter Anne," Hal said carefully.

Henry sipped his wine, trying not to look too interested. Or insulted. They did not get that far with him. "What else has he offered? We need to know what land and jewels he plans to send with her. Is Burgundy prepared to pay for whatever expedition he expects from us? Is he willing to help with the recovery of Guyenne?"

"I have sent my own envoys with those very questions," Hal assured him.

Henry was quick to respond. "Who did you send?"

"Earl Thomas of Arundel led the embassy along with the Bishop of St. Davids, my chamberlain Hugh Mortimer, and other retainers of mine." He got up and paced the floor. "Surely you agree that an alliance with Burgundy can only enhance our trade with Flanders, and even resolve some of those old commercial disputes."

Henry nodded reluctantly though he was far from mollified. "What is the size of this entourage you sent?"

Again, Hal hesitated. "He went with 200 men-at-arms and 800 archers."

"That's not an embassy. You sent him with an army!" Grabbing the arms of his chair, Henry attempted to stand but fell back, defeated.

Hal swallowed, determined to stand firm. "A mercenary force, to be ready if required. We need Burgundy as an ally, not an enemy. Already you declared your will to defend Calais. We can't have him threatening our backs. So they will be there as a deterrent. Besides, if our forces go to the aid of the duke, he has already offered to pay for their wages."

His father shook his head. "I'm not sure I trust the man. That dreadful murder! You know I didn't get along with Orléans. But I cringe every time I think about it. And Burgundy got away with it. How was that even possible?"

Hal knew better than to express his thought. *How was it possible to get away with decapitating an archbishop?* That wouldn't improve matters. He pursed his lips, thinking of a different approach. "As terrible as the assassination was, it helped our cause. Burgundy has good reason to ally with us."

Henry shrugged. "I don't necessarily disagree with your aims, son. It's your methods that upset me." He found himself breathing too hard. "Who is running this country? You or me?"

This was the crux of the matter and both of them knew it. Hal knelt by his side. "Your council and I are doing our best to represent your interests."

"Doing your best," Henry muttered. "Leave me, Hal. I have much to do."

Getting up slowly, Hal breathed a sigh of relief, even though he had just been dismissed. They were uncomfortably close to an argument, and he wasn't ready for a confrontation. Maybe when he was surer of himself. As Hal backed from the room, Henry had already turned away. That wasn't a good sign.

If the prince had known what his father was referring to when he said *much to do*, he might not have been so eager to escape. Once Hal was safely gone, Henry called for his secretary and started issuing writs for a new parliament to meet on 3 November. It was time to put his house back in order, and he needed to do it publicly. He saw now that he had given his son too much power, and he had better assert himself before it was too late. There was only one king in England. He had worked too hard to let his authority slip away.

After dismissing his secretary, Henry looked up with a smile when Queen Joanna came to say goodnight. He needed her comfort and she always seemed to know.

She refreshed his wine and poured one for herself, sitting beside him. "You're troubled. I can see it in your face."

His hand tightened around the cup. "It's Hal. He's determined to support the Duke of Burgundy."

"Is that such a bad thing?"

"Not in itself. But he's taking matters into his own hands."

"Ah." She stretched out her legs. "You would prefer a more biddable son, like Thomas."

A brief smile flashed across Henry's face. "Like Thomas. Sometimes I wish…"

"I know. He's a loyal son, but Hal will make a better king."

"Perhaps." This was not something Henry was willing to admit—not the way he was feeling. He shifted uncomfortably in his chair.

"You're no better, are you," she said, stroking his hair. She noticed once again how thin it had become. "Aren't you planning to travel to Calais?"

"Yes, by the end of the week. Preparations are almost finished. Dear God, I must go this time. What will people think of me if I cancel?"

"You can't have them carry you to the boat. What would they think of you then?"

He knew what they would think. The humiliation would be almost more than he could bear. Henry took her hand and held it in both of his. "My poor Joanna. You married a strong, able warrior. And look what you ended up with. A decrepit wretch, old before his time."

She smiled sadly. "That's not how I see it. I married a warm, loving partner. What matters is on the inside."

"You rescue me from myself, my dear."

Joanna pretended not to notice when Henry brushed a tear from his eye. "If I had the chance to do it all again," she said, "nothing would be different. You have made me very happy."

They sat for a while in silence. She watched his eyes close and his breathing deepen. He *had* become old before his time. How much longer would he survive?

Waiting until the last minute, Henry was finally forced to announce the cancellation of his expedition to Calais. He gave no reason why, but his advisors knew it was due to his health. The following day he was visited by his son bringing a small deputation from the council. He expected this to happen and had already prepared his excuses. But as the little group filtered into the room, there was something about their evasive looks that made him suspicious. Gesturing to his squire, the king summoned Erpingham and Norbury to attend. And his son Thomas.

They gathered around the table in his cabinet and the servants offered refreshments while he waited. The prince had brought six knights including Sir Roger Leche, who was once esquire of the royal body but now served Hal as steward of his household. Sir Thomas Chaworth had also been one of the king's knights who had gravitated toward the prince. This was a natural trend, but Henry was a bit deflated by it. Worse than that, his own half-brother Henry Beaufort sat at Hal's side, obviously ill at ease; he kept adjusting his shoulders and cracking his neck.

From his set mouth, Bishop Beaufort looked ready to stand by some uncomfortable decision.

The king glanced to the side as Erpingham and Norbury came into the room. Between the two of them, they were worth a dozen knights. Thomas came running up and stopped short at the gathering in the room.

"All right, I am here." Henry kept his voice low and expressionless. "What do you need to discuss with me?"

"Sire." It was Beaufort who spoke first. "We are here as representatives of the council and are acting in the best interests of your kingdom." He cleared his throat. "Now that you have summoned another parliament we feel we should review the issues at stake. Since the next instalment of the 1410 subsidy has not yet been gathered and you agreed not to ask for further taxation until then, there must be another reason you called parliament."

They waited in vain for an answer. Henry's reason had much to do with taking back control of the kingdom, but he was not ready to discuss the matter.

Prince Hal had plenty to say, however. "Father, the wool exports have collapsed this year and we're still replacing corrupt customs collectors, the exchequer is terribly short of funds—"

"Especially since three-quarters of the last subsidy went to *your* Calais!" interrupted Prince Thomas. "I'm still owed over twelve thousand pounds for Ireland!"

"And why should you be paid for a job you haven't fulfilled?" shot back Hal. "As far as I am concerned, you should receive nothing unless you return to your post."

"We've already discussed this," the king muttered helplessly.

"You're complaining about money," said Bishop Beaufort angrily, "while at the same time you seek to marry my brother's widow before he's even cold in his grave!" This was another argument that had been brewing, and Thomas had just inadvertently left himself open to attack. King Henry had no problem with the marriage; it would solve Thomas's financial difficulties without depleting the crown's resources. However, he did not reckon on Henry Beaufort's strenuous objection; as executor of his brother's will, the Bishop was opposed to seeing the Beaufort inheritance pass into Thomas's control.

The king raised his hand. "This has nothing to do with parliament. Let us move on."

Henry's timely interruption gave everyone in the room a moment to cool down. Hal's steward smoothed a parchment on the table and read out a list of deficiencies that needed to be covered. After an hour's worth of discussion with no conclusion, Bishop Beaufort decided to come to the point of their meeting. He looked at Hal and cleared his throat.

"Sire, as I said earlier, we are here as representatives of the council." He nodded at the group of knights who sat quietly at Hal's other side. "Due to your continued illness which has debilitated you to the point where governing has become an encumbrance, we are here to suggest that you retire in favour of the Prince of Wales."

There. It was said. A silence blanketed the room.

Then Hal stood. "My father, we only propose to relieve you of the stresses of ruling this country."

Henry moved his stare from Beaufort to his son. His lips were pursed and his face had grown red. Erpingham moved behind the king and put a hand on his shoulder, leaning down and whispering.

For a moment it seemed that Henry was oblivious to his words, but he finally exhaled deeply, coming to a resolution. Gritting his teeth he grasped the edge of the table and pulled himself up.

"I will govern for as long as I draw breath. Do you understand?"

Hal opened his mouth to speak but thought better of it.

Lowering himself back into his chair, Henry gestured to the assembled knights. "Thomas Erpingham, arrest these men and put them into the Tower. All except the prince and Bishop Beaufort."

This was unexpected and Hal paled, but he dared not interfere. His companions all went quietly while he watched them go out the door. Returning to his father, he realized just how much the king had been restraining himself up to this point.

"If it weren't for the fact that I require your support in the upcoming parliament, you would have gone with then," Henry growled. "I will not permit any kind of novelty during this session and I intend to exercise the same liberties my predecessors have done. Make no mistake, my lords. My patience is at an end."

While King Henry prepared for parliament, on the other side of the Channel the Earl of Arundel offered his services to the Duke of Burgundy. His instructions from the Prince of Wales were to use his own judgment and favour the duke's plans if he felt he would gain an advantage.

Since late August, the Armagnacs had attempted to blockade Paris, having been repudiated by King Charles, who was under Duke John's control. They were not successful. Burgundy was popular with the people and managed to get into the city along with Arundel's troops. Together, one November night, their combined forces slipped out of Paris and stormed the hamlet of St. Cloud, across the Seine. After heavy fighting they dislodged the Armagnacs, winning great renown. Arundel's men impressed the Parisians and the Burgundians with their stout and efficient performance and were richly rewarded. The Duke of Burgundy paid their expenses as promised, and most of the army was back in England within the month.

Parliament met on 21 September, though Henry was too ill to attend the first three days. He came on the fourth, however, determined to assert himself. After repeating the same words to the speaker that he had said to Hal and Beaufort about no novelty, he agreed to get down to the business of taxation. The month of November passed without incident, and on the 30th King Henry called Prince Hal, Bishop Beaufort, the Earls of Warwick, Westmorland, and Arundel along with the others from the council. Kneeling at the king's feet, they received formal recognition for administering the State.

"I thank you all," Henry said, nodding graciously. "And henceforth, your services will no longer be required. I will appoint a new council in the next year."

Backing from the room, the freshly dismissed councillors kept their silence while the king addressed the speaker with his next order of business. But once outside, Hal stood with his arms crossed over his chest and glared at the closed doors. He knew that many of the members—like Westmorland—would be recalled to the council. But he would certainly not be among them. Nor would Henry Beaufort.

The bishop put a hand on Hal's shoulder. "It could have been much worse," he said. "Think of it this way: the king has given you leave. Take a holiday. You have worked very hard."

Still gripping his arms, Hal turned his head. "You know, I think I'll do just that. It's time I did something for myself." He turned swiftly away and the bishop watched him stomp off—not like a man who has just been given his freedom, but more like a soul who was mad at the world. Sighing, Hal's uncle tapped a forefinger against his cheek, trying to determine whether he should follow the prince, then decided against it. Let him work out his frustrations. He had a good head on his shoulders.

Bishop Beaufort knew his nephew very well. In his mood, Hal would have welcomed an opportunity for a fight, but that wasn't really his focus. He wanted to get drunk. Good and drunk.

Westminster Palace was a busy place. Not only did the council regularly meet there, the king's main residence also took up most of one wing. King Henry had recently granted the queen her own tower next to the great gate of the palace to conduct her business and for her archives. As Hal strode across the cobblestones, he saw Humphrey walking in his direction—waving. Hal had to stop and think a moment. He had been too busy to pay any attention to his youngest brother, and he was stunned to realize Humphrey was no longer a boy. He must be twenty-one years old by now.

Humphrey stopped before him with a big smile on his face. Hal's heart warmed toward the stripling—as he saw him—and he was almost ashamed he had given him so little thought. "Where are you headed?"

The other shrugged. "I was thinking of food."

"Ah. Just the perfect opportunity. Let's find some place together."

Humphrey's face lit up. He wasn't used to getting his brother all to himself. Pleased, Hal put an arm around his shoulders and together they went out through the gates and into the city. After a few blocks they found a quiet public house where they could eat and talk. Humphrey was shy and Hal ordered food and drink for the both of them.

"How go your studies?"

"Well, I finally got a new English translation of Aristotle. I find the Greeks to be most enlightening..." He paused; this wasn't what he wanted to talk about. He put his elbows on the table, leaning forward. "Hal, of course I enjoy my studies. But I'm not going into the Church. I don't know what father has in mind for me. He has given me no responsibility, no commands. I'm not fit for anything. I feel so useless."

Hal sat back, considering his brother's frustration. He had never given it any thought. "I see what you mean. Maybe father is trying to protect you..."

"But from what? I can't learn from my mistakes if I don't get a chance to make any. I've certainly learned from his."

"Maybe that's the problem. He's running out of time and you're the only one left. Thomas hasn't helped matters any." Hal frowned. "But you're right. Though I'm not sure where he could send you."

"Anywhere would be a start." A serving wench put down a platter of meat slices and a pitcher of ale. Humphrey grabbed a piece of bread and tore off the end. "I follow the court wherever he goes, like a spare horse."

"Do you get away?"

"Like now?" Humphrey chuckled, despite himself. "Rarely."

"Hmm." Hal poured some ale into his brother's cup. "Listen, Humphrey. I've been remiss. We need to make up for lost time. Are you with me?"

The other laughed. "I thought you'd never ask."

Freed from restraints, they forgot about trying to get to know each other better and just started drinking. Moving on, they found a rowdier pub and Hal bought drinks for everyone in the room. Appreciating his generosity, a big brawny fellow with a red beard started singing, pointing at Hal:

As for the liquor, the juice of the grape
Sometimes it makes man wise as an ape
But whilst we are sober, more civil we stay,
And ever account it our duty to pay
Like brothers together in friendship doth hug,
A worthy respect to the mug, yes the mug!

"That's more like it," Hal exclaimed, holding up his own. "You know, Humphrey, I haven't had a chance to forget about my duties, which is the opposite side of your coin. I'll need to find a way to shift some responsibilities onto your shoulders." He reached out to a passing serving girl and pulled her onto his lap. "My brother here needs a little education," he said as she leaned toward him. "Can you give him some instruction?"

Looking embarrassed, Humphrey took a drink. The girl smiled and went over to him, curling a lock of his hair around her finger. "Wait a while," she said, bending toward his ear. "I'll be back."

Not knowing what to say, Humphrey watched her walk away. Her hips swayed in the most creative manner. "I don't know…"

"Am I correct?"

The other was glad the room was too dim to see his blush. "I haven't had the opportunity—"

"That's the first thing we need to fix. You're too old not to know something about women."

"What about you?"

"I'm not going anywhere. You'll see."

More drinkers gravitated toward their table and before long, Hal had his choice of buxom serving maids. While the bearded man sang a couplet that begged for an answer, Humphrey's waitress came back and sat on his lap, plucking a grape from a platter and feeding it to him.

Ignoring his brother, Hal added his own verse and the drinkers around them laughed and called to each other, shouting out more bawdy stanzas. Extra pitchers of ale appeared on the table and more singing followed, until Humphrey forgot about his embarrassment.

As the evening wore on, Hal seemed captivated by a willowy gal with long black hair. When she sat on his lap, he took a little peek down the front of her dress.

"Someone told me you're the Prince of Wales," she said, laughing.

"I am."

"Pshaw! Don't fool me. What would the Prince of Wales be doing here?"

"Looking for a girl like you."

"Ha! You'll have to do better than that."

"Ask my brother," said Hal, pointing at Humphrey, who nodded. "Can't a prince have a good time?"

After a few more drinks, Hal's chosen companion led him up the stairs to her room, but before he left he winked at Humphrey, who seemed to be getting along just fine. "I'll see you in the morning," he said, enjoying his brother's momentary expression of surprise. It passed quickly when the girl kissed him on the lips.

The next morning, Hal awoke in a strange bed with a strange partner and a throbbing headache. Groaning, he sat up and pulled on his hose.

"Hmm?" the girl said, rolling onto her side.

He bent over and kissed her on the cheek. "What's the name of this place?"

"The Boar's Head," she said, trying to pull him back down.

"I wish I could, my pretty one. I must return to my duties. And what is your name?"

"Ella. Don't forget. Come back any time."

"I will. Come back, that is. You pleased me very much."

Pulling on his tunic, Hal looked at her wistfully. But he was a bit concerned about his little brother. He left some coins on the chest and wasted no more time going into the main room. He spotted Humphrey, sitting in a corner and sipping on a spoonful of gruel. And looking more than a little dishevelled.

"There you are," said Hal, ordering a mug of ale before sitting at the table. "Everything all right?"

Putting a hand to his forehead, the other gave him a bemused smile. "My head aches, but the rest of me is quite well exercised."

"Well done. Shall we come back again tonight?"

"Um, not sure I should."

"Worried about father? You're a grown man, Humphrey. And remember, even father was young, once."

Shrugging, Humphrey threw up his hands. "How can I refuse?"

"Good. It's time for you to stretch your wings. It gets easier all the time. We'll bring John Oldcastle with us. He's good company."

"He's back from France?"

"Just a couple of days ago. If we buy him enough drinks, maybe he'll tell us about it."

Oldcastle was a bit of a hero to the younger generation of knights. About ten years older than Hal, he had proven himself many times over on the battlefield. With intense, deep-set blue eyes and blond hair that always looked to be windswept, Oldcastle was a natural leader. When he smiled it seemed like the sun came out, and he smiled often. Gladly accepting Hal's invitation to drink, he met both brothers at the Boar's Head, and clapped Humphrey on the shoulder as he sat next to him.

"You look so much like your father," he said to the surprised lad. "It's truly amazing."

"Do I really?"

"Don't you think so Hal? Where has Humphrey been hiding?"

"Our father has kept him close," said the prince. "Too close. I've decided to take over his education."

"Oh, ho! You'll have to rein in your bad behaviour!"

"On the contrary. I haven't had enough opportunity to misbehave. I intend to catch up with you."

As they both knew, for years Hal had his hands full trying to stay ahead of the Welsh rebels. He had little free time to spend with the soldiers and even less time to himself. All of a sudden he had no immediate responsibilities.

But it wasn't by choice! What to do with his limitless energy? In addition, now he needed to burn off his anger. The hell with his father. The hell with the council. Let them fend for themselves. He turned around, looking for Ella.

Not entirely aware of Hal's circumstances, Humphrey was impatient for action. "Tell us about St. Cloud," he said eagerly.

"St. Cloud. It was our finest moment." Oldcastle reached for the pitcher. "Between St. Cloud and St. Denis, the Armagnacs were in a position to block all supplies to Paris from the north and west. There were fifteen hundred men holding the bridge over the Seine. Since there was no wall protecting the town, they dug a trench and threw up a stockade composed of barrels full of stones. The three roads into St. Cloud were blocked with wagons and rough masonry."

"Sounds impossible," said Humphrey.

"They hoped so. But by the time the Parisians and Burgundians joined us, we were nine thousand strong. We set out from Paris about ten o'clock in the evening and marched all night. The roads were frozen and the wind blew ice in our faces. By dawn we finally arrived and situated ourselves on the southern bank, which was higher than their side. So the archers were able to start a barrage that threw them into confusion. The cavalry charged across the bridge and pushed back the defenders. I'm happy to say our English contingent forced our way through the barriers and took the Armagnacs in the flank. They retreated into the town and fought like devils but finally broke in all directions. Unfortunately for them, the Gascons who were supposed to hold the tower panicked and raised the drawbridge. Many of the poor bastards fell into the river and drowned like sheep." He shook his head. "Over nine hundred knights and squires lay dead after only three hours, and it's said we only lost twenty."

Humphrey whistled in admiration.

"How fared the Earl of Arundel," asked Hal.

"The Duke of Burgundy gave him his due. Not only did he pay for all the wounded to be treated—and our wages, too—he feasted Arundel at the Louvre and gave him a seat at his side. Our contingent performed well and was adequately rewarded."

"We'll greet him like a hero!" Humphrey raised his mug.

"And so we shall. Drinks for everybody," Hal shouted at the barkeep. "A toast to the Earl of Arundel!"

Enjoying the boisterous response, Hal got up and traded quips with men at the other tables. Humphrey admired his easy way with people, no matter what social class. "I wish I could be like him," he said to Oldcastle, who was in the middle of a draught.

The older man turned to him thoughtfully. "I think Hal told me you have been shut up in your father's court."

"Well, not exactly shut up. But I'm usually part of his entourage wherever he goes."

"Not much opportunity to gather your own household, then?"

"I have some friends…"

"Well, consider me one of them," Oldcastle said, giving him a nudge. "Between you and me, we'll keep Hal out of trouble." He pointed to the prince who had an arm around two women. "Or maybe we'll have to join him."

CHAPTER 17

Before December had passed, Hal's treasurer had been replaced with Henry's choice, Sir John Pelham; Thomas Beaufort was supplanted as chancellor by Archbishop Arundel. Again. Prince Thomas was given a seat at the council table—but not Hal, as expected. The six knights who had been arrested were examined and released, somewhat chastened but none the worse for wear.

Although Hal was absent from the ranks of the king's counsellors, he stayed in London and kept himself informed of events. The Duke of Burgundy, emboldened by his success against the Armagnacs, sent an embassy to England. They were entertained by both princes, Hal and Humphrey, and discussed further marriage proposals. The same ambassadors met with King Henry at Coldharbour, and again at Rochester. By early March, they returned to Paris glowing with excitement.

Unfortunately for the Burgundian envoys, at the end of January another set of ambassadors—sent by the Armagnacs—also called on King. This time Hal wasn't consulted, but he found out soon enough what was happening.

His recent rapport with Humphrey was bearing fruit in a way he never expected. Grateful for his attention and hungry for more approval, the youngest prince had taken his brother's cause to heart. They had made a habit of gathering at the Boar's Head in the evening, along with a growing circle of friends. But this night, Humphrey had something important to relate. Appreciating the look in Humphrey's eye, Hal took him aside in a back room and ordered supper. A delicious meat pie started their meal and Hal pulled his knife from its sheath. "I can see something is troubling you," he said. "What has happened?"

"It's father. He met with envoys from the Armagnacs today."

Stopping in mid-cut, Hal put the knife down. "Representing the Dukes of Berry, Orléans, and Bourbon?"

"And the Counts of Armagnac and Alençon."

"You were there?" Hal considered the implications as Humphrey nodded. "I had a suspicion they would come. The Duke of Burgundy must have given them a good scare. And father welcomed them?"

"With open arms."

Suppressing his annoyance, Hal cut two pieces of pie and put them on trenchers. "I suppose they made an enticing proposal."

"Oh yes. They offered no less than the restoration of the ancient Duchy of Guyenne, 'as fully and freely as any of his predecessors held it,' they said. I assume that means including the counties that have been lost over the years. In return, they request England's support against Burgundy."

Hal leaned back for a moment. "By the blood of Christ, father could never refuse. Even if they couldn't possibly deliver on their promises."

Nodding, Humphrey went on. "They also agreed to hand over twenty castles right away, and help him conquer the rest. There's more, but I couldn't remember it all."

"That's enough," Hal said bitterly. "Burgundy will be outraged. He expects our support, especially after St. Cloud."

"I wanted to prepare you," Humphrey said. "Please don't let father know I told you."

"Never. You have done me a great service and I realize the risk you are taking. Has father said anything about your disappearances?"

"Oh." Humphrey laughed uncomfortably. "He must have sent spies after me because he knows all about this place."

"Ha! I'm not surprised."

"He wondered what I am doing at night. And why."

"What did you tell him?"

"That I'm a grown man. You should have seen the look of shock on his face."

"His baby boy," laughed Hal. "He's lost control of you. But he still has Thomas."

"His favourite," said Humphrey casually, picking up the pie wedge. Then he looked up. "Watch out for him. They often quit speaking when I walk into a room. I don't trust him."

"Neither do I, brother. Neither do I."

It didn't take long for the Duke of Burgundy to discover the treachery. One of the Armagnac's envoys was captured with compromising dispatches. Burgundy brought the evidence to the King of France, who was under his control at the moment. Immediately they started planning their own offensive against Guyenne, to punish the English. King Henry discerned that time was of the essence, and he agreed to sign the Anglo-Armagnac Treaty of Bourges in May, while announcing his plan to go to Guyenne in person.

Commanded to meet his father, Hal was glad he was prepared, for there was no explanation connected to the summons. He was disappointed to see that there were a host of witnesses to this meeting; no chance to discuss matters privately. Archbishop Arundel was waiting, as well as the queen, Thomas Erpingham, John Norbury, and all of his brothers.

The king's face had broken out again in a terrible rash and his clothes hung on his fragile limbs like a scarecrow. Once again, Hal was amazed he had the energy to host such a meeting. It looked like he could barely sit up straight.

Perching himself on the edge of a bench, Hal waited for his father to start.

"I've brought everyone here," Henry started, "because I have decided to sign a treaty with the Armagnac dukes." The king stopped, studying Hal. He suspected his son knew something, though Hal's face was inscrutable. "You know they have approached me, and I feel our interests more closely coincide with theirs."

Hal felt something was expected of him. "I don't understand. Our financial interests align with Flanders, who is our most important trading partner."

"Yes, I recognize that. We will have to negotiate that treaty separately. What's more important to me is to maintain our lordship in Guyenne and protect Calais. Everything else is secondary. That's always been my policy."

"Burgundy will feel betrayed. How am I going to explain this reversal?"

"That's your problem," shot Thomas. "You should have thought about that before sending Arundel."

Henry gestured for Thomas to be quiet.

"The duke will most certainly attack Guyenne," pursued Hal.

"All the more reason we require the assistance of the Armagnacs," insisted the king. "You must understand, Hal. They have finally acknowledged me as the King of England and offer to do whatever is in their power to restore the duchy of Guyenne to me. All they ask in return is a thousand men-at-arms and three thousand archers to resist the Duke of Burgundy."

"They've made other offers as well," added Thomas. "Their children in marriage, according to father's discretion."

"Except for you," growled Hal, "since you're so intent on marrying Margaret Holand."

Henry looked wearily at his sons. "The details are yet to be worked out. What's important is that all of you sign the treaty." He held up his quill. "I've already sent out a mandate that no one is permitted to go to France and fight for either side. I'll need all the men I can muster for my own campaign. Is this understood?" He looked at his sons, all of whom grunted an answer. "Good. The envoys are waiting in the other room. Have them come in."

248

The Armagnac ambassadors duly made their entrance, dressed in their most extravagant robes. Henry nodded his greeting.

"My sons are prepared to swear, in your presence, to uphold the terms of this treaty and refrain from making any alliance with the Duke of Burgundy, his children, or his kinsmen. Is that not so?" He signed the document and then looked directly at Hal, holding out the quill.

Reluctantly, Hal stood. "I do so swear," he said, signing below his father's name. His brothers did the same.

The servants came in with wine and poured a chalice for each person in the room. Henry stood. "To your illustrious masters. May we all prosper." Everyone took a drink, though the king noted that Hal made a face as if the wine was sour.

After the envoys took their leave, the king talked a bit about raising loans to pay for the expedition and gathering troops. "Hal, I would have you bring fifty men to serve under my banner," he said.

The prince had been standing by the window and looked around. "Sire, I would prefer to bring more men, which would enable me to serve you more honourably and provide me with more security." He glanced briefly at Thomas.

"I'm sorry, son. This all the exchequer can afford."

"Then I'll have to make up the difference from my own estates. With your permission, I would consult with my kinsmen and friends with a view to recruiting additional retainers."

Henry considered briefly and nodded. "Very well. Now, Thomas, how many men do you think the Duke of York and Thomas Beaufort would recruit?" And at that, the conversation moved on. Hal's contribution was at an end and he excused himself at the first opportunity.

Before he left for his estates in the west, Hal wrote a letter to the Duke of Burgundy, stressing that the Armagnac offer was just too compelling for his father to refuse. Much though he desired a Burgundian marriage, he had no choice but to withdraw from any alliance they were considering. Because the King of England made Guyenne a priority, the English were obliged to defend their allies—meaning the Armagnacs. Hal signed the letter, hoping the duke would be able to accept it in the spirit it was written—as a dutiful son and loyal subject.

At the same time, the Earl of Arundel also wrote a similar letter, thanking the duke for his generosity and expressing that he was bound by the king's treaty.

"Come with me to Coventry," Hal said to the earl. "We need to put some distance between ourselves and the court." He had been feeling increasingly rebuffed by his father's friends who seemed to feel that they could get away with showing him disrespect—in small ways. His response had been to spend more time carousing with his drinking companions at the Boar's Head. They didn't care what his politics were.

But this would not do. The more he escaped, the more scurrilous stories they spread about him. Gathering a score of retainers, Hal made ready to leave. Humphrey wanted to go with him, but this might have been seen as an affront to their father. "You would best serve me here," the prince told him, "if you agree. I don't need to tell you there are certain people..." he hesitated at the word, rolling his eyes, "who would do me harm. Please let me know if I need to hurry back."

"I will, Hal. You can count on me."

"I can. I do." Hal gave him a little cuff on the chin. "Your time will come. Never fear."

There was one other person Hal had to see before he left for Coventry. Henry Beaufort was waiting for him at the Abbey and they walked together along the East Cloister.

"Such a peaceful place," sighed Hal. "I wish my mind was as serene as these halls."

"These are not settled times," said the bishop.

"I feel like everything we have been working for has failed. I couldn't be any more out of favour."

"Well, the king has certainly shown us he will not relinquish any of his hard-earned authority, no matter how incapable he is of sustaining it."

"He's not the only one. I don't think we can stand against the archbishop, either."

Beaufort sighed. "At least for now. Patience, my son. This will not last."

Hal glanced at him uncertainly. "You mean my father's health?"

"It's in God's hands." They both crossed themselves, knowing what each other was thinking. How much longer would Henry live?

When Hal and Arundel reached Coventry, they had already gathered more followers and expected additional recruits. They had been gone for ten days when a letter from the king caught up with them, bundled with another message from Humphrey. Hal read his father's letter first, and Arundel gathered from his expression that the news was not welcome.

"I knew this was going to happen," Hal said, putting the paper on the table. "The king has taken a turn for the worse. He cannot go to Guyenne." He frowned at his friend. "Guess who is going to lead the expedition?"

"It certainly won't be you," said Arundel.

"No, thank God. Burgundy would never forgive me. No, this is going to be Thomas's big chance to prove himself."

Arundel shrugged. "He's been itching for a command."

"Well, he may be good at it. We'll find out." Hal pointed at the letter. "It says here that I am relieved of all responsibility. I'm to stay home. Not that I object. At least father won't try to force me to serve under my brother."

"Ah. And we're gathering all these retainers."

"At my expense," he said wryly, opening the second letter. His frown deepened.

"What is it?"

"Here." Hal handed over the letter. "Read it to me. I can't finish it."

Looking worriedly at Hal, Arundel smoothed the paper. "Dear Hal. It was fortunate that you left me behind after all. For some reason, no one has paid any attention to me and I've been able to sit quietly in the room while your enemies plot your downfall, for I can't find any other word to use. You already know Archbishop Arundel sees you as a direct threat, and Thomas will take any opportunity to poison father's mind against you." He stopped reading, looking up at Hal who sat with his forehead in his hand. "This is treacherous!"

Hal let out a groan. "Father has many advisors who are threatened by me. Those two are not alone." He waved for Arundel to go on.

The earl took a deep breath. "They accuse you of trying to obstruct the campaign to Guyenne. They say you are in league with Burgundy. Someone has come forward with an accusation that you have misappropriated the funds for the Calais garrison. Outrageous!"

"My brother, I'm sure," Hal said bitterly.

"By God's wounds, it gets worse." Arundel's lips started trembling. "They say you are raising a rebellion to seize the throne for yourself!"

Raising his head, Hal's hand drew into a fist. "This has gone too far! We have to go back." Fighting tears, he looked around almost as if expecting an assassin to fall on him. "I have to think. One mistake and I'm ruined."

"You're the Prince of Wales! What are you saying?"

"There's no doubt father would prefer Thomas as his heir. If his hold on the crown was firmer, he might have tried to make it so."

Horrified, Arundel could only stare.

"Listen," said Hal, getting up and pacing the room, "we cannot give this time to grow out of control. I need to write a memorandum and send it to every part of the realm explaining my position. Can you get my secretaries?"

"Give me a moment." Arundel dashed from the room and soon returned with the requested clerics and a pile of writing materials.

"Good." Hal was still pacing, and he immediately dictated a letter stating why he had come to Coventry with his father's permission. "But even as I was traveling to this city," he went on, "certain children of iniquity and disciples of dissension were sowing base treachery. Desiring to upset the ordered succession, they have suggested to my most revered father that I am contemplating a rebellion to seize the throne for myself. With a serpentine cunning they claim I am trying to hinder the departure of the campaign to Guyenne. I intend to make it known that both of these rumours are false, spread by those who seek to stir up civil war in place of peace. As God knows, I feel nothing but love, obedience, and filial humility toward my father and would strive with all my power for the recovery of Guyenne and the other rights of the crown. This is the unfeigned truth of my innermost heart, and I am sending this letter so that all should know."

Stopping his pacing, Hal watched his scribes who were busily scratching with their quills. "We'll send a copy to my father, Bishop Beaufort, St. Albans, all the major bishoprics. A copy must go to Bristol, Lichfield, Chester, the Mayor of London... wherever else you deem appropriate. And now, I must think..." He turned away and went out the door, alone. No one dared follow him.

Hal's footsteps led him through the garden and right up to the Priory Gate, attached to the new city wall, still being built. He climbed the stairs to the top of the little tower and leaned over the battlements, taking in the view of the countryside. Although his inclination usually took him into a church where he felt the presence of the Trinity, on this day he was drawn to the serenity of nature—a tranquillity never encountered in London.

Just out of sight, he heard the tapping of stonemasons, and a few men laughed at some joke. In the distance a herd of white sheep stood stark against the deep green of the pasture. He watched as a pair of wrens hopped from one tree branch to the other, right below him, searching for food. When was the last time he did that?

What had happened to his peace of mind? How in the world had he found himself bitterly opposed to his father? Somehow he had been diverted from reforming the country's finances to leading a faction opposed to royal policies. That had never been his intention. And look what happened. He had been sharply put in his place, due to his inexperience and lack of sensitivity. At least he understood belatedly how disastrous it was to suggest that his father retire. He hadn't seen it as opposition, but undoubtedly Henry did.

He bit his lip. No, it had always been Archbishop Arundel he objected to, not his father. The man's overbearing convictions drove everything before him, including Henry, who was no longer strong enough to stand up to him. As far as Hal could tell, the king didn't even realize he was being manipulated. What the Prince of Wales needed to do was take back control. He needed to redeem himself. He wanted his father's love, of course, but also his approval.

Hal sighed, turning back to his lodgings. It was time to make a statement, proving to the world he had such a strong following he could not be ignored.

His secretaries were just finishing when he joined them. Arundel looked up worriedly, but Hal shook his head gently, sitting by his side.

"I've come to a decision," he said. "We shall continue to increase my entourage and take them to London. The more, the better. This will not be an army, since none is required. They will be my supporters. My advocates. I will enter the city, not as a military threat but as a popular force to be reckoned with. My brother Thomas is well-liked, but I am the one who will lead this country, and there will be no mistake about it."

And so it was. Prince Hal returned to London accompanied by a great force of lords and gentles; the multitude was widely remarked upon by chroniclers. It was almost like a triumph. Hal took up lodging at Bishop Langley's palace on the Strand and requested an interview with the king. Henry was ill but agreed to see him. This was not to be an ordinary visit. First, Hal solemnly made his confession at Westminster Abbey and took the sacrament. Then, he apparelled himself in a dark blue velvet gown encrusted with golden threads. A band of gold esses encircled his left arm—a smaller version of the Lancastrian collar.

Conspicuous in this unusual garment, he walked across to the palace along with a host of friends. When they entered Westminster Hall he admonished them not to proceed beyond the fire pit in the middle of the floor. Advancing alone toward the king, he was aware of the hostility among the courtiers; even the Biblical saints, painted on the walls, eyed him with malice. Stopping a respectful distance from his father, Hal dropped to one knee.

"May I have a private audience with you?" he said.

Henry sat on his portable chair draped in a heavy cloak. A knitted hat covered his bald head and his eyes were sunken in a wan face with a heavy copper beard. But those eyes were piercing, and for a moment they widened in exasperation. He thought about refusing, but changed his mind at the earnest expression on Hal's face. Nodding once, he raised a finger in consent. Responding to this, a handful of men picked up his chair and carried him into his secret chamber, followed by Erpingham and Norbury. The litter bearers and the king's friends stayed put and Hal entered the room by himself. He looked around. This was not exactly his idea of private, but perhaps a few witnesses were preferable. Then no one could misinterpret his intent.

"Well," said Henry without preliminaries, "what is it you want?"

This was more difficult than Hal expected. Kneeling at Henry's feet, he said, "Father, I have learned of the rumours against me and I wanted to proclaim my undying loyalty. I assure you they are totally false." He hesitated, and saw no alteration in his father's face. "Tell me. If there is any person in the world whom you fear, I would see it as my duty to punish that person, to erase that sore from your heart."

Henry clutched and unclutched his hand but made no other gesture.

"Father, before I came here I prepared for this moment by confessing myself and receiving communion. My soul is pure." Reaching into his gown he pulled out a dagger and extended it to the king, hilt first. "I desire you, if you truly believe these accusations, for the easing of your heart to slay me with this dagger. My life is not so precious that I would live one day further in your displeasure. Your goodwill and welfare are infinitely more important than my life. I offer you this dagger in the presence of these lords and before God, so that all know I clearly forgive you my death." He then closed his eyes and waited. This was no performance; Hal was truly prepared for the worst.

Henry was astonished. But seeing that Hal was in earnest, he broke into tears, throwing the dagger to one side and holding out his arms. "My son, my son. It is true I partly suspected you, as I now see, undeservedly on your part."

Overjoyed, Hal threw himself into his father's embrace. Seeing that the danger had passed, the witnesses slipped from the room, leaving them alone.

They stayed thus for longer than a normal hug, and when Hal finally pulled away, Henry still had tears running down his face.

"Never again will I succumb to any dissension," Henry said. "I promise you, henceforth I will trust you absolutely."

Hal pulled up a chair and sat beside his father. "I understand why we misunderstood each other," he said solemnly, "when well-meaning actions are seen through the eyes of men intent on harming me. I have no trouble with those who disagree with me. But I very much resent those who aim to bring me down." He wanted to mention Thomas but bit his tongue. No need to spoil their rapprochement.

Pulling out two scrolls from his pouch, Hal put them in his father's lap. "Here are my accounts for Calais. Review them and I'm certain you will find nothing to complain about."

Grasping the rolls like a lifeline, Henry acknowledged his gesture. Indeed, in the next council, Henry declared that his son was blameless and Hal was exonerated. All was well between the two of them.

Arrangements for the army to Guyenne proceeded as planned, and King Henry saw the need to create two peers—the first of his reign after Hal—so that his commanders wouldn't be outranked by the enemy. Thomas Beaufort was created Earl of Dorset, and Prince Thomas was made Duke of Clarence and lieutenant of Guyenne. At the same time, Thomas married Margaret Holand and received a satisfactory allotment from her dowry. Hal was not present at either ceremony. He had withdrawn to Bishop Langley's palace.

At the beginning of August, all was ready for Thomas's expedition. The king was not well enough to accompany him to Southampton, so the new Duke of Clarence took his leave at Westminster. The two of them were alone in Henry's privy chamber, and for once Thomas was at a loss for words.

Henry was seated in his throne and Thomas knelt by his side, taking his father's hands. "I promise to do you proud," he said. "It shall be as though you are with me every step of the way."

Not even trying to stop the tears, Henry squeezed his fingers. "I have always been proud of you, son. You have been my joy and my consolation."

Almost embarrassed, Thomas cleared his throat. "Do not listen to anything they say against me. Everything I do shall be for your benefit."

"No one will dare speak against you. Never fear." Henry swallowed, his mouth suddenly dry. "Thomas, I may not be here when you return."

This was something that had never been mentioned before. Thomas closed his eyes, willing it otherwise.

"No, son. I am ready to go to a better place. My life gives me no joy anymore and I can barely stand the humiliation my body has inflicted upon me. Give me your blessing, Thomas, and leave with the knowledge that I love you more than life itself."

Putting his forehead against his father's, Thomas fought back a sob. "I cannot bear the thought."

"You must trust in the Lord. And Thomas, learn to live with your brother in harmony, for he *will* reign after me and he will need your strong arm. Now kiss me, my son, and God be with you."

Gently placing a kiss on Henry's lips, Thomas stood and gave him one last long look, ignoring the lesions on his face and the trembling of his head. "Goodbye, father. May God bless."

Not trusting himself any farther, Thomas left the room, gesturing to his guards who stepped in behind him. It was time to look forward and he was anxious to be gone.

A fleet of fourteen large ships sailed from Southampton to the sound of musicians playing and citizens cheering. Long flags embroidered with the cross of St. George flew from the masts, sea gulls squawked and encircled their boats, though higher waves than usual promised a choppy crossing. They were driven back to Southampton by adverse weather but soon sailed again and landed in Normandy with fifteen hundred men-at-arms, three thousand archers and two thousand light-armed infantry.

On his arrival, Thomas learned that the Armagnacs and Burgundy had signed a peace treaty at the insistence of King Charles—who had finally bestirred himself. Only the Count of Alençon adhered to the agreement with the English, so an angry Duke Thomas continued the invasion in his name. He captured Chateauneuf, St. Remy, and Belleme before passing into Anjou and then the Duchy of Orléans. The French were anxious to get rid of the invading force, and through a combination of a huge bribe—paid in instalments—fabulous gifts, and hostages they managed to mollify the English. Thomas spent a comfortable winter in Bordeaux and moved on to his command in Guyenne.

Would things have gone any better if the English had supported the Burgundians? Considering the disarray in France, probably not. Poor King Charles was yanked back and forth between his feuding nobles, and he didn't know who to believe from day to day. He tried to stop the civil war from proliferating, but his efforts were feeble and didn't last long. So perhaps Thomas's expedition was not a total loss. At least his unchallenged march through France struck terror into the hearts of their enemies and strengthened England's hold on Guyenne, which was the king's ultimate goal, anyway. It was Hal's goal, too, even when he questioned his father's decisions.

CHAPTER 18

King Henry spent the last Christmas of his life at his beloved Eltham Palace with his wife and sons—all except Thomas. By then he was barely able to walk and his physical appearance was repugnant to anyone who was not used to seeing him. One of his contemporaries described him as "cruelly tormented with festering of the flesh, dehydration of the eyes, and rupture of the internal organs." Another said "he was all sinews and bones" and "completely shrunken and wasted by disease".

He had called Parliament for 3 February, the anniversary of his father's death, but was unable to attend opening day. No significant business was done, and the members lingered at Westminster, wondering if they were going to witness the government passing on to the next generation. Henry went to stay at Lambeth, for he preferred the company of Archbishop Arundel to anyone else besides his wife. Toward the end of February, he was ferried across the Thames to make an offering at the Shrine of Edward the Confessor.

The king's attendants carried him into Westminster Abbey on his litter and placed him behind the high altar. Retreating respectfully, the men watched as Henry painfully lowered himself to his knees and prayed, lifting his hands and silently moving his lips. Suddenly, he swayed, trying to support himself on the litter; as his companions watched in alarm, he fell backwards to the floor.

Letting out a cry that echoed from the vaults, Squire William dashed forward, followed by the others. He knelt beside the king and lifted Henry's head into his lap. A gasp escaped from Henry's lips but his eyes remained closed.

"We need help," exclaimed the squire, trying to stay calm. He didn't have to wait long; drawn by his cry, four monks drew near and bent over, quickly assessing the situation.

"The abbot's palace," one of them declared, "through the cloisters. Can you get him back into his chair?"

William nodded. "He is as light as a feather," he said, taking hold of Henry's shoulders. As a monk was sent to prepare the way, the others picked up the king and carefully placed him into the litter which was designed for sitting. "I'll hold him," the squire insisted as the king's attendants lifted the chair.

Moving very slowly, the little cortege exited from a side door and made its way through the cloisters. The new part of the palace had just been added in King Richard's reign, and Henry had not seen it. They brought the king into a large, long chamber and laid him on a pallet in front of a stone fireplace surmounted by carved wood panelling stretching to the ceiling. The walls were painted with biblical scenes.

The monks sent for Queen Joanna and Prince Hal, who were both at Lambeth.

For a long time Henry lay insensible, until finally his eyes fluttered open. He looked at the fire then up at the beautiful vaulted ceiling which reminded him of the great hall.

"Where am I?" he asked, licking his lips. Squire William raised his head and gave him a drink of water.

One of the monks leaned over. "You are in the Jerusalem Chamber."

The king let out a laugh that sounded more like a choke. "The Jerusalem Chamber. Praise be to the Father in Heaven! Now I know I shall die in this chamber. Do you remember William," he said, taking hold of his squire's arm, "the old prophecy that I would die in Jerusalem? I always thought it meant the Holy Land." He visibly relaxed. "I will be released soon from this torment."

Friar Tille, Henry's confessor, was the first of his intimates to show up, and he knelt by the side of the pallet. William stuffed a large pillow behind the king so he could sit a little, then backed up to give the two privacy.

"I'm here to give you your last confession," the friar said, putting the stole around his neck.

"What would you have me confess, father?" Henry said weakly.

"There are three things I think you need to repent. First, your share in the deaths of King Richard and Archbishop Scrope, and lastly, for your usurpation of the crown."

This must surely be the end, Henry thought, *because Tille had never brought these up before*. "Father, I've already written to the pope about the first two and received absolution. As for the third, there is no remedy to be had, for my children will not suffer that the regality go out of our lineage." Tille was not terribly convinced by this answer, but he gave Henry the last rites anyway, for he wasn't sure how much longer the king would live.

As he prayed over Henry's head, Hal entered the room. The king was surprised at his own surge of affection for his firstborn. He extended his arms. "My son! Come to me so I may kiss you."

Hal hurried to his bedside while the confessor withdrew. He knelt, pecking his father gently on the forehead and receiving a kiss in return.

"I am so glad you are here, Hal, for my time has come and I would counsel you." He coughed and reached for a cup of water. "Look at me, once so strenuous in arms and now adorned with bones and nerves. My bodily strength is gone, but my soul is braver and more devoted than before."

Hal sat on the floor, tucking in a cover around Henry's frail form.

"I beg you to pay my debts, Hal, and reward my friends. Choose wise confessors who are not afraid to tell you the truth." He coughed again and took a rattled breath. "Hal, there is something I fear above all else. After my death, I fear that there will be discord between you and Thomas." Hal made to say something but he held up a hand. "You are both of such great stomach and courage. Maybe you are too much alike. But listen to me: Thomas could be a pillar of support for you, if only you would let him."

A succession of emotions crossed Hal's face. For the first time, he was forced to see his quarrelling with Thomas from his father's point of view. Could it be that his prejudices coloured his judgment? Was he simply jealous of his brother? Hal wasn't prepared to admit such a thing to himself. Not yet, anyway. On the other hand, as king there was no longer any need for resentment. Things could be different between them. To an extent.

He took a deep breath. "Father, I will love and honour my brothers above all men so long as they remain true to me. But if they conspire or rebel against me, I assure you that I shall as soon execute justice upon any one of them as upon the worst and simplest person within your realm."

He could see from his father's face that he had said the right thing.

"It's only just," Henry nodded, "and I am content." He looked to the side where his crown had been placed on a pillow. Hal noticed his glance and picked it up, placing it on Henry's chest. The king grasped it with both hands. "Many have said I had no right to this bauble. God forgive the crooked paths I trod. But I have tried to do the right thing, though so many rebellions threatened the peace of my kingdom. You, my son, shall reap the benefits of my hard-won achievements. Wear the crown well, and do not act in haste, but also do not hesitate to punish those who threaten the Church, from where all your honour comes."

He handed the crown to Hal who took it carefully with both hands. "My lord, as you have held this by right of your sword, it is my intent to hold and defend it in the same way during my life." He knew, as soon as he said it, that these words also took on a new meaning. He would be responsible for everything, good and bad. Kingship was more than just a series of trials. A king had to look deeper into the hearts of men surrounding him; he had to use judgment rather than emotion. Hal saw how the crown weighed heavily on Henry's conscience, for when he failed to remember this precept, he had brought disaster on his own head.

He looked up at that moment, to see Joanna by his side, and Humphrey behind her. The queen had tears in her eyes.

"My lord, I came as quickly as I could."

Henry held out a hand and Hal stood, stepping back. She knelt in his place. "My dear love, I can see your suffering is almost at an end." She stroked the king's forehead as he leaned back against the pillow.

Erpingham and Norbury came into the room, followed by Archbishop Arundel, the Duke of York, and many of Henry's other retainers. As Joanna sat by his side, they came over one at a time to pay their last respects. Such an end was all Henry could have wished for, though he did linger all night before finally taking his last breath on St. Cuthbert's day 20 March, 1413.

Hal took one last look at the small crowd surrounding his father's deathbed before slipping from the room. He found his way to the abbot's private chapel and knelt in the semi-darkness. The altar was lit by only one candle, and he found comfort in the small pool of light directing his eye toward the crucifix. The room was inundated with the slightly nutty smell from the melting wax. Taking a deep breath, Hal was surprised at the jumble of emotions fighting for precedence. Having expected to feel relief at the passing of his father, he was overwhelmed with a sense of inadequacy. Was he truly prepared for the onerous task of ruling the country? He saw how repeated uprisings dragged his father down from a healthy, spirited leader of men to a pathetic, worn-out carcass—dead before his time. Would he do any better?

264

He spent many hours before the altar, way past the time the candle burned down to nothing and a monk silently replaced it. Getting up, he rubbed his knees and looked around, still unsettled. Praying was not giving him any answers.

Remembering the anchorite that famously lived in a cell at the end of the Abbey's south transept, Hal determined to make his confession. He walked through the silent Abbey lit by rows of candles toward Edward the Confessor's tomb. Climbing the few steps to the saint's chapel, he stopped for a moment, looking up at the vaulted ceiling which was shrouded in darkness. Edward's tomb was raised high over a tall stone base with arched openings, commissioned by King Henry III for his new edifice. It, too, was lit by candles on long holders at each corner. He put his hand on a plain black slab beside him, underneath which lay King Edward I. Moving on, he caressed the tomb of Edward's father, Henry III. Then Hal walked across the chapel and knelt before the glorious gilt-bronze effigies of Richard II and Anne of Bohemia lying side-by-side. Tears filled his eyes as he thought about the deposed monarch, shunted away to King's Langley while his Queen lay in this big tomb, all alone. Crossing himself, he swore that fixing this travesty would be one of his first tasks after his coronation.

Comforted by this promise, Hal made his way to the anchorite's cell. He knocked on the door and waited for an answer. It opened slightly and a stooped old man with a grey beard observed him with glittering eyes. "I was expecting you," he said, stepping aside. "Come in."

Suppressing his surprise, Hal entered the tiny space. It was clean and sparsely furnished, with an altar opposite the door. "Did you hear about the death of the king?"

"I knew he was dying," the old man said, "and that you would be troubled."

"That I am."

The anchorite sat on a folded-up blanket on the floor and pointed to a spot in front of him. "I am ready to listen."

265

Hal felt an unusual wave of relief as he knelt before the old man. The friar had no interest in advancing himself, no ulterior motives. He was an impartial and confidential witness to Hal's uncertainties. "I fear that I am not prepared for what is in front of me."

"That is only natural."

"I think I am unworthy. I have not given my father the respect he deserved."

"Were there reasons for this disrespect?"

"Why, yes. I had many enemies and they influenced him unfairly. I fear I reacted with hostility."

"You will always have enemies."

Hal nodded. That didn't help.

"As did he," the anchorite went on. "Unlike yourself, your father was not raised to be a king. Unlike yourself, he spent his whole reign fighting against the stigma of usurper. And he survived, bequeathing to you a kingdom intact. This is a great accomplishment, and a great gift. You will have a fresh start, and you will have far fewer battles to fight than he did."

Even in the semi-darkness, Hal imagined he could see the anchorite's eyes sparkle. "Surely you must realize," the man said, "that your anticipated sovereignty is part of God's grand plan. Our Lord has paved the way for the House of Lancaster to bring the world into a more enlightened future and restore the unity of the Church."

Blinking tears away, Hal looked at him, his heart swelling. This humble man had just answered questions he couldn't express to himself. He had just laid out a divine objective Hal could easily follow. Perhaps he was prepared, after all.

It was as if all his doubts were falling away like melting ice. "Will you listen to my confession?"

"Gladly, my son."

And several hours later, Hal closed the door of the hovel and walked slowly back to the Jerusalem Chamber. Opening the door slightly, he observed the people gathered around his father, waiting. His stepmother was crying. The king lay with his eyes closed. The air in the room was heavy. He knew it was his duty to sit there among this mournful group, but after what he'd just been through, he didn't want the grieving to drag his thoughts away from higher purposes. Besides, there was no one in the room he could comfort, nor was there anyone on earth who could comfort him. He had never felt so alone in his life. At least his father had a loving wife.

So Hal directed his steps to his own chamber and fell on his bed, fully clothed. Tonight, he suspected, he would sleep for the last time without the weight of the world on his shoulders. Tomorrow, he would have to face the court as a new man. With these last thoughts on his mind, Hal slept the sleep of exhaustion, and he woke up to the news that his father was dead.

Henry's friends and churchmen would already be taking care of the body, moving it to a place where it would be washed, eviscerated, embalmed, filled with spices and wrapped in waxed linen.

The sun was barely up when Hal entered his father's cabinet, walking around the desk, picking up loose parchments and putting them in a pile. He opened his father's favourite book and ran a finger over the gold-embossed illumination. A knock at the door interrupted his thoughts, and he grunted for whoever it was to enter.

It was Archbishop Arundel—the last person Hal wanted to see right then. But there was no point in delaying the inevitable, and he sat at his father's desk as Arundel entered and quickly bent his knee.

"I have come to extend my condolences," the archbishop said. Hal nodded. "And to tender my resignation." He laid the great seal on the desk. "I have God's work to do, and you need a chancellor you are in accord with."

Hal could barely control his face. He didn't want Arundel to see his relief, for the man had done his best for his father. He leaned forward, picking up the seal. "I know you keep this country strong in your fight against Lollardy. May God be with you."

Arundel looked a little disappointed, but there was really nothing else to say. Backing from the room, he nodded one last time and disappeared through the door.

Leaning back in the chair, Hal was impressed by the difference in the way Arundel conducted himself. Whereas before, the man only paid attention to him when he had to; now, he was respectful—even submissive. How would his friends act?

Hal spent the rest of the morning in his father's cabinet. No one bothered him. Once he was ready to make a public appearance, he preceded a pair of guards and directed his steps to the great hall in the palace. Yes, there were many people waiting for him. When he stepped into the room, everyone bowed. He turned this way and that, taking in the faces. His two brothers, John and Humphrey, stood near the throne. Next to them, his stepmother was talking with Bishop Beaufort. Many of his father's advisors and officers were present, probably wondering whether they would be replaced. When Hal made his way to the throne, they parted for him. The room was deadly quiet.

What else was there to do? He sat on the throne beneath the canopy of state and waited for people to come up to him. The first was Queen Joanna, who knelt.

"Sit, my lady," Hal said, patting the empty seat next to his: her seat—or at least, formerly. They were on friendly terms, but never did they have a chance to really get to know each other. For now, since he had no queen, she could continue in the role she was accustomed to.

Graceful as ever, Joanna took her place by his side. She studied him for a moment. "The throne suits you."

"I'll grow into it." He smiled briefly. "I understand your dowry is in arrears."

She laughed. "It's been in arrears from the first day. I cannot complain. Your father was more than generous."

Too generous, Hal thought. His words were more judicious. "He was a good husband to you."

"And a good father. He loved you very much."

"Did he?" Hal wasn't so sure. "I hope I live up to his expectations."

"I have no doubt." She held out her hand as John and Humphrey came up the two steps. She smiled gratefully; at least she had had a chance to play mother to them. Both bowed then kissed her on the cheek.

"Father is laid out in state at the Abbey," John said. "We are ready to take you there."

Joanna smoothed her skirt. "I am ready. With your permission, Sire."

Unused to being asked for permission, Hal nodded. He had run out of things to say and was relieved to see his stepmother go.

Next to pay his respects was Bishop Beaufort. That was much easier.

Once again Hal patted the chair next to him. "I've already seen Archbishop Arundel."

"Oh?"

"He resigned." Permitting himself a brief smile, Hal enjoyed a moment of triumph. "He saved us both a lot of trouble. I believe we will all get along much better now, as he will be busy tending his flock."

"I wish him well." Beaufort crossed himself automatically.

Only delaying a moment, Hal pulled out the great seal from its pouch. "I beg you to accept this."

"Sire!" There was no surprise between them, only satisfaction. "Gladly. We have much to accomplish."

"I dare say we do. Our work was interrupted just as it looked like we were making progress."

"Fortunately, the way is clear ahead. As for now, the first thing we must do is issue the usual command that no one leaves the country without special permission. We can't have our enemies taking advantage of any change of government. Then we need to instruct the sheriffs to proclaim the King's Peace in the capital and all the counties throughout England. They will announce your succession and warn against disturbances. Justices of the Peace need to be confirmed in their positions so the transition will go smoothly."

Hal leaned back in his chair, feeling better already. The bishop was the perfect man for the job, and his experience would cover any gaps in the new king's education. Suddenly, with a thought, he sat straight again. "My father's hostages."

Beaufort nodded wisely. "I think we need only concern ourselves with the King of Scotland, Murdoch, the son of the Duke of Albany, and Gruffydd, son of Owain Glyndwr."

"Yes, they are the most important. Give orders to bring them back to the Tower for safekeeping. We can't afford to take the chance that someone might attempt to rescue them."

"I shall do it at once." The Bishop got up with a bow and stepped away to carry out the king's bidding. *It's as simple as that*, Hal thought. *Make a request and it's done. How seductive power is!*

For the rest of the afternoon, Hal received officers and civil servants from all stations, reassuring most, staying neutral to others. Inspired by his confession with the anchorite the night before, he felt surer of himself than he expected. This was his destiny. Prince Hal was another lifetime ago, and already he felt like a new man.

King Henry lay in state for a week, accessible for all to see him. He was clothed in a long robe and mantle, his beard brushed carefully across his chest, with his head and face covered by a silk handkerchief. He wore a crown and his hands were covered with gloves decorated by a band of embroidery; a gold ring was placed on the middle finger of his right hand. In the same hand he held a gilded orb and a golden rod surmounted by a cross which lay on his chest—and in his left hand a gilded sceptre reaching to his ear.

After the viewing was over, the king's body was stripped of its finery and wrapped five times in leather. Then it was sealed in a lead shroud. They laid him in an elm box so large they had to wrap the body in ropes of twisted hay—or hay-bands—to hold it steady. In his final resting place, the regalia would be placed next to his wrapped body. King Henry's coffin was loaded onto a barge and taken downstream to Gravesend. It was surrounded by oil lamps and the barge was accompanied by eight other vessels carrying Joanna, Hal and his brothers, and a host of barons, ecclesiastics, and other notables. At Gravesend, the old king was transferred to a horse-bier covered with a cloth-of-gold.

A torchlight procession accompanied the king to Canterbury where he was laid to rest in Becket's Trinity Chapel between two pillars on the north side of the shrine, next to the Black Prince's tomb. Henry had chosen this spot many years ago, in the company of the knight he had always seen as his particular hero.

Plans for the coronation went on apace, and within a week Hal was back in London. On Friday, 7 April he rode in state to the Tower of London where he hosted a magnificent feast. There he was served by fifty young nobles who were chosen to be made Knights of the Bath on the morrow. The members were promoted from the ranks of knights bachelor—the knights who fought under someone else's banner. This would lift these new members one level higher in the order of precedence.

One by one the knights carried up a platter and presented its delicacy for the king's pleasure; some cut Hal's meat and others poured his wine or offered a bowl for him to wash his hands. The minstrels played and choristers filled the hall with sweet harmonies. Hal was gracious to one and all, but he rarely smiled. Archbishop Arundel sat by his right side, given his rank, and the two had little to say to each other. Bishop Beaufort sat at Hal's left, and was the only one at high table who appeared to be enjoying the food. Hal's other brothers—except for Thomas, who had not yet returned from France—flanked the churchmen. They were still getting used to their brother's new status and didn't quite know how to behave toward him. At least Humphrey had the advantage of drinking with Hal in his freer days; poor John had spent the last several years in the North, and he barely knew Hal at all.

The following morning, the great hall in the Tower was prepared for the bath ceremony. The Order of the Bath was instituted by Henry IV at his own coronation, and Hal wanted to retain the best aspects of his father's rule. Among these fifty were Lord le Despenser and John Holland—both sons of men who had been executed for treason by Henry IV. Surprisingly, Edmund Mortimer was also included, who had just been set at liberty on the king's accession. More than anything, this demonstrated Hal's intent to start fresh, and bring back the noble families who had been delegitimized.

This morning, fifty baths were set up in the hall, filled with warm water and draped with white sheets. The ritual of bathing was for purification. Each bath had a canopy draped over it and a bed set up behind it with rich hangings. All fifty knights proceeded to bathe themselves, and then Hal entered in procession. One by one the king approached the knight, dipped his finger in the bath and made the sign of the cross on the man's naked back. The king said, "You shall honour God above all things; you shall be steadfast in the faith of Christ; you shall love the King your Sovereign Lord and defend his rights to the best of your power." Then he moved on to the next knight and repeated the blessing.

Once finished, the king processed out of the hall and the knights dried themselves off and lay in their beds to rest. When the curfew bell rang, they all got up and dressed in long brown gowns like monks, with the help of their squires. All were instructed to move on to St. John's Chapel as music played in the background. There they knelt beside their armour and stayed at vigil the rest of the night. At dawn, the knights attended confession and mass, then returned to their beds until full daylight.

The king was waiting. Senior knights buckled spurs onto each knight-elect's heels, strapped a belt around his waist, and then the king tapped him on the neck with his sword. That same afternoon, they processed with the king and a large crowd of lords through the city to Westminster Palace where they spent the night.

The following day, in the midst of a terrible snowstorm, the new Bath Knights accompanied Hal to Westminster Abbey, where he was crowned by Archbishop Arundel as Henry V. After the ceremony, the new king and his entourage trudged back across the palace yard through deepening snow to the great hall, their heads bent against the blizzard. Once inside, everyone shook off the snow, ignoring the pools of water gathering on the floor. The minstrels struck up their tunes and the guests moved into the great hall where Henry took his place all alone on a marble chair raised above the other tables. Soon they were enjoying themselves, and all applauded as servants on horseback brought in the main courses, balancing a plate on each arm. Queen Joanna had ordered lampreys from Brittany, William Croisier presented a large pike, and Sir John Pelham brought in two Sussex does. Happy courtiers stuffed themselves with boar, peacock, venison, pork, hen-brawn ground with rice and milk of almonds, figs boiled in small ale, and cheese fried and baked in pastry, among other courses. Beautiful subtleties were brought out between courses such as sugar and paste swans and gilded eagles. Ribbons came out of the animals' mouths with sayings such as "out of court be banished tort" and "one and no more with God before".

Just as people remembered from Henry IV's coronation feast, John Dymoke rode into the hall, armed as St. George and bellowed his challenge three times to anyone who would dispute Henry V's right to the throne. The first challenge was given at the entrance to the hall, the second challenge in the middle, and the third before the king's throne. With each challenge, he threw his gauntlet on the floor. Once satisfied that no one would answer his defiance, Dymoke bowed to the king then backed his stallion from the hall without doing any damage to the banquet tables.

Many people said that Henry looked like an angel beneath his cloth of estate. It was also said that he barely ate a bite and didn't eat for three days afterwards. The blizzard which made his coronation so memorable lasted for two days, burying houses in the country deep in snow.

It wasn't until after the coronation that Thomas returned from France. On the way to London he stopped at Canterbury and prayed over his father's grave. Between the choir and the high-altar, a tall iron *herce*, or candle-frame, towered over him. Many candles and torches still burned in the king's memory. The *herce* was hung with forty pennons and other painted hangings depicting religious figures. Thomas came away filled with peace, for his parting with Henry had been tender and loving. But now he had to face his brother, and his mind was filled with trepidation.

When he got to Westminster, Thomas's first inclination was to search out his younger siblings. They could give him any warnings about the king's temperament, for he had absolutely no idea where he stood. He found them together in the library, poring over a manuscript recently brought over from Paris. Humphrey was the first to look up.

"Thomas!" He jumped down from the dais and ran to his brother, taking him into a big hug.

A little flustered, Thomas nonetheless hugged him back and held him at arm's length. He wasn't used to a show of emotion. "It's good to see you, brother. And you, John. It's been a long time."

John was more reserved. "Welcome back, Thomas. It looks like soldiering agrees with you."

The other nodded. Having finally taken charge of a real army, he had gained confidence over the last several months. His men responded to his leadership and he found he liked this new responsibility. He carried himself more proudly and his brothers couldn't help but notice. "I think I was born to it," he said with a slight smile. "I hope our brother the king finds more work for me to do." He hesitated. "How is he adjusting?"

Humphrey smiled. "He is a changed man. He is taking his duties more seriously than ever. He will welcome you, Thomas."

"I don't know. There was a lot of tension between us."

"There is no longer any occasion for it," John assured him. "Many of the conflicts have been removed. He no longer needs to prove himself."

"Perhaps. This won't be easy."

"I think you'll be surprised. We were."

Raising his eyebrows, Thomas patted Humphrey on the shoulder and turned away. It's not like he had any choice! He might as well get this over with.

King Henry was going over some exchequer rolls with the Earl of Arundel, who had been made treasurer. When Thomas was introduced, Arundel greeted him then got up to leave. Both brothers stared at each other, barely noticing the other's exit.

Raising his chin a little, Henry gestured for the chair. "Sit, brother. How was your crossing?"

"Uneventful, thank God. I'm glad to be home. I stopped by Canterbury on the way back and saw father's grave." Thomas hesitated. "How were his last days?"

"He lost consciousness while praying at Edward the Confessor's tomb and they moved him into the abbot's quarters. He was awake long enough to speak to all of us, though he was in great pain."

"I'm so sorry I wasn't here."

"I wish you had been," said Henry, and was surprised that he meant it. "Thomas, his last words to me were about you."

"Oh?"

275

"He feared there would be discord between us. I think he feared I would do some harm to you."

Thomas shifted in his chair. "How did you respond?"

Henry leaned forward. "I told him that as long as you were loyal to me, I would love and honour you above all men." He narrowed his eyes. "I meant that, Thomas."

The other blinked in amazement. This wasn't what he was expecting.

"Your old antagonist, Prince Hal, is gone," the king said, reassuring the both of them. "I am a new man, now, and I accept my responsibilities. I can no longer be ruled by my temper." He reached out a hand. "You are my heir now, Thomas. We must work together so that the Lancastrian dynasty prospers."

Whatever ill will Thomas harboured dissipated when he grasped his brother's hand. He never would have seen himself give in so gracefully, but perhaps his father's wishes had something to do with his acceptance. "I pledge myself to you, King Henry. Let nothing ever come between us."

CHAPTER 19

There was one grand gesture that King Henry insisted on carrying out. He had his heart set on bringing King Richard's body from King's Langley to Westminster and laying it to rest in the tomb next to his beloved Queen Anne. When he announced his intention, Sir Thomas Erpingham requested a meeting with him. This was nothing unusual; Erpingham had been appointed steward of the household, so he was already working closely with the king. But this day, as he took his normal place at the table, his face was unusually pale.

"I'm glad you are here. We have much to do." Henry glanced up at Erpingham and looked a second time. "Are you well?" he asked.

"Quite well. But there is something I must discuss with you and it is a great burden."

Henry was naturally intrigued. He had a servant pour some wine then sent everyone from the room. Erpingham had served his family faithfully for three generations; he was always there. The king gave him a little smile. "Surely you can tell me anything."

"I hope so." He took a drink and Henry noticed that his hand was shaking.

"What is it?"

Putting his cup down, Erpingham sighed. "It's about Richard."

"Is there a problem?"

"I'm not sure how to tell you this, Sire. You know all the rumours."

Henry was starting to get agitated. "You mean about his death."

"Yes." Henry's face was not encouraging. "The pseudo-Richard."

Henry slammed his cup on the table. The wine splashed over his hand. "No. It can't be."

Erpingham was afraid to go on. He waited while Henry stood and walked to the window. Then, whirling around, the king strode back and leaned on the table.

"Tell me," he said.

Erpingham took a deep breath. "As far as we could tell, Hotspur sent a man to help him escape from Pontefract."

"Hotspur. I should have known." Henry straightened. "Why didn't my father tell me?"

"He was afraid of what you might do. It was just before the Epiphany Revolt, and we didn't even know if we would survive, remember. Everyone thought Richard might come back at the head of an army. And when he didn't, we weren't sure when he would come."

"And father thought I would go after him?"

Erpingham shrugged. "You might have. He couldn't take that chance."

Even through his anger, Henry admitted to himself that his father was probably right. "So it really was Maudeleyn in the coffin."

Nodding, the knight wiped his forehead.

"You might have told me," Henry growled.

"I was sworn to secrecy. Now that the king is dead, I owe you the same loyalty. I just couldn't let you go through with the reburial without knowing."

Discouraged, Henry sat heavily, putting his face in his hands. "Dear God in heaven. All these years."

"We can only assume he doesn't want to come back. From what I understand, he's had plenty of opportunities to do so."

Lifting his head, Henry let his misery show. "That doesn't excuse what happened. Any of it."

Erpingham shook his head sadly. "I had hoped you wouldn't have to put yourself through this again."

The king grunted. "In a way, it was easier once I accepted he was dead." He looked down, waving his hand. "I need to be alone."

Relieved, Erpingham quickly went to the door. But before he put his hand on the lever, Henry called out to him. "Thank you, Thomas. I know that wasn't easy."

Looking back, Erpingham wished he could have offered more solace. But Henry just wasn't the kind of man to accept comfort from others.

As the door closed, Henry looked at his hands. They were closed into fists, and he had to consciously relax. He twisted the signet ring on his finger—the same Richard had relinquished to Henry.

"This doesn't belong to me," he said out loud. "Oh, Richard. What have we done to you?"

He couldn't help himself. All the memories came flooding back...when King Richard knighted him in the forest in Ireland...the conversations they had together—especially the last one in Dublin, when Richard told him he thought of Hal as the son he never had. He remembered that day in Chester, when he found the captive king despairing that he couldn't strike a flint to make a fire. He cringed at the forlorn king riding his broken-down horse all the way to London. And there was nothing Hal could do for him.

Was there anything he could have done at any moment? It was his father who betrayed the king—his father who took the crown so defiantly. He couldn't have stopped him. On the other hand, did he complain when he was made Prince of Wales?

Would he have gone after Richard if he had discovered the exiled king was in Scotland? What purpose would that have served? Even if Richard had been willing to return—even if he found his way back to the throne by some strange twist of fate—what would have happened to King Henry? Then Hal would be responsible for his own father's death.

No. He couldn't dwell on that.

Too many years had passed. He had to be honest with himself; he couldn't give up the kingship. Not now. Not ever.

But there was one thing he could do. Go ahead with his plans to transfer the king's remains to Westminster. All right, Maudeleyn's remains. The point was, in doing so he was showing respect for King Richard's memory. There was a possibility Richard would learn of this gesture, and even appreciate it.

He would swear Erpingham to secrecy. That wouldn't be too difficult.

King's Langley was twenty-one miles northwest of Westminster. This was destined to be a long and expensive distance, for Henry V had every intention of showing the world his respect for his unfortunate predecessor. Kneeling at the tomb of his great-uncle, Edmund Langley the Duke of York, Henry begged his forgiveness for removing King Richard from his church. He knew York had been honoured to be laid to rest in the same place as his former king. At least he occupied the tomb Richard had originally designed for himself, years before Anne died.

"I'm taking him to his desired resting place," Henry whispered, "next to his beloved queen. I trust you will not feel mortified by his removal. I will bestow alms on the brothers of Langley in your honour."

Hoping this pledge would assuage the spirit of his great-uncle, Henry attended the removal of the body from its inconspicuous tomb in the priory. He had commissioned a wooden bier and coffin to carry the body to Westminster, as well as candle wax and 120 torches to burn alongside the hearse as it made its stately way. He even borrowed the fabric trappings used at Canterbury during Henry IV's funeral. Riding a black horse, King Henry accompanied the procession the whole way, distributing alms along the route amounting to a thousand marks. This was a tremendous sum, especially when contrasted with the mere twenty shillings distributed by Henry IV during the original funeral cortege.

Upon finally reaching Westminster Abbey, the Abbot presided over a lavish ceremony and mass. A host of monks removed the gilt effigies from the tomb and carefully deposited the king's body next to his wife. They placed a jewelled bible on his chest and a bronze crown upon his head. The king stood by quietly as they lowered the effigies and sealed the tomb. When it was all over, he knelt at its side and lay his forehead against the marble.

"I pray through you, Richard Maudeleyn, to my true king Richard Plantagenet, who henceforth shall be my spiritual father. From you, King Richard, I owe my legitimization, just as I legitimized your burial before the world. Henceforth, I shall wear the crown proudly, since you had yourself foretold and blessed my elevation. I fear I shall never see you in this lifetime, but know, King Richard, that I revere you as my royal patron."

When Henry finally came down the steps from Edward the Confessor's shrine, he saw his brother Humphrey on a bench against the partition across the way. The poor lad was exhausted and sat with his head back, deep asleep. As Henry crossed over, his brother woke guiltily, wiping his eyes and standing.

"You were waiting for me?" This came out more as a statement than a question.

"I was concerned," Humphrey said, shrugging.

"Well, brother, I think I am safe in saying this crown had lain heavily upon our father's brow. I feel the weight myself, but after today I think I can bear it." He put an arm around Humphrey's shoulders. "For better or worse, I've closed the book on King Richard's life, and it's time for us to move on.

Come, Humphrey. I have great plans for this country and with God's help we'll bring in a new golden age."

END OF BOOK FOUR

AUTHOR'S NOTE

It's a great pity that once Henry IV finally put his major rebellions to rest his body betrayed him and he never achieved his greatest desires. Time and again he announced that he would be leading expeditions, and time and again he had to cancel his plans, though not always giving an explanation. Historians have largely assumed it was his health—and with good reason. It's nearly impossible to diagnose an illness from the past, and theories have ranged from leprosy (though modern medicine has pretty much discarded this one—at least Hansen's Disease, as we know it), to psoriasis, to syphilis (usually thought to have been introduced later), to even yaws, a tropical skin disease from Africa. The arguments against leprosy were many: most importantly, he recovered after his first couple of attacks. Also, he wasn't exiled like a leper by his contemporaries. The most significant clue was when his tomb was opened in 1832. Although his face disintegrated quickly after being exposed to the air, enough was seen to determine that his nose cartilage was intact (apparently one of the first casualties of leprosy) and his features were not disfigured.

Whether King Henry experienced his first attack the very night after Scrope's execution is open to interpretation. But a significant number of chroniclers reported this as such—too many to dismiss out of hand. There was no question that everyone—including probably the king himself—saw this as divine retribution. According to Peter Niven (*The Problem of Henry IV's Health*) "Leprosy was the disease *par excellence* associated with God's punishment of sinners". No wonder he couldn't shake the stigma.

Modern historians think Henry must have experienced a combination of illnesses, because a skin disease would not account for his episodes of unconsciousness which lasted for extended periods of time. Perhaps he suffered from strokes or serious circulatory problems. Blood clots could explain the sudden pains in his legs. Coronary heart disease or rheumatic heart disease could explain his deteriorating health. And we can't ignore the effects of stress and—let's face it—possible guilt over the usurpation and execution of an archbishop.

The murder of Archbishop Scrope was a huge upset to the northerners. Henry IV is often criticized by historians for allowing his brethren to bury Scrope in his own minster—near the great altar, no less. The archbishop was soon seen as a martyr to Lancastrian oppression. Miracles were reported at his grave and pilgrims began to flock to his tomb with offerings, which was a boon to the church but an embarrassment to the government. Henry ordered a log barrier to be built around the tomb, and when that didn't work the barrier was replaced by a wall of stone and logs. That didn't work either, and eventually the government allowed the barrier to come down. The donations were put to good use; a tower in the minster had collapsed previously and was badly in need of restoration. Even as late as 1462, efforts were made to canonize Scrope, but as the Yorkist regime took hold, his usefulness faded away and the martyr's following faded as well.

Immediately after Scrope's execution, an irate Pope Innocent VIII excommunicated Henry IV, but Archbishop Arundel declined to publish the bull in the current troubled political situation. Because of the schism, Innocent had to be very careful in his relations with any of his allies and he didn't make much of a fuss. Shortly thereafter he died anyway, and after appropriate donations were given, the new pope reversed the previous censure and issued a new bull relieving the king of responsibility.

After Richard II's reburial at Westminster Abbey, rumours of his return diminished dramatically—although not altogether. As you will see in the next book, he was brought up again in the Southampton Plot against Henry V, although with less conviction. The Scottish pseudo-Richard, or Mammet (or real Richard II) lived out his life in peace at Stirling. The Duke of Albany paid his expenses until the end, regardless of his usefulness. He died in December of 1419 and was buried near the altar of the Blackfriars in the same town. (The foundations of this friary were discovered in 2014 along with the skeletal remains of one unidentified individual.)

A great deal has been written about Henry V's alleged outrageous behavior in his youth. As usual, we owe most of our perceptions to Shakespeare. And the great bard is a hard act to follow! So much depends on which historian we believe. Henry V's biographer (and apologist), J. Endell Tyler, says absolutely not. Others are not so adamant, and many do believe that Shakespeare often played fast and loose with the "facts". Even Wylie assumes there is some credence to Hal's misconduct, and refers to a "learned educational book" called *The Governour*, written by Sir Thomas Eluyot in 1532. However, a later historian, S. Solly-Flood, wrote an article entitled *The Story of Prince Henry of Monmouth and Chief-Justice Gascoign* referring to this exact book. Flood gives us a very convincing argument that "it never was intended by its author to be accepted otherwise than as a romance composed for the edification and amusement of his patron, Henry VIII". Flood seems to think that historians referring to *The Governour* never actually read it! So in the end, because Shakespeare portrayed Hal as a bad boy from his early years (when he was historically waging war on the Welsh), I concluded he just didn't have the time to misbehave. But I could at least allow the possibility that he "let his hair down" in the year-and-a-half after he was dismissed from the council.

As long as we're talking about Shakespeare, I'd like to add a quick note on Falstaff. Interestingly, many critics believe Shakespeare originally wrote that part for Sir John Oldcastle (in

Henry IV Part 1), who was still widely known 150 years after his martyrdom (you'll see that in my next book). This theory is by no means universal, and a dizzying array of articles can be found about it. Allegedly Falstaff was a caricature of a heretic and Shakespeare's audience took delight in portraying him as a wastrel. As the story goes, Shakespeare changed the name to Falstaff before his 1598 quarto edition, some say because Oldcastle's descendant, Baron Cobham objected. Others say the Puritans protested Oldcastle's name being taken in vain. Why Shakespeare chose John Falstaff which is an obvious alteration of Sir John Fastolf (a wealthy knight and contemporary of Henry V) is another mystery. Though I did read that Fastolf owned the Boar's Head in Henry V's day, so that might be enough of a link.

Henry IV's reign has largely been forgotten, sandwiched as it was between two dynamic kings. In my next volume, I'll be tackling the story of our famous Agincourt king, who took his personal vision of destiny to a whole new level. Like it or not, Henry V owed much to his father. If he hadn't inherited a country finally at peace, he could never have pursued immortality in France.

BIBLIOGRAPHY

Allmand, Christopher, HENRY V, The University of California Press, Berkeley, 1992

Davies, R.R., THE REVOLT OF OWAIN GLYN DWR, Oxford University Press, 1995

Dodd, Gwilym and Biggs, Douglas, *Editors*, HENRY IV: THE ESTABLISHMENT OF THE REGIME, 1399-1406, York Medieval Press 2003

Dodd, Gwilym and Biggs, Douglas, *Editors*, THE REIGN OF HENRY IV: REBELLION AND SURVIVAL, 1403-1413 York Medieval Press 2008

Given-Wilson, Chris, HENRY IV, Yale University Press, London, 2017

Goodrich, Norma Lorre, CHARLES DUKE OF ORLEANS, MacMillan & Co, New York 1963

Livingston, Michael, OWAIN GLYNDWR'S GRAND DESIGN: "The Tripartite Indenture" and the Vision of a New Wales, from *Proceedings of the Harvard Celtic Colloquium, vol. 33*

Lomas, Richard, THE FALL OF THE HOUSE OF PERCY 1368-1408, John Donald, Edinburgh 2007

McFarlane, K.B., LANCASTRIAN KINGS AND LOLLARD KNIGHTS, Oxford at the Clarendon Press, 1972

McNiven, Peter, THE BETRAYAL OF ARCHBISHOP SCROPE, in Bulletin of the John Rylands Library, Vol. Issue 1, University of Manchester

McNiven, Peter, HERESY AND POLITICS IN THE REIGN
OF HENRY IV: THE BURNING OF JOHN BADBY, The
Boydell Press, Suffolk, 1987

McNiven, Peter, PRINCE HENRY AND THE ENGLISH
POLITICAL CRISIS OF 1412, History, Vol. 65, no. 213, 1980
pp. 1-16

McNiven, Peter, THE PROBLEM OF HENRY IV'S HEALTH,
1405-1413, The English Historical Review, Vol. 100, no. 397
(Oct. 1985), pp. 747-772

Monstrelet, Enguerrand de, CHRONICLES Containing an
account of the Cruel Civil Wars between the houses of Orleans
and Burgundy, Vol. 1-4, Longman, et.al, London, 1810

Mortimer, Ian, THE FEARS OF HENRY IV; The Life of
England's Self-Made King, Vintage Books, London, 2008

Ross, James, SEDITIOUS ACTIVITIES: THE CONSPIRACY
OF MAUD DE VERE, COUNTESS OF OXFORD, 1403-4,
from The Fifteenth Century III: Authority and Subversion Edited
by Linda Clark, the Boydell Press, Woodbridge 2003

Strickland, Agnes, LIVES OF THE QUEENS OF ENGLAND
From the Norman Conquest, Blanchard & Lea, Philadelphia,
1852

Towson, Kris, HENRY PERCY, FIRST EARL OF
NORTHUMBERLAND: Ambition, Conflict and Cooperation in
Late Medieval England. A Thesis submitted for the Degree of
PhD at the University of St. Andrews, 2005

Vaughan, Richard, JOHN THE FEARLESS, Barnes & Noble,
New York, 1966

Wylie, James Hamilton, HISTORY OF ENGLAND UNDER HENRY IV (In 4 volumes), Longmans, Green & Co., London, 1884

Printed in Great Britain
by Amazon

32821884R00165